Donald Westlake won the Edgar Award three times and was named a Grand Master of the Mystery Writers of America. Amongst his numerous awards he also received a Lifetime Achievement Award from the Bouchercon committee and his screenplay for *The Grifters* won an Oscar nomination. He is known for the great ingenuity of his plots, his believable and clever characters and his lively and witty dialogue. Born in Brooklyn, he died in New York on 31 December, 2008.

Praise for Donald Westlake

'Westlake is a crime-writing machine bordering on genius ... twists and turns, masses of snappy dialogue and a ton of humour.'
Daily Mirror

'Dortmunder and his pals, whose status as fictional characters does not prevent them from seeming more real than anyone who has ever appeared on *Big Brother*, will be sorely missed.' *Daily Telegraph*

'The entertainment offered by Westlake lies not only in his own enjoyment of the gang's ability to outwit sophisticated organizations but in the subtleties of his characterisations ... the humour is one of Westlake's most endearing and enduring qualities as a writer ... Westlake has left a wonderful legacy.' *Irish Examiner*

'Westlake is the undisputed King of comic capers.' *The Times*

'So laden with irony it almost has you thinking that crime doesn't pay. But of course it does pay, when the criminals involved are Westlake's congenitally depressed master thief, John Dortmunder ... a full cast of bizarre characters and enough plot twists to keep them all tied up in knots.' *New York Times*

BY DONALD WESTLAKE

NOVELS

Money for Nothing • The Hook • The Ax • Humans • Sacred Monster •
A Likely Story • Kahawa • Brothers Keepers • I Gave at the Office •
Adios, Scheherazade • Up Your Banners

THE DORTMUNDER SERIES

What's So Funny? • Watch Your Back! • The Road to Ruin •
Bad News • What's the Worst That Could Happen? • Don't Ask •
Drowned Hopes • Good Behavior • Why Me • Nobody's Perfect •
Jimmy the Kid • Bank Shot • The Hot Rock

COMIC CRIME NOVELS

Smoke • Baby, Would I Lie? • Trust Me on This • High Adventure •
Castle in the Air • Enough • Dancing Aztecs • Two Much •
Help I Am Being Held Prisoner • Cops and Robbers •
Somebody Owes Me Money • Who Stole Sassi Manoon? •
God Save the Mark • The Spy in the Ointment • The Busy Body •
The Fugitive Pigeon

CRIME NOVELS

Pity Him Afterwards • Killy • 361 • Killing Time • The Mercenaries

JUVENILE
Philip

WESTERN
Gangway (with Brian Garfield)

REPORTAGE
Under an English Heaven

SHORT STORIES
Tomorrow's Crimes • Levine •
The Curious Facts Preceding My Execution and Other Fictions •
A Good Story and Other Stories • Thieves' Dozen

ANTHOLOGY
Once Against the Law (coedited with William Tenn)

DONALD WESTLAKE
GetReal

Quercus

First published in Great Britain in 2009 by Quercus
This paperback edition published in 2010 by

Quercus
21 Bloomsbury Square
London
WC1A 2NS

A CIP catalogue record for this book is available
from the British Library

ISBN 978 1 84916 107 7

10 9 8 7 6 5 4 3 2 1

Printed and bound in Great Britain by Clays Ltd, St Ives plc

Television isn't something you watch.
Television is something you appear on.

NOËL COWARD

I

DORTMUNDER DID NOT like to stand around on street corners. A slope-shouldered, glum-looking individual in clothing that hadn't been designed by anybody, he knew what he looked like when he stood for a while in one place on a street corner, and what he looked like was a person loitering with intent. The particular intent, as any cop casting an eye over Dortmunder would immediately understand, was beside the point, and could be fine-tuned at the station; the first priority was to get this fellow in charge.

Which was why Dortmunder didn't like standing around on street corners: he hated to give cops the feeling there was duty to be done. And yet, here he was, in the middle of a weekday morning in April, as obvious as a carbuncle in the pale glare of the weak spring sunshine, the near-beer equivalent of real sunshine as in, say, August, but still plenty bright enough to pick out a questionable detail as large as John Dortmunder, who happened to be waiting, in fact, for a cab.

But not just any cab. The cab he wanted to see before he became a known loiterer would be driven by Stan Murch's Mom, Stan being a fellow with whom Dortmunder had engaged in for-profit activities from time to time in the past. Murch's specialty was driving; when it became necessary to leave a location at speed, Stan was your man. And his Mom drove a cab; so that was probably an argument for nurture.

Earlier this morning, Stan had phoned Dortmunder to say, "My Mom had an interesting fare yesterday, she wants to tell us about it."

"Whadaya mean, an anecdote?"

"No, I think something interesting for us."

So they were making a meet, except it hadn't happened yet. Amid the coughing buses and snarling delivery vans of Madison Avenue the occasional empty cab did go by, cheerful rooftop light gleaming its invitation, some even pausing fractionally to see if Dortmunder felt like hailing anything, but none of them was piloted by Murch's Mom, so he let them pass.

But then one did arrive with Murch's Mom herself glaring out from behind the steering wheel. It angled to a stop at Dortmunder's feet, and he quickly took shelter in the back, already occupied by Stan, a carroty-haired guy with a skeptical slant to his brow.

"Harya," Dortmunder told him, and to the driver's reflection in the rearview mirror, "Morning."

"It is," she agreed. "Hold on, let me get over to Eighth Avenue."

Dortmunder nodded. "That's where we're going?"

"I need a traffic jam," she explained, "so I can talk without distraction."

"Oh. Okay."

As Murch's Mom headed across Thirty-seventh Street toward her traffic jam, Dortmunder said to Stan, "How we doing?"

"I don't think we *are* doing," Stan told him. "I think we come to a stop. The last time I looked in my wallet, we're growing mushrooms in there."

"Does your mother's anecdote have a cash crop in it?"

"I hope so. Mom wanted to wait and tell us both together."

"So you don't know what the story is here."

"Nope. Mom wanted to wait and tell us both together."

Since the conversation had deteriorated to a loop, Dortmunder abandoned it and looked out his window instead at the thin sunlight out there, until Murch's Mom made the right turn onto Eighth Avenue and sank contentedly into the perpetual blockage there, a traffic snarl well into its second century, running—or not running—from below Penn Station up to above the Port Authority bus terminal.

"Now," Mom said, half turning in the seat, back against the door, one negligent hand on the steering wheel, "we can talk."

"Good," Dortmunder said.

"Yesterday I had a fare."

"So Stan tells me."

"Coming in from Kennedy," she said. "You know, when you pick up a fare at Kennedy, you don't throw the flag, it's just a flat rate."

"Says so on the back of your seat here."

"That's right. So there's no point you do anything but

the shortest quickest route. Not that any of them *are* short and quick."

"Right."

"So we were in a mess on the Grand Central," she said, "kind of like this here— Hold on." And she moved the cab two car-lengths forward toward the next light. Then, "So the guy and I get into a conversation, he's a TV guy, they do productions in New York, I started to tell him about Stan here—"

Stan said, "Hello? You started telling him *what* about me?"

"I'm looking to see," his mother told him, "could he get you a job."

"In TV? What am I gonna do, sports?"

"Whatever," his mother said. "Face it, Stanley, your previous occupation is coming to an end."

Stan frowned at her profile. "How do you work that out?"

"Cameras," his Mom said, and pointed at one mounted on a nearby pole. "Security. ID. Tracking. Records of everything. Global positioning. Radio chips. It's harder for people like you and John every day, and you know it is. It is time, Stanley, you underwent a career change."

Dortmunder said, "It isn't that bad."

"Oh, it's all right for you," she told him. "You go on doing what you're doing because what else have you got, but Stanley's possessed of an actual marketable skill."

"Mp," said Dortmunder.

Stan said, "Which skill is that?"

"Driving," she said. "Keeping your wits about you. Anyway, the point is, I liked this guy, Doug Fairkeep his name is, so I wound up I gave him a little more of your background than I originally planned."

"Oh-oh," Stan said.

"It's okay," she promised him. "Turns out, what he is, he's a producer of those reality shows, you know the deal, and when he figured out what sort of driver you are and your kind of associates and all that, he got very interested."

"Oh, did he," Stan said.

"He did. He wants to do a reality show of you guys."

Dortmunder said, "That's the shows where they follow real people around while they do real things. Kinda real."

"That's right," she said. "Hold on." And she burrowed the cab forward all the way across the intersection, at the same time shifting one lane to the left.

Dortmunder waited till that maneuver was complete, then said, "What does he want to follow *us* around while we're doing?"

"A job."

They both looked at her as though she'd lost her mind. Dortmunder said, "He wants to make a *movie* of us, committing a crime?"

"A TV show."

"Where's it gonna play? Court TV?"

"He's got some ideas," she said. "How you could do it and not have anything fall on you. He wants to talk it over with you." Drawing a business card from her shirt pocket, she extended it toward Stan, saying, "Use your cell, give him a call."

"When you're committing a felony," Dortmunder pointed out, "the idea is, you don't want witnesses. What you want is privacy. And you especially don't want the entire television-watching population of America for a witness."

Stan, who had taken the card from his mother's fingers to study it, said, "Well, John, the guy does look legitimate."

"Of course he's legitimate," Dortmunder said. "*We're* the ones that aren't."

"While I'm over here anyway," Murch's Mom said, "I might as well pick up a fare at the Port of Authority. Unless you want me to deliver you two somewhere, only I'd have to throw the flag. I still got a living to make."

Dortmunder and Stan looked at one another. "Weather like this," Dortmunder muttered, "I like to walk."

"Me, too," Stan said.

"Well, we're stopped anyway," Murch's Mom observed, "so you might as well get out. I got my Port of Authority right over there."

"Fine," Stan said. "See you later, Mom."

As they stepped out of the cab into this diorama of unmoving transportation at its worst, she opened her window to say, "Call Fairkeep, Stan. The rest of your future starts right here."

2

ONE OF THE PRODUCTION assistants had a problem. A short overweight girl named Marcy Waldorf, a very recent hire, she wandered into Doug Fairkeep's office at *The Stand* looking bewildered, which is to say looking mostly like a chipmunk on steroids. She held some script pages in her hand and waved them vaguely as she said, "Doug, I'm sorry, but this just looks to me like writing."

"Marcy," Doug said, turning his attention with some relief from the budget for next week's shoot, "what have you got there?"

"The script I've been writing, Doug," she said, and held it out to him as though he'd never seen a script before. "And it's just— I'm sorry, Doug, this is *writing.*"

"That is not writing, Marcy," Doug assured her, being patient and kind. This was not the first time he'd explained the facts of life to a newbie. "Those are *suggestions.*"

Marcy now held the pages out in front of herself with both hands, as though she intended to sing them, but intoned instead: "Grace: Why don't we display the strawberries right next to the melons? Maybe then some people will buy both. Harry: That's a good idea. Worth a try, anyway."

"Very realistic," Doug said, approving. "Very nice. Totally on message."

Looking over the pages at Doug, she said, "That's writing."

"It is not writing, Marcy," Doug said, "for two reasons. In the first place, *The Stand* is a reality show, the cameras catching real life on the fly, not a scripted show with actors. The Finches aren't actors, Marcy, they are an actual family struggling to run an actual farmstand on an actual farm on an actual secondary road in upstate New York."

"But," Marcy objected, "they're saying the words we write, down here in the production assistants' room, Josh and Edna and me."

"The Finches often," Doug allowed, "follow our suggestions, that's true. But, Marcy, even if they followed your suggestions one hundred percent of the time, you still wouldn't be a writer."

"Why not?"

"Because *The Stand* is a reality show, and reality shows do not have actors and writers because they do not need actors and writers. We are a very low-budget show because we do not need actors and writers. If you were a writer, Marcy, you would have to be in the union, and you would cost us a whole lot more because of health insurance and a pension plan, which would make you too expensive for our budget, and we would very reluctantly have to let you go and replace you with another twenty-two-year-old fresh out of college. You're young and healthy. You don't want all those encumbrances, health insurance and pension plans."

Doug's secretary Lueen, a cynical youngish woman in training to be a battle-axe, stuck her head in the door and said, "Doug, you got a party named Murch on the line."

Surprised, Doug said, "She *did* call? I didn't think she would."

"A male party named Murch."

"Oh, my God, the son! That's even better." Putting his hand on the phone as Lueen vacated the doorway, Doug said to Marcy, "You're a very good production assistant, Marcy, we all like you here, we'd hate to lose you. Just keep those suggestions coming." And into the phone he said, "Mr Murch?"

"I don't know about that," said a voice much warier than Marcy's. "My Mom said I should call you, make a meet. Me and a friend of mine."

"John," Doug said, remembering that other name, smiling at the phone. Oh, this was going to be a thousand times richer than *The Stand*. *The Gang's All Here.* "Your mother told me all about him."

"He'll be sorry to hear that," Murch said. "For a meet we were thinking about now."

Surprised, Doug said, "Today, you mean?"

"Now, we mean. Across Third from where you are there's a sidewalk restaurant thing."

Doug had often wondered who those people were at those tables on the sidewalk, one lane away from all those huge buses and trucks; it would be like having lunch next to a stampede. He said, "Yeah, I know it."

"Come on over, we're there now."

Oh, of course; that faint noise behind Murch's voice was traffic. Doug said, "If you're there anyway, why not come up to the office? It's a lot more comfortable."

"We're already settled in down here. Come on down."

"Well—" Murch was clearly trying to control his environment, protect himself from the unknown. Didn't he know there *was* no self-protection? Apparently not. "Okay," Doug said. "How will I know you?"

"We'll know you," Murch said, which sounded ominous, and broke the connection before Doug could say anything more.

All right; let's work this out. He called, "Lueen!" and when she appeared in the doorway he said, "Get me Marcy."

She smirked, just slightly. "Your standards are slipping," she said, and vacated the doorway.

Rising, Doug shrugged into the soft suede jacket he wore to the office at this time of year, then took a moment to wire himself, with a radio-microphone in his shirt pocket and its receiver in a pocket of the car coat.

As he finished, Marcy appeared in the doorway, now looking like a frightened steroidal chipmunk, meaning she expected she was about to be fired. "You wanted me, Doug?"

"Indeed I did. Do. Have you got your cell on you?"

"Sure."

"You know that sidewalk café across the street."

"Trader Thoreau, sure. I can't afford a place like that."

"I," Doug told her, "am going to meet with a couple fellows over there. I want you to leave a minute or two after I do, go down there, and get pictures of them both."

"Okay, sure."

"Be discreet, Marcy."

She nodded, with a fitful smile. "Sure, Doug."

"Nice clear pictures."

"Sure."

Doug headed for the door, patting the receiver in his pocket. "We don't know each other," he said.

"Oh, sure," she said.

3

DORTMUNDER WAS DUBIOUS about this. "What's in it for us?" he wanted to know, employing the plural form of the motto on his (stolen) family crest: *Quid Lucrum Istic Mihi Est*.

"Well," Stan said, "according to my Mom, he'll wanna pay us."

"To let him make a movie of us boosting something."

"That part can't be exactly right," Stan said. "We'll just listen to what he has to say. Is that him?"

They had taken an outdoor table at Trader Thoreau along the line of black wrought-iron fence separating the dining area from the pedestrian-and-vehicle area, which gave them an excellent view of the broad facade of the office tower across the avenue. Out of those doors now had come a purposeful youngish guy in a tan jacket, who paused to peer across at this café, then looked to left and right to see which intersection was nearest (neither), then struck off to his right.

"That's him, all right," Dortmunder said. "He's wired. See him pat the pocket?"

"I see him."

"I'll keep him," Dortmunder said.

"Good."

Which meant Stan would keep an eye on that building entrance to see what else might come out, while Dortmunder followed Doug Fairkeep's progress to the intersection, where he had to stand fidgeting while he waited for the light to change.

"Fat girl in red."

Dortmunder looked, and Stan was right. The girl was young and short and very nervous. Also, that shin-long red coat was too heavy for this time of year, making her look more like a sausage than a person. She too started off to the right, then apparently saw Fairkeep still stuck at the DON'T WALK sign, and veered around to hurry off in the opposite direction so abruptly that she knocked two other people out of their orbits, though neither actually fell to the ground.

Meanwhile, Fairkeep's traffic light had finally changed, permitting him to cross the avenue, and as he came nearer they could see he was a pleasant-looking guy in his early thirties, with that kind of open helpful manner that people's mothers like. Which didn't mean he was trustworthy.

Or particularly swift. He reached the entrance at the far end of the wrought-iron fence, then stood there gaping around, apparently not able to figure out who anybody might be, until Dortmunder raised an arm and waved at him.

Then the guy came right over, big smile on his face, hand stuck out for a shake from several yards away, and when he got close enough he said to Dortmunder, "You must be Mr Murch."

"In that case, I got it wrong," Dortmunder told him. "I'm John. This is Murch. Siddown."

Still smiling, Fairkeep put his unshaken hand away and said, "I'm Doug Fairkeep."

"We know," Dortmunder said. "Siddown."

So Fairkeep sat down and said to Stan, "I had a very pleasant chat with your mother yesterday."

"I heard about that," Stan said. "Usually, she's a little better at keeping her lip buttoned."

"Oh, don't be hard on your mom," Fairkeep said, with a little indulgent smile. "She could tell I didn't mean any trouble for you guys."

Dortmunder said, "What *do* you mean for us guys?"

"I work for Get Real," Fairkeep explained. "We produce reality shows and sell them to the networks. Maybe you've seen some—"

"No," Dortmunder said.

Fairkeep was almost but not quite hurt. "No? How can you be *sure* you never saw even—"

"John and I," Stan explained, "don't do much TV."

"I do the six o'clock news sometimes," Dortmunder allowed, "for the apartment house fires in New Jersey."

"Well, reality TV," Fairkeep told them, regaining the wind in his sails, "is the future. You don't have these fake little made-up stories, with actors pretending to be spies and sheriffs and everything, you've got real people doing real things."

Dortmunder gestured at Trader Thoreau and its surround. "I got all that here."

"But not *shaped*," Fairkeep said. "Not turned into *entertainment*."

Stan said, "Why doesn't she come sit with us?"

Fairkeep looked at him. "What? Who?"

"Your friend," Stan said, and pointed to where she lurked just outside the fence in crowded pedestrian land, being knocked about by elbows and shoulders as she tried to pretend she wasn't taking pictures with a cell phone. "The fat girl in red."

For just an instant, Fairkeep turned as red as the fat girl's coat, but then he laughed, open and cheerful, and said, "You guys are something. Sure, if you want. Where is she?" Not waiting for an answer (because he obviously knew she would be behind him to focus on the other two at the table), he twisted around and waved to her to join them.

She obeyed, but hesitantly, as though not sure she'd interpreted the gesture properly, and when she neared them Fairkeep said, "Join us, Marcy. Marcy, this is John and that's Stan Murch."

Marcy perched herself on the leading edge of the table's fourth chair, but as she opened her mouth to speak a waiter appeared, harried and hurried but somehow with a smooth still inner core, to say, "For you, folks?"

Stan said, "We all want a beer. Beck."

Fairkeep said, "Oh, nothing for me, thanks."

"You're paying for it," Stan told him, "so you might as well take it." He nodded to the waiter, who was anxious to be off. "That was four Beck."

Slap, four paper napkins hit the table and the waiter was gone.

Stan said, "Marcy, let me look at that phone."

"Sure." She handed him the phone, and he smiled at her as he pocketed it.

Fairkeep said, "Hey—"

"While we're at it," Dortmunder said, "why don't you give me that receiver now? It's there in your right pocket."

"My what?"

"The thing that's recording us," Dortmunder said.

Fairkeep bridled. "I'm not going to give you any company equipment!"

Stan said, "You know, we could get the same effect if we just throw you under that bus there."

Fairkeep turned and looked at the bus. "It's moving pretty slow," he said.

Dortmunder said, "That could make it worse."

Fairkeep thought about that, while Marcy sat and stared from face to face. Whatever was going on, she was pretty sure she wasn't qualified at this level.

Then all at once Fairkeep offered a broad smile, like the sun coming out on a previously cloudy day, and said, "You guys really are something. Here." Taking the little gray metal box from his pocket, handing it to Dortmunder, he said, "You don't want the mike, do you?"

"No need."

The waiter returned then, to slap bottles and glasses and a check on the table. "That'll be twenty-six dollars," he said.

Fairkeep, about to reach for his wallet, reared back and said, "Twenty-six dollars!"

"I just work here," the waiter said.

Fairkeep nodded. "Maybe I should," he said, and put two twenties on the check. "I'll need a receipt."

"I know," the waiter said, and sailboarded away.

Dortmunder said, "Cash? I thought guys like you always used credit cards."

16

"Cash," Fairkeep told him. "I leave a ten percent tip and put in for twenty."

Stan laughed. "Doug," he said, "you're a desperado."

"No," Fairkeep said, unruffled, "but you guys are. Here's what I'm offering, if I get an okay from you and an approval from my bosses up above. Twenty thousand a man, plus six hundred a working day per diem. That's for up to five men, and what you're selling us is permission to film you at work, doing what we needn't go into in any detail but that which makes you of interest to us. We would expect to be filming a few days a week for no fewer than six and no more than twelve weeks."

Dortmunder said, "Filming us doing what we do."

"That's right."

"What we do for real."

"That's why it's called reality."

"And then," Dortmunder said, "you're gonna show all this on TV."

"That's the whole point of it."

"The part I don't get," Dortmunder said, "is the part where we don't go to jail."

"Oh, I know there's gonna be a few problems along the way," Fairkeep said, cheerily confident. "There's always a few problems, and we work around them, and we'll work around the problems this time. Believe me, this one is gonna be easy."

Dortmunder looked at him. "Easy," he said.

"Compared to the dominatrix series we did," Fairkeep told him, "this is a snap. *That* one was nothing but problems. And laundry."

"So what we're gonna do that you're gonna make a movie of is break the law. I mean, break a bunch of laws; you never get to break just one."

"We'll work around it," Fairkeep assured him. "We got a great staff, crack people. Like Marcy here."

They all contemplated Marcy. "Uh-huh," Dortmunder said.

"So we'll all kick it around," Fairkeep said. "Beat the bushes, burn the midnight oil. You'll bring your expertise, we'll bring ours. And you guys never have to go one step forward if you're not comfortable."

Dortmunder and Stan looked at each other, and Dortmunder knew Stan was thinking just what he himself was thinking: We don't have anything else. Twenty grand to playact with a bunch of clowns with cameras. Plus the per diem.

Dortmunder nodded at Fairkeep. "Maybe," he said firmly.

"Me, too," said Stan.

Fairkeep beamed. "Great!" From inside the jacket came a fancy pen and a cheap pad. "Give me a contact number," he said.

"I'll give you my Mom's number," Stan told him. Since he lived with his Mom, this was also Stan's number, but Dortmunder felt Stan wasn't wrong to try for a little distance here.

Fairkeep copied down the number Stan rattled off, then said, "Where is this? Brooklyn?"

"Right."

"What is it, her cell?"

"No, it's her phone," Stan said. "On the kitchen wall." He wouldn't give out her cell phone number in the cab; Mom wouldn't like that.

"My mom has a phone like that," Fairkeep said, sounding sentimental, and smiled again as he put away pen and pad. "I'll talk to my bosses," he said, "and I'll be in touch."

"Fine."

They were all about to stand when Marcy said, "Excuse me."

They looked at her, and she was looking at Stan, so he was the one who said, "Yeah?"

"That's my only cell phone," Marcy said. "It's got all my friends on it, and my speed-dial, and just about my entire life. Couldn't you just delete the pictures out of there, so I could get my phone back?"

A little surprised, Stan said, "Maybe so," and pulled out the phone. Studying it, he said, "It's different from mine."

"I know," she said. "They're all different, I don't know why they do that. Push that button there to get to the menu."

It took the two of them a few minutes to burrow together down into the depths of the phone, but they finally did find where some slightly out-of-focus long-shot pictures of Dortmunder and Stan were located, and successfully removed them. Then Stan handed the little machine back to her and said, "I wouldn't want you to go around without your life."

"I appreciate it," she said. "Thank you very much."

4

Andy Kelp, a sharp-featured guy with a friendly grin, casually dressed in black and dark grays, said to the checkout clerk, a skinny doorknob-nosed seventy-year-old supplementing his Social Security with some minimum-wage retail work, "I wanna see My Nephew."

The clerk scratched his doorknob with a yellow fingernail. "Oh, no," he said, "there is no such person." Gesturing at this cavernous big-box discount store all around them, he said, "It's just the name of the place."

Kelp nodded. "He's about five foot one," he said, "and he weighs over three hundred pounds, all of it trans fats. He dresses out of a laundry basket and he always wears a straw hat and he talks like a frog with a sore throat."

"Oh, you *know* him!" the clerk said. Reaching for the phone beside his cash register, he said, "Most people don't. They don't know My Nephew's a real guy."

"Lucky them. Tell him it's Andy from the East Side."

"Okay, I will."

Kelp stepped aside while the clerk was on the phone, to let the next customer, a short round Hispanic lady totally concentrated on her own business, wheel into place an enormous shopping cart piled sky-high with Barbies, all different Barbies. Either this lady had an awful lot of little nieces or she was some kind of fetishist; in either case, Kelp was happy to respect her privacy.

"Okay," the clerk said to him, getting off the phone. "You know the office?"

"It's my first time here."

"Okay." Pointing with his doorknob, the clerk said, "You go down to the third aisle, then right all the way to the end and then left all the way to the end."

Thanking the man, Kelp left him amid the Barbies and followed the directions through this big near-empty space, with not quite enough customers and not quite enough merchandise to create confidence.

This was the My Nephew experience. He tended to open his discount centers in marginal areas of the city and New Jersey and Long Island, never pay the rent or the utilities, and get thrown out twelve to fifteen months later, with the loss of a certain percentage of his stock. Since his landlords and his suppliers were usually as iffy as he was, and since he created a new corporation with every move, there were never any very serious consequences, so My Nephew could always go on to open another marginal store in another marginal area of Greater New York that hadn't heard from him for a while. It was a living.

At the end of the clerk's directions stood a closed door, bearing two pieces of information: MEN painted in black at eye level, and OUT OF ORDER handwritten in red Flair pen on a shirt cardboard masking-taped a few inches lower down. Kelp knocked on OUT OF ORDER and heard a frog croak, "What?"

That was invitation enough; he opened the door and stepped into a small windowless messy office with My Nephew seated at the dented metal desk, looking exactly like Kelp's description of him, or possibly worse. "Hello," Kelp said.

"Andy from the East Side," My Nephew croaked. "You're a long way from home."

"I had a bit of luck," Kelp told him, and frowned at the wooden kitchen chair facing the desk. Deciding it was neither diseased nor likely to collapse, he sat on it.

"I don't like luck," My Nephew said. He sat hunched forward, fat elbows splayed on the desk to left and right.

"It has to be treated with respect," Kelp agreed. "And that's why I'm here."

"Luck don't usually bring people to this neighborhood," My Nephew said. "Tell me about it."

"It seems," Kelp said, "there's a spring storm out in the Atlantic. Way out in the Atlantic."

"So I shouldn't worry."

"It's an ill wind, you know. And what *this* ill wind means, there's two semis in a lot over by the Navy Yard hooked to containers full of flat-screen TVs supposed to be on their way to Africa right now."

"Only the storm."

"That ship may not get here at all. So I'm told by the warehouseman gave me the tip."

My Nephew shook his heavy gray head beneath his gray straw hat. "I would not be a seaman," he said.

That was too obvious to comment on. Kelp said, "It could be, I could move those semis."

"What make are we—?" My Nephew interrupted himself. "Second," he said, and reached for his phone, so it must flash a light instead of ringing.

Kelp sat back, in no hurry, and My Nephew said to the phone, "What?" Then he nodded. "Good," he said, hung up, and said to Kelp, "Gimme a minute."

"Take two."

Now My Nephew got to his feet, a complicated maneuver in three distinct sections. In section one, he leaned far forward with his broad palms flat on the desktop. In section two, he heaved himself with a loud grunt upward and back, becoming more or less vertical. In section three, he weaved forward and back, feet on floor and palms on desk, until he found his equilibrium. Then, lifting the palms from his desk and taking a loud breath, "Be right back," he said, turned, and waddled more briskly than you would have thought possible to a metal fire door in the wall behind the desk. He opened this door, stepped through a space barely wide enough for the purpose, and left, the door automatically shutting behind him.

Kelp had seen street out there. My Nephew's in a business conversation, he gets a phone call, he says one word, he leaves the building. This sequence suggested to Kelp that it could be some previous purveyor of irregular goods, not unlike Andy Kelp himself, had been a bit sloppy and had led police attention to this building, giving My Nephew the motivation to vacate. Probably it would be Kelp's smart move now to follow My Nephew's lead.

The door My Nephew had taken, which Kelp now took, led to a side street of warehouses across the way from the blank rear of the big-box store. Trucks of various sizes and descriptions were parked on this side only. My Nephew was nowhere to be seen. In a minute, neither was Kelp.

Three blocks from My Nephew—the building, not the man—and very close to the subway station that was his current goal, Kelp felt the cell phone in his jacket pocket vibrate against his heart. (He much preferred, in all situations, silence to noise.) Unpocketing it, opening it, he said, "Yeah."

"Maybe a conversation." The voice, Kelp recognized, belonged to a frequent associate of his named John Dortmunder.

"I'm very open," Kelp said, which was more true now than it had been ten minutes ago.

"Where are you?"

"Outer rings of Saturn."

"Brooklyn, huh? How long to get here?"

"Forty minutes," Kelp said, and was exactly right.

5

DORTMUNDER FINISHED DESCRIBING the situation and waited to hear what Kelp had to say, but Kelp just sat there, nodding slowly, looking at Dortmunder as though he were a rerun on that turned-off television set over there. They were seated together in Dortmunder's living room on East Nineteenth Street, with its view of the airshaft, Dortmunder in his usual armchair and Kelp on the sagging sofa. Kelp wouldn't take the other armchair because it was the exclusive property of Dortmunder's faithful companion May, who at the moment was still at her supermarket checkout job at the Safeway, bringing in the more or less honest part of their joint income.

Dortmunder nudged a little. "Well? Whadaya think?"

"I think," Kelp said judiciously, "I think I need another beer."

Dortmunder hefted the can in his own fist, found it empty, and said, "Yeah, me too."

Rising, Kelp said, "You stay there, John, I'll get it. The

exercise will do me good. Give me a chance to think about this."

"I know, it's a little different."

Heading for the hall, Kelp said, "The twenty G I kinda understand. It's the other parts."

"I know."

"I'll be back," Kelp said, but as he stepped through the doorway Dortmunder heard the sound of the apartment door open, down at the end of the hall. Kelp looked to his right, smiled in a way that suggested he now felt no ambivalence at all, and said, "Hey, May."

She appeared in the doorway, a tall slender woman, her neat black hair with gray highlights. She was lugging a grocery sack, her daily self-bestowal bonus for working at that place. "I just have to take this stuff to the kitchen," she said.

Kelp said, "I was on my way to get us both a beer. You want one?"

"I'll bring them," she said. "You sit down." And she headed on down the hall toward the kitchen.

So Kelp came back and settled once more onto the sofa, putting his empty on the coffee table as he said, "I tell you what. When May comes in, tell her the story. Maybe I'll get a better read on it if I look at it from the side, like."

"Good idea."

So, a minute later, when May reappeared, unencumbered except for three beer cans that she distributed, Dortmunder said, "I got a very strange proposition today."

She didn't quite know how to take that word. Settling into her chair, she said, "A proposition?"

"A job, kind of. But weird."

"John's gonna describe it to you now," Kelp said, and looked at Dortmunder, as alert as a sparrow on a branch.

Dortmunder took a breath. "It's reality TV," he said, and went on to describe how Murch's Mom had introduced Doug Fairkeep into their lives and what Doug Fairkeep had proposed, including the payoff.

Somehow, every time he told that story he got the same kind of dead-air silent reaction. Now May and Kelp both gave him the glassy-eye treatment, so he said, "That's the story, May, that's all there is."

She said, "Except the next day, when they drag you all off to jail."

"Doug Fairkeep says we'll work around that."

"How?"

"He doesn't say."

May squinted, much the way she used to squint back when she chain-smoked. "I'll tell you another question," she said. "What is it you're supposed to steal?"

"We didn't go into that."

"It might make a difference," she said.

Dortmunder didn't get it. "How?"

"Well," she said, "if they were going for laughs, like. Like if you hijacked a diaper service truck, something like that."

Kelp said, "*I'm* not gonna hijack any diaper service truck."

"*Like* that," she said.

Dortmunder said, "May, I don't think so. What they do is, they find people got some sort of interesting lifestyle or background or something, and they film the people doing what they do, and then they *shape* it, to make it *entertainment*. I don't think they're goin for jokes, I think they're goin for real."

"Jail is real," she said.

27

Dortmunder nodded, but said, "The problem is, so is twenty G."

"Looks to me," Kelp said, "as though you oughta go back and see this guy and ask him a lot more questions."

"I'm realizing that," Dortmunder admitted. "You wanna come along?"

"Oh, I don't think so," Kelp said, as casual as an aluminum siding salesman. "No need for me to poke my face in at this point. Murch's Mom didn't rat *me* out to the guy."

"No, she didn't," Dortmunder said.

"But I tell you what I'll do," Kelp said. "Come home with me and I'll Google him."

Dortmunder frowned. "Is that a good thing?"

"Oh, yeah," Kelp said.

6

DOUG FAIRKEEP'S IMMEDIATE BOSS at Get Real was a barrel-bodied bald sixty-year-old named Babe Tuck, who had come over from the news side after thirty years as a foreign correspondent. In the company bio online, a hair-raising read, were listed the times he'd been gassed, kidnapped, shot, abandoned in mid-ocean, set fire to, poisoned, dropped from a helicopter, and tied to the railroad tracks. "I've had enough of the real world," he'd announced, when making the transfer to Get Real. "Time to retire to reality."

Everybody was a little afraid of Babe Tuck, partly because of his history and reputation, but also because his mind was seriously twisted. He not only came up with the most outrageous ideas for reality series, he then went on to make them work. *The One-Legged Race,* for instance. All those wheelchairs, all those colostomy bags, all that bitching and complaint. Apparently, the fewer the limbs you had, the bigger the ego, to compensate.

So Doug had been pretty sure Babe wouldn't immediately reject the idea of filming professional criminals performing a professional crime. All it needed was for Babe to see how the idea could be made practical. Therefore, all he said was, "We'll have to run this by legal," when Doug finished describing the layout of the show.

Doug smiled. "We'll have to run this by legal," was obviously a way to say, "Yes, if . . ." That was fine. The if would work itself out; all Doug had needed was the yes.

"I'll talk to them over there," he offered, "or you can. Whatever you want."

Making a note on the legal pad on his desk, Babe said, "I'll make an appointment. Now we come to the question, violence."

Doug sat back in the leather visitor's chair, Babe's office being grander than his own, which was only right, but not garishly so, which was gratifying. "The cabbie," he said, "Mrs Murch, told me her son and the other guys didn't like violence, avoided it whenever they could."

Babe nodded, frowning at the note he'd just made. "Does this make them a little too Milquetoasty?"

"When I didn't want to turn over the recorder," Doug said, "Stan offered to throw me under a bus. A moving bus."

Surprised, Babe said, "*That's* a little violent."

"I didn't take it literally," Doug assured him. "I took it to be Stan telling me he would do what it took, so he was showing me the extreme case. Naturally, I gave him the recorder before we got anywhere near there."

"So there's a *threat* of violence," Babe said, "without the actual violence. That's good, I like that."

"These guys," Doug said, "have a certain grungy kind

of authenticity about them that'll play very well on the small screen."

Nodding, looking at his notepad, sucking a bit on his lower lip, Babe said, "What are they gonna steal?"

"That's up to them," Doug said. "We didn't get that far."

"No widow's mites," Babe cautioned. "No crippled newsie's crutches."

"Oh, nothing like that," Doug said. "Our demographic would like to see some snooty rich people get cleaned out."

"Clean out the Saudi Arabian embassy," Babe suggested.

Laughing, Doug said, "I'll pass that idea on."

"But not yet," Babe said. "Let's clear it with legal first, make sure we know what we're doing and we can actually do it. Not too much contact right at first."

"I won't move," Doug promised, "until I get your say-so."

"Good thinking," Babe said. "I'll get back to you."

Doug smiled all the way from Babe's office to his own, where Lueen looked up from her suspiciously clean desk (what did she actually *do* around here?) to say, "Somebody named John called for you."

Ah, John: the gloomy one. Following on Babe's desire for no premature contact, Doug said, "It's late in the day, Lueen, I'll get back to him tomorrow."

Pushing a pink *While You Were Out* slip across her desk toward him, she said, "He especially said he wanted to talk to you today. 'No surprises,' he said."

Doug frowned. "No surprises? What's that supposed to mean?"

"Beats me. There's the number anyway."

Doug picked up the slip, looked at it, and saw immediately Lueen had made a mistake. "No, it isn't," he said.

She gave him a skeptical eyebrow. "What do you mean it isn't?"

Holding the pink slip in his left palm, he tapped the phone number with his right index finger. "Lueen," he said, "this is *my* phone number."

She seemed pleasantly surprised. "Well, how'd he do that?"

Doug felt the earth shift slightly; an unpleasant sensation. Pushing the phone slip back toward Lueen he said, "You dial it. And I would very much prefer it if you got my answering machine."

"No skin off my nose," she said, made the call, and said, "John?"

Doug moaned minimally, and Lueen said, "Sure, Doug is right here. Hold on."

"I'll—I'll take it at my desk," Doug said, and fled to his office, where he picked up the phone with both hands, as though it just might make some kind of fast move on him. Into it he said, "Hello?"

"Doug?" John's voice.

"What are you doing in my apartment?"

"It's a nice place, Doug, you got good taste. Only that woman Renee moved out, I guess."

"A year ago," Doug said, and then thought, I can't have a calm conversation with the man, he's in my *apartment*. "What are you *doing* there?"

"Waiting for you. Quiet place for a meet. Only could you bring a six-pack? We like Heinekens."

"Heinekens," Doug echoed, and hung up the receiver.

What pier had he walked off here?

7

A T FIRST, Dortmunder couldn't figure out why he was suddenly hearing a jangly version of "The Whiffenpoof Song" on chimes. He looked across Fairkeep's neat if anonymous living room at Andy, seated at his ease on the other tan leather armchair across the kilim carpet, and as the final *bah* ricocheted around the gray-green walls, leaving only a metallic echo of itself, Andy said, "Doorbell."

Dortmunder said, "He's ringing his own bell?"

"Well," Andy said, being an understanding sort of guy, "he's not used to the situation. You oughta be the one that lets him in, he knows you."

Andy's decision to attend this meeting after all had been the result of that Google search done on the computer in Andy's apartment, which had not only given them Fairkeep's address, and Ivy League college record (low Bs), and marital status (un), and DVD rental preferences (date movies, mostly), but had also, once Andy switched to a different question, described the entire corporate Christmas tree of which Get Real Productions was a shiny but small bauble on a lower branch. Armed with this knowledge, and being in possession of Fairkeep's residence, Dortmunder rose, crossed to open the apartment door, and said, "You made good time." (He felt it would be better to begin with a pleasantry.)

Eyes wide, straining to scan every bit of the room at once, Fairkeep said, "I took a cab."

"Well," Dortmunder said, to reassure him, "ourselves, we didn't take anything."

Fairkeep's stare froze on Andy. "Who's this?"

"This is Andy," Dortmunder said, closing the door. (Fairkeep flinched, then tried to cover it.)

"How ya doing?" Andy said.

"Andy," Dortmunder explained, "will be another one on the payroll if it comes to that."

Seeing nothing amiss, and nothing missing, Fairkeep grew a lot calmer, saying, "Well, if it comes to that, we're gonna need something more than first names."

"When we're just batting it around," Andy said, "first names are friendlier. Yours is Doug, right?"

Before Fairkeep could answer that, Dortmunder gestured generally at the room and said, "Which chair is yours, usually?"

"What?" Fairkeep gaped around, apparently baffled by the question, then pointed at the chair where late Andy had sat. "That one."

"Fine," Dortmunder said, "I'll take that one over there."

"And I'll," Andy said, "be very happy on this sofa here." And sat down with a big smile.

Seeing both his guests seated on his furniture, Fairkeep

belatedly and abruptly also sat, rocking the armchair a bit. "You wanted to talk to me."

"We had some more questions," Dortmunder told him. Having plotted the whole thing out in his mind, he started with question number one: "What is it you want us to steal?"

Surprised, Fairkeep said, "*I* don't know. What do you usually steal?"

"Things that turn up," Andy said. "But you don't have any particular valuables in mind."

"No. *We* don't supply the story line, you do. We film you doing what you do—"

"And then you shape it," Dortmunder said, "and make it entertainment."

"That's right," Fairkeep said. "Even if the setup's kind of artificial sometimes, you—— Let me give you an example."

"Good," Dortmunder said.

"Let's say we rent a house, and we furnish it," Fairkeep said, "and we put spycams all through the house, and we get a bunch of college kids, boys and girls, and we pay them to live in the house. But the gimmick could be, they have to spend the whole summer vacation there, they can't ever step outside the house. Anybody leaves the house, they're out of the game. We ship in food, and they can watch TV, and like that. And they don't know each other before they start. And we can make up any rules we want to make up, make it different from any other show like that."

Dortmunder said, "And you get people to do this? All summer?"

"We've got waiting lists," Fairkeep said.

Dortmunder nodded. "And people watch this."

"You'd be surprised."

"I am surprised."

"The point being," Fairkeep said, "in a situation like that, what's gonna happen? Who falls in love, has a fight, can't hack it. We do the setup, but then they just do themselves. Same with you."

Andy said, "Only, where's our setup?"

"Well, with you," Fairkeep told him, "*you're* the setup. Like we're shooting one now, *The Stand*, it's a farm family upstate, they're running a vegetable stand out by the road, they're a quirky family, kind of kooky, but they've got to make this stand work, they really need the money. Maybe you've seen it. *The Stand*."

"Never," Andy said.

"Oh, well," Fairkeep said, "they did that stand thing anyway, long before we came along, but now we shape it—"

"—And make it entertaining."

Fairkeep's nod at Dortmunder was a little uncertain. "That's right," he said. "So whatever you want to do, that's what you do, and we'll film it."

Andy said, "Well, we were thinking, if it was gonna be like that, maybe it would be good, you know, what you call your tie-in—"

"Product placement," Dortmunder suggested.

"That, too," Andy agreed. "What we were thinking, Doug, if we lifted something that was connected to your own company some way, it might give us an inside track on things."

"A mole, like," Dortmunder said.

"And the other thing," Andy went on, "if the cops suddenly showed up to bust us, we could all just laugh and say it was all in fun, we were never gonna lift anything anyway."

"An insurance policy," Dortmunder said.

Fairkeep looked doubtful. "Take something from Get Real? There isn't anything at Get Real. We want you to aim a little higher than office supplies."

"We weren't," Andy said, "thinking of Get Real."

"Oh, you mean Monopole," Fairkeep said, sounding surprised that Andy would know about that. "Our big bosses?"

"Well, not your *big* bosses," Andy told him, taking a folded sheet of paper from his shirt pocket. Opening it, consulting it, he said, "What we got from Google is, Get Real is a subsidiary of Monopole Broadcasting, doing commercial TV and cable and Internet broadcasting and production and export. Sounds pretty good."

"Yes," Fairkeep said. "But Monopole isn't—"

"Now, Monopole," Andy said, frowning at his list, "is sixty percent owned by Intimate Communications, and that's owned eighty percent by Trans-Global Universal Industries, and that's owned seventy percent by something called SomniTech."

"My God," Fairkeep said, sounding faint. "I never worked it out like that."

"Now, all of these are East Coast companies," Andy said. "Among them, they're in oil, communications, munitions, real estate, aircraft engines, and chemistry labs."

Fairkeep shook his head. "Makes you feel small, doesn't it?"

Dortmunder said, "Doug, somebody in that mob has to have some cash."

Fairkeep blinked at him. "Cash?"

"Doug," Andy said, "we can't resell an aircraft engine."

"But there is no cash," Fairkeep told him. "Per diem for the crew on the road, that's all."

"Think about it, Doug," Dortmunder urged. "Somewhere in all those companies, all those businesses, and a lot of them are overseas, somewhere in all that there's got to be someplace with cash."

Shaking his head in absolute assurance, Fairkeep said, "No, there isn't. I have never seen cash in—" And then he kind of stuttered, as though he'd just had one of those mini–power outages that makes you reset all your clocks. In a second, less than a second, power was restored, but Fairkeep continued the sentence in a different place. "—Anywhere. It just isn't done. Even Europe, Asia, all those transactions are wire transfers."

Dortmunder had seen that little blip, and he was sure Andy had, too. He said, "Well, Doug, will you at least think about it?"

"Oh, sure," Fairkeep said.

"Good." Getting to his feet, because the explanation for the power outage would not be found in this room, not today, Dortmunder said, "We'll be in touch."

Surprised, Fairkeep said, "Is that it?"

"For today. We'll get back in touch when we fill out the roster."

"Oh, the five men, you mean," Fairkeep said. "But you don't even know what the robbery is yet, so you don't know if you'll need all five."

Rising from the sofa, Andy said, "Here's a rule for you, Doug. Never go in with fewer crew than you need."

8

JUDSON BLINT WAS TIRED of opening envelopes. Oh, sure, every envelope he opened was another check, twenty percent of which would go directly into his own pocket, the easiest money he could ever hope to find, and slitting open envelopes with a very good letter opener was not exactly hard labor, but still. Here he was, at a desk in a seventh-floor office in the Avalon State Bank Tower in midtown Manhattan, slitting open envelope after envelope, scanning into the computer the return addresses, keeping track of the check totals, and even though he knew very well what he was actually doing was mail fraud—in fact, three different mail frauds, as any federal law officer would know at once—there were still some moments, and this was one of them, when what he was doing here just felt like a job.

So here he sat, late on this Wednesday afternoon in April, when spring fever should by all rights have had him in its grip, and still he was making these repetitive movements, with the envelopes and the letter opener and the check piles and the scanner and the pen and the ledger, and if this wasn't work, Judson wanted to know, then what the hell was it?

The inner office door opened and J. C. Taylor came through. A dangerous-looking black-haired beauty in her mid-thirties, she paced forward like a predator who'd just picked up a fresh scent. Behind her in her office was Maylohda, the fictitious South Pacific island nation she used in her developing-country scams. (So many people want to help!) Looking at Judson, she said, "You still here?"

"Pretty heavy today, J. C.," he said. "I'm done with the detective course and the sex book and I'm just finishing up with the music."

"Don't stay too late," she advised. "You don't want to get stale."

"No, ma'am, I won't."

"Ma'am," she said, with a scornful look, and left. Judson shrugged—it was so hard to know the right reactions to people when you were barely a person yourself at nineteen—and went back to, face it, work.

He always saved the music business for last, because those people were the most fun. The people who just wanted to be a detective at home in their spare time or just wanted to look at dirty pictures at home in their spare time were pretty cut-and-dried, merely sending in their money, but the people who sent music to Super Star Music to have lyrics set to it, or alternatively, lyrics for an infusion of music (sometimes A's request meshing just fine with B's, so what came in could be shipped right back out again, neither participant any the wiser), tended to write confessional letters of such mawkish cluelessness that Judson wished there were, somewhere in the world, a publisher gutsy enough to put out a collection of them.

But that was not to be, since dispassionate self-knowledge is not a quality held in much esteem by the majority of the human race, so not enough people would find the product funny. Oh, well; at least he could enjoy the sincerity of these simpletons, to ease his own stress in the workaday world.

Ah; this grandmother of eight had been compelled at last to her true vocation as love-song lyricist by the flaming car-crash death of her favorite seventeen-year-old grand-daughter. Well, Grandma, lucky for you she bought it.

And this is the last of today's talents. Judson totted up the three totals and pushed his chair back from the desk, and the phone rang.

Answer? If he had already gone, the voice mail would take it. On the other hand, not too many phone calls came to this office, and he was bored enough and curious enough to pick up the receiver and deliver into it the standard patter: "J. C. Taylor. Mr Taylor isn't in at the moment."

"That's okay, Judson," a known voice said. "We're trying to get the book group back together again."

"John," Judson said, delighted. "I haven't heard from you for a while."

"I haven't had anything to say for a while."

Hope leaping in his breast, Judson said, "But now you do?"

"That's why we wanna get the book group together," John said. "We thought maybe the OJ at ten tonight."

"That sounds very good, John," Judson said, because it did, and smiled at the phone as he listened to John hang up.

Very good; yes. Though there was unlikely to be a book group involved in tonight's meeting, Judson knew from past experience that this sort of get-together often ended in gains much more ill-gotten than these little scammed checks here, but on the other hand far much less like work.

Whistling, he double-locked the office and legged it to the elevator.

9

WHEN DORTMUNDER WALKED into the OJ Bar & Grill on Amsterdam Avenue that Wednesday night at ten, the big low-ceilinged square room was underutilized. The booths along both sides and the tables in the middle were all empty. At the bar, along the rear of the room, Rollo the meaty bartender, off to the right, was slowly carving tomorrow's specials onto a black blackboard with a stub of white chalk, a gray rag in his other hand. The regulars, as usual, were clustered along the left side of the bar.

It being April, the regulars were discussing taxes. "I might declare my bowling ball as an expense," one said.

The guy to his right reared back. "Your *bowl*ing ball!"

"We wager certain amounts," the first regular explained. "Only then I'd have to declare how much I won, and then pay tax on *that*. I asked the guy at the drugstore, which way do I come out ahead, he said he'd get back to me on that."

As Dortmunder angled toward Rollo, he saw that the

barman was groping in the direction of "lasagna," but hadn't quite reached it yet. Seeing Dortmunder, he nodded and said, "Long time no see."

"I been semiretired," Dortmunder told him. "Not on purpose."

"That can be a drag." Rollo pointed his jaw at the black-board. "Whadaya think?"

Dortmunder looked: LUHZANYA. "I don't know about that H," he said.

Rollo considered the entire word. "At least I'm sure of the L," he said, as Andy Kelp joined Dortmunder and said, "How you doin? It isn't a Z."

Dortmunder turned to him. "What isn't a zee?"

Kelp pointed. "That thing there. It's an S."

Rollo went akimbo, chalk staining the seam of his apron as he brooded at the blackboard. "It sounds like a Z," he decided.

"Yeah," Kelp acknowledged, "but you gotta remember, it's a foreign tongue."

"Oh, lasagna," Dortmunder said, catching up. "I think you're right. I don't think those languages even have a Z. Except the English do."

"And the Polish," Kelp said. "What *they* don't have is vowels. And Rollo, what I don't have is a drink."

Rollo at once put down rag and chalk. "You two," he said, "are bourbon on the rocks." Reaching for ice and glasses, he said, "Who else we got tonight?"

Understanding that Rollo preferred to know his cus-tomers by their drink preferences, as being conducive to good customer relations, Dortmunder said, "Well, we got the beer and the salt, and the vodka and red wine, and I don't know what the kid drinks."

"He hasn't settled down yet," Rollo said. "He's still making up his mind." And he pushed forward toward them a round metal bar tray on which appeared RHEINGOLD WORLD'S FAIR 1939, atop which now stood two glasses containing ice cubes, a white plastic bowl with more ice cubes, and a bottle labeled *Amsterdam Liquor Store Bourbon—"Our Own Brand."* "I'll send them back," he said.

Picking up the tray, Kelp said, "Good luck with the menu."

"I'll need it." Rollo frowned at the blackboard. "Anyway," he said, "I know there's got to be a Y in there somewhere."

Dortmunder followed Kelp as he carried the tray down along the bar past the regulars, where the third was now saying, "The idea of the flat tax is, you just pay the same as one month's rent."

Rounding the turn at the regulars, Dortmunder and Kelp trooped down the dim-lit hall, past the doors marked POINTERS and SETTERS over black dog silhouettes, and past the crammed-full narrow storage space for boxes of deposit bottles that had been a phone booth before the communications revolution and a certain amount of vandalism. At the end, while Kelp waited, Dortmunder pushed open a door on the right to reach in and switch on the light. Then they both entered.

This was a small square room with a concrete floor. Beer and liquor cartons were stacked ceiling-high against all the walls, leaving an area in the middle just big enough for a beat-up old round wooden table with a once-green felt top, surrounded by half a dozen armless wooden chairs. The light Dortmunder had switched on was a single bare bulb under a round tin reflector hanging from a long black wire over the center of the table.

Dortmunder and Kelp went around this furniture to left and right, Kelp putting down the tray as they took the chairs that most directly faced the open door. The first arrivals always took the chairs facing the door, leaving it to the latecomers to be made uneasy by the proximity of an open door behind their backs.

As he poured Amsterdam Liquor Store Bourbon over the ice in their glasses, Kelp said, "You tell them the story. I like to listen to it."

"Well, Stan already knows the story," Dortmunder pointed out. "It's only Tiny and the kid."

"So those are the ones you tell."

The hallway out there abruptly dimmed, as though there'd been a partial eclipse of the hall. Seeing that, Kelp said, "Here comes Tiny now."

As Dortmunder nodded, the doorway filled with enough person to choke Jonah's whale. This creature, who was known only to those who felt safe in considering him their friend as Tiny, had the body of a top-of-the-line SUV, in jacket and pants of a neutral gray that made him look like an oncoming low, atop which was a head that didn't make you think of Easter Island so much as Halloween Island. In his left fist he carried a glass of what looked like, but was not, cherry soda. When he spoke it wasn't a surprise that bass notes of an organ sounded: "I'm late."

"Hi, Tiny," Kelp said. "No, you're not."

Ignoring that, Tiny said, "I hadda take the limo driver back."

"What, to the car service?"

"That's where I got him. Turns out, he's from California." Tiny shook his Halloween Island head and came over to sit at Dortmunder's right, so at least he had the doorway in profile.

Kelp said, "That could be okay, Tiny. There's okay people in California."

"In California," Tiny said, "he's also a limo driver."

"So he knows how," Kelp said.

"Every year," Tiny said, "he drives people to the Oscars. Celebrities. He wanted to tell me, every year, every year, the celebrities he drove to the Oscars."

"Oh," Kelp said.

"There's only so many," Tiny said, "celebrities goin to the Oscars you can put up with. So finally I took him back, dropkicked him through the door, and said, gimme one doesn't speak English. So how are you people?"

Dortmunder took over the conversational ball: "Just fine, Tiny."

"I hope you got a good one here," Tiny said.

"So do we," Dortmunder said.

"It's been a while," Kelp said.

"Oh, I'm doin okay," Tiny said. "I always do okay. I squeeze out a little livin here and there. But I'd like a little cushion for a while."

"So would I," Dortmunder said, and Stan and Judson came in together.

Stan carried a draft beer in one hand and a saltshaker in the other. As a driver, he preferred to limit his alcohol intake to the occasional sip, but beer left to its own devices soon grows flat, which nobody likes. A sparing shimmer of salt over the beer every once in a while causes the head to magically return.

Judson, on the other hand, was carrying a drink nobody recognized. It was in a tall cocktail glass with ice and was a kind of palish rose color, as though it were Tiny's drink's anemic sister.

When they came in, while the others were sharing greetings, Stan looked around, made a quick assessment, and said, "We're late." Then he homed in on the chair to Kelp's left, leaving the kid to choose one of the chairs on the vulnerable side. But that was all right; he was a calm sort.

Once they were all seated, Kelp said, "Kid, if you don't mind a nosy question, what's that?"

"Campari and soda," the kid said, with the proud smile of ownership.

"Campa—" Kelp pointed at the glass. "And what's the yellow thing?"

"Lemon peel."

"Uh-huh. If you don't mind, how come?"

"Somebody had it in a movie, and it sounded nice. So I thought I'd try it."

"And is it nice?"

"Yeah." The kid shrugged. "Makes a change from beer."

Everybody agreed with that, and then Kelp said, "John's gonna tell the newcomers the story here."

Stan said, "I picked up the kid at his place, and filled him in on the way over."

"Oh," Kelp said.

Looking around, Tiny said, "Does this mean I'm the last to know? I don't like that much."

Hastily, Stan told him, "What it is, Tiny, yesterday my Mom picked up a fare at Kennedy, he's a reality television producer, turns out, he wants to film us pulling a heist, for twenty G a man plus per diem."

Tiny nodded, but not as though he agreed with anything. He said, "And the get out of jail free card?"

Dortmunder said, "The guy says we'll work around that."

"Twenty years at hard labor," Tiny commented. "That's a lot to work around."

Dortmunder said, "Andy and I had a discussion with the guy this afternoon, at his apartment."

Stan said, "Oh? Where's that?"

"One of those Trump buildings on the west side."

"And how is it?"

Dortmunder shrugged. "Okay."

"A little too bronze," Kelp said.

Tiny said, "Over here, I'm still working around this."

"Okay," Dortmunder said. "Andy did some computer trick—"

"It's no trick," Kelp said. "I Googled."

"Oh, sure," Stan said.

"Whatever," Dortmunder said. "Turns out, this guy's little company is owned by a bigger company, owned by a bigger company, and like that. Like those cartoons where every fish is getting eat by the bigger fish behind him."

Tiny said, "So? What does this have to do with you and me?"

"We asked him," Dortmunder said, "did he have something in particular he wanted us to boost, and he said no, dealer's choice, he just wants to make the movie."

"The evidence."

"Yeah, that. So Andy had a suggestion for him."

"I'm ready to hear it," Tiny said.

Kelp said, "Why not boost something from one of those companies up there on top of him? That way, if law suddenly shows up, we were just foolin, never gonna do it for real."

"That's not bad," Tiny admitted.

"In fact," Stan said, "that's good. An escape hatch."

"So then," Kelp said, "he asked what kind of thing we'd like to lift, and we said cash, and he said there's no cash anywhere in all these big corporations. And all of a sudden—"

"Yeah," Dortmunder said.

Kelp nodded. "We both saw it. All of a sudden, he remembered something. But then he clammed up, pretended like nothing happened."

Stan said, "Why that son of a bitch."

"Somewhere," Dortmunder said, "somewhere in his working hours, Doug Fairkeep has seen cash."

Tiny said, "Where?"

"That's what we gotta figure out."

Kelp pulled some sheets of paper from his pocket. "I printed out the companies and what they do," he said. "Three copies. Tiny, here's yours, Stan, you can share with the kid, and I'll share with John."

The room became quiet, as though it were study period. Everybody bent over the lists, looking for cash, failing to find it. Finally Tiny pushed his list away and said, "There's no cash there. Real estate, movies, aircraft engines. Forget cash."

"It hit him," Dortmunder insisted. "We both noticed."

The kid said, "What was it, like he just remembered?"

"Yeah, like that."

The kid nodded. "So it's not cash he's around all the time," he said. "It's just some cash he happened to see a couple times. Or once."

Tiny said, "That still doesn't help."

"Well, wait a minute," the kid said. "What were you

50

all talking about when he suddenly remembered the cash?"

Dortmunder and Kelp looked at one another. Dortmunder shrugged. "How there was no cash."

Kelp said, "How even with Europe and Asia it was all wire transfers."

The kid looked interested. "That's what he was saying just before he remembered? Wire transfers to Europe and Asia?"

Dortmunder said, "No, Andy, that was after. Before, I said there were all these companies, and some of them overseas, so there had to be some cash around somewhere."

The kid said to Dortmunder, "So *you* talked about overseas first."

"Yeah, I did. And then he did that stutter-stop thing—"

"And *then*," Kelp said, "he said how, even to Europe and Asia, it's all wire transfers."

"So it's something foreign," the kid said. "It's cash, and it has something to do with Europe and Asia."

"But Doug Fairkeep isn't foreign," Dortmunder said. "He doesn't work foreign. His work is right here."

"So where he saw the cash," the kid said, "was here, on its way to Europe and Asia. Europe *or* Asia."

Stan said, "Am I following this? We now think this Fairkeep guy at least once saw a bunch of cash around where he works, that was going to Europe or Asia. What the hell for?"

Kelp said, "They're buying something?"

"What happened to the wire transfers?"

"Oh!" said the kid. When they all looked at him, he had a huge happy grin on his face. Lifting his glass, he toasted them all in Campari and soda, then knocked back a good swig of it, slapped the glass down onto the felt, and said, "Now I get it!"

That was the annoying thing about the kid, who was otherwise okay. Every once in a while, he'd get it before anybody else got it, and when he got it, he got it. So Tiny said to him, "If you got it, give it to us."

"Bribes," the kid said.

They looked at him. Stan said, "Bribes?"

"Every big company that does business in different countries," the kid said, "bribes the locals when they want to come do business. Here, buy our aircraft engines, not that other guy's aircraft engines, and you look like you could use another set of golf clubs. Here's a little something for the wife. Wouldn't you like to run our TV show on your station? I know they don't pay you what you deserve; here, have an envelope."

"I've heard about this," Kelp said. "There's a word everybody uses, it's *chai*, it means 'tea,' you sit down together, you have a cuppa tea, you move the envelope."

Tiny said, "So? That's what they call business."

"Somewhere around thirty years ago," the kid said, "the US Congress passed a law, it's illegal for an American company to bribe foreigners."

Stan said, "*What?* No way."

"It's true," the kid said. "American companies have to be very careful, it's a federal crime, it's a felony, they all gotta do it, but they really don't wanna get caught."

Kelp said, "So we're shooting ourself in the foot, is what you're saying."

"Both feet," said the kid. "And not for the first time. Anyway, what this guy Doug saw was the courier, the guy who carries the cash. He's a known guy to everybody, he works for this television outfit, he travels for them all the time, they're used to seeing him go back and forth, he always carries all his movie equipment with him."

Tiny said, "That's very nice."

"And one time," the kid said, "maybe more, Doug saw the cash going into the DVD boxes. So the guy who carries the money works in Doug's outfit."

"Him," Dortmunder said, "we'll find. It may take a little time, but him we'll find."

"What's extra nice about this," Tiny said, "it's like those guys that knock over drug dealers. You heist somebody already committing a crime, he doesn't call the cops."

"At last," Kelp said. "The perfect crime."

On his way out, Dortmunder saw that the blackboard of tomorrow's specials was now complete, and included LASAGNA. "Very good," he said, nodding at the board.

Rollo smiled, happy again. "We called the Knights of Columbus," he said.

IO

WHEN THE PHONE on the Murch kitchen wall sounded at eight-fifteen on Thursday morning, both mother and son frowned at it from their twinned breakfast helpings of white toast, much grape jelly, black coffee, and a matched set of *Road & Track* magazine. They watched the phone through its ensuing silence, and when it sounded a second time Stan said, "That isn't for me. I don't know anybody up at this hour. It's taxi business."

"You don't do taxi business on the phone," she said, but nevertheless she got to her feet, crossed to the phone, slapped it to her ear, and snapped, "Go ahead," giving nothing away.

Stan, striving to appear as though he wasn't watching and listening, watched and listened, and was surprised when his mother abruptly smiled and said, with no ill will at all, "Sure I remember. How you doing?" Then she turned, still smiling, extended the phone toward Stan, and said, sweetly, "It's for you."

Oh. Getting it, Stan said, "Reality check," got to his feet, and took the phone, while his triumphant mother went back to her breakfast and her SUV comparison appraisals. Into the phone, Stan said, "Yeah, hello. You're up early."

It was Doug from yesterday, all right, "Reality," he said, "waits for no man, Stan."

"Where are you, a Chinese fortune cookie factory?"

"Ha ha. Listen, it's time we got started."

"Doing what?"

"*The Gang's All Here*. You like it?"

Stan had the feeling he was in the wrong conversation somehow. He said, "Like what?"

"The title. *The Gang's All Here*. You like it?"

"No."

"Well," Doug said, sounding just a little hurt, "it isn't written in stone."

"No, it wouldn't be."

"What we've got to do," Doug said, determinedly getting down to business, "is make a start here. I don't need the whole five men yet, but I want to get together with you and John and Andy soonest."

Stan still wasn't comfortable with the idea that this civilian knew everybody's name. He said, "Where do you want to do this, your office?"

"No. We've got a rehearsal space downtown, we—"

"Wait a minute," Stan said. "You got a rehearsal space for reality shows?"

"It isn't like *that*," Doug said. "It's a big open space, like a loft, it gives us the chance, try out some ideas, smooth out some problems before we really get moving."

"Okay."

"When do you think you guys could get there?"

"Well, I'll have to talk to the other two, they probly aren't up yet."

"Out burgling all night? Yuk yuk."

"No." Stan could be patient, when he had to be; it comes with being the driver. "We don't punch a clock, see," he explained, "so we like to sleep in."

"Of course. I tell you what. I'll give you the address, my cell number, call me back and tell me when we can meet. Okay?"

"Sure."

"It's down on Varick Street," Doug said, "below Houston, the freight elevator opens onto the sidewalk, that's where the bell is."

"Okay."

"We're the fifth floor, that's the top floor, the name on the bell is GR Development."

"I'll call you back," Stan said, and hung up.

"Taxi business," his mother said, and snapped a page in *Road & Track.*

II

When Kelp came strolling down Varick Street at two that afternoon, he saw Dortmunder ahead of him, facing a building in midblock, frowning at it while he frisked himself. Kelp approached, interested in this phenomenon, and Dortmunder withdrew from two separate pockets a crumpled piece of paper and a ballpoint pen. Bending over the paper held in his cupped left palm, he began to write, with quick glances at the facade in front of him.

Ah. The right third of the building, at street level, was a gray metal overhead garage door, graffiti-smeared in a language that hadn't been seen on Earth since the glory days of the Maya. To the immediate left of this was a vertical series of bell buttons, each with an identifying label. These were what Dortmunder was copying onto a cash register receipt from a chain drugstore.

Reading the labels directly, since Dortmunder's handwriting was about as legible as the Mayan graffiti, Kelp saw:

5 GR DEVELOPMENT
4 SCENERY STARS
3 KNICKERBOCKER STORAGE
2 COMBINED TOOL

The building, broad and old, was made of large rectangular stone blocks, time-darkened to a blurry charcoal. On the street floor, to the left of the garage, were two large windows, barred for security and opaque with dirt, and beyond them at the farther end a gray metal door with a bell mounted in its middle at head height. The upper floors showed blank walls above the garage entrance and three windows each, all looking a little cleaner than the ones down here.

Putting paper and pen away, Dortmunder acknowledged Kelp's presence for the first time: "Harya doin?"

"I wanna see the inside of the place," Kelp told him.

"We can do that," Dortmunder said, and pushed the button for five.

They waited less than a minute, and then a mechanical voice from somewhere said, "Yeah?"

"It's John and Andy," Dortmunder told the door.

"And Stan," Stan said, having just walked up from farther downtown.

"And Stan."

"I'll be right down."

They waited about three minutes this time, while beside them the slow-moving traffic of southbound Varick Street oozed by, the two nearer lanes headed for the Holland Tunnel and New Jersey, the farther happier lanes not. Then, with a lot of metallic groaning and creaking, the garage door lifted and there was Doug Fairkeep with the grin he wore like a fashion statement, saying, "Right on time."

They boarded. The elevator, big enough for a delivery truck, was just a rough wooden platform, with no side walls of its own. Ahead of them the building was broad and deep, and this level was used as a garage, for a great variety of vehicles. There were cars and vans and small trucks, but also what looked like a TV news truck, a small fire engine, an ambulance, a hansom cab without the horse, and a lot more. If it had wheels, it was in here.

Doug stood next to a compact control box attached to the building's front wall, and when he pressed a button on it the door began noisily to lower. The elevator started up before the door finished coming down, which was a surprise, though nobody actually lost his balance.

The platform they rode rose slowly through the building, too noisily for conversation. On the second floor—Combined Tool—a clean off-white wall stood at the side, but no front wall. Out there a hall extended to the left, also off-white, with one closed office door in the part they could see.

Third floor: Knickerbocker Storage. On this level too there was a wall to their left, not recently painted anything. This wall extended straight back to the rear of the building, with double doors spaced along the way. Apparently the idea was, a truck or a van could come up the elevator to this floor, then drive along that hall and stop to unload at one or another set of doors.

Four: Scenery Stars. No wall either left or straight ahead, and no interior walls either except in the far right corner; probably a bathroom. In the far left corner a flight of black iron stairs rose up from rear to front, and thick black iron

59

columns stood at intervals to bear the weight. The large space was full of stacks of lumber, piles of paint cans, tables covered with tools, tall canvas stage flats. A bald man in sunglasses sat at a slanted drafting table near the stairs, drawing on a large pad with pen and ruler under a bare bulb with a broad tin shade like the one in the back room at the OJ. He didn't look toward them as their platform rose up past him.

Five: Another big open space with black iron support columns and corner bathroom, but this one brighter, with large windows and skylights. The iron stairs at this level rose up to a closed trapdoor. Sofas and chairs and tables were scattered around in no order, as though waiting to be assembled into a stage set, but still the space seemed mostly empty.

Three men rose from sofas toward the middle of the room and waited to be introduced. Doug led the way to them, then said, "Andy, John, Stan, this is my boss, Babe Tuck."

Babe Tuck, a tough-looking sixty-year-old with the barrel shoulders of a street fighter, nodded without smiling and said, "Doug has high hopes for you."

Dortmunder said, "We feel the same way about him."

Nobody offered to shake hands. Babe Tuck put his own hands in his pockets, rocked back on his heels a little, nodded again as though agreeing with himself, and said, "I suppose you've all been inside sometimes."

"Not for a while," Dortmunder said.

Stan said, "We don't go where that's likely to break out."

"You're probably like most guys," Babe Tuck told them. "You got no idea how lucky you are to be inside an American prison. Except for the rapes, of course. But the rest of it? Heated cells, good clothes, regular food. Not even to talk about the medical care."

"I wish I'd looked at it that way," Kelp said, "back then."

Tuck grinned at him. "Make the time pass easier," he suggested. "Do you know the longest life expectancy in America is in our prisons?"

"Maybe," Kelp said, "it just seems longest."

Tuck liked that. His eyes lighting up, he turned to Doug, gestured at Kelp, and said, "Keep a mike on this one."

"Oh, I will."

"Well," Tuck said, "I just wanted to see our latest stars, and now I'll leave you to it." Nodding toward Doug, he said to his three latest stars, "You're in good hands with Doug."

"Glad to hear it," Dortmunder said.

Walking off toward the platform elevator, Tuck said, "I'll send it back up."

"Thanks, Babe."

No one said anything until Tuck reached the platform, crossed it to the control panel on the building wall, and pressed the down button. He was patting his pockets, frisking himself like Dortmunder, as the platform descended, leaving a startlingly large rectangular hole.

Doug now turned to the last introductions. "Fellas, this is Roy Ombelen, he's your director."

"Charmed, I'm sure," said Roy Ombelen, a tall man thin enough to be a plague victim, dressed in a brown tweed jacket with leather elbow patches, bright yellow shirt, paisley ascot, dark brown leather trousers, and highly polished black ankle boots. On a gold chain around his neck, outside the shirt, hung what looked like a jeweler's loupe.

Kelp gave this vision his most amiable grin. "And charmed right back at you."

Ombelen looked faintly alarmed, but managed a smile. "I'm sure," he said, "we'll all hit it off just famously."

"You got it."

"And this," Doug said, "is our designer, Manny Felder."

Manny Felder was short and soft, in shapeless blue jeans, dirty white basketball sneakers large enough to serve as flotation devices, and a too-large gray sweatshirt with the logo *Property of San Quentin.* He peered at them through oversize tortoiseshell glasses taped across the bridge with a bit of duct tape, and, in lieu of "hello," said, "The most important thing we gotta consider here is setting."

"Setting what?" Dortmunder asked.

"*The* setting." Felder gestured vaguely with unclean hands. "If you got your diamond, and you put it in the wrong setting, what's it look like?"

"A diamond," Stan said.

Ombelen said, "Why don't we all sit, get comfortable? You— John, is it?"

"Yeah."

Pointing, Ombelen said, "Why don't you and Andy slide that sofa around to face this way, and Doug, if you could help Manny bring over those easy chairs . . ."

Following Ombelen's brisk instructions, they soon had an L-shaped conversation area and sat, whereupon Ombelen said, "What Manny was talking about was mise-en-scène."

"Oh, yeah?" Dortmunder said.

"The setting," Felder insisted.

"Yes, Manny," Ombelen said, and told the others, "what

we're looking for is places you frequent, a background to place you in. For instance, do you lot have a lair?"

The three latest stars compared bewildered looks. Dortmunder said, "A lair?"

"Some place the gang might gather," Ombelen explained, "to plan your schemes or—what is it?—divvy the loot."

Kelp said, "Oh, you mean a hangout."

"Well, yes," Ombelen said, "But not, I hope, a corner candy store."

Stan said, "He's talking about the OJ."

"Ah," Ombelen said, perking up. "Am I?"

Dortmunder said to Stan, "We can't take these guys to the OJ. That blows everything."

Ombelen said, "I understand we're dealing with a certain delicacy here."

"No matter how good your boss thinks American prisons are," Dortmunder told him, "we don't want to be in one."

"No, I can see that," Ombelen said, and frowned.

Doug piped up then, saying, "Roy, we don't have to use actual places. We'll make sets." To Dortmunder and the others, he said, "For this show, because of the special circumstances, we won't have to use authentic *places*. Just the guys in them and what they're doing, that has to be authentic."

"Well," Ombelen said, "the site of the robbery, wherever that is, that can't be a set. That has to be the real place."

"Of course," Doug said.

"I'd wanna see this OJ," Manny Felder said.

Stan said, "Why? If you're not gonna use it."

"I gotta get the feel for it," Felder said. "Whatever I make, I gotta make it so when you're in it it's the place that looks right for you."

"This OJ," Ombelen said. "What is it, a bar?"

"We use the back room of a bar," Dortmunder told him. "It just looks like the back room of a bar, with a table and some chairs."

"But Manny's right," Ombelen said, as across the way the elevator/platform rose noisily into view, and stopped. Once its racket ended, "We would need," Ombelen explained, "the feel of the entire place, the ambience, the bar itself, the neighborhood, the customers. There must be a bartender. He's an important character."

Kelp said, "That doesn't work. We can't let you have Rollo."

"That's the bartender?" Ombelen shook his head. "Not a problem. We'll cast that."

Doug said, "Maybe a good spot for some comic bits."

"But," Ombelen said, "we'll have to see what the original looks like, so we know how to do our casting."

"Agreed," Doug said, and turned to the others. "We're not gonna use anybody's real name, or any*thing*'s real name, so your OJ will stay private, it's yours. But Manny's right, we've got to see it."

The three exchanged glances, frowns, minimal head-shakings, and then Dortmunder said, "All right. This is what we do. We give you the address and you go there— maybe tonight, it's better after dark—and you look around, maybe take a picture or two. But not suspicious or sneaky, not like you're from the state liquor authority. No conversations. You go in, you buy your drink, you drink it, and get outa there."

Felder said, "What about this back room?"

"You do it, only by yourself," Kelp told him, "You can take all the pictures you want back there."

"That's good, Andy," Dortmunder said.

"Thank you."

"All right," Felder said. "How do I get to this back room?"

"The johns are down the hall from the left end of the bar," Dortmunder said. "Nobody can see you back there. At the end of the hall is a door on the right. That's us."

"Easy," Felder said.

Stan said, "But only one of you guys goes. We don't want everybody running into the men's room together, it isn't that kind of joint."

Doug said, "Understood. We'll probably go tonight. I take it you won't be there?"

"Absolutely not," Dortmunder said.

Doug looked around at his creative team. "Is there anything else?"

Felder looked unsatisfied. He said, "Any more settings?"

"Manny," Doug said, "I don't think so. Just generic Manhattan streets, apartments." To the others he said, "You all live in apartments, right? In Manhattan?"

Again they exchanged troubled looks. This time, reluctantly, Stan said, "I live in Canarsie."

"But that's wonderful!" Doug said, and Ombelen too lit up in a way that the name "Canarsie" doesn't usually evoke.

Stan said, "You can't use it, it's just where I live, it doesn't have nothing to do with nothing."

"But you come to Manhattan for the heists," Doug said, eyes bright with pleasure. "Stan, you commute!"

"Yeah, I guess. I never thought of it like that."

"But that's good," Doug said. "Gives us another demographic. The burglar who commutes to his job."

"I like it," Ombelen said. "I could do some very nice visuals with that."

Doug peered at them all with his freshest, most bright-eyed face. "Anything else? Any little details I should know?"

"I don't think so," Dortmunder said. "In fact, I know so. No."

"Well, this has all been very good," Doug said, and actually rubbed his hands together. "We're moving along here. I'll be back in touch when we've got something to show you. And meanwhile, see if you can decide what exactly you're gonna steal. That's Manny's other setting, and he'll need to know it pretty early."

"One little favor," Felder said.

They looked at him. Dortmunder said, "Yeah?"

"Nothing too dark, okay?" Felder spread his hands, looking for understanding and assistance around here. "Somewhere where we can see what you're doing."

Kelp laughed, mostly in amazement. "You know," he said, "usually, everything we do, what we're trying for is just the reverse of that."

12

Doug felt buoyant all the way uptown from Varick Street, cheered by the meeting with *The Roscoe Gang* (tentative), cheered by the way Roy Ombelen and Manny Felder had immediately seen the potential, and cheered by Babe's genial manner when he'd left them. Then, the instant he stepped into the office, he sensed something was wrong, and all his mellow mood was instantly flushed away.

What was it? The atmosphere was somehow not its usual self; his antenna tingled with it. He headed straight down the hall toward Lueen, to ask her what had broken down and how much it would spoil his day, but then he saw, in the production assistants' room, Marcy and Edna and Josh, the three nonwriters, all huddled together, whispering, apparently in a state of shock.

Writers whispering together; never a good sign. Entering

their room, Doug said, as though cheerfully, "Hello all. What's up?"

The three young faces that turned to him were bleak. Marcy said, "It's Kirby Finch."

Kirby Finch was the younger son of the family running the farmstand, a strapping handsome boy, nineteen, known to the viewers as a fun-loving cutup. This year he'd be finding a girlfriend, a warm little G-rated romance to keep the audience numbers up. Doug said, "What about Kirby Finch? There wasn't an accident, was there?"

"Worse," Josh said. His eyes were wide, and his voice seemed to be coming from an echo chamber.

"He says," Marcy explained, "he doesn't want to do all that stuff with Darlene Looper."

Josh said, "He just saw next week's script, and he says he won't do it."

"Oh, come on," Doug said. "Kirby *shy*? I don't buy it."

Marcy said, "It isn't that, Doug." She seemed reluctant to spell out what the problem was.

"I'll tell you," Doug said, "*I* wouldn't kick Darlene out of bed."

"Kirby would," Marcy said, and the other two sadly nodded.

Doug said, "Does he have a *reason*?"

"Yes," Marcy said. "He says he's gay."

"*Gay!*" Doug made a fist and pounded it into his other palm. "No! We shall have no gay farm boys on *The Stand*! Who gave him *that* idea, anyway?"

Marcy, on the verge of tears, said, "He says he *is* gay."

"Not on *our* show, he isn't. In the world of reality, we do not have surprises. Kirby has his role, the impish younger brother who's finally gonna be okay. No room for sex changes. What does Harry say?" Harry being the father of the Finch family.

Josh shook his head, with a weak apologetic smile. "You know how Harry is."

Not an authority figure; yes, Doug knew. *Whatever they want is okay by me, you know?* So far, that had been a plus, meaning there was never any argument with the producers' plans for the show. Except now.

Marcy said, "I think Harry has the hots for Darlene himself."

"No, Marcy," Doug said. "We aren't going there either. This is a clean wholesome show. You could project it on the wall of a megachurch in the South. Fathers do not hit on their sons' girlfriends. Come next door, fellas, we've got to solve this."

Next door was the conference room. Once they'd settled themselves in there, Doug said, "This *is* our story line, you know. We've been setting it up for this. In the third season, Kirby gets a girlfriend, just when the audience thinks they already know everything about the Finch family. And next season, the wedding, in sweeps week. Wedding episodes *always* get the biggest numbers of the year. Kirby and Darlene, true love at last."

Marcy said, "I'm sorry, Doug, but he won't do it. I asked him if he could just pretend and he said no. He won't kiss her, he doesn't even want to put his arm around her. He says her boobs are too big."

"Oh, God." Doug closed his eyes, in an attempt to leave the world behind.

But he hadn't yet learned the worst. Speaking right through his eyelids, Josh said, "And now that Darlene knows what Kirby thinks of her boobs, *she* doesn't want to work with *him*. She says she wants off the show."

"Which wouldn't be terrible," Marcy said, also talking through the wall of his closed eyelids. "You know, she hasn't even been introduced on the show yet."

Doug opened his eyes to find the awful world still unchanged. "Well, it is terrible," he said. "Are they shooting up there tomorrow?"

"Yes," Marcy said.

"I'll have to go up," Doug decided. "Marcy, you come along, just in case there's some other throughline we can work out, put it together on the fly up there. But for now, fellas, all three of you, I beg of you. Do not sleep tonight, not for a minute. If we don't have Kirby and Darlene, what *do* we have?"

Josh said, "Could it be Lowell and Darlene?" Lowell being Kirby's big brother.

Doug squinched his face in pain. "No," he said, "it's too late for that. We've already established Lowell as the loner, the gloomy genius going off to engineering college. He represents the life of the mind, which is why we've made sure nobody likes him." Doug smacked his palm against the table, making everybody jump. "*Why* didn't that little pansy tell us before this?"

"Be fair, Doug," Marcy said.

"I don't want to be fair."

"We don't tell them the story line ahead of time," Marcy reminded him, "so they won't be tempted to play something they're not supposed to know yet. Kirby didn't find out until today."

"That he's gay?"

"That he's supposed to fall in love with Darlene."

Doug let out a long moan and then just sat there, jaw slack, shoulders sagging.

Marcy, hesitant, said, "How did *The Gang's All Here* go?"

"What? Oh." The thought of that bunch restored just a bit of his spirits. Sitting straighter, he said, "The first meeting was wonderful. We're gonna have a winner there, boys and girls. But there's nothing for us to do on *that* score, not now. The Finch family is our problem today, so don't even think about the gang. We won't hear a word from them for a couple of weeks."

13

NINE P.M. The Holland Tunnel–bound traffic along Varick Street moved more freely now, and two groups of men, pedestrians, a trio and a duet, converged from north and south toward the GR Development building. As the groups came together on the sidewalk in front of the metal fire-door entrance to the building, greeting one another as though this were a happy coincidence, three miles to the north Manny Felder took many Weegee-style photos of the back room at the OJ while out front Roy Ombelen nursed his white wine and listened with growing astonishment to the regulars discuss the possible meanings of the letters D, V, and D, and farther east, in midtown, Doug Fairkeep, unable to keep his appointment with the other two at the OJ due to the revelation of the sexual orientation of Kirby Finch, brainstormed with his production assistants, while growing stacks of Dunkin' Donuts coffee containers kept a kind of score.

Andy Kelp liked locks and locks liked Andy Kelp. While the others milled around and chatted to cover his activities, he bent to the two locks in this door, bearing with him picks and tweezers and narrow little metal spatulas.

Judson took the opportunity to ask Dortmunder, "You think we're gonna find that cash down here?"

"I think," Dortmunder said, "Doug has seen cash somewhere and it has to be somewhere he works. The two places we know where he works are that midtown office building and here. Maybe they wouldn't want bribe money laying around the office, so we'll see what we come up with down here."

"*There* we go," Kelp said, and straightened, and pulled open the door.

Pitch-black inside. They all piled in, and only when the door was shut did flashlights appear, two of them, one held by Kelp and one by Dortmunder, both hooded by electrical tape to limit their beams. The flashlights bobbed around, then closed on the iron interior staircase along the rear part of the left wall. At this level, it rose from front to back.

Holding the light on the stairs, Kelp moved off across the crowded garage toward it, followed by Tiny, who used his hips and knees to clear a path through the underbrush of vehicles. Judson went next, then Stan, who said over his shoulder to Dortmunder, bringing up the rear with the other light, "This reminds me of Maximillian."

"I know what you mean," Dortmunder said, Maximillian being the owner and operator of Maximillian's Used Cars, a fellow known to purchase rolling stock of dubious provenance, no questions asked. He didn't pay much, but he paid more than the goods on offer had cost the offerer.

"A fella," Stan said, "could switch the cars around in

here, waltz out with one a day for a week, they'd never notice."

"You could be right."

Kelp had reached the stairs and started up. The others followed, and when Kelp got to the second floor he turned to his right, tried to open the door there, and it was locked.

As the others crowded up after him, wanting to know the cause of the delay, he studied this blank door in front of him and said, "That's weird."

"What's weird?" everybody wanted to know.

"It's locked."

"Unlock it," everybody suggested.

"I can't," Kelp said. "That's what's weird. It isn't a regular door lock, it's a palm-print thing. There's no way to get it open unless it recognizes your palm."

Judson said, "Down on the street they put a little simple lock you went through like butter, and up here they've got a high-tech lock?"

"Like I said," Kelp said. "It's weird."

Tiny, next nearest to Kelp, reached past him to thump the door, which made a sound like thumping a tree. "That's not going anywhere," he said.

Dortmunder, well back in the pack and therefore unable to see clearly for himself, called up the stairs, "Then that's the one we gotta get into."

"Can't be done, John," Kelp called back.

Judson said, "What about from upstairs?"

"What, down through the ceiling?" Kelp shook his head and his flashlight beam. "This time," he said, "we don't want to leave any marks we were here."

"I can't *see* anything," Dortmunder complained.

74

"Okay," Kelp said. "John, we'll go on up the next flight."

Everybody thudded up the stairs, which from the second to the third floor reversed and rose from back to front, and when at last Dortmunder got to the impassable door he stopped to frown at it all over, to look for hinges to be removed—no, they were on the inside—and to press his palm to the circle of glass at waist height. But the door didn't know him, and nothing happened.

The others had gone on up to the third floor so, abandoning the door, Dortmunder trudged on up after them. At the top, he found them all lolling around at their ease in what looked like a dayroom combined with an office. A few sofas and soft chairs and small tables were scattered around this part of the building from front to back, with filing cabinets and stacks of cardboard mover's cartons along the inside wall. Somebody had even switched on a floor lamp by one of the sofas, making a warm soft cozy glow.

"John," Kelp said, from the depths of a green vinyl easy chair, "take a load off."

"I will." Dortmunder did, and said, "It's that door, that's what we want."

Tiny said, "Not without demolition."

"Tiny's right," Kelp said. "We can't get into it, John. Not tonight. Not without doing some damage. And right now, we don't want to do damage."

"We want to know what's in there," Dortmunder said. "We need to know, what's the setup."

"Won't happen," Tiny said.

Dortmunder took from his pocket the drugstore receipt on which he'd written the firm names in this building.

"What we got on this floor," he said, "is Knickerbocker Storage. It's all storage areas the other side of that wall."

Stan said, "There's a john down at the end there."

"Fine." Dortmunder consulted his list. "Up one flight, that's Scenery Stars, that's the people gonna make the sets, like the imitation OJ. And up top is GR Development, their rehearsal space for their reality shows. The question is, what the hell is the thing *down* one flight? It's called Combined Tool. What would that be? If your name is Combined Tool, who are you?"

Stan said, "Do they make tools?"

"Where? How? That's not a factory."

At a side table, Judson had found phone books, and now he turned from consulting them to say, "Not in any phone book."

Dortmunder looked at him. "Not at all?"

"Not in the white pages under Combined Tool, not in the yellow pages under Tools-Electric, Tools-Rentals *or* Tools-Repairing & Parts."

Stan said, "So who the hell are they?"

"You got a company gets big enough," Dortmunder said, "it's got a dark side."

"But it's still a company," Kelp said, "so it's still got to have records and meetings and a history of itself."

"Down in there," Dortmunder said.

Stan said, "But what would *Doug* be doing in there? He's not that important. That door doesn't know *his* palm print."

"He's close to the operation," Dortmunder said. "He works sometimes out of this same building. He works for them, and they trust him, and he happened to see something once."

"You open a door in New York," Tiny said, "you never know what's in there."

Rousing himself from his easy chair, Kelp said, "We might as well take off now. We're not gonna do anything else in here tonight."

Dortmunder was reluctant to go, with the mystery of Combined Tool still unsolved, but he knew Kelp was right. Another day. "I'll he back," he vowed.

As they trooped back down the stairs, Stan said, "I think I'll pick up a car along the way. Won't take a minute."

14

B Y MONDAY, Doug knew he just had to get out of Putkin's Corners, *Stand* or no *Stand*. He'd been here since Friday, struggling with the problem of Kirby Finch's inversity—if that was a word—and he could feel himself on the very brink of going native. Even Marcy was beginning to look good.

Fortunately, he had Darlene Looper on hand to remind him what a proper object of lust was supposed to look and sound like. A talented if unagented actress, Darlene was a corn-fed beauty who, like for instance Lana Turner long before her, could show glints of a darker side. It was that darker side Doug was determined to tap into.

She was off *The Stand* now, no salvaging that situation. But how about *Burglars Burgling* (tryout)? Given the right makeup and wardrobe, Doug could just see her as a continuation of the long line of blonde sexpot gun molls extending back to before movies discovered sound. Give her a short slit skirt, fishnet pantyhose, and a nice small silver designer pistol slipped under the black frilly garter on her thigh, and there wasn't a felony on the books a man wouldn't be happy to commit with her. Doug saw her as the candy on the arm of Andy; surely *he* wasn't gay. So back to New York Darlene would come, traveling in Doug's Yukon with himself and Marcy. Marcy in the backseat, of course.

None of which dealt with the real problem that had forced him to drive one hundred miles north from the city last Friday. Now that this year's story line for *The Stand* had been fatally wounded by young Kirby Finch, what could replace it? What was their throughline story for the year, culminating in spring's sweeps week?

Many useless solutions were proposed, starting with the all-night brainbender session at Get Real on Thursday. For instance, Josh: "Kirby decides to become a priest. The family's ambivalent, and just when they're coming around, just when they're learning acceptance, he decides he'd rather stay with the family, at least until the farmstand succeeds." Doug: "No."

Or Edna: "Kirby's big brother, Lowell, the intellectual, carrying too heavy a load of books out of the library, trips and falls and is paralyzed. There's one slim chance an operation will give him back the use of his arms and legs, and at the end of the season, where we were going to do the wedding, he walks!" Doug: "No."

Or Marcy, Friday morning, on the trip up: "We go with the reality. Kirby comes out of the closet." Doug: "He isn't *in* the closet, that's the problem." Marcy: "He comes out to his family. They don't know what to do, what to think, and they finally decide blood is thicker than prejudice, and they'll stand by him. Everybody learns a wonderful lesson in tolerance." Doug; "No." Marcy: "Doug, it could be very real." Doug: "But it couldn't be reality, Marcy, reality shows do not solve society's problems. They don't even *consider* society's problems. Reality is escapist entertainment at its most pure and mindless."

All weekend the suggestions kept coming in. Harry Finch, father of the fairy: "What I say is, we bring that Darlene back. Turns out, she's my daughter. Wrong side of the blanket, you know. Family's all upset, thinks she's trying to horn in on the success of *The Stand*, they finally come around, see she's just a poor lost girl, needs a family, at the end we all hug and kiss and have a big celebration." Doug: "Let me think about that, Harry," which is how you say no to a civilian.

Finally, Monday morning, when Doug went along the walk from his motel room to Darlene's room to see if she was packed and ready for the trip, he found her appropriately dressed but seated on the bed among her unpacked goods, frowning into space.

"Darlene? What's up?"

She looked startled out of her reverie. "I was just thinking," she said.

"We gotta get going, Darlene."

"Oh, I know that. But I was thinking about the problem here, and I was wondering if something that happened to a friend of mine might be any use."

Another "solution" to the problem, eh? Well, might as well listen. "Sure," he said. "Go ahead."

"Her folks eloped," Darlene said. "You know, years ago, just before they had her. I think it was gonna be pretty close, which came first."

"That happens sometimes," Doug agreed.

"Only if you're not paying attention," she said, and shrugged. "Years and years later," she told him, "they found out, that preacher wasn't any preacher at all. He was a fake."

Interested despite himself, Doug said, "The one who married them?"

"Except they wasn't married," Darlene said. "You know, they had six kids by then, most of them half grown up, they didn't know what to do."

"A tricky situation," Doug agreed.

"At first," she said, "they was just gonna go to some city hall somewhere, get married on the sly, not tell anybody about anything. But then they thought it over, they decided, the first time they had to run away and elope, didn't have any proper family wedding, so now they could. Get the whole family in on it, great big church wedding, big party, the girls were the bridesmaids, the youngest boy was the ringbearer, it was the best time anybody ever had anywhere."

"Darlene!" Doug cried. "You're a genius!" And he flung himself on her on the bed in a massive embrace that was almost entirely pure.

Which is where Marcy found them a minute later, when she opened the room door. "Oh!" she said, embarrassed, backpedaling. "I thought we had to, ah, start going, uh, away."

Doug sat up and gave her the most dazzling smile of her life. "Marcy," he said, "Darlene has just saved *The Stand*!"

"She has?"

"Get the family together, before we leave we can give them the good news, let them start working out some of the details."

Confused but agreeable, Marcy said, "Okay, Doug. Should I close this door?"

"No, no, Marcy, we'll be right along."

Marcy took her departure, and Doug turned his dazzling smile on Darlene. "And Kirby," he said, "can be the bridesmaid."

15

WHEN STAN MURCH TRAVELED interborough while not in his professional role of getaway specialist, he preferred public transport. It was always possible to pick up private wheels when and where needed. Therefore, when he left the Murch manse early Monday afternoon, where he walked was to the final stop of the L subway line, being Canarsie/Rockaway Parkway, a line which, at its other extreme, a world and more than an hour away, culminated at Eighth Avenue and Fourteenth Street in Manhattan. (He was a commuter! Think of that! He'd never known that before.)

While walking down Rockaway Parkway, which it was impossible not to think of as Rockaway Parkaway, Stan cell-called John at home, expecting it to take three or four rings to get an answer, since John had only the one phone in his house, which he kept in the kitchen even though he was never in the kitchen except when eating, when, of course, his mouth would be full.

Four rings. "Yar?"

"Stan here. You gonna be around in an hour?"

"Even two hours."

"I'm on my way. I'm commuting, John."

"Uh-huh," John said, and when he opened his apartment door to let Stan in an hour and ten minutes later he said, "You're pretty good at that commuting."

"Practice makes perfect."

As they walked toward the living room, John said, "You want a beer?"

"A little early in the day," Stan said. "I'm trying to cut down on sodium."

In the living room, John settled into his chair and Stan onto the sofa, where he said, "I been thinking. That's why I'm here."

John nodded. "I figured it was something like that."

"What I been thinking about," Stan said, "is this reality caper thing."

"I guess we're all thinking about that," John allowed.

"So here's what I come up with," Stan said. "This is more complicated than it looks, because we're tryin to come up with two heists at the same time."

John thought about that, then nodded and said, "Yeah, that's right. The one they see and the one they don't see."

"While *they*," Stan said, demonstrating with arm movements, "think we're doing something to put in front of their camera, we're *actually* doing something we don't want them to know about, because it's stuff *we're* not supposed to know about."

"The cash in Combined Tool," John said. "If there *is* cash in Combined Tool."

"There's something in there," Stan said. "Something with a value on it. That high-tech door tells you that much."

"I think," John said, "what we gotta do is their heist first, collect our pay, and then pick up the tools."

"Well, that's what I was thinking about," Stan said. "Once we do their heist, we got no more access to that building."

"Well," John said, "we've always got *access.*"

"Yeah, but not so easy," Stan insisted. "If there's an excuse for us to be around that building anyway, it gives us more elbow room, like."

John shook his head. "We can't do Combined Tool first," he said. "They've got to know it's us that did it. They'll call off the other thing *and* they'll call the cops."

"So what we do," Stan said, "we do them both at the same time."

John frowned at that. "What, a couple of us one place, a couple another place?"

"No, that's not the idea." Stan spread his hands. "I know you think it's a mistake for drivers to come up with ideas."

"Not exactly a mistake," John said, being diplomatic. "Just unnecessary."

"Well, I did my thinking anyway," Stan said, "and I'm gonna tell you what I come up with."

"I'm listening," John said, but couldn't entirely hide a hint of skepticism in face and voice.

"We haven't given Doug our target yet," Stan pointed out, "because we didn't pick it yet."

"Right."

"And Andy, sometime back, suggested to Doug we make the target one of the outfits in that corporate spaghetti they got over there. People thought maybe that was a good idea."

"Maybe," John said. "I don't seem to remember Doug being really excited about it. So what do you want to do?"

"The storage place," Stan said. "One floor up from the tool place. People put things in storage if they got no use for them right now but they're too valuable to throw away."

John said, "Wait a minute. What? You want to knock over Knickerbocker Storage? In the same *building*?"

"At the same time," Stan said. "We're right there already, we can get alarms shut down, we can get the electricity off if it comes to that. We can probably go right down through the floor from one of the storage units."

"That you're not gonna do," John told him. "That isn't just some little thin wood floor like a house in the suburbs. That's a building you can drive trucks around in, every floor. Those floors are gonna be concrete, thick slabs of concrete."

"All right, some other way," Stan said. "Maybe there's a fire escape in the back."

"I don't think so," John said. "There's that inside metal staircase, with the trapdoor to the roof. That's the second exit, all you need for the fire code."

"Then some other way," Stan said, shrugging that off. "The point is, we're *there*."

"Yeah, we would be," John said. "You're right about that. The question is, would Doug go along with this?"

"We ask," Stan said. "If you think it's a good idea, we ask."

"I think," John said, "it could possibly be a good idea."

Heady praise indeed. Grinning in relief, Stan said, "I'll take that beer now. And what the hell, I'm not driving. Hold the salt."

16

WHAT WITH THE MASSIVE last-minute changes in the story line of *The Stand*, Doug didn't get home on Monday evening till well after seven. There were so many subsidiary decisions to be made, or remade, so much new research to be done. For instance, they had to be certain the actual officiator at the Grace-and-Harry wedding twenty-some years ago wouldn't come out of the woodwork to sue everybody in sight for calling him a con man. So much to do, so little time.

Fortunately, to make up for all this sudden scrambling, Doug was bringing Darlene Looper home for an evening of confabs. A little later, they'd go out for dinner in the neighborhood, during which he would describe to her the concept of *Heist!* (provisional), but for now, there was time to relax and get to know one another a little better. "It's a humble hovel," he announced grandly, unlocking the door, "but it's my own," and he pushed it open to everything wrong.

In the first place, he would never leave the lights on in the empty apartment all day long, and in the second place, this was not an empty apartment. There were several people in the room, the most prominent being someone who could retire the phrase "most prominent" if he wanted to. A giant in black trousers and a vast black turtleneck sweater who suggested somehow a black hole that had come to Doug's living room from deepest space, he was turning in his huge mitts the life-size brass banana with Doug's name etched into it that had been given him by his employers in celebration of the completed first season of *The Stand*. That the banana was not a crop that could be grown on the Finch's upstate New York farm had been completely irrelevant; the operative consideration, Doug believed, as with most things, had been phallic.

Now, in the corners of the room not occupied by the giant, Doug saw faces he recognized, that at least suggested some explanation for this invasion: Stan, Andy, and John, all pawing through Doug's artifacts. Plus, in another corner, a young guy with the eager look of a born pickpocket.

"The householder," said the giant, in deep organ tones, and Andy looked around, dropping several of Doug's books onto the coffee table as he said, happily, "*There* you are! We thought you'd never get home." Then, noticing the dumbfounded Darlene peeking over Doug's shoulder, his happy smile switched to a look of concern, and he said, "Doug? Is this a bad time?"

In the reality business, Doug had learned to recover fast when hit with surprises; adapt, play the scene you've got, fix it later in the editing room. "As a matter of fact, Andy, this is a very good time. I was going to tell Darlene all about you guys at dinner, so now we can all get on the same page at the same time."

Stan, never far from paranoia, said, "Tell her all about us? Which all is that, Doug?"

"Come in, Darlene," Doug said, and when she sidled past him into the room he shut the apartment door and said, "Darlene, these guys are going to be in another reality show we're just putting together, that I want *you* for. That's Andy, that's Stan, and that's John, and I don't know these other two."

Andy, a natural master of ceremonies, said, "The kid is Judson, and the guy with the banana is Tiny."

Doug said, "Tiny?"

"It's a nickname," the big man growled, and put the banana down.

Darlene, who also adapted fast, grinned a little loosely at Tiny and said, "It doesn't do you justice. I'm *sure* it doesn't."

Andy said, "Doug? You want her for the show? Walk me through this."

"Let's all sit down," Doug said. "As long as we're all here."

There were chairs and sofas to accommodate them all, but not much over. Once they were all seated, Darlene said, "Doug? What kind of reality show are they going to be in? Not a farmstand."

"How do I phrase this?" Doug wondered, "The fact is, these guys are, uh . . ."

"Crooks," John said.

"Criminals," Tiny grumbled.

"Thieves," Stan said.

"Professional thieves," Andy expanded, and grinned. "Licensed and bonded."

Darlene said to Doug, "You're going to do a reality show about professional thieves? Doing what?"

"Thieving," Doug said,

"Professionally thieving," John explained.

"I don't understand," Darlene admitted. "These people even *say* they're thieves, and you give them the keys to your apartment?"

"I didn't give them the keys to my apartment," Doug told her. "Apparently, they don't need the keys to my apartment."

Stan said. "How is this— Darlene, is it?"

"Yes," she replied simply.

"Darlene," he repeated, and said to Doug, "what's she gonna do on the show?"

"You can't have an all-male national television series," Doug explained. "Not even professional wrestling. Darlene was going to have a part on *The Stand* this year, but it didn't work out, so it occurred to me she could be a very good addition to our show."

"As?" Stan asked.

"As," Doug told him, "a gun moll."

Everybody else looked blank, while Darlene looked appalled. "A *gun* moll!"

"Sure." Doug spread his hands, "What's a gang without a gun moll?"

"I don't have a gun," Darlene said.

"That comes with your costume."

"And I don't *want* a gun."

"No bullets," Doug assured her, "Just the gun, as a prop. On your thigh, I thought."

The kid, Judson, said, "Darlene, how old are you?"

She looked at him with curiosity. "Twenty-three."

To Doug, the kid said, "A moll is going to have to be hooked up with one of the guys in the gang." Smiling at Darlene, he said, "I'm almost twenty, and I've always liked older women."

This development came as a very unpleasant surprise to Doug, who realized at once that he hadn't thought the ramifications through. Darlene was going to slip through his fingers even before he ever got his fingers onto her.

And had already slipped, from the grin she was now bestowing on the kid. "Your name is Judson?"

"Right," he said, grinning back.

"What do they call you?"

"The kid," everybody said,

She laughed. "Well, kid," she said, "it's nice to meet you."

"You, too."

Nose now firmly out of joint, Doug said, "What *I* don't get is, what's everybody doing here? How come everybody's in my apartment?"

"I'm glad you brought that up, Doug," Andy said. "What with romance rearing its head and all—"

"And gun molls," John said.

"Those too," Andy agreed. "We were about to forget the whole point of this meeting."

Doing his best not to show how peeved he was, Doug said, "Oh, there's a *point* to it?"

"We want to talk over with you," Andy said, "the place we're gonna rob."

Darlene said, "You're really gonna *rob* something?"

"Otherwise," Doug told her, "it isn't reality." Turning to Andy, he said, "You picked something? What, a bank, something like that?"

"Not exactly," Andy said. "You remember, we talked about, if we took something from one of those corporations up above you, then, if we got caught, it was always just gonna be a gag anyway."

"I remember," Doug said. "I feel quite ambivalent about that, if you want to know the truth. But you picked a target for the heist?"

"Knickerbocker Storage," Andy said.

The name might have rung a bell for Doug in its proper context, but not here. He frowned, thinking this idea seemed like awfully small potatoes for an entire gang of professional crooks, and said, "Storage? You want to break into some storage place? What for?"

John said, "Storage is what people do when they don't want to throw something away."

"It's valuable," Stan explained, "but they got no use for it right now."

"People put all kinds of things in storage," the kid said.

"Gee," Darlene said, smiling at the kid, "I guess they do. Prom gowns and jewelry and everything."

"Antique cars," Andy suggested. "Paintings. Jewelry. Furniture."

"All right," Doug said, though reluctantly. "But you'll have to, uh, case the joint first, be sure there's stuff in there worth taking. That's the kind of thing we want to film, you know, all the lead-ups."

Andy said, "Oh, sure, we'll take a look ahead of time. We're not out to get somebody's old collection of LPs."

"Videotapes," the kid said.

"Back issues of *Road & Track*," said Stan.

"Dial telephones," said John.

Andy gave him a look. "You've *got* a dial telephone."

"Not in storage."

"All right," Doug said. "If you go in there to check it out, and it looks like there's things worth taking, then that's where you— What do you call it? Pull the heist?"

"The job," Andy said.

Doug, his irritation over Darlene forgotten, at least for the moment, said, "Really? You call it a job?"

"It's what we do," Tiny said.

"All right, fine," Doug said, accepting the point. "But where exactly is this storage place? You have one in particular in mind?"

"I told you," Andy said, sounding surprised. "Knickerbocker."

"In your rehearsal building," John added. "Down on Varick Street."

"My— *Varick* Street? Our own building?"

"That was the idea," Andy said. "Remember?"

"But—" Dumbfounded, Doug said, "Let me think about this."

"Take your time," Andy offered.

Doug stared at his switched-off, but at least still here, television set. The idea of watching a group of burglars doing their burglaries had been amusing and interesting in the abstract, but when it was suddenly a case of watching them burgle from yourself, it was quite something else.

The instinct to say, "Take from those people, not from me," was a very strong one. But wasn't it the same, no matter who the victim was? Get Real had stumbled heedlessly into a project of aiding and even encouraging a felony. That these people would be performing their felonies anyway, with or without Get Real's encouragement, didn't make it any more right. In fact, if Monopole, the corporate entity that owned the building and also owned Get Real, took the loss in this matter, rather than some innocent bystander, it might even be a moral mitigation, mightn't it? Mightn't it?

"They'll be insured," Stan told him, to help his thought processes. "Nobody'll lose a thing."

"I just can't do this on my own," Doug said. "I've got to describe it to Babe. I mean, maybe he'll say we just can't do anything like that."

"Here's the thing," Stan said. "At first we were thinking about something else. There's a Chase bank on the corner."

"There's a Chase bank on every corner," Tiny said.

"There's a Chase bank on *this* corner," Stan insisted, "on Varick Street. We thought about it, Doug, because it'd be convenient for your camerapeople and all, but you'd have to do it in the daytime and there's too much tunnel traffic right outside the door. But this place, this Knickerbocker, we can go in there anytime at night when there's no traffic at all, we can take a truck or two from downstairs, load them up, zip zip, we're through the tunnel into Jersey."

"I can't say anything about it," Doug said. "Not till I talk it over with Babe."

"Back at the start," Andy said, "you said anytime we didn't feel comfortable about something, we could call the whole deal off. We won't feel comfortable unless we hit Knickerbocker Storage."

"I'll talk to Babe," Doug promised. "Tomorrow morning, first thing."

"Then we shouldn't keep you hanging around any more," Andy said, and Stan said, "Leave me a message with my Mom."

"I will."

They all trooped out, and it wasn't until they were well gone that Doug realized Darlene had gone with them.

17

DARLENE DIDN'T BELIEVE they were really serious. This was her third reality show—fourth, if you counted *The Stand*, though you probably shouldn't—and in her experience nothing that happened in reality was serious. She'd been a contestant on *Build Your Own Beauty Parlor* and a survivor on *The Zaniest Challenge of the Year!* and would have been a fiancée on *The Stand* if that fellow hadn't turned out to be all icky, and she had to say that not one of those shows had been any more serious than first love.

This one, that Doug Fairkeep kept calling *The Gang's All Here* although apparently he really didn't want to, would just be more of the same. This "gang" wasn't going to steal anything. They were just a bunch of guys who could look like bank robbers in some B movie somewhere, that's all.

Just look at the variety of people inside the "gang": that was the giveaway. All of these cast-to-type characters, the ugly monster for the "muscle," the sharpie with the line of patter, the gloomy mastermind, the testy driver, and the innocent youth, that last one so the audience would be able to see it all through *his* eyes. Everything but a black guy, so maybe you didn't need a black guy any more.

One good thing about the arrival of the "gang" at Doug's apartment was that it opened Darlene's options considerably. She had just reached the point where she'd have to decide if she would go to bed with Doug (a) now, (b) indefinitely later, or (c) never, when circumstances suddenly changed and off she could go for an evening's mixer with the fellas.

Darlene Looper was a product of North Flatte, Nebraska, a town that had had its peak of population and importance in the 1870s, after the railroad arrived and before the drought arrived. The railroad turned out to be a sometime thing, but the drought was the natural condition of the Great Plains, it being a kind of a joke on the European settlers that they got there in the middle of a rare rainy streak.

All the time Darlene was growing up, North Flatte was getting smaller, until there was nobody left who cared enough to correct the POP. sign on the edge of town, which would apparently read 1,247 forever. (In truth, the comma had moved out a long time ago.)

When your town is too small for a movie theater and your combined regional high school is an hour away by bus and too small to have a football team—much less anybody to play against—you are a deprived teenager, and there wasn't a teenager in town who didn't know it and didn't dream of the day when the Trailways could take them away to anywhere in the world that wasn't N. Flatte, Neb.

The first place the Trailways took Darlene was St. Louis, where she got a waitress job at a diner, lost her virginity, had an abortion, and learned how to avoid that sort of thing in the future, by which she didn't mean abstinence. The waitress job gave her money and independence and leisure to go to the movies a lot, which was already an improvement over North Flatte, where the choices had been television or comic books, and not much of either. The movies taught her that a girl with looks and self-confidence and native wit could do well for herself, at least for a few years, as an actress, and so the Trailways next deposited her in LA.

Where she lucked into an apartment-mate named Bette Betje, a few years older than herself and trying her hand at the same racket, who gave Darlene some invaluable advice. Never do porn; once you enter that ghetto, even the Pope couldn't get you out. Make sure there are never any naked photos of you anywhere. Never screw more than one man on any job location. Don't gamble on anything, don't get a weird haircut, and don't fall in love.

Following Bette's rules and her own sense of self-preservation, Darlene did moderately well in LA. She was always going to be soft-bodied, which would prove a problem someday but for now meant she could play younger than herself. At twenty-three, she could still audition for high school roles in commercials and infomercials and lesser horror films, and occasionally get one. Then came reality.

Reality was a revelation to Darlene. It seemed to her it must be very like the way the soap operas used to be, when they were the hottest thing around. Sure you're all professionals, but nevertheless you're getting together every day like kids in a barn to put on a show. It's open-ended, it's seat-of-the-pants, and it's *fun*.

It also, through *The Zaniest Challenge of the Year!*, brought her to New York and a new roommate, Lauren Hatch, an investigative reporter wannabe, currently a gofer for an online gossip columnist. A skinny, sharp-featured laser-eyed workaholic, Lauren was Darlene's age but appeared to have no interest in sex of any kind unless it concerned other people and could be spread on the Slopp Report.

The Stand was supposed to have been Darlene's big break, playing a real-life bride on prime-time television, known and loved by the whole world. Doug had explained to her that the marriage would have to be a legal one, but the fix was in and an annulment would be the easiest thing in the world. All she had to do was swear in court she hadn't meant it when she said, "I do," which would be the truth, and there she'd be, single again, with an already guaranteed exclusive on the Slopp Report (a four-hour exclusive) in which she would explain that marriage wasn't for her, she was wedded to her career.

Well, that hadn't happened, entirely because Kirby Finch was something that had never been seen in North Flatte, Nebraska, at least not by Darlene, so far as she knew. He was entirely unnatural, Kirby was, and Darlene considered herself well out of it, particularly with the "gang" already in place to give her another chance of a lifetime.

Of course, if she were to hook up with the "gang," she'd have to hook up with one particular member of it. Group sex could be implied in the world of reality, but not confirmed. Besides, Darlene, who hadn't tried it, didn't think she'd like it.

So it kind of came down to the kid and the sharpie, and it wasn't an easy decision. They were very different, but both were fun, both were quick-witted, both could look appropriate as her escort; at an awards dinner, say.

The question was, which would be right for *her*, her needs, her future, her image. There was a lot to be said for both of them. Fortunately, she didn't have to decide right away.

From Doug's place they walked, not very far, to a bar/restaurant on West Fifty-seventh Street called Armweary's, a funky dark wood place, pretty full for a Monday night, with waiters who appeared to be waiters and not actors between gigs. The place was loud, but not too loud to hear the people at your table, and Darlene quickly noticed that, while everybody had a lot to say, nobody had anything at all to say about the show they were going to be on or the "robbery" they were going to pretend to commit. All of that seemed to be off-limits somehow, so, even though there was a lot about this crowd and their series she would love to know, she was smart enough not to push the envelope.

They all chipped in to buy her dinner, which was sweet. Then it was time to go, and out on the sidewalk, while she was preparing herself to say it had been a wonderful evening but she was really tired right now, all the others were telling one another so long and planning when they would meet again.

The kid did finally turn to her and say, "How do you get home?"

"Oh, I just walk up to Seventy-sixth Street," she said. "It's nothing, I do it all the time."

"Oh, okay," he said, and everybody took off, in various directions.

Walking up Broadway, Darlene found herself brooding over the fact that not one of them had even tried to come home with her. She hadn't wanted any of them to, but still.

Awful thought. They weren't all Kirbys, were they?

18

B ABE TUCK SAID, "You agreed to *what*?"

"Well, we didn't exactly agree," Doug said, seated across the pockmarked old wooden desk Babe had brought with him from his foreign correspondent days. "Andy just suggested, if we could find a target from inside our own corporation, then, if something went wrong, we could all claim it was never going to be a real robbery anyway."

"But we *want* a real robbery," Babe pointed out. "That's the whole idea. Reality on the edge."

"I think they're a little insecure," Doug said. "They're not used to doing a burglary with cameras pointed at them."

"You told them we'd cover their asses? Halo their heads? Alter their voices?"

"They know all that," Doug agreed. "It's just, I think, it's just all a little too strange. They want some kind of reassurance."

"An escape hatch," Babe suggested.

"Exactly."

"I can understand that," Babe said. "There've been times when I wouldn't have minded an escape hatch myself."

"So in theory," Doug said, "it's not an idea we'd reject out of hand."

"A little strange to steal from yourself," Babe said, and shrugged. "But I suppose the network could stand it. Might even be something salutary in it."

Politely, Doug said, "Salutary?"

"See our own vulnerabilities from the outside," Babe explained. "Find out where we need to shore up our defenses. So they've picked some underbelly of ours, have they?"

"Yes, sir."

"What?"

Doug seemed reluctant to speak, and then he said, "Sir, before that, let me—"

"You're calling me sir a lot," Babe said, not as though he liked it.

"Am I?" Doug could be seen to replay his mental tape. "Oh, yeah, I guess I am. I guess I'm nervous."

"About what, Doug?"

"First, si—Babe, let me say we agreed at the beginning, if anything ever made them uncomfortable, they didn't have to do it."

"Of course."

"They now say it's *this* target, or they're not gonna be comfortable."

"Then," Babe said, "you'd really better tell me the target."

"The storage facility on Varick Street."

"The— *Varick* Street?"

"They say they wanted a place in that neighborhood to make the filming easier," Doug explained. "There's a Chase bank on the corner—"

"Of course there is."

"They say they considered doing that," Doug said, "but they'd have to do it in the daytime, and there's too much tunnel traffic out front, and they'd never get away. So they decided to go with the storage facility in our building."

"On Varick Street."

"It's called Knickerbocker Storage."

"I know what it's called," Babe said.

"They say the losses will be covered by insurance, and that's true, so that should make it even easier for us to say yes."

"Doug, Doug, Doug."

Doug said, "I know. Babe, I thought about this, and thought about it, and we've got a double problem here."

"How so?"

"If we say yes," Doug said, "we're exposing ourselves in ways we can't even be sure of. But if we say no, if we scrub the whole operation, Babe, what do we tell them is our *reason*?"

"We don't want to do it," Babe said. "We don't have to give reasons."

"Babe," Doug said, "these are professional burglars. They can smell profit around corners. If we say no, not that place, you can hit anywhere else in our whole corporate structure, but you can't do anything to Varick Street, they're going to wonder why."

"Let them wonder."

"Babe," Doug said, "I live in an apartment in a new high-tech building. My door has a hotel-type card instead of a key." He took it from his shirt pocket to show it. "We've got doormen, closed-circuit TV. Those guys have taken to dropping by my apartment."

"They have?"

"They just walk in, don't ask me how. They don't raise a sweat, and they don't leave a mark."

Babe frowned over this. "What you're saying is, if we say no to the specific after we already said yes to the general, they're going to be curious."

"And they have a capacity to satisfy their curiosity."

Babe nodded. "So, do you want to give them the go-ahead?"

"I don't *know* what I want," Doug said. "Either we give them the green light and hope for the best, or we find some *reason* to say no, some reason that doesn't have them wandering around Varick Street just to see what's what."

"And you don't have that reason."

"No, sir."

Babe made a face. "There's that *sir* again. You know, Doug, any reason we give them is going to make them curious. And if they walk off the series, if they're out of our lives, there's no motivation for them to not move *in* to Varick Street and try to find out just what we were keeping to ourselves."

Doug said, "That's why I wanted to come directly to you first thing this morning."

"Thanks," Babe said, with some ironic emphasis. Brooding across his office, past the tattered and blood-stained and smoke-smeared mementos of a long life reporting from the edge, he said, "If we say yes, then it's only Knickerbocker Storage they'd be after? Only the—what is it—third floor?"

"Well, the first floor, too," Doug told him. "They'll need to steal some vehicles to put the stolen goods into."

"Oh, of course," Babe said. "Silly of me not to think of that. But if we said yes, could you *keep* them to just those two floors?"

"I think so," Doug said. "I'm pretty sure I could."

"Not by telling them, 'Don't think of a blue elephant.'"

"No, no, I know better than that. I wouldn't even mention the second floor." Doug leaned forward, pretended to consult a clipboard, and said, "Now, for our camera crews, you're gonna need footage on the third floor, and footage on the first floor, and footage out front, coming and going. That's really all you need."

"Good," Babe said.

Putting the imaginary clipboard onto his lap, Doug leaned back and said, "You know, there might be a kind of silver lining in all this."

"Shoot it to me at once," Babe said.

"Inside the company," Doug said, "there are rumors and questions sometimes, you know that."

"Of course," Babe said. "That's true in any large organization."

"Some of those rumors have centered on Varick Street."

"Which is very bad," Babe said, "We really *don't* want people wondering about Varick Street. I've wished there was a way to get everybody to think about something else."

"Well, if we pull off *The Gang's All Here*," Doug said, "and stage a robbery in that same building, nobody will believe for a minute there's anything *else* going on in Varick Street."

Babe, for the first time in the conversation, smiled. "If we could bring that off," he said, and shrugged. "Well, we'd *have* to bring it off."

"Scary," Doug said.

"Scary we eat for breakfast," Babe told him. Suddenly decisive, he said, "Green-light it."

"Thanks, Babe."

Doug got to his feet, the imaginary clipboard falling to the floor, and Babe said, "Oh, by the way."

"Yes?"

Babe shook his head. "I don't like that title."

19

A WEDNESDAY NIGHT, just one week since the organizational meeting at the OJ, and Dortmunder and Kelp were walking, not for the first time in their lives, on a roof. It was the roof of the GR Development building, sixty feet above Varick Street, and out around them the night was well advanced, it now being not quite four in the morning.

It was a cloudy night, not cold, and not particularly dark. The city generates its own illumination, and on cloudy nights that glow is reflected down onto the streets and parks and rooftops, for a soft Impressionist cityscape.

Dortmunder and Kelp, dressed in dark grays to blend into the prevailing color scheme, walked the roof above Varick Street and looked around to see what they could see. The building they stood on was flanked by two much larger, taller, heftier structures extending both ways to the corner. To the north was the stone pile containing the Chase bank at basement level and street level and one level up. From the look of the many sentry lights visible in the upper windows, most of the tenants above Chase had also thought long and hard about the issue of security.

To the south, the other building's ground floor housed a restaurant supply wholesaler, whose strategy in the realm of security lighting was one illuminated wall clock at the rear of the showroom, in the pink glow of which were tumbled all the fast-food counters, bartops, banquettes, ovens, walk-in freezers, and wooden cases of dinnerware recently collected from enterprises that had unfortunately stumbled into nonexistence and whose gear was now awaiting the next hopeful entrepreneur with a certified check in his pocket. The floors above this bric-a-brac were uniformly dark except for the red neon EXIT sign the fire code requires at every level.

That had been Dortmunder and Kelp's route in. A low-security door on the side street, leading to the woks and barstools, had given them easy access to the building and then its stairwell and eventually the sixth-floor office of an olive oil importer through whose window they had stepped to get here on the roof.

There were several protuberances on this roof, and all were of interest, but the most interesting of all was the three-foot-by-five-foot cinder-block box, seven feet tall, in the left rear corner. This would be the terminus of the iron staircase that zigzagged up the interior. Inside that gray metal door would be the top of that staircase, and down that staircase would be GR Development, and then Scenery Stars, and then Knickerbocker Storage, and then, last but far from least, Combined Tool.

While Dortmunder held a shrouded flashlight to marginally increase the illumination, Kelp studied the staircase door, bending over it, squinting at it, not quite touching it. "It's got an alarm on it," he decided.

"We knew that," Dortmunder said.

"It looks like it's connected to a phone line," Kelp said. "So it won't make a lotta noise right around here."

"That's good."

"It'll do something somewhere, though. Lemme see what we can do here."

While Kelp continued to study the problem before him, Dortmunder braced his wrist against the doorjamb to keep his light beam steady while he studied the world around them. Although he saw many lit windows in the wall above the Chase bank, it didn't appear to him that any of those rooms were currently occupied. The windows in the wall down the other way were dark, and the buildings across Varick Street were too far away to matter, so it seemed to Dortmunder they were unobserved at this moment and would be likely to go on being unobserved anytime they happened to come up here at three-thirty in the morning. It was a reassuring thought.

While he was thinking, Kelp was taking from one of his many pockets a short length of wire bounded at each end by an alligator clip. The first clip he attached quickly to a bolt head jutting from the door just above the lock and handle. Then he thought a while before attaching the other to a screw head on the door frame. Nodding in agreement with himself, he took another wire from another pocket, this one with an earphone at one end and what looked like a stethoscope at the other. Earphone into his ear, he listened at a wire on the door, then said, "Listen to this."

Dortmunder took the thingy and listened at the same wire. "It's a little hum."

"That's right. If it stops humming when I cut this here, we go."

"Gotcha."

Dortmunder listened intently. Kelp watched intently, clipper in hand, and snipped a wire.

"Still humming."

"We like that," Kelp said.

Now Kelp worked with more confidence. The alarm wires led to a metal plate on the door that extended beyond the edge of the door to its metal frame. If the door were opened, the plate would lose contact with the frame and sound the alarm, somewhere, to somebody.

As Dortmunder stepped back to give him room, Kelp loosened the plate and turned it so its contact was only with the metal door. The ends of the wire he'd snipped he bent back and stuck to the door with bits of nonreflecting electrical tape. He studied what he'd done, then nodded and said, "Listen some more."

"Right. Still humming."

"If it stops, we're outa here."

"You bet."

Kelp turned his attention to the lock on the door. Needle-nose pliers and a thin metal plate came from more of Kelp's pockets. The faint humming in Dortmunder's ear was really very soothing, and then the door eased open, outward. Kelp cocked an eye at Dortmunder, who, ear to earphone and stethoscope to wire, had moved with the door.

Dortmunder nodded. "Humming."

"We're done."

Kelp pocketed his equipment and then, by Dortmunder's muffled flashlight, they went down the iron stairs, closing the roof door behind themselves. At the bottom of that flight, GR Development, they started confidently forward and then abruptly stopped.

"It's different," Kelp said.

"It's all walls or something," Dortmunder said, shining the light around.

"We need more light," Kelp decided.

Guided by the stone side building wall, they worked their way around the newly obstructed space until they came across light switches, which turned on glaring overhead fluorescents, and in that light they could see these several pieces of walls, all eight or ten feet high, rough wood or canvas, propped up with angled two-by-fours nailed into the floor.

"It's like a set," Kelp said.

"From the wrong side," Dortmunder said. "Is there a way in?"

There was. Around the rough unfinished wall they came to an opening, and now they could see that what had been built was a broad but shallow three-walled room without a ceiling. A dark wood bar, a little beat-up, stretched along the back wall, on which were mounted beer posters and mirrors that had been smeared with something that looked like soap, so they wouldn't reflect. A jumble of bottles filled the back bar, plus a cash register at the right end. Barstools in a row looked as though they'd come directly from the wholesale restaurant supply place next door, and so did the two tables and eight chairs in the grouping in front of the bar. At the right end of the bar stood two pinball machines, and at the left end a doorway into darkness.

Kelp, in wonder, said, "It's the OJ."

"Well, it isn't the OJ," Dortmunder said.

"No, I know it isn't," Kelp said, "but that's what they're going for."

"Pinball machines?"

"I know what Doug would say," Kelp told him. "Visual interest."

"You can't talk next to a pinball machine."

"They won't have pinball machines in the back room," Kelp said.

"Let's take a look at it."

But the space at the left end of the bar didn't lead to anything but a canvas wall painted a flat black. Standing in front of it, they looked at one another and Kelp said, "It's gonna be some of these other walls."

It was. Out of the stubby bar set and down to the right they found two parallel walls propped up to look something like the hall at the OJ, except twice as wide and many times cleaner. Instead of the catchall onetime phone booth there was a many-shelved wooden hutch piled with neat stacks of tablecloths and napkins. There were two doors on the left side, marked DOGGIES with a cartoon dog in a cardigan smoking a pipe and KITTIES with a cartoon slinky cat in a long tight black gown smoking a cigarette with a long holder. Also, the doors didn't open.

The door at the end of the hall did open, but didn't lead anywhere, and particularly didn't lead to the back room. That they found in another quadrant of the rehearsal space with two of its walls propped on dollies so they could be rolled forward and back to accommodate a camera. The table was the right shape, round, and the chairs were the right era, old, but there were no liquor cartons stacked up in front of the cream-painted walls.

"No boxes," Dortmunder commented.

"Probly," Kelp said, "it makes it too busy behind people's heads when they're filming."

"Probly."

Dortmunder sat at the table, automatically taking the chair that faced the open door. The hanging light was a little too high and a little too clean and it didn't have a bulb in it. "You know what I feel like," he said.

"No," Kelp said, interested. "What?"

"One of those guys fakes an autobiography," Dortmunder said. He gestured at the table, the chairs, the walls. "We haven't done anything and already this is a lie."

"We aren't in this for an autobiography," Kelp reminded him. "We're in it for the twenty G."

"And the per diem."

"And the per diem."

Dortmunder got to his feet. "Anything else around here?"

There wasn't; at least, not of interest to them. So they switched off all the fluorescent lights and, by Dortmunder's blurred flashlight beam, went on down one flight to Scenery Stars, where there was nothing that caught their eye, except, on a table, scattered photos of the real OJ and the real Rollo in profile and the real sidewalk outside.

Dortmunder said, "I hope Rollo didn't see them take that."

"No, it looks okay," Kelp said. "But even so, those guys could pass for tourists."

"Easily."

On down they went to Knickerbocker Storage, the "target" of their robbery, where two security cameras were installed at opposite ends of the hall where they hadn't been before. Their view was down along the line of closed storage spaces toward one another. They didn't appear to be operating.

"Looks like they're giving us a little extra work," Kelp said.

Dortmunder glowered. "I don't need that."

"We'll talk to them."

"Not right away. We don't want them to know we've been here."

"When we come back," Kelp said, "to see their idea of the OJ, to get a little tour, we'll be very surprised on the way up. 'Oh, cameras!'"

"No cameras would be better," Dortmunder said.

Kelp said, "Well, let's see what other surprises they got for us."

They went on down the next two flights, skipping past Combined Tool because they knew there was nothing they could do about that now. On the ground floor, among the automobile menagerie, they skirted the corners of the building and found the main electric service, which someday they might want to interrupt, in a large black metal box in the left rear corner, under the stairs.

Next to this service box, almost impossible to see, was another find, a gray metal fire door, blocked by a few cardboard cartons and a couple of spare tires. They cleared it, Kelp did his stethoscope trick, and they found that this door too was alarmed. They used the same methods to declaw it, and stepped outside, not having to move the boxes and tires because the door opened outward.

This was a cul-de-sac, a completely enclosed space blocked by the inner walls of buildings on all four sides, each of them with a fire door for access. Looking up by the very uncertain light back here, not wanting to chance a flashlight out here, they could see one small window on the left at each story, which must be for the bathrooms. There were no bars over the second-story window.

Dortmunder nodded at that window. "I bet that isn't as easy as it looks."

"You know it."

They went back inside, made sure their changes to the door didn't show, and made their way through automotive world to stand on the platform of the elevator and look up at the second floor opening.

"We can't unalarm the elevator," Kelp said.

"I know." Dortmunder waved the flashlight beam along the floor edge above them. "Next time we come here," he said, "we'll have to bring a ladder. Either to go up through here or out to that window."

"We can stash it out there."

"Good."

Stepping off the elevator platform, Kelp said, "Okay, we're done for tonight. What do you think, should we bring Stan a car?"

"All the way to Canarsie?"

"I guess not."

So they climbed the stairs back to the roof and headed for the olive oil importer's exit, leaving the GR Development building as ready as a Thanksgiving turkey at noon.

20

HAVING BEEN SUMMONED to Babe Tuck's office Thursday morning, Doug arrived to find a very dapper fortyish man with a large brushy-haired head and a wide op art necktie seated in one of the big leather chairs facing Babe's beat-up desk. This fellow stood as Doug entered the room, as did Babe on the other side of the desk, and the new man turned out to be very short, out of proportion to both the large head and the neon necktie. Doug guessed at once that he was an actor.

Babe made the introductions: "Doug Fairkeep, producer of *The Crime Show*, this is—"

Doug said, "*The Crime Show*?"

"Temporary title," Babe told him.

"I'll think about it."

"This is," Babe insisted, "Ray Harbach. With your agreement, I think I want to add him to the show."

Surprised, Doug said, "As the bartender?"

"No, one of the gang."

Now Doug frowned, deeply. "Babe, I don't know," he said. "They're pretty much a unit."

"I feel," Babe said, "what with one thing and another, we need eyes and ears inside the gang. You know what I mean. We don't want any surprises, Doug."

"No, I don't suppose so."

"We *deliver* surprises," Babe told him. "We don't collect them." Gesturing at the chairs, he said, "Come on, at least let's get comfortable."

As they all sat, Ray Harbach took a small magazine from his jacket pocket and extended it toward Doug, saying, "I thought, to introduce myself, I'd show you my bio from my last *Playbill*." He had a deeply resonant voice, as though speaking from a wine cellar. "We write those ourselves, you know."

"Yes, I know."

Ray Harbach had left the *Playbill* conveniently folded open to the page with his bio, which was fifth among the cast, and which read:

RAY HARBACH *(Dippo) is pleased to be back in the Excelsior Theater, where he appeared three seasons ago as Kalmar in the revival of Eugene O'Neill's* The Iceman Cometh. *Other theater roles have included work by Mamet, Shaw, Osborne, and Orton. Film:* Ocean's 12; Rollerball. *Television:* The New Adventures of the Virgin Mary and the Seven Dwarfs at the North Pole; The Sopranos; One Life to Live; Sesame Street. *I want to dedicate this production to my father, Hank.*

"I see," Doug said, and handed the *Playbill* back. "Thanks."

Pocketing the *Playbill*, Harbach said, "I get the idea this is something a little different here."

"To begin with," Doug said, "it's a reality show."

Harbach smiled with the self-confidence of a man who will never run out of small parts to pay the rent. "Then what do you need me for?"

Babe said, "The fact is, it's a reality show with a difference. Explain it, Doug."

"We will follow," Doug said, "a group of professional robbers as they plan and execute an actual robbery."

Harbach cocked a large head. "An *actual* robbery?"

"Not entirely," Babe said.

Doug said, "Babe, if they don't do it, what's the show *about*?"

"I understand that, Doug," Babe said, "which is why we're going along with the target, even with the additional complications." To Harbach he said, "Get Real has corporate owners, and one of the thieves came up with the idea, if they chose a target that was owned within the umbrella corporation, it would give them a fallback position if the police happened to get involved."

Harbach nodded. "I get it. Pretend it was never gonna be real."

"Right." Babe made a little fatalistic shrug gesture he'd learned many years ago in the Orient. "Unfortunately, the target they chose is a sensitive one, for reasons we don't want them to know about."

Harbach did his own shrug. "Tell them to pick something else."

Doug said, "Then they'll know we're hiding something, and they'll want to know what it is, and we don't want them curious because we *are* hiding something."

Harbach looked interested. "Oh, yeah? What?"

Babe said, "We're hiding it from you, too. That way, if

they start to think something's going on, you won't know what it is, but you'll be right in there with them, you'll know what they're thinking, and you can pass it on to us."

"So I'm the mole." Harbach didn't seem to mind that.

"The reason we cast you," Babe said, "we were looking for a guy who's a good solid actor, good credits, good rep, but also has some little dodgy elements in his past."

"Oh, come on," Harbach said. "I had a few wild times in my youth, but that was over long ago."

Doug said, "Ever do time?"

Harbach was appalled. "*Prison?* My God, no!"

Babe said to Doug, "What Ray has is just enough of a background to make him plausible for our group."

Harbach said, "You know, I don't emphasize that stuff on my résumé."

"This time," Babe told him, "you need to. We want the gang to accept you as one of them."

Doug said, "Babe, why are we adding him to the show? I mean, I know why we are, to have a spy inside the gang, but what do we tell *them* is the reason?"

"They are experts," Babe said, "at crime. Ray here is an expert at acting in front of a camera, at selling a scene. He'll be able to coach them, help them be more realistically what they already are."

Harbach said, "I'm gonna need legal protection here, if this is gonna lead to an actual robbery."

"Oh, absolutely," Babe told him. "Legal's putting together a contract addendum now, explaining what you're doing and why you're doing it. We'll get it to your agent this afternoon."

"That sounds good," Harbach said. "When do I meet this gang?"

Doug said, "Our sets are about ready. I was gonna call them this afternoon to make a first run-through tomorrow." To Babe he said, "They don't like it if you call them in the morning."

Harbach laughed. "Already," he said, "they sound like actors."

21

THIS WAS PROBABLY the most exciting day of Marcy's life. She'd been working for Get Real only four months now, and *The Crime Show* was only her second reality series, and it was so *much* more interesting than *The Stand*, which was, after all, finally only about a family selling vegetables beside the road. But *The Crime Show*! Real criminals committing a real crime, right there in front of your eyes! In front of her eyes.

Yes, Doug had given her the assignment: she was the designated production assistant on *The Crime Show*. Therefore, late Friday morning, her shoulder bag so loaded down with documents she was bent almost double, so she looked like the Hunchback of Notre Dame's little sister, she joined Doug and Get Real's personnel director, a dour skinny nearly hairless man named Quigg, in a cab from the Get Real offices in midtown down to the company's building on Varick Street, a place about which she'd heard vaguely from time to time, but before this had never actually seen.

And which was not that impressive, once she did lay eyes on it. Some kind of warehouse thing, apparently, on a commercial street with an awful lot of one-way traffic headed south.

"We'll be the first, so we'll go in this way," Doug said, unlocking and opening the graffiti-scarred metal front door, but what other way would you go in? Through the graffiti-scarred garage door over there to the right?

Maybe so; the three entered a space like a very crowded parking garage and Doug, saying, "We'll have to take the elevator up," switched on overhead fluorescent lights and led them a zigzag path through all the parked vehicles to a big open rectangle, like a rough-wood dance floor.

But once they were all there, he pushed a button on a control panel on the front wall and suddenly the floor jolted upward! Marcy was so startled she wrapped both arms around her shoulder bag, as though it could help her stay upright, and gaped without comprehension as floor after floor went by.

There. It stopped, at a level with almost no walls, no sensible rooms, just odd pieces of furniture here and there, and Doug said, "The sets are one flight up, but we'll be more comfortable down here for the paperwork."

"I'll need a table," Quigg said, stepping off the platform elevator with a sniff, looking around as though he wanted to fight with somebody.

"Everything's here," Doug assured him. "Just pick what you want and push it all together." Turning back to Marcy, he said, "Come on, you can put your stuff over here."

She followed him, saying, "Doug? What is this place?"

"This is where we build the sets," he told her. "Upstairs is the rehearsal space."

"And downstairs?"

He shrugged. "Businesses. Tenants. Nothing to do with us."

Off to the right were a dining room table and half a dozen accompanying chairs, in light maple, furniture in some old-fashioned style, the cushioned seats shabby and peeling. But it was all solid, with good working space on the table, so Marcy dumped her shoulder bag there with a thud, like a body thrown out a window.

Doug said to Quigg, who'd barely moved, but stood in one place looking disapproving, "Sam? Use the same table as Marcy, you've both got to process these people."

So Marcy and Quigg shared the table, though not much else, and Doug wandered around, whistling behind his teeth. "This is a very interesting moment, boys and girls," he said, looking at the floor as he paced. "The beginning of the new adventure."

Marcy thought, are Quigg and I boys and girls? But then a loud ringing sound came from downstairs and Doug looked startled, then consulted his watch and grinned. "They're early," he said, "but we were earlier. You two sit tight." And he walked back to the elevator, pushed the button, and descended in a great cone of noise.

Quigg, not looking at Marcy, slapped his attaché case on the table and sat in front of it to click its lid open. He too had carried a lot of paperwork here, but somehow he'd done it much more neatly than she. Oh, well, some were neat and some were not.

Marcy took a chair across the table from Quigg, dumped out her shoulder bag, and was sorting through its contents (Quigg's materials were now neatly stacked in front of him) when the cone of noise came back, this time carrying, in addition to Doug, five more or less scruffy people, two of whom were the ones she'd met with Doug almost two weeks ago at Trader Thoreau.

The whole crowd came this way, Doug saying, "This is most of us, only two more to come. Marcy, Sam—"

But the introductions, if that was what he'd planned, were interrupted by the loud bell-ringing again, and Doug said, "Here they are. Introduce yourselves, I'll be right back." And off he went to the platform to make that noise again.

The youngest of the newcomers, a nice-looking boy of a kind Marcy hadn't expected to see on a show called, even temporarily, *The Crime Show*, stepped forward, grinning at them, and said, "Hi. I'm Judson, and this—"

"We'll need full names," Quigg said. He didn't sound at all friendly or welcoming. "Did you bring an attorney?"

They looked blankly at one another. One of them, a gloomy slope-shouldered guy Marcy remembered from Trader Thoreau as being named John, shook his head at Quigg and said, "You mean a lawyer? In our line of work, if you need a lawyer it's already too late."

"And no agent," Quigg said. "So you are all principals in this matter."

"We're the new stars," said John.

"Well, I'm Quigg," Quigg said. "I'll be dealing with your payroll matters, tax matters, workmen's comp, all of that. So what I'll need from each of you is full name, address, Social Security number."

Another general blank look. A sharp-featured guy among them said, "It sounds like we're being booked."

"And not being paid," John pointed out.

"You'll all receive an advance payment," Quigg snapped, "but not until *after* the processing."

It seemed to Marcy that Quigg was alienating every-body, which wouldn't be a good thing for her own pur-poses. And here came that cone of noise again. "Maybe we should wait," she said diplomatically, "for Doug to get back and explain everything."

"That sounds good," said the young one, Judson. Somehow, Marcy found herself thinking of him as the kid.

This time, Doug brought with him on the elevator a short man in black leather jacket, black turtleneck, scuffed blue jeans, and serious workboots. Leading the newcomer over to the others, he said, "Okay, group, this is our first story session on *The Crime Show*, a title that may change, and we have some preliminary stuff to set up. So that's Sam Quigg of—"

"We met him," John said. He didn't sound all that excited about it.

"Okay, fine," Doug said. "And this is the latest member of our cast, Ray Harbach. Ray, you'll get to know all these people."

"I'm sure I will," Ray said. He had a swell voice, which went with a rich full head of luxuriant dark hair.

The sharp-featured guy said, "Doug? What does Ray do in this cast? Not another gun moll."

"No," Doug said, chuckling as though somebody had made a joke. "Ray has some experience in your world, which he'd rather not talk too much about—"

"Then he's smart," said a guy that Marcy had been trying not to notice. He was a man monster, very scary looking. He didn't so much remind her of one of those wrestlers on television as of three or four of them rolled into one.

"But, Tiny," Doug said (Marcy blinked at the name),

126

"he also has experience in the worlds of television and theater and he'll be a great help to you guys in working out your parts."

John said, "What experience?"

"I did a very good *Glengarry Glen Ross*," Ray said, "in Westport."

"Oh," John said. "An actor." He said it in a very flat way, as though he hadn't made up his mind what he thought about it.

Ray didn't take offense. Grinning at John, he said, "It makes a very nice cover."

"I can see it," said the sharp-featured guy. "The cop says, 'What are you doing with that fur coat?' and you say, 'It's my costume.'"

"When I'm doing *The Entertainer*," Ray said.

"Well, anyway, boys and girls," Doug said, more accurately this time, "first Sam is going to do all the personnel stuff with you people, and then you'll get together with Marcy here and start to work out our story line. Marcy," he told the others, "is the production assistant on the show, she's the one to keep control of the throughline."

"She *shapes* it," John said, "and makes it *entertainment*."

"That's right," Doug said, in the same flat tone as John when he'd said "actor." Then, ebullient again, he said, "The sets are one flight up, but we don't have to look at them today, we'll come back Monday for that. For now, we want to get the paperwork squared away and start to work out our plotlines and our character arcs."

"One thing I noticed, coming up," the sharp-featured guy said. "There's cameras now at Knickerbocker Storage."

Grinning, Doug said, "Andy, that just makes it a little more dramatic."

"No, it doesn't," Andy said. "It makes it a no deal."

Taken aback, Doug said, "No deal? What do you mean?"

The kid said, "You can't just follow us around and toughen up your act when you see what we do."

"That's right," John said. "Doug, you can't keep changing the place, so every time we get here it's different."

"And tougher," Andy said. "Look, Doug, if you got cameras, you got people watching them, right?"

"Not all the time," Doug said. "They feed to our central security office uptown, those people have a lot of cameras to monitor."

"Monitor means watch," John said.

Doug said, "But can't you— Can't you work around them somehow?"

"How do we do that?" Andy wanted to know. "If we leave them there, the guys watching the cameras watch *us*. If we turn them off or cover them, the guys watching the cameras know something's wrong, and who do they call?"

"Nine one one," John said.

Deeply troubled, Doug said, "I thought you'd have some cute way around that. You know, do footage of the place, empty, and then run a film of that for the cameras, something like that."

In a very flat voice, John said, "Now we're making movies, and then we're putting the movies inside surveillance cameras. We're pretty good."

After a short unhappy silence, Doug sighed and shrugged and said, "We'll remove them."

"Thank you, Doug," John said.

★　　★　　★

That was the low point of the day. The high point came later, unexpectedly, and involved Ray. Sam Quigg had finished his own work and departed in less than half an hour, but then it had been Marcy's task to find out who these people were and what each of them would contribute to the ongoing plot of *The Crime Show* (tentative).

As in robbery movies, each of the gang had a specialty. There was the driver, there was the muscleman, there was the lock expert, there was the planner (though not quite the leader, somehow) and there was the kid.

Which left Ray Harbach. What would his role be in the gang? Was there another specialty to be filled? It seemed as though the gang was already complete.

Marcy talked to each of them, getting a sense of his skills, his character, his position within the group ethos, and it was interesting how it all fit together. It really didn't seem as though it needed a Ray Harbach, though Doug definitely did want him aboard. "Ray's gonna be a real addition to the group dynamic," he insisted.

"How?" Marcy asked.

"A real addition."

So Marcy, in the interviewing, asked the man himself. "Ray," she said, "do you have some specialty, some expertise, some way you'll fit in with the rest of the group?"

"I can pretty much fill in most character roles," he told her, not boastfully, but merely as a fact.

"No," she said. "I mean *here*. In *this*."

He looked blank. "In this?"

The others were all within earshot, lolling on couches and chairs, idly listening in, commenting on each other's comments from time to time, and now the monster called Tiny, sprawled across much of a settee nearby, growled,

"What she wants to know is, whadaya contribute? How you gonna pull your weight?"

"When you're not being King Lear," said Andy, not unkindly, "whadayado on *our* team?"

"Oh," Ray said. "Gotcha. I'm a wall man."

Nobody seemed to know what that was. Stan the driver spoke for them all when he said, "And what does that look like?"

Again Ray looked around the big space, thinking. Then he got to his feet, said, "It looks like this," and walked over to the rough stone side wall. Without fuss, he climbed it, finding toe- and fingerholds in the tiniest crevices and crannies, moving steadily, angling over to the right as he went.

This building had ten-foot ceilings, which didn't give Ray much room to show his skill, but it was immediately apparent he had some. "Wow!" Doug cried, leaping to his feet. "What a visual!"

"It's wonderful," Marcy said, in awe. "Just wonderful."

They all loved it, and all got to their feet now as Ray moved horizontally along the wall, just beneath the ceiling, until he reached the rear of the building. There he made the turn onto the back wall and continued on as far as the first window, then descended easily to the floor. There, Darlene gave him a huge bear-hug and kiss that made him blink, but then he grabbed her and gave her the kiss right back again.

The gang's acceptance of Ray now, as they congratulated him and patted him on the back, was so clear that it became apparent, by contrast, that they had not actually accepted him before, but had just been going along with Doug with a wait-and-see attitude.

Andy, when the congratulations died down, asked Ray, "So how do you do this? Single-o?"

"No, I had two or three guys I'd work with," Ray said. "I'd go up a wall to some window nobody'd think to lock, let myself in, come downstairs, deal with any alarms and then open the front door. Usually then I'd leave, I wasn't gonna carry a lot of stolen goods around with me, and later they'd give me my share."

Andy approved. "That sounds like a very good plan."

"That's why," Ray said, "when the crew got caught, and nobody could figure out how they got into the place, somebody finally squealed, you know, for a better deal—"

"Always," said Tiny.

"Ain't that the truth," said Ray. "So they had my name, they had a witness, but he's a guy under indictment and they can't really prove anything against me. I kept saying it was a mistake, all I am is an actor, I'm no human fly, so what could they do? I got leaned on a lot but then they hadda let me go."

"Good thing for us," Stan said, which was the final seal on Ray's acceptance.

After that, Doug said it was time to quit for the day, they'd all meet again on Monday to start working out the story details, and then, when everybody left, Doug took Marcy to lunch at a diner near the tunnel (wow!), where she spent the first part of the meal trying to absorb it all. "That Ray," she said, still in wonderment.

"Babe told me he'd done some shady stuff in the past," Doug, said, "but he didn't say what. Maybe he didn't know."

"You know, Doug," Marcy said, her mind beginning to work again, "that kind of gives us our opening, doesn't it? The first scene of the first episode."

"Tell," he said.

"We open on Ray," she said, waving her fork, on which a piece of chicken breast was cooling, "climbing the outside of the building on the corner."

"The Chase bank."

"Either corner, whichever works. We see him looking in windows, climbing all the way up, then going across the roof and back down the other side to the roof of *our* building."

"And over the side," Doug said.

Marcy nodded. "That's right. He goes down the back of our building, where nobody can see him. He's alone, so there's no dialogue, just city noises. He looks in windows, and when he looks in at the storage place he does a big reaction. Then he leaves, and he goes to the bar, and he tells the others what he's seen."

Beaming like a lottery winner, Doug said, "Take the weekend, Marcy, write it up, we'll lay it on the guys on Monday. All of that movement without dialogue. What a grabber. We've got *Rififi* here, Marcy. Write it up!"

22

NOBODY WAS HAPPY with the meeting just past. Once Doug and Marcy had walked away southward, waving and smiling, cheered by recent events, and once Ray had hailed a cab to take himself and Darlene somewhere else, the two of them also expressing pleasure at the unfolding of their adventure, the other five stood on the sidewalk on Varick Street and frowned together.

"Dortmunder," Tiny said, "this is not good."

"I know that," Dortmunder said.

"Nothing is happening," Tiny said.

Dortmunder nodded. "I know that, too."

Kelp said, "The trouble is, these clowns are in no hurry to get their reality up and running."

"And meanwhile," Stan said, "what are we doing on our own plan? Nothing."

"We don't have a plan," the kid said. "We have a door we can't get through, to something we don't know what it is behind it."

"I can feel," Tiny said, "discouragement creeping on. We gotta sit and meet."

Kelp said, "You mean tonight, at the OJ?"

"No," Tiny said, "I mean now, at Dortmunder's. Stan, use your cell, order out a pizza, extra pepperoni, I'll whistle up the limo." And he stomped off around the corner, to the limo he never left home without, due to his size and his disinclination to rub shoulders with the civilian world.

"Tiny's right," Stan said, breaking out his cell.

"Well, yes and no," Kelp said. "Get two pizzas, one with hold the pepperoni."

Midafternoon at the Dortmunder abode, May still at her supermarket checkout register, pizza shreds and beer cans creating their festive litter across the living room, and Tiny saying, "We don't have all the time in the world like those reality geeks."

"We've only got," Kelp said, "until they try to check the IDs we gave them."

"I do have this situation," Stan said, around a mouthful of pepperoni. "On account of my Mom, they got my last name and her home phone number."

"That's an easy one," Tiny said. "I already got that one scoped."

Everybody wanted to know how, so Tiny told them. "They're not gonna come back at us about the phony names and the phony Social Security numbers until the earliest Tuesday, so before then, we see Doug, we explain we threw Murch out."

"Hey, wait there," Stan said. "Threw me *out*?"

"Everything," Tiny told him, "takes place in that building on Varick, everything they know about and everything they don't know about. Where's the driving?"

"Gee, you're right," Kelp said.

"Hold on a minute," Stan said. He was about to get on his feet.

The kid said, "No, wait, Stan, you don't get it. Monday we tell them you're out, and anything that happens after that you aren't part of. You set up an alibi for whenever it is we do whatever it is we're gonna do—"

"About which," Dortmunder said, "it wouldn't hurt to do some thinking."

Stan said, "But I'm not *out*. Not out out. Just as far as those people I'm out."

"There's gonna be driving, Stan," Kelp told him, "only they don't know about it."

"We can say," the kid said, "this new guy means the pot's smaller all the way around, so we gotta unload somebody to bring the numbers up, and Stan, you're the guy. We'll tell him Monday."

Tiny said, "Quicker than that. Dortmunder, you and Kelp go by his place tonight, tell him the story. Then he's got days and days to get used to it. Murch is out, the human fly is in."

Kelp said, "Speaking of, whadawe thinka this human fly?"

"He's a human plant," Tiny said.

"Yeah," Kelp agreed. "They put him on us to watch us, but why?"

"Because," the kid said, "they're afraid we might start thinking about Combined Tool, as long as we're in the building, and they wanna know if that happens."

"Which brings me," Dortmunder said, "back to my point. When *do* we start to think about Combined Tool?"

"Tonight," Tiny decided. "When you're done with Doug, and later on tonight, we all come to Varick Street. I'm not gonna run around on roofs, so at one o'clock I'll be at the front door. In the limo."

Dortmunder said, "Tiny, would there be room in that limo for an extension ladder?"

Tiny lowered a gaze on Dortmunder, thought a moment, then smiled, an unusual and not an entirely comforting sight. "That would be a first, wouldn't it?" he said. "You're on."

They didn't stay to help with the cleanup.

23

Not having the hoped-for comfort of Darlene in his life, Doug had dinner with a couple college friends, also bachelors, also beginning to get querulous about it, and got home at quarter to ten to find the lights on and John and Andy seated in his living room, reading his magazines. "Oh, come on," he said. "Don't you guys have homes of your own?"

"Where do you get your magazines, Doug?" Andy wanted to know. "A dentist's office?"

"I've been busy lately," Doug explained. "I'm behind on my reading." And he thought, I'm apologizing to these people! They're in my home. I don't want them here.

Dropping last year's *TIME* on an end table, Andy said, "We don't wanna take up a lotta your time. Particularly when it's that old. We just wanted to drop by, tell you, there's a little change in the personnel."

"Change? What do you mean, change?"

John said, "A couple facts come together today and we

saw we didn't have the exactly perfect string for this job."

"You're changing the crew?" Doug didn't get it. "That's what this is about? Why do you want to change the crew?"

"Because you did," John said.

"See," Andy said, "Ray's a nice addition to the group, climbing up the walls and all that, but it means we got one guy too many."

"You don't wanna work in a crowd," John explained.

"So what are you saying?" Doug asked. "One of the group is leaving?"

"Stan," Andy said.

"Stan? What, *Stan*? He's the one *started* this thing. His mother. But he's the first one in."

"But he's a driver," Andy said. "There's no place in this thing for a driver, it's all on the third floor of that building on Varick."

Doug, trying to wrap his head around this change, said, "What does Stan think about it?"

"There's always another job," Andy said, with a shrug. "Always another day."

"Is he happy about it?"

"Happy doesn't come into it," John said. "After we saw you people today, we thought it over, and we all agreed, the string's got to change. So Stan's out."

Struck by a sudden horrible thought, Doug said, "You didn't— You didn't *kill* him, did you?"

They were both clearly astonished. John said, "What are you talkin about?" and at the same time Andy said, "We're the *non*violent crowd, remember?"

"But you're criminals," Doug reminded them. "Is there

really any such thing as a nonviolent criminal? Except politicians, you know, white collar."

Andy, speaking with great sincerity, said, "I can guarantee you, Doug, we stay away from violence completely unless there's absolutely no way it can get back at us."

"Which is never," John added.

Doug was unconvinced. He said, "Tiny? Are you saying Tiny isn't ever violent?"

"Look at Tiny," John suggested. "Does he *need* violence?"

"We don't want to take up your whole night here," Andy said. "All we wanted was to come by and tell you, Ray's in, so Stan's out, and you can tell that payroll guy."

"Quigg," John said.

"Yes, I will." Doug frowned at them. "That was worth a whole trip? You couldn't call me tomorrow? You're gonna *see* me Monday."

"We wanted you to know when it was fresh," John explained. "You've got your girl Marcy working on it, shaping it, making it entertainment, we didn't want her to waste any time shaping Stan, because he's out."

"I'll tell her," Doug said.

"Thank you, Doug," John said, with dignity, and they both got up and left.

Doug brooded at the closed door through which they'd just passed. Something's wrong here, he told himself. Something smells funny about this. But what? And why?

24

ONE A.M. A gleaming black limousine comes to a stop on Varick Street. The building door beside it opens and two men come out and cross the sidewalk to the limo. The limo's rear door opens and an extension ladder slides out horizontally into midair. First one of the men grasps the oncoming ladder, then the other. The two men turn and carry the ladder to the building doorway, open into darkness. The limo's passenger says a word to the driver and climbs out to the sidewalk. He shuts the door, crosses to the building, enters into the same darkness as the other two men and the ladder, and shuts that door behind himself. The limo purrs away around the corner.

Crash.

"Turn on a light," Tiny said. "You're gonna bust every windshield in here."

Kelp found the light switch and turned on the overhead fluorescents. "No, it was a side window," he said. He was at the front end of the ladder.

Dortmunder, at the other end, said, "We'll do the indoor stuff first."

Kelp looked across the massed vehicles to the elevator platform way over on the other side. "I think," he said, "we got to carry it over our heads."

"Save a lotta glass that way," Tiny commented.

Holding his end of the ladder up in the air over his head, Kelp started the dodging and weaving necessary to thread the needle in here. Dortmunder followed, his end of the ladder also up in the air, and Tiny followed as caboose. They would use the ladder to get to the second floor because they didn't know what would be alarmed when the building was supposed to be empty, and the elevator seemed like a prime candidate for security.

As they neared the elevator, Stan and the kid came up out of a horseless hansom cab, both yawning a little. (Stan was out of the public part of events, but not out of the inner circle parts.) The kid said, "That's really comfortable, that thing."

"Not much scenery, though," Stan said, and nodded at the ladder. "Good. Now we find out if the damn place is worth the trouble."

"It better be," Kelp said. "I'm not doing this for *wages*."

At the elevator at last, Kelp put his end of the ladder down while Dortmunder walked the other end up toward the vertical. The other three came in at that point to lay hands on the ladder, to help and hinder, and when it was upright they pushed up the extension, elongating the ladder into the upper darkness.

"Ouch!"

Kelp looked over at Dortmunder. "You okay?"

"Not until you lower it a little so I can get my thumb out."

"Sorry."

They completed the extension without further incident, and Tiny said, "We don't have to do a mob scene up there, everybody in everybody's way. Dortmunder, you and Kelp go on up, see what it looks like."

"Right."

So Kelp went up the ladder, Dortmunder following, and on the next level they came to the empty space fronting Combined Tool. Six feet back from the hole for the elevator an off-white wall stretched across from the right-side outer wall, with the one brown door in the middle of it they'd seen before. Just to the left of the elevator area, a second wall came forward, perpendicular from the first one, running beside the elevator hole to the front of the building.

So this empty rectangle of space with the door in it was all at this level they could see. Of course this door too was equipped with palm-print recognition. They stood back—not too far back—and considered the situation.

"Wires," decided Kelp.

"You're right."

They both had flashlights out now, shining them on the walls and ceiling. Kelp said, "Electricity. Phone. Cable. Security. A cluster of wires."

Dortmunder pointed his light at the stone side wall of the elevator space. "They gotta do surface-mount. You can't bury wires in a stone wall. See, like that." And his light shone on a gray metal duct, an inch square, coming down from above. "That's where they put in those cameras, to screw us outta the storage space."

"Well, let's see." Kelp turned the other way, looking at the side wall where it came close to the front of the building. "There we go."

His light showed another gray duct, a little larger, coming out of that side wall, very low and almost to the front. The duct emerged, made a left turn to go downward, then another left and headed off toward the door they'd come in.

Kelp called, "Tiny! You see that duct? I'm shining the light on it."

"I got it."

"Find where it goes, I'll be right down."

Dortmunder said, "And what am I doing?"

"Same as last time. Comere."

They went over to the impregnable door, and Kelp withdrew from one of the rear pockets of his jacket the stethoscope and earphone gizmo. As Dortmunder watched, he bent to the door, listening here, listening there, then saying, "Hah."

"You got it."

"We know the thing has to be alarmed," Kelp said, "and here it is. Only this time I want it to stop."

"Okay."

"Give me a couple minutes to get set," Kelp said, "then you listen, and you tell me when it switches off." He tapped a fingertip on the appropriate spot on the door. "Right there."

"Done."

Kelp went away down the ladder, and Dortmunder experimentally listened to the door's faint hum for a minute, then, tiring of that, walked around in this blank, supremely uninteresting area until Kelp, from far away at the ground floor rear, yelled, "John!"

"Yar!"

"Start listening!"

143

"You got it."

Bending to his work, Dortmunder listened through the gizmo to the humming of the door. It was a very soothing kind of hum, really, especially when you positioned yourself so your back could be comfortable. It was a nonthreatening hum, an encouraging hum, faint but unending, assuring you that everything was going to be all right, all your troubles were over, you'd just sail along now on the calm sea of this hum, no nasty sur—

"JOHN! WHAT THE HELL'S THE MATTER WITH YOU?"

The scream, about an inch from his non-gizmo ear, was so loud and unexpected he drove his head into the door to get away from it, and the door bounced his head back into the scream with a new ache in it. Staring upward, he saw what appeared to be Kelp's evil twin, face twisted into a Kabuki mask of rage. "What? What?"

"Can't you *hear* anything?"

"The hum." Dortmunder straightened, pulled the earphone out of his unassaulted ear, assembled the tatters of his dignity about himself, and said, "You wanted me to listen to the hum, I listened to the hum."

Now Kelp frowned at the door. "It never stopped."

"Never. It was gonna stop, I'd tell you."

"I shouted up from downstairs," Kelp said. He was growing a bit calmer.

"I," Dortmunder said, self-respect now totally intact, "was listening to the hum."

Again Kelp frowned at the door. His rage with Dortmunder seemed to be forgotten. "I did everything," he said. "I shut down everything, I bypassed everything."

"Hum," Dortmunder said.

Kelp stood frowning, thinking. From downstairs voices were raised, full of questions for Kelp, but he continued to frown at the door.

"They're calling you," Dortmunder said. "Pretty soon they'll come up and yell in your face."

Slowly, Kelp was roused from his studies, and called down, "I'll be right there!" Then, to Dortmunder, he said, "I didn't yell in your face, I yelled in your ear."

"Very similar."

Kelp nodded. "I'm sorry," he said.

"Accepted," Dortmunder said.

"I was upset," Kelp explained.

"I am remaining calm," Dortmunder said. "You wanted to go down the ladder?"

"Well, there's nothing we can do here," Kelp said. "We are not gonna get through that door."

"Not tonight, anyway," Dortmunder said, and Kelp didn't say anything.

So they went down the ladder, Kelp first, to find the others at their ease in the hansom cab. Tiny pretty thoroughly occupied the rear-facing front seat, with Stan and the kid opposite. The seats were well-cushioned, to accommodate the needs and expectations of tourists.

Kelp clambered up to the driver's perch, above and behind the others, not quite so padded, but not bad. Dortmunder stood there, and then the kid said to him, "Grab something and sit."

"Sure."

Dortmunder looked around. A motorcycle with a sidecar stood alertly nearby. He rolled it over next to the hansom cab, settled himself into the surprisingly comfortable sidecar, and said, "It looks as though Kelp doesn't know how to get past that door." He might be remaining calm, but that didn't mean he'd forgiven or forgotten.

"I've been thinking about it," Kelp said, too absorbed with the problem to take offense. "The only thing I can figure, they've gone wireless. And why wouldn't they? They've got TV and the Internet and all that, so why not go wireless?"

The kid said, "Andy? What do we do about it?"

"Nothing," Kelp said. "If it's wireless, we're screwed."

"Well, that isn't the only possibility," Dortmunder said. "We haven't tried out back yet."

"I don't know," Kelp said. "It's lookin tight."

"If this thing isn't gonna happen," Tiny said, "it's time for us to start packing tents."

"It's going to happen," the kid said, suddenly energized. Clambering over the other passengers, he climbed out of the hansom cab and said, "Bring the ladder out back, I'll climb up it and see what the windows do."

"They won't open," Tiny told him.

But the kid refused to be daunted. "Come on," he insisted. "Let's go see what's what."

"If we're gonna keep on with this," Tiny said, rising from the hansom's front seat, causing a smallish tremor that rattled Stan around on the backseat like a lone die in a padded cup, "I'll carry your ladder, kid."

"Thank you, Tiny."

First Tiny retracted the ladder, getting more help than he needed along the way, and then he held it up horizontally over his head and set out across the valley of vehicles. If the world wore a propeller beanie, this is what it would look like.

They all made their way diagonally across the interior of

the building, to the rear door Kelp had earlier tamed. He opened it again now, and everybody got out of the way as Tiny carried the ladder outside. He extended it, all by himself, then leaned it against the wall next to the leftmost second-floor window, which was smaller than the other windows at that level, and said, "Okay, kid, do your thing."

"Right."

The kid scrambled up the ladder, took his flashlight out of his jacket pocket, and shone it in through the window. "It's a bathroom," he reported.

Stan said, "We already figured that. All the johns are in the back corner there."

"This is a very nice one," the kid said. "Big walk-in shower, a painting of some castle on the wall, and one of those things girls use."

The others all looked at one another, baffled. Stan hazarded, "A hair dryer?"

"No, no," the kid said, rattling the ladder a little. "One of those things that's like a toilet but isn't."

"Oh," Kelp said, "a bidet," pronouncing the T.

Dortmunder said, "Is that how you say that?"

"How would I know?" Kelp asked. "I never had to ask for one."

Tiny said, "Kid, come down, move the ladder, see what else is up there."

"Right."

The kid came down, over, and up, and shone his light in the next window. "It's a kitchen," he said.

Dortmunder, unbelieving, said, "A *kitchen*?"

"A really nice one," the kid said. "Big refrigerator, microwave, all kinds of stuff."

Dortmunder said, "In Combined Tool? This is getting weirder."

The kid said, "It's big, too. It looks like it goes almost all the way across the back."

Tiny said, "Go to the last window, see what's in there."

So the kid did, and said, "It's a pantry. Big one, lots of nice shelves, but not much in there. Some pots and pans, some dishes. No food."

"Let me see this," Kelp said, and suddenly hurried up the ladder.

The kid, feeling the tremors in the ladder and looking down to see the top of Kelp's head getting nearer, said, "Hey. You think this is a good idea?"

"Yes," Kelp said. "Lean to the left." And he muscled upward to the kid's right, while the kid held on with all of his fingers and many of his toes.

"I think I'll hold the ladder now," Tiny said, and did so.

With the two of them side by side on the same rung up there, Kelp peered intently in at the sides and bottom of the window, pushing the kid's head out of the way and saying, "Shine the light over there. No, on the jamb. Okay, and down. Okay." And back down the ladder he zipped, followed a bit shakily by the kid.

Dortmunder said, "So whadaya think?"

"I think we aren't gonna know what's in there until we go in there," Kelp said. "So we don't know if it's worthwhile until we do it."

"And then," Stan said, "it could turn out not to be cash at all, but some big boss's love nest."

"That would irritate me," Tiny said.

Dortmunder said, "With the palm-print locks? I don't

think so. Andy, do you see any way to get in there through a window?"

"One way," Kelp said, "and one way only. But it's gonna use the place up, I don't think we'll be able to do the same thing twice."

Tiny said, "You mean break the window."

"No, I don't," Kelp said. "You break the window, you make a vibration, and that sets off the alarm."

Dortmunder said, "In that case, you can't open the window either."

"I don't wanna open it," Kelp said. "This is not an easy thing here. What we're talking about is at least two more trips."

Tiny said, "Back twice more? This is beginning to look like a career."

"We're in it this far," Kelp said, and nodded toward the far end of the areaway. "In the meantime, we can leave the ladder in the corner back there. Nobody's gonna notice it."

Dortmunder said, "Two more trips and still the ladder, but you don't want to open the window and you don't want to break it. What *do* you want to do in these trips?"

"The first one," Kelp said, and gestured up toward the pantry window, "we bring epoxy and seal that window to the frame. I looked at it, and nobody ever opens it, so they're not gonna notice."

Tiny said, "Why are we doing that?"

"Vibrations again," Kelp said. "Because when we come back the second time we've got our glass cutter and our suction cup with the handle on it."

Dortmunder lifted his head, with a sudden surge of that unexpected quality: optimism. "I see it!" he said.

"If we do it right," Kelp said, "we cut out the whole pane in one piece, prop it inside, go in, do what we're gonna do, and on the way out we epoxy the glass back in place."

The kid said, "The line will show, where it was cut."

Kelp said, "What do we care?"

"Oh, yeah," the kid said. "Right."

Tiny said, "I'm not gonna get through that window."

"That's okay, Tiny," Stan said. "I'll take pictures up there with my cell, you won't miss a thing."

Dortmunder said, "Glue tomorrow night, glass cutter Sunday night, and then on Monday morning we tell Doug we don't want reality after all."

"As we don't," Tiny said.

25

D OUG WAS WORRIED about Stan Murch. Not worried about him, exactly, but more worried *for* him. The news that he had been peremptorily kicked out of the gang had come as a real shock. Weren't gangs supposed to stick together? Wasn't it the gang against the world, and they relied on one another because there was nobody else they *could* rely on?

And what made it even worse, in some way it was Stan Murch who had put this gang together. His mother had sent Stan to Doug, and Stan had shown up with John, and then at the next meeting Andy was there, and it really looked as though this was a tight-knit group, people who had known and trusted one another through many nefarious experiences. Tiny and Judson had come in to complete the crew, and it had all made sense.

But then, because he himself had added Ray Harbach to the mix, all at once they threw Stan out. No regrets, no good fellowship, just cold calculation. It had changed the way he looked at the gang, and not for the better.

And how would Stan have taken it? Oh, John and Andy had dismissed all that, as being nothing of importance, because Stan knew the ways of the world and there would always be another job, but did that make sense? Would Stan not be resentful even a tiny bit?

Nonviolent, Doug thought. They're supposed to be nonviolent, but who says so? They do. Do they *look* nonviolent?

He remembered asking them, John and Andy, when they'd told him Stan was out, asking them because he so much didn't want anything really bad to happen, asking them if they'd actually killed Stan—the way the mobsters on television always do a reduction in staff—and he clearly remembered Andy's answer:

"I can guarantee you, Doug, we stay away from violence completely unless there's absolutely no way it can get back at us."

And that's a slippery sentence once you start to look at it, isn't it?

What if they *had* killed Stan? Tiny, with those big hands of his. Killed him to keep him from betraying the gang to the police as revenge for his ouster, or to keep him from spying on them and robbing *them* once the job was done. Didn't honor among thieves, really, go out with Robin Hood?

Doug fretted the entire weekend about Stan, where he was, what he thought about what had happened, and by Sunday afternoon, two days after he'd been told about Stan's downsizing, he couldn't stand it any more. He had to find out. No matter what the truth was, he had to know it.

So finally, Sunday afternoon, giving up his futile attempts to read the Sunday *Times*, he took the only route he knew to get in touch with Stan, and phoned his Mom, only to get her answering machine, with her distinct impatient voice: "If I know you, say so, and I'll call you back."

"Mrs Murch," he told the machine, "this is Doug Fairkeep. Would you please have Stan call me as soon as possible?" And he hung up, to fret some more.

She called back at seven that evening. "He's outa town," she said.

"Out of town?"

"He went to California for maybe a month," she said. "He had a couple possible job opportunities out there."

"Do you have a contact number for him?"

"Not me," she said. "He'll check in, I'll tell him you called."

"I'd really like to hear from him."

"You know how often people call their mother," she said. "When he gets a minute off his busy schedule and gives me a ring, I'll give him your message."

"Thank you," Doug said.

That was his own mother. *She* wouldn't cover up for them, would she, if they'd . . . done . . . anything? Or had she been intimidated? (Though she hadn't sounded particularly intimidated.)

But the more he thought about it, if they did decide to eliminate Stan because he knew too much, wouldn't that mean Doug also knew too much? Not a happy thought.

All in all, he had a troubled night.

26

"HE CALLED my Mom this afternoon," Stan said, as Kelp got into this nice Chevy Gazpacho that Stan had borrowed half an hour ago from a perfectly legal parking place on West Forty-ninth Street.

Shutting his door, putting on his seat belt—because who wants to listen to all that ping-ping-ping—Kelp said, "Doug? What'd she tell him?"

Stan put the Gazpacho in gear and continued on downtown. "What we said. I'm out of town into California a while, considering my job prospects."

"Good."

Last night's expedition to Varick Street, like this one tonight, had been only the two of them, since they didn't need a whole crowd to gaff one window. They'd brought a different car from a different neighborhood last night, gone through the house like smoke, Kelp up the ladder while Stan held it, and sufficient epoxy glue was spread there to hold USS *Intrepid* in place. A gas-pipe explosion could take out the entire block, but that window would not leave that frame.

Tonight would be step two of the plan: Cut out the lower pane, carefully place the pane inside the room, case Combined Tool to find out at last what the hell was in there, gently epoxy the pane back in place, and depart. John had wanted to come along tonight, just because it was a kind of a matter of personal pride for him to walk around inside that forbidden city, but he'd come to understand it wasn't necessary; soon they'd be going in for real.

Now, Stan parked in a temporarily legal place a couple blocks from Varick Street, and he and Kelp used paper towels to wipe down anything they might have touched in the car. When they were done here, Kelp would cab uptown and Stan would subway to Canarsie, and eventually the city would take charge of the Gazpacho. In the meantime, Kelp carried the thick tube of epoxy and the strong suction cup with a handle.

The walk to Varick Street and through the building was uneventful, but when they went out the back door to the areaway and looked up the lights were on in Combined Tool. "What the hell," Stan said.

"Ssh," Kelp whispered. Pointing toward the ladder, he whispered, "We gotta see."

"Good."

They went over to get the ladder, extended it without difficulty, and leaned it against the wall between two of the kitchen windows. Stan whispered, "I'm not doing that thing like you and the kid did, with two people at once up on this thing. You go up and come down, and then I'll go up and come down."

"I like that."

Stan held the ladder and watched Kelp climb. The light
from the kitchen was bright enough that he'd have to be
careful up there looking in. His head bent far back, Stan
watched as Kelp eased up and over, and then the light was
on part of Kelp's face including his right eye, and he was
looking in.

Well? Get on with it. Stan wanted to call up to Kelp,
Come on, what're you looking at up there, what's going
on, but he knew he couldn't do that, and eventually Kelp
did come back down the ladder. He looked at Stan, shrugged
in a manner that didn't communicate anything, and gestured for Stan to take his turn.

Stan said, "What's up there?"

"Look at it," Kelp advised.

So Stan did. Up he went, and slowly eased his face into
the light, and what he was looking at was the profile of a
man seated at the kitchen table eating a bowl of cereal and
reading a newspaper. The word "Zeitung" was the biggest
word Stan could see on the newspaper, so it was in
German.

The man himself was about fifty, thin, balding, spectacled, wearing a pale yellow dress shirt and dark patterned
tie under a buttoned-up black vest, plus dark pants and
black shoes. Very formal dress for eating cereal on Varick
Street in Manhattan at one in the morning.

Stan went down the ladder. "We can't do it," he whispered. "Not with him in there."

"I know it."

"And you were all supposed to meet Doug here tomorrow.
Except you weren't going to."

"Well," Kelp said, "it looks as though we're gonna meet
Doug here tomorrow."

27

WHEN DORTMUNDER WALKED into the fake OJ at ten o'clock on Monday morning, Doug was there with Ray Harbach and Darlene Looper and Marcy and the flamboyant director, Roy Ombelen, plus a stocky fiftyish man in a bartender's white apron and white shirt—though rather too white, in fact—who looked as though he might be Rollo's mild-mannered cousin from San Francisco. More tofu than meat.

"Good morning, John," Doug said. He had the harried look of a man having to remind himself to look cheerful. "Where's the others?"

"They'll be along," Dortmunder said. He himself was feeling grumpy, since he'd thought everything would be done by now. They would set things up for the break-in, that was the plan, then disappear from Doug's Global Positioning System, wait a week, and clean out Combined Tool *and* Knickerbocker Storage. Let Doug and his pals believe anything they wanted to believe, they wouldn't be able to prove a thing. If they went so far as to look at a lot of old mug shots they might eventually identify one or more of their former reality-stars-to-be, but they still wouldn't be able to prove anything, and Dortmunder and associates would all have rock-solid alibis for the night in question.

But it wasn't to be. All at once, Combined Tool had turned into a pied-à-terre for a guy reading a Zeitung. They obviously couldn't do their pre-heist survey with him there, and there seemed to be no way to find out who he was, or how long he intended to stay, or what he had to do with Combined Tool.

So there was nothing for it but to stick around a little longer, because none of them, not even Tiny, wanted to just walk away with no profit *and* no answers. Which was why he was here again, saying to Doug, "You wanted to start something today?"

"Roy's going to tell you about it," Doug said, "but it ought to wait till the rest arrive."

"Fine," Dortmunder said, and went into the non-OJ to sit at a booth on the right, which was, in fact, a little more comfortable than the ones in the original. Looking around he saw three cameras, hulking black things on big elaborate swivel-chair-type wheel arrangements, each camera attached by a black wire to the earphones of a cameraperson slouched negligently in a chair, reading a tabloid, while Doug and the others murmured together a little ways off.

He had barely made himself comfortable in this booth when that loud doorbell sounded, signaling the arrival of the rest, brought here in Tiny's current limo. Doug hurried off to let them in.

Dortmunder had come here separately because he'd wanted a little solitary time to think over this unpleasant new development and had therefore decided to walk down from Nineteenth Street, hoping to find a solution to their problems along the way. Some hope.

Soon Kelp and Tiny and the kid appeared, and when they came over from the elevator they all started in about how terrific this imitation OJ was, and Dortmunder suddenly remembered, That's *right*! I'm supposed to be seeing this thing for the first time. Instead of which, he'd just moped in and said something grumpy and sat down.

Well, fortunately, Doug and the others hadn't noticed that slip, and now everybody else was making up for it; maybe overdoing it just a bit, but not bad.

Should he join them, suddenly overcome by this OJ clone? No; better just leave it alone.

Once everybody calmed down, Roy Ombelen assembled them at the tables in the non-OJ while he described what was going on. (Today his shirt was fuchsia, ascot teal, corduroy trousers café au lait, shin-high boots apricot.) "I realize," he told them, "the security concerns you fellows are constricted by go a bit beyond the, shall we say, run of the mill? It is our firm intention not to recognizably film your faces, because such film we wouldn't be able to use anyway."

"You got that right," Tiny told him.

"Well, that's my job," Ombelen said. "But in this particular instance, it's your job as well. We will photograph you from above, from below, from behind. We will photograph your ears, your hands, your elbows. But we need your help to do this right, so here's the one rule you must remember. If you can see the camera lens, the camera can see your face. Tell us at once if the camera has moved into the forbidden zone, and we'll reshoot."

"That sounds good," Kelp said.

"It's the only way," Ombelen assured him, "we can make this *peculiar* situation work. Now, your opening scene, you will all be at the bar, and Ray Harbach will join you with some news. Our production assistant, Marcy, will describe the scene to you."

Marcy, showing evidence of stage fright, took a position in front of them and said, "First, I want to introduce you to your bartender." Gesturing at the obvious bartender to come forward, she said, "This is Tom LaBrava, he's a professional actor."

"Hi, guys," LaBrava said. He showed no stage fright at all.

Marcy said, "Tom isn't going to be part of the actual robbery plot, in fact he isn't going to hear anything about it at all, so his face will be seen."

"Better for the résumé," LaBrava said, and grinned around at them.

Kelp said, "So he's Tom? 'Hi, Tom,' like that?"

Doug stepped forward again, saying, "No, we decided we had to make it clear his part was fictional, so he has a character name." Chuckling a bit hollowly at them, he said, "We felt you wouldn't like it if we called him Rollo—"

"That's right," several people said.

"—So we've decided to go with Rodney. If that's okay with you guys."

Kelp said, "Rodney?" He sounded uncertain. Turning to LaBrava, he smiled in an amiable way and said, "Hi, Rodney." He then made a thoughtful face, like somebody tasting a new recipe, mulled, and finally said, "Sure. Why not?"

"Hi, Rodney," Tiny growled.

"How you doin, Rodney?" Dortmunder asked.

"Just fine," LaBrava said. "I kinda like Rodney. It's a name I can work a character into."

"It's you, Rodney," the kid said.

"Okay, that's fine, then," Doug said. "Marcy?"

Marcy came back into her place, looking slightly less self-conscious. "What's going to happen," she said, "you're all going to be at the bar, and Ray will come in and say he's got something really interesting to tell you all. You want to know what it is, and he says it isn't really something for public consumption, and you—John, I think—say to Rodney, 'Okay if we use the back room?' and he says, 'Fine.' And then you all head off that way for the back room. Let's try it once or twice without the cameras."

Then Roy Ombelen took over, to place them here and there at the bar, angling them in ways that felt a little weird but were apparently going to look okay in the film. Once he had them where he wanted them, he said to Harbach, "Now, when you come in the bar you come over to about here, where you can see everybody, and you tell them you've got this interesting information."

"Okay, great."

"Places, please," Ombelen said. "Rodney, a little farther away along the bar, if you would. That's fine. Ray, a little farther back. I want you completely off the set, and then you come in. That's it, that's perfect. All right, everybody. Action."

And, on that word, the loud elevator machinery jolted into its racket, and the elevator began to sink, as everybody turned to stare and watch it go.

Obviously, nobody was going to rehearse anything with

that going on. Doug moved a little closer to the elevator, shaking his head in irritation, and as the sound receded he turned to tell them, "There isn't supposed to be anybody else coming here now. We left strict instructions, everybody stay away from Varick Street, we're putting together a new show here."

The elevator snarl, having receded, now advanced again, and soon it appeared, with Babe Tuck standing on it, arms akimbo, expression deeply annoyed. As Doug and Ombelen both approached him, both trying to say something to him, he marched straight across from the elevator to the set, glowered at everybody, and said, "This show is canceled. Shut it down."

28

Doug was stunned. Shut it down? Cancel? But it was coming together so well. It was going to be wonderful, the most exciting innovative new reality show since *Sitcom Reunion*. So much more fun to work on than *The Stand*. Cancel it? Shut it down? What did Babe mean?

Doug voiced the question: "Babe? What do you mean?"

Babe, looking the angriest he'd been since he quit the news beat, said, "I talked with Quigg this morning."

Doug nodded, not sure why. "About what?"

"About these *phonies*," Babe said, jabbing a thumb in the general direction of the cast.

Now Doug was shocked. "Phonies? Babe, you mean these people aren't crooks? They aren't hardened criminals after all? They're just people, like everybody else?"

"I don't know and I don't care what they are," Babe said. "Every single piece of ID they gave Quigg on Friday is a phony."

"Of course it is," John said. "You gotta know we can't give you our real names."

"Names shmames," Babe said. "What I need is legiti-mate rock-solid Social Security numbers. Not those soy-bean statistics you gave Quigg."

"I don't think we're following this," John said.

But Andy said, "John, maybe they got a legit problem."

"And I," John said, "got an *il*-legit problem." Then he looked around and said, mostly to Babe, "We're kind of a crowd here. Why don't you and him and him and me"—pointing to Doug and Andy—"siddown at a booth there and talk this over. Everybody else takes a break some-where."

Roy Orbelem said, "There's some nice sofas over there. Beyond the hallway set."

"All right," Babe said, though grumpily. To John he said, "If you think you got something to say."

"Let's find out."

Everybody started to move, and Andy said, "Rodney?"

The actor/bartender looked alert. "Yes, sir?"

"You got any actual beer around here?"

It was Doug who answered. "We do, for the shoot. It's in a cooler under the bar."

"I'll get it," the new Rodney offered, and went away to do so.

So Doug and Babe and John and Andy, all of them looking grim in a variety of ways, settled into a booth to wait for their beer to be delivered. Doug took that hiatus to notice a change that had occurred in the dynamic of the gang. Before this, the impetus or spark plug had usually been Andy, sometimes the now-gone Stan, occasionally Tiny. But now, in the face of some unknown and unexpected apparent disaster befalling them, John had quietly taken over and everybody had tacitly agreed he had the right to do so. Interesting. See how that dynamic could be worked into the show. If there was a show.

Rodney soon brought four cans of Budweiser, solemnly said, "Call me, gentlemen, when you're ready for more," then grinned and winked to show he was merely getting into the part, and left.

Andy picked up his beer can, looked at it, and gave Doug a skeptical eye. "Product placement?"

"They will be providing the beer," Doug agreed. "It's a perfectly fine beer."

"Uh-huh," Andy said, popped open his can, and took a noncommittal slug.

Babe turned to John. "Just so you know what's happened here," he said, "the Social Security numbers are much more important than the names. You can call yourself Little Bo Peep for all I care. But a corporation like ours simply cannot employ anybody who cannot demonstrate, with a valid Social Security number, their right to work in this country. We absolutely cannot hire wetbacks."

Andy said, "Wetbacks?" sounding incredulous.

Babe patted the air in his direction. "Listen, I know you guys are homegrown, I know you're not illegal aliens."

"We are," John said, with dignity, "illegal citizens."

"And we can't hire you," Babe said. "It's as simple as that. The feds require that we vet every hire and make them *prove* they have the right to work in this country."

Doug said, "John, when they took me on, I showed them my passport."

Babe said, "All right, I apologize. When Quigg first gave me the news, I got really pissed off, I don't know if you noticed—"

"Kinda," Andy said.

"Well, now I see," Babe said, "you just didn't understand the situation. You thought all you had to do was spread a little fantasy and then get on with the job. But I'm sorry, guys, it's more serious than that."

"I can see it is," John said, and started to brood.

Doug found that fascinating, the way the man's eyes seemed to go out of focus, as though he were actually looking at something on a hillside in western Pennsylvania or somewhere, while his head from time to time nodded, and the other three at the table sipped their beers and watched. Until, some time later, his eyes refocused, and focused on Doug, and he said, "Passport."

"That's right," Doug said. "I had to show them my—"

"We talked, one time," John said, "you said wire transfers."

"Wire transfers?"

"Money going to Europe, on account there's nothing in cash any more."

"Oh, that's right. I forgot about that."

Babe said, "You talked about wire transfers?"

"When they were looking for things that might be robbery targets," Doug explained.

"Well, how about that, then?" John asked.

Doug didn't get it. "How about what?"

"Wire transfers," John said. "We don't work for you any more, we work for some European part of that big company up above you. *They* hire us, they send us here to do this show, all the pay comes from Europe, we don't have to be anybody's citizens."

Andy, sounding excited, said, "Why wouldn't that work? Let's say in England you own a show called, I dunno, *You Better Believe It*, and—"

"I think we do, in fact," Doug said.

"So there you are." Andy lifted his beer can in a toast. "We work for those people. You don't have to tell the Americans about us at all."

"This," Babe said, "would not be as simple as you think."

"But possible," John said.

Babe shook his head. "I'm not sure yet. *Do* any of you have a passport?"

"I can always get a passport," Andy said. "I wouldn't wanna get on a plane with it. I might drive a car into Canada and back with it."

"That's been done," John said.

Doug suddenly thought of a way that might be even better and simpler, though even less legal, but when he turned his wide eyes in Babe's direction he saw that Babe had just thought of it, too.

Combined Tool.

Years of foreign correspondence had taught Babe how to keep his cool. "Let me work on this," he said. "I don't know if we can make anything happen or not, but we've come this far with it, we might as well go on, at least a few more days. Then, if we *can* make it work, we haven't lost any time."

"We're thinking of a September launch," Doug confided.

"*If* there's a launch," Babe said. He knocked back the

rest of his beer and heaved out of his seat. "You all keep going here. Doug, when you come back uptown, come see me."

"I will, Babe," Doug said, and just managed not to give a conspiratorial wink.

29

WHEN THEY FIRST started to do the camera thing, Dortmunder found himself, to his surprise, itching all over. That was completely unexpected, the idea that all of a sudden he'd be feeling this great need to scratch, all different parts of his body. He didn't *want* to scratch, he just felt *compelled* to scratch, but he fought it off, because he was damned if he was going to stand there and look like an idiot, scratching himself like a dog with fleas in front of a bunch of cameras.

And the cameras themselves were intrusive in ways he hadn't guessed. They were like those barely seen creatures in horror movies, the ones just leaving the doorway or disappearing up the stairs. Except that the cameras weren't disappearing. They were there, just incessantly there, at the edge of your peripheral vision, their heads turning slightly, polite, silent, very curious, and big. Big.

Between the nudging presence of the cameras and the maddening need to scratch all these itches, Dortmunder found himself tightening into knots, his movements as stiff as the Tin Woodman's before he gets the oil. I'm supposed to act natural, he told himself, but *this* isn't natural. I'm lumbering around like Frankenstein's monster. I feel like I've been filled up with itchy cement.

Roy Ombelen had them go through the scene, and Dortmunder thought it went along pretty good, except for the stiffness and the need to scratch, but then Roy said, "Cut," and then he said, "Guys, let me make one other thing clear here. We know we don't want the cameras to look at your faces, but the other part of that, we don't want you to look at the cameras. You're in a conversation, so be in the conversation. Look at the people you're talking to. There are no cameras here, okay?"

Okay, they said, and Roy started the scene again, and they all caught on to that part pretty quick, all of them. In fact, Dortmunder noticed, once he wasn't thinking about the cameras, the itches started to fade. Another plus.

But then Roy cut them again and said, "Doug, I think we need the girlfriend in on this. Give the cameras something else to look at."

"You're absolutely right," Doug said.

So Darlene came over from the sofa where she'd been reading a *People* magazine, and Marcy told her who she was and what was motivating her and gave her a couple of things she might want to say. The idea was, she came to the bar with her boyfriend Ray, but then she would wait in the bar while the others went to the back room to talk business. Also, because she wasn't part of the robbery story, the cameras wouldn't mind looking at her, which everybody thought was okay.

They rehearsed it the new way, with Darlene, and people

were getting more relaxed, more into the flow of things. Gradually, Dortmunder grew less stiff and itchy, and it was even becoming kind of fun, sitting around, pretending to be tough guys in a tough bar talking tough to each other. It was very different, this new OJ, not having the regulars around to sing a cappella.

They did it three times, all the way through, with the cameras on, and it all seemed to go very smoothly. Between takes Marcy would suggest small changes in what people would say, and after a while it all got to be so easy and natural that Dortmunder found he was actually enjoying himself, as though he were really in a real bar having a real conversation with a real bartender.

It was a short scene, which was probably a good thing for those members of the cast not used to this sort of activity. It opened with Dortmunder and Kelp and Tiny and the kid sitting at the bar, talking with Rodney, ordering drinks— somehow they all seemed to be drinking Budweiser beer— and then Ray Harbach came in with Darlene. Marcy gave Kelp a couple of flirty things to say to Darlene, which he did mostly as though he was trying to lift her spirits rather than put the moves on her, which was just as well, because Marcy hadn't given Darlene any reaction instructions, so Darlene just stood there with a vacant smile on her face while Kelp's witticisms wandered off away from the set.

On the one hand, Darlene didn't add much to the occasion, basically having not been given anybody to be or any reason to exist, but on the other hand her presence did completely change the dynamic and everybody felt it. The gang became more confident, somehow, and more united. The same things said by the same people in the same way became more *interesting*.

After the third taped run-through of the bar scene, Roy Ombelen told Darlene and Rodney the barman they were finished for the day and they'd be getting a callback when they were next needed, which would be sometime after tomorrow. They left, and when the receding elevator racket finished, Ombelen led his five players and his camerapeople and two other guys who had something to do with light and sound and his producer to the hall set with the fake restrooms.

And now there was a delay because the lighting was all wrong and something was screwed up with the sound, so the reality stars of tomorrow were told they could go back and lounge on the OJ set while the hall was being perfected.

Once away from the cameras and the role-playing, Dortmunder found himself returning to his right mind, and he wished he could talk with the others, or at least with Kelp, about this situation, but of course he couldn't, not with Harbach here. So he sat in silence, telling himself the things he would have been telling Kelp, things he already knew, until he couldn't stand it any more, and that's when he stood and said, "Andy, let's walk a little."

"I was thinking the same thing," Kelp said.

Harbach looked briefly as though he might volunteer to walk with them, but the kid, recognizing what Dortmunder was up to, chose that moment to say, "Ray, I keep thinking you look familiar somehow. Would there be any television shows I might've seen you on?"

"Well," Harbach said, "I don't suppose you've watched a lot of soap operas," by which time Dortmunder and Kelp were already on their feet and out of the OJ set, so that danger was averted.

This was still a pretty big building, and there was still a lot of underused floor space away from the three sets. Dortmunder and Kelp strolled through this, and Dortmunder said, "What are we gonna do here?"

"Well," Kelp said, "we still got the problem of the tenant."

"I know that. We gotta come back tonight and see if he's still there. And this time, I gotta come along, because if we can go in, I wanna be there."

"Okay, sure. But what if he's still there?"

"I dunno about this TV thing," Dortmunder said. "I mean, it wasn't too bad after a while—"

"Once you got used to the cameras. And the guy carrying the microphone in the air over your head."

"He didn't bother me so much," Dortmunder said, because he'd barely noticed that guy. "But, Andy, this isn't what we *do*. What we do is, we go in, we pick up what we pick up, we go out. One, two, it's done. This thing, they *rehearse* it over and over."

"Maybe," Kelp said, "the guy will be gone tonight. And we can give up our TV career."

"Hey, Andy! Hey, John!"

It was Doug, over by the sets, waving to them, so they went over there and Kelp said, "Are we ready for my close-up?" which Dortmunder didn't get, but which apparently Doug did, because he laughed and said, "Just about, Norma. I wanted to tell you guys, when they're done taping today, I'd like you to stick around a little. Babe's coming back downtown, and he thinks he might have the solution to our problem."

Kelp said, sounding as enthusiastic as though he actually intended to go through with this reality thing, "That's great, Doug. I figured we could count on Babe."

"Oh, yeah," Doug said. "Babe's been around the block a couple times. He knows what's what. You're not gonna put anything over on Babe."

"That's great news," Dortmunder said.

The taping in the hallway, once they got their technical problems out of the way, didn't take long at all. Two of the cameras were used, both behind the group, one high and one low, panning forward as the group moved.

Even being wider than the hallway in the original OJ, this one was still not wide enough for all five to walk abreast, so they proceeded in a little cluster, telling each other the made-up stuff they'd been given by Marcy, about how they hadn't seen one another in a while, and how it was good to get the gang working together again, and how they couldn't wait to hear Ray's news.

Three times they did this, walking down the same hall to the same doorway to nowhere, the cameras trailing like large black dogs, and the third time, when Ombelen called, "Cut!" Dortmunder turned around and looked back there, and saw, just beyond the cameras and the camerapersons and the soundman with the long sound boom and Ombelen and Doug, there was Babe Tuck. And standing beside Babe Tuck was a very rigid-looking guy, balding, spectacled, in a three-piece black suit and pale blue shirt and dark blue tie.

Beside Dortmunder, Kelp coughed a little, putting his hand up to his mouth. Behind that hand, "Zeitung," he muttered.

30

DOUG WAS ASTONISHED when he turned around to see Babe walking toward the set with Herr Muller at his side, and for just a second he thought, Did he send all the way to Munich for Herr Muller, and how did he get here so *fast*? Then he realized Herr Muller must have already been here in the States, maybe even staying in Combined Tool, and the coincidence just seemed like a good omen. Well, Herr Muller owed him a good omen, didn't he?

Doug wasn't originally supposed to know anything about the double life of Herr Muller, and still wouldn't, if it hadn't been for a strange event that had happened almost three years ago during *The Stand*'s first season and just after Babe came over to reality from news. Until then, Doug had only known Richard Muller the way most people did, as a well-thought-of serious documentary filmmaker on subjects like South African gold mining or contemporary Arab slave trade that the American commercial television market hadn't much use for but that the Europeans ate like candy.

He had known that Herr Muller had a production deal with Trans-Global Universal Industries (TUI), one of the highest business levels above Get Real, and that on his occasional trips to the United States he might use Get Real's facilities for interviews or editing, and in the normal course of events that's all he would have known.

The day it happened, Herr Muller was in a morning meeting with Babe and, just by coincidence, he and Doug took the same elevator down, Doug on his way to lunch, Herr Muller apparently on his way to a plane, given the large garment bag he carried over one shoulder and the wheeled suitcase he towed behind. Doug knew the man well enough to nod and smile, and Herr Muller did likewise.

When they reached the lobby, all hell had broken loose. The space from the elevators to the revolving doors onto Third Avenue was full of milling querulous people, demanding explanations, being ignored. The doors were blocked by uniformed city police, frisking everybody before letting them leave the building, checking into all handbags and other parcels: a very slow process. Two more policemen by the elevators kept announcing that no one was to go back upstairs. Everybody had taken the elevator down, and everybody would now leave the building. Slowly.

The cops guarding the elevators would not answer any questions, and in fact would say nothing but that nobody was permitted to make a U-turn. It was a bit like rush hour in Hell.

"Well, this is a mess," Doug said, and looked at Herr Muller to see the man as pale as a white wine spritzer. He really did look as though he might faint. Doug said, "What is it?"

"I cannot be searched," Herr Muller said. He did not have a marked accent, but the kind of overcareful pronunciation that marked the foreign-born.

Doug was aghast, but in the film business this sort of thing is never entirely impossible. Leaning closer to the ashen man, pitching his voice under the clatter of the crowd, he said, "Drugs?"

"No no!" Herr Muller almost gained strength from the accusation, but then his terror struck him again, and he clutched at Doug's arm, saying, low but shrill, "It is money. Cash money. Company cash money."

"Money?"

"A half a million US dollars. I cannot explain such money to the police." Herr Muller's hand on Doug's arm fluttered like an imprisoned butterfly.

Speaking hurriedly, Doug said, "Don't call attention to us. Get on line, one of the lines here."

Herr Muller obeyed, but also whimpered, "I cannot be searched."

Doug said, "But you were gonna take a plane. How can you take that stuff on a plane?"

"We have a relationship with the airline. I am known as a filmmaker. I am never searched." Looking out ahead at the unfortunately meticulous cops he said, with woebegone fatalism, "I am ruined, you know."

"Hold on," Doug said. "Just wait." And, pulling out his cell phone, he speed-dialed Babe, got through his secretary, and said, "Babe, we got a mess in the lobby."

"A mess? What kind of mess?"

"Something's happened, the cops are searching everybody before they let them out of the building."

"Is Richard Muller there?"

"He's with me," Doug said. "He told me about the— I think he's gonna faint."

"I am usually stronger than this," Herr Muller said, but he kept a tight grip on Doug's arm.

"I'll be right down," Babe decided.

Doug said, "No. Don't do that. The cops aren't letting anybody back into the elevators. If you come down, they won't let you back up. Does the company have any influence with the New York police?"

"With street-level cops? Of course not. Doug, they can't find all that, it'll get back to the company, it'll make all kinds of trouble."

"Well, Herr Muller wouldn't last long in interrogation, I can tell you that," Doug said, and beside him, attached to his arm, Herr Muller moaned.

"Doug, it's up to you," Babe said. "You're the only one there, the only one can do anything."

"Do what?"

"Doug, you're a producer. Produce something. You've thought your way out of bigger jams than this."

"I have?"

"What if he does faint?"

"Babe, they'd search him before they put him in the ambulance. I don't—" And then he did. With a sudden sunny smile at the frozen Herr Muller he said, "Oh, yes, I do."

"You do?"

"I'll call you later, Babe," Doug said, broke the connection, and said, "Herr Muller, you work for me."

Herr Muller looked at him with the tremulous beginnings of hope. "I do?"

"Yes, you do." Doug found and handed over one of his business cards. "That's me. I'm doing a reality show now called *The Stand*, and you work for me, and we're heading upstate to where they're shooting the show."

Herr Muller turned Doug's card over and over, as though it might contain some important clue to something. "How can this help us?"

"Just let me do the talking," Doug said. "You're my assistant, you work for me. Better put that card away."

It took nearly a quarter hour to get to the revolving doors of the exit, and when they did get there at last Doug pointed at the wheelie bag and said to the cop there, "I don't want you to get too excited, but we got half a million in play money in there."

The cop frowned at him. Cops don't like to have their leg pulled. "Oh, yeah?"

Doug handed over another of his business cards. "I'm with Get Real, a reality show producer, our offices are upstairs here."

The cop held the card, but eyeballed Doug. "Oh, yeah?"

"We've got a show, *The Stand*, we're gonna do a gag with play money."

The next cop over to Doug's right looked up from his study of a lady's handbag. "Did you say *The Stand*?"

"That's right," Doug said. "You've seen it?"

"A couple times," this second cop said. "It's pretty good. It's about these people upstate, right? They're selling vege-tables."

"The Finches."

"That's right," the cop said. "Finch. That's a funny name, Finch."

"Well, they're a funny bunch," Doug said.

The first cop, tone a little softened, said, "So you've got fake money in there, for the show?"

Realizing they were actually going to have to do something like this on the show now or risk trouble down the line, Doug said, "Yeah. The stunt is, they've been collecting all this cash, make a mortgage payment, and a sudden wind comes up—"

"Oh," said the lady with the handbag. "That's terrible."

"Oh, but it's all right," Doug assured her. "They get almost all of it back."

The first cop said, "Let's see this money."

So Herr Muller lay the wheelie on the floor on its back, knelt over it, and unzipped the top. He peeled it back, and they all looked in at five hundred thousand dollars in bright crisp new hundred-dollar bills, the largest denomination now printed by the US Treasury, all of it banded into blocks. They looked damn real.

"Those," the first cop said, "look damn real."

"They're supposed to," Doug said. "We'll do close-ups in their hands and all of that."

The first cop looked at Doug's clearly legitimate business card. He looked at his fellow cop, now picking through a messenger's tote bag of documents. He shrugged. "Okay," he said. "Go on through."

It turned out later that a big-ticket jeweler on the third floor of the building had been robbed, by two men and two women pretending to be customers. They'd tied up the staff, but one employee got loose almost immediately and phoned the building's security, who sealed the doors and brought in the city police at double time, so the robbers should still have been inside, though they and the jewelry were never found.

The experience, however, did create a bond between

Doug and Babe, who was both grateful and admiring of Doug's quick-witted cool. The same closeness did not evolve with Herr Muller, who had felt shamed by his weakness and who since then, on his trips to New York, had subtly avoided Doug, as an unhappy reminder of the day that he had failed.

Too shaken to go on with his flight to Europe on that fateful day, Herr Muller had been grateful for an escort and had wanted to go to the company's building on Varick Street, where, before leaving the cab, he said, "Please tell Babe Tuck I will spend one more night at Combined Tool."

So here they were again, all of them together on Varick Street, where Babe said, "Roy, are you finished shooting for today?"

"All done," Ombelen said. "We'll do the back room scene tomorrow. And Babe, it's really coming along very well."

"Glad to hear it," Babe said, sounding as though he didn't give a damn. "You and the crew can take off now, I need to talk to our performers a minute."

"Of course," Ombelen said.

"And take the stairs down. That's how we came up, so we wouldn't make a racket while you were taping."

"Very nice. Thank you."

As the others left, Babe led Doug and Herr Muller and the four robbers to the bar set, where they took a couple of adjoining booths and Babe said, "We've got it worked out. Gang, this is Richard Muller, he's got a production company in Munich, he's gonna hire you for a reality show they've got over there. You'll shoot the show right here, but the company's over there."

Andy, the quick one, said, "So this means no Social Security numbers?"

"That's right," Babe told him. "And you can call yourself anything you damn please, just so you remember to use the same name every time."

"And signature," Herr Muller said.

"That's right," Babe said. "Herr Muller has employment forms for you, you put in whatever fairy tales you like, but then it's got to be your own handwriting for the signature. Muller's going back to Munich tomorrow, he'll file the papers, start the production company, and you're all set. He'll pay you in cash. US cash."

Herr Muller said, "Please," and held a hand up. When he had everybody's attention, he said, "Do not become arrested while you are in my employ."

John, the gloomy one, nodded at Herr Muller. "We'll do our best," he said.

31

As far as Dortmunder was concerned, it didn't feel at all like the back room at the OJ. For one thing, it was all too clean, and the lights were too bright. And for another thing, nobody at the OJ was moving walls back and forth all the time, so the cameras could get a different slant. And when they talked together at the OJ they said what they wanted to say, not what Marcy thought up.

Well, this was the last of it. They were going along with Doug and Get Real for this one extra day, but now that they knew Muller was clearing out of Combined Tool today, that would be the end of it. Go in that back window tonight—and he would definitely be going in there with them—look the place over for whatever was valuable, leave it behind, then go back in two weeks and clean it out. Finally.

They spent a couple hours on the back room scene Wednesday afternoon, and the television people all seemed pleased by how it came out. Roy Ombelen congratulated them and then said, "You can take the day off tomorrow. Marcy's working out a little subplot with Darlene and Ray, so we'll be shooting them tomorrow in Central Park. We'll want you back here Friday at ten, we'll do some building exteriors to go along with Ray's walking on the walls."

Friday, Dortmunder figured, would probably be a good day to take May and go for a ride on the Staten Island Ferry. She could use a day off, and they hadn't been to sea for a long time. From the happy smiles he saw on the other members of the gang, he could tell the whole group had plans for Friday that did not involve watching Ray Harbach walk up and down on walls.

People were all just saying so long, see you around, when here came Babe and Muller again, up the stairs. "Hold on," Babe called, and walked over to say, "I'm glad I caught you. I got something I want you to see." Turning to Muller, he said, "It'd be more comfortable downstairs, wouldn't it?"

"Of course," Muller said. "There is nothing to hide."

Dortmunder cocked an ear at that. Nothing to hide? Downstairs? What was going on?

Babe explained. "What I've got here," he said, flashing a DVD, "is the first cut of yesterday's work. It's just rough, the sound isn't perfect, there's no musical stings, but you'll get the idea. I think you'll like it."

Roy Ombelen said, "I can hardly wait to see it."

"Me, too," Doug said.

The reality people were very excited now, but what Dortmunder wanted to know was, what downstairs? What nothing to hide?

Babe soon showed them. He led the way to the stairs, then down two flights to the door to Combined Tool. Pressing his palm to the glass eye in the door, he pushed gently and the door said *snick* and opened inward. Babe entered, switching on room lights, and the others trooped in after him.

We've been trying to get in here forever, Dortmunder told himself, and now they just open it up and *invite* us in. This is not good.

What they had entered was a large pale green living room, stretched most of the way across the front of the building, except where the elevator would go. The windows were clean and soundproofed against the Varick Street tunnel traffic. The furniture was expensive but anonymous, and so were the pictures on the walls, so that the room looked more like an upscale hotel lobby than a living room, except for the television and entertainment area and the wet bar. To add to the hotel lobby impression, a wheeled suitcase stood near the door, with a garment bag draped over it.

As Babe welcomed everybody into the place, telling them to sit down and put their feet up, Dortmunder said to him, "That's some lock you got on that door."

"That's left over," Babe said. "This location used to be part of a TUI research and development operation. They had a lot of very valuable metals in here, platinum and like that."

"And secrets," Muller said.

"That's right," Babe agreed. "New technologies, that sort of thing."

"All in Asia now," Muller said.

"So now," Babe said, "it's mostly used to store the files from those days and take care of our people from overseas when they visit, like Herr Muller here."

"Or shipments," Herr Muller said.

Babe shrugged that off. "Oh, sure, the occasional shipment," he said, and made a little dismissive wave of the hand. "The kind of thing doesn't need to go through customs. Business stuff. All businesses have their secrets."

"You know, Babe," Muller said, glancing very slightly toward the luggage by the door, "this time, perhaps it ought to stay here."

Babe didn't want to hear about that. "We'll discuss it," he said, curt, closing off that conversation, and turned a more cheerful face to the others. "But the point is, you want to see what you people did yesterday. Everybody take a seat."

It was a spread-out living room, with all seating angled toward the large flat television screen. Babe grabbed a handful of remotes and got it all fired up, and then inserted the DVD and stepped back, grinning comfortably at the screen.

And there it was: the OJ. Dortmunder looked at it, and couldn't believe it. Not only did the bar look a lot more real on television than it did in reality, but it looked more like the OJ, the real OJ.

And there *they* all were, seen from behind, from the side, from above. Never angled enough to show a face, but always making it clear which character was speaking, and always making sure the characters' personalities came through.

Dortmunder watched himself and Kelp and Tiny and the kid and Rodney the bartender discuss the latest ball scores, and he could almost believe he was watching something that had happened. That was *them*. The lighting was a little distorted, the shadows a little angular, so that everybody and everything seemed more menacing, tougher, more interesting, but nevertheless still them. Look at that.

And here came Ray and Darlene, he looking like a finger-snapping crook in a Broadway musical, she like the singer in the honky-tonk, and not at all bad to look at. There were greetings, Kelp's little remarks to Darlene no longer seemed so stupid, and then Ray announced he had news, and asked Rodney for the use of the back room, and it was over.

It had only been about three minutes long, but they all reacted as though they'd been asleep for hours, or maybe it was more like the sleep that goes on for years after you've eaten the poisoned apple. In any case, they all roused themselves from lassitude, blinked at one another, and the kid spoke first: "That was neat!"

Babe stood, smiling around at them all, and said, "Doug, I think you have a winner here. We just want to be sure to keep that tone."

"Oh, I know we can," Doug said. He was grinning from ear to ear, "Can't we, Roy?"

"Absolutely," Ombelen said. "This is very gratifying, fellows. I'll see you all here at ten a.m. on Friday, day after tomorrow."

"See you then," the gang said.

As they all trooped down the stairs, Tiny spoke, only loudly enough for his own group to hear: "A meet, at Dortmunder's."

32

Doug watched them go down the stairs, listened to the fire door slam, then closed this upper door and turned to the group, to Babe and Marcy and Ombelen and Muller, now on their feet in the Combined Tool living room, and beamed as he said, "*That* went very well."

Babe said, "You notice, the first thing John asked about was the lock on this door here."

"Well, it is pretty elaborate, Babe. Anybody's likely to notice it."

Muller said, "They were all very interested in this place. They wanted to know, what are the secrets here?"

"Well," Babe said, "what we told them is almost completely true. Secrets that don't concern any of us here." Nodding at Muller's wheelie suitcase, he said, "Except for a little cash going through, every once in a while."

Muller said, "They might very well be interested in that cash, if they knew it existed."

"Well, it's leaving with you today," Babe said. "And the

next time there's our cash in here is when the Brits wire the gang their payments and we draw it out of the New York bank." He grinned and spread his hands. "If they want to steal their own pay, they're welcome to it."

"But something like that," Marcy said.

They all looked at her. Babe said, "Something like what?"

"What if," Marcy said, "they were going along with all this only because they wanted to steal something *else*?"

Babe frowned. "Like what?"

"I don't mean for real," Marcy said. "I mean, in our story line. Could we get that in, get an audience to understand that the gang is agreeing to be filmed only because they really intend to steal something else entirely?"

Babe said, "I keep asking, steal what from us? We don't have anything useful to them."

"I don't know," Marcy said. "A camera truck? Those are very valuable."

Scoffing, Babe said, "What are they gonna do with a camera truck? Peddle it under the table to NBC?"

"I don't know," Marcy said, "but it would be a nice complication if they meant to steal from us as well as from the storage place. Okay if I think about it a while?"

"Think all you like," Babe told her.

Doug said, "But, Marcy, I'll tell you what you do have to think about. Factions."

Marcy looked abruptly guilty, as though suddenly realizing she hadn't prepared her homework. "I know," she said. "I'll work on that, Doug, I really will."

Muller said, "Excuse me, I am only an outsider here, but if you do not object to the question, factions? What factions?"

Doug gestured at the television screen where they'd recently watched the snippet of their still-unnamed show. "In that footage," he said, "they're all agreeing with one another all the time. There's no factions, there's no arguments, there's no choosing sides. You can't have drama that way."

"I see," Muller said, though he sounded doubtful.

Marcy said, "Doug's right. They have to struggle toward a consensus, it can't all be too easy. The only problem is, it seems as though they *do* all get along. It's up to me to find a way to get them to disagree about something."

"You have to," Doug told her. "We want them fighting with each other. We want some yelling, people waving their arms around. They're all too happy with one another. We need some conflict."

"If possible," Marcy said.

33

"Y<small>OU PEOPLE ARE CRAZY</small>," Dortmunder snarled. "You want to *do* this thing?"

They were seated with beers in Dortmunder's living room, Dortmunder and Kelp and Tiny and the kid, and to Dortmunder's appalled disbelief it turned out the rest of them all wanted to go on with the show.

"It'll be fun," the kid said, not for the first time, but what would you expect from the kid?

What you would *not* expect is for Kelp to say, "I thought we looked pretty good on that thing. I want Anne Marie to see it," referring to his live-in friend.

And what you would *really* not expect is for Tiny to say, "Whadaya in such a hurry for, Dortmunder? We're in no hurry to go anywhere."

"The whole idea," Dortmunder said, "is go along with these people until we know what our target is, then disappear and wait, then clean them out. That's the whole idea. That's what we're doin all this for. We're not here to be in a *movie.*"

"TV show," Kelp corrected.

"Reality show," the kid amended.

Tiny said, "Dortmunder, you know as well as I know what was in that bag by the door in there that's goin out by plane today. Now we know what that place is used for, and we were almost right, it's for their money courier, but that doesn't mean there's money in there all the time, only when they're moving it. And today they're moving it, so now there's nothing in there."

"Which was the reason to wait," Dortmunder said. "Disappear, let them start to forget us, *then* clean them out."

"John," Kelp said, "the next time there's gonna be money in that place it's gonna be *our* money, from England. You wanna go steal your own money?"

"Money from wages," Dortmunder said, "is not the same as the same money from theft. Money from theft is purer. There's no indentured servitude on it, no knuckling under to whatever anybody else wants, no obedience. It isn't yours because you swapped it for your own time and work, it's yours because you *took* it."

"Basically, Dortmunder," Tiny said, "I agree with you. But there's an extra little spin on it this time."

"Because it's fun," said the one-note kid.

"Also," Tiny said, "I agree with Kelp. I want Josie to see this thing. I want to tell you, Dortmunder, I'm impressed by every one of us, and that's also you. I looked at those guys in that back room, I *believed* them."

Dortmunder sat back, appalled. "I don't know what's happening here," he said. "You people have completely forgot who and what you are. You *want* to go down to that place, day after day, and pretend to be, pretend to be I don't even know what."

"Ourselves," Kelp said.

"You don't have to pretend to be yourself," Dortmunder said. "You *are* yourself."

"But this is fun," the damn kid said. "John, listen, just relax into it. We'll do this for a while, and then we'll get paid something, and then it'll be over or it'll stop being fun or whatever, and then we'll go in and clean them out."

"We'll keep an eye on Varick Street," Kelp said, "until some other time Muller's staying there, so we'll know there's money there, and we'll know it isn't ours, and it'll be just as pure as anything you want."

Rising, the kid said, "I'll get us another beer while you guys talk. There's more beer in the refrigerator, isn't there, John?"

He took Dortmunder's sigh for a yes.

Early that evening, he was alone again in the apartment when May came home with her daily donation from Safeway. She reached the living room doorway, looked in, and said, "John? What's wrong?"

"You won't believe this, May."

She said, "Is there time for me to put the groceries down and get a beer?"

There was. When she was back in the living room, in her chair, Dortmunder said, "You think you know people," and then told her about his day. When he was finished, he said, "So? Whadaya think?"

"What do I think?" She shrugged. "John, honestly, it doesn't sound that bad." Smiling, she said, "I'd like to see that show myself. Tell you the truth, it kind of sounds like fun."

Dortmunder sighed into his beer.

34

STAN DIDN'T LIKE having nothing to do, and so, when he had nothing to do, he did something. Wednesday afternoon, while the others were off taping their debuts with the reality people, Stan subwayed from Canarsie to Manhattan, walked over to Varick Street, took up a position across the way from the Get Real building and up at the next corner, leaned against a light post as inconspicuous as a Russian spy in a fifties movie, folded his arms, and waited.

After a while he saw his own group come out of that building and walk away toward Tiny's limo around the corner, discussing things. He didn't join them or call to them or anything because he was working his own gag now, single-o.

A while later another limo arrived and the Get Real people came out of the building, including the German guy he'd seen through the Combined Tool back window, who was now lugging a garment bag and a wheelie suitcase. The limo driver stored his stuff in the trunk while the tunnel traffic struggled around them, and then that group was away, too.

Once they were gone, Stan crossed the street, walked down to that building, and entered it by using the dummy key he'd made the last time he was here. Inside, he switched on the overhead fluorescent lights and looked around.

Vehicles, vehicles everywhere. Big ones, little ones, new ones, old ones, valuable ones, junk. Whistling behind his teeth, Stan wandered among all these wheels and used his cell phone to take pictures of the ones he thought might be of interest. He stopped after he'd chosen six, not wanting to be greedy, then picked for tonight's transportation a rel-atively modest black Dodge Caliber, mostly because it was pretty close to the garage door and wouldn't require shifting too many other vehicles around to get it out of here.

The Caliber had apparently been used one way or another in movie- or television-making, because the pas-senger floor in front was littered with several random screenplay pages and the entire back area was a foot deep in plastic coffee cups and fast food trays. The glove box con-tained four different lipsticks, a package of condoms, and a cell phone; people are always leaving their cell phones.

Well, all of this would be somebody else's problem, far-ther down the line. Stan merely drove the Caliber out to Varick Street, then left it athwart the sidewalk as he ducked back in to close the garage door.

Satisfied with the day's work, he steered the Caliber down through the Brooklyn-Battery Tunnel and thence by many secondary streets across Brooklyn to Canarsie, pausing along the way to pick up from a closed movie rental place a DVD of *Pit Stop* (1969, Brian Donlevy, with a cameo from George Barris, famous custom car builder) to watch that night with his Mom.

Leaving the Caliber at the curb on a side street a couple blocks from home, he returned to it Thursday morning to find it was still there, so he drove it onto an even more remote area than Canarsie, a neighborhood—if that isn't too fancy a word—somewhere out there that was in a way Brooklyn, in a way Queens, and very nearly but not quite, Nassau County.

Along a commercial boulevard of quiet desperation, one particular enterprise, Maximillian's Used Cars, seemed so natural, so inevitable, it might have grown there, from a seed dropped by a passing asteroid. Under flapping three-sided pennants in bright crayon colors huddled a wan fleet of cars that hadn't known love for a very long time, despite the whitewashed words bellowing from their windshields: !!!CREAMPUFF!!! !!!ULTRASPECIAL!!! !!!TRIPLE-A-ONE!!! And behind this assembly of sad sacks stood the office, a small pink stucco structure that looked vaguely as though it might have been transplanted from some arid part of inland California.

Stan drove the Caliber—a thoroughbred, in this neck of the woods—past the lot and turned in at the anonymous driveway that would go behind the place. He stopped in an area of tall unkempt weeds beside the white clapboard backs of garages, and got out, taking the Caliber's keys with him. Stepping through an unlocked gate in a chain-link fence, he followed a shrubbery-flanked path to the rear of the pink office structure. A back door here opened into a gray-paneled office populated by a thin severe hatchet-faced woman typing rapidly on an off-brand computer with a sound like a cocktail party for crickets. She looked up, but didn't stop typing as she said, "Hello, Stan. Long time."

Stan, with some amazement, said, "Harriet, Max bought you a computer?"

"The motor vehicle forms are online now," she said, still cricketing away. "He hated it, he hated the whole idea of it, but then he worked out my taxi fares all the time to the DMV, and this was cheaper."

Stan nodded. "That must have been a bitter blow."

"He got so mad," she said, "he said he was gonna sell the place and retire. I said, 'From what?' and he went into his office to sulk."

"How long ago?"

"About three weeks."

Stan looked at the closed connecting door to the front office. "You think he's over it by now?"

She laughed, a mirthless sound. "He's in there now," she said, gesturing with her jaw at the connecting door while continuing to cricket. "Go cheer him up."

"Well, I'll say hello, anyway," Stan said, and crossed to step through to the outer office, closing the door behind himself. The cricket sound disappeared.

This office was dominated by its windows, giving a different but no more lovely view out onto the wares under offer. Within, the office was dominated by Max himself, a big old man with heavy jowls and thin white hair, wearing a dark vest hanging open over a white dress shirt smudged across the chest from his habit of leaning forward against his used cars. There was a time when he had smoked cigars, until the doctor told him the cigars were actually smoking *him*, so he didn't do that any more, but still kept all the moves, so that people looking at him kept thinking they were missing something.

At the moment, Max was crouched at his desk like a leopard at a water hole, watching the two or three potential customers wandering the lot, their needs perhaps being attended to by Harriet's nephew, an eager faun in a three-piece suit. Stan observed for a minute, but then, when Max made no move to acknowledge his presence, he forced the issue: "Whadaya say, Max?"

Max exhaled as noisily as if he still smoked those old cigars, dropped back into his swivel chair, continued to glare outward, and said, "I say I don't like it, that's what *I* say."

"Don't like what, Max?"

At last Max looked Stan in the eye, and nodded, though not with much satisfaction. "Morning, Stanley."

"Good morning. What don't you like?"

For answer, Max glared again out the window. "Any of those birds look like a television person to you?"

"What, a repairman? I don't think they have those any more."

"No, a reporter," Max said, as though the word were synonymous with "dungheap." "Ever see any of those people on the air?"

Interested, Stan stepped closer to the windows and considered the candidates. "Not unless it was a perp walk," he decided. "What's up, Max?"

"Siddown, Stanley, you'll give me a crook in my neck."

So Stan sat in the client's chair and said, "You've had a problem with reporters?"

"No, and I don't want any. But one of these local channels, busybodies, on their six o'clock news, they been doing a deep investigative thing on customers and the people that sell to customers."

"Aha."

"If you ask me," Max said, "what they're investigating is people that sell to customers without using their crappy TV station for advertising."

"That makes sense," Stan said. "You don't want to bite the hand that feeds you."

"I wanna bite *some* hand. They're goin after all kinds of legitimate businessmen, Stanley. Furniture stores where you don't pay any money down. *That's* a worthy thing, isn't it?"

"Sounds it."

"So what if they come to take the stuff back next year and sell it all over again to the next yo-yo? It was never anything but junk anyway."

"You're right."

"And appliance stores, those too," Max said, "and—you know it—used car dealers."

Stan nodded. "They been to see you, Max?"

"No, but they hit one in the Bronx, and they hit one in Staten Island, nailed them for perfectly ordinary business practices, but, you know, the stuff that's difficult to explain to the layman."

"I know what you mean."

Max did his best to look pathetic. "Stanley," he said, "*I* don't want to be under scrutiny, you know that."

"None of us does, Max," Stan agreed. "It's like a contagious disease."

"You know it."

"Maybe they'll pick a competitor."

"Your lips to God's ear. In fact, I got a couple suggestions, only I'm not about to attract attention." Max shivered all over, relit his imaginary cigar, and said, "But why should I borrow any trouble? Usually, you come to see me, you got a vehicle, it's a fine vehicle, only the dog ate the registration."

"That's what happens, all right," Stan agreed.

"Also," Max said, now smiling on Stan like some son or other close relative in whom he was well pleased, "you understand the ways of the real world, how, when you bring me these orphans, how it costs me out of pocket to bring them back into the world of ordinary commercial trade, which is why there's gotta be a little discount from book value between us from time to time."

Stan, who found his cost of raw materials not burdensome, said, "We help each other out, Max, and I appreciate it."

"So now," Max said, finished with the emollient of human empathy, "what have you brought me today, Stanley?"

"To begin," Stan said, "a black Caliber, maybe two years old."

Max looked at him. "To begin?"

Unpocketing his cell phone, Stan reached it across the desk to show Max the pictures he'd taken. "I can get you," he said, "one of these a day, as many as you think you like. After that, maybe a few more, who knows?"

Max took the phone and scrolled through the pictures, then frowned at Stan. "What'd you do?" he asked. "Follow them to their nest?"

"Where they are now," Stan said, "they're kind of goin to waste. They were used on TV shows, but now they're just like in storage, like an old costume."

"TV shows?" Max didn't like that. "Stanley, I don't want somebody from television news to come in here and recognize one of these vehicles. Hey, I used to drive that, call the cops."

"Not that kind of TV," Stan assured him. "Nothing to do with the news, these are reality people, they don't come to the outer boroughs."

"If you're sure."

"I'm sure. And these cars, I think they'll be happier out and about in the world."

"You're a very thoughtful boy." Handing back the phone, he said, "I'll give a new home to every one of these, you pick the rotation. You want I should run a tab?"

"Oh," Stan said, carelessly, "I think pay as you go is easier, you know. Less paperwork. We look at each of these when I bring it in, we tell each other what we think it's worth, we come to an agreement, and then I'll take the cash. Simple. Friendly."

"Some do it that way," Max agreed, as though it didn't much matter one way or the other. Heaving himself to his feet, he said, "Well, let's look at your first episode." But then he stopped, to stare out the window again. In some astonishment, he said, "Look at that."

Stan looked. The new customer who'd just joined the random molecules slowly crisscrossing the lot was a huge man with a huge black beard and a whole lot of woolly black hair. He was dressed in a kind of muted orange muumuu, so that he looked mostly like the king of the apricots.

"Wow," Stan said. He meant it as a compliment.

Leaning forward over the desk, hissing toward the window, Max said, "Could he be undercover?"

"As what? A blimp?" Stan shook his head. "Come on, Max, lemme show you the car."

But Max was still staring out the window. "Look what he's doing."

The new arrival had taken a big interest in a Volkswag-en Rabbit, not a particularly big car. Stan said, "What's he gonna do with that?"

The big man opened the Rabbit's driver-side door. Before Harriet's nephew could get there to discuss the situation, he'd started to insert himself behind the wheel.

"That's not gonna work," Max said.

The man kept squeezing and twisting himself farther and farther into the Rabbit. Stan said, "Is he gonna drive it or wear it?"

"If he can't take it off," Max said, "he's bought it. Let them work it out for themselves, Stanley, come show me what you brought."

So off they went to have a look at Stan's ex–Caliber.

35

THIS TIME it WAS REAL. Darlene knew it, and she knew Ray knew it, too, so they both knew it. At long last love, the real thing.

And to think it was all because of a reality show. The irony of it. To find true love in such an artificial setting, it just went to show, didn't it? You never knew what was going to happen, you just never did.

It all began on the Thursday, the second day of taping, when the gang got the day off while Darlene and Ray and Marcy and Roy Ombelen and the tape crew went to Central Park to work out some improv, which was just simply fun to do. Inject some of your own personality, your own feelings, your own ideas, into the story line.

The setup was this: Ray, the wall-walking specialist of the gang, had recently met Darlene and had wanted to show her off to the guys, but when he did, the contrast between her nearly fresh innocence (it's all in the acting) and their jaded disbelief (no acting required) had shown him his life in a whole new light.

So they'd gone off to Central Park together, that was the idea, to be away from the others, unobserved, so they could talk things over. What was their relationship, really? (In reality show terms, that is.) What was their future? Did they have a future together?

They spent most of that day filming all over the park, with all the necessary permits, that was part of what made the day so special and so much fun and so liberating. They rowed a boat together on the lake, they wandered together in the Ramble, they watched the joggers endlessly circling the reservoir (without joining them, although Marcy would have dearly loved it if they had), they walked around Belvedere Castle, they observed the imposing stone buildings that stood like sentinels in long straight rows all around the periphery of the park, and they talked it all out, coming to several different conclusions in the course of several different takes of each sequence, because Roy wanted to keep his options open. (At that time, so did Ray.)

And they shared one brief tentative tremulous kiss, late in the day, on the path beside the Drive, surrounded by taxis and hansom cabs and joggers and bicyclists, all of whom, this being New York, ignored the smoochers in their midst.

And then they all went home, walking out of the park, Darlene and Ray and the others, and they didn't even hold hands. But they knew, they both knew, and a little later that evening they confirmed their knowledge.

Ray had a very nice apartment in a small old gray stone

building on West Eighty-fifth Street, pretty near Central Park, a third-floor walk-up, at the back, large living and bedrooms, very modern kitchen and bath. He was after all a financially successful actor, in everything from off-off-Broadway Strindberg revivals to Christmas-season electric shaver commercials. He was also a member of three actors' unions, SAG, AFTRA and Actors' Equity, which was too poor to have an acronym.

The show didn't need them any more that week, so they spent all that time in Ray's apartment, getting to know one another from every angle. He had a callback for an incontinence commercial Friday afternoon (he didn't get it), and she spent that time searching the place for secrets, careful to leave no traces. She didn't find any secrets, which was both pleasing and a little disappointing, and rewarded Ray on his return (also making up to him for the incontinence rejection) by some very special attention.

By Sunday night, sticking close to Ray's place, they'd ordered out Thai, Italian, Mexican, Brazilian, and Bangladeshi. Monday morning they were expected back at Varick Street at ten o'clock, when Marcy would tell them where their story line was going. Ray's shower was above the bathtub, which meant it was plenty big enough for them to shower together, again, which made them a little later leaving the apartment than they'd planned, but they were lucky in catching an immediate subway downtown and were hardly late for the call at all.

With everybody assembled on the OJ bar set, Doug was still giving them all today's pep talk, prior to Marcy unclosing the future to them, when the sudden clank-and-*broowwrrr* of the damn elevator started again. Doug, already stressed and irritated by the responsibilities of reality, loudly said a couple of things his father wouldn't have said in front of the ladies, and then the elevator snarl stopped and here came Babe again, this time accompanied by the stone-faced personnel man, Sam Quigg.

"Babe?" Doug called, no longer showing his irritation; in fact, showing a desire to be of use somehow, if a use for him could be found. "What's up, Babe?"

For answer, Babe stopped flat-footed in front of them all, arms akimbo, as he raked them in a turning pivot of rage, like a big cannon on a battleship, and grated, "This show is canceled. Shut it down."

36

DORTMUNDER COULDN'T believe it. Again? Now what? Over the last week, he and the others had gotten used to this weird business. Dortmunder was still basically opposed to the whole thing, he assured himself of that, but there was just something about actually doing it. It was fun in some sort of unexpected way, and it drew you in.

For instance, last week they kind of took the show on the road. All of them except Ray, since there was to be no actual planning or wall-walking involved, went to a real pawnshop and talked to a real pawnbroker, who wasn't like old suspenders-wearing pawnbrokers in the movies, but was some kind of Asian guy, very thin, who talked very fast with a hard click-like thing at the end of every word. He thought what they were doing was hilarious, and he kept cracking up with high-pitched giggles, his whole face scrunched around his laughing mouth. Marcy and Doug kept at him to stay serious, to remember the actual cash money they'd be paying him, and eventually he did settle down enough so they could get through it.

But it wasn't any good. That is, it wasn't any good on purpose. The whole point of the week was that Tiny knew this pawnbroker, so they all went over to talk with him (taxi scenes, with Tiny all over the front seat, and another reason not to include Ray), because this pawnbroker would be willing to take whatever it was they would be removing from the storage company.

But then it turned out he was only willing to take the stuff on consignment, and consignment was not going to cut it. Thieves don't work on consignment. Thieves obtain the goods, they sell the goods, they take cash on the bar-relhead. That's why they finish with such a small percentage of the value of whatever they've taken, which was all right, because it meant they had something where they had nothing before.

So the pawnshop guy didn't work out, at least in terms of what Doug kept calling the arc of the story. But in terms of what they were really doing, the pawnshop did exactly what it was supposed to do. Face it, in truth, if you and a group of friends decide to knock over this or that, what you do, you discuss it once (the OJ back room scene), you case the place (scout the location, in Doug's term), you go in and get what-ever it is and bring it out, and if it isn't cash you discuss it with a fence, and that's it. Over and done with.

There's no way to get a whole television season out of a scenario like that, which is why the fertile little brain of Marcy was called upon to find frustrations and interruptions and roadblocks along the way. For a whole season, they'd start to plan the job, they'd move along setting it up, and then Marcy would throw a monkey wrench into the works, so that off they'd go back to the OJ for another confab.

That's part of what made this whole thing strangely

interesting: you never actually did anything, you just kept planning to. And at some point every day you'd sit in front of a television set and watch what you did yesterday, and agree you weren't half bad. None of them; they were none of them half bad.

But here comes Babe again, with his shut it down you're canceled. So now what's up?

Doug voiced the question for them all: "Babe? Now what's up? What's gone wrong?"

"These people," Babe snarled, pointing at them all, "are thieves. They're rotten thieves."

Doug, sounding as bewildered as everybody else, said, "Of course they are, Babe. That's why they're here."

"They're stealing," Babe snapped at him, "from *us*."

"The storage business," Doug agreed. "Yes, we know, we—"

"Cars," Babe said.

In that instant, Dortmunder knew. And without looking at the others, he knew they also knew. Stan was going free-lance.

Doug, who didn't share this knowledge, said, "Cars? Babe, what are you talking about?"

Now, Babe pointed floorward. "At least four of the vehicles downstairs," he said, "are missing. One of them was needed for a show yesterday, and when the driver got here it was gone."

"Oh, guys," Marcy cried, heartstruck. "You wouldn't."

"We didn't," Dortmunder said.

Babe said, "We have people coming downtown to do an inventory, find out exactly how many these people took."

"Not us," Dortmunder said.

Babe didn't even bother to look at him. "I know there's

no honor among thieves," he told Doug, "but this goes too far. We're *paying* them, Doug, Each and every one of them has twenty-four hundred dollars out of us already."

"Less taxes," Kelp said, sounding bitter. "I don't know where *that* money's going."

Doug turned to this new problem. "We talked about this, Andy," he said. "It's true your money's coming from out of the country, but US citizens have to pay income tax no matter where they're working, or where they get paid. You understood that, you agreed with it."

"And," Babe said, ice-cold, "it doesn't make up for stealing our cars when you're supposed to be cooperating with us."

"Not us," Dortmunder repeated.

Kelp pointed at Dortmunder and said to Babe, "He's right, you know. It wasn't us."

Babe put hands on hips and lowered his head at Kelp. "Are you going to try to tell me," he said, "you and your *friends* here didn't rig the front door, and the back door, too, for some reason, so you could get in and out of this building whenever you want?"

"Of course we did," Kelp said.

Dortmunder said, "Sure we did. That's what we do."

Now Babe managed to glare at the entire crew of them at once. "You *admit* it?"

"That's how it works," Kelp said. "You never go into a place unless you know how to get back out again. It's called an exit strategy."

Dortmunder explained, "You never want to be in a box with only one way out."

Kelp said, "We rigged the roof door, too, did you know that?"

"What?" Babe could not hide his astonishment. "You can't take cars out the roof!"

"We don't take cars anywhere," Dortmunder said. "The only time we take a car is when we need transportation to where we're gonna take what we're gonna take."

Darlene suddenly announced, "Well, Ray and *I* didn't take any old cars." She sounded as though she couldn't decide if she were angry or weepy. "We have alibis," she told the world. "We both have alibis. We alibi each other every second."

"Darlene," Ray said, a note of caution in his voice.

Doug said, "Darlene, nobody thinks you *or* Ray did anything you weren't supposed to."

"And neither did we," Kelp said. "Maybe even more so."

Babe was beginning to look bedeviled. "If you people didn't take those cars," he said, "and I don't believe that for a second, but if you didn't take them, who did? Who else would?"

"Babe," the kid said, surprising everybody. When Babe met his look, he said, "How many people have keys to this building?"

Babe frowned at him. "I have no idea," he said. "So what?"

"A hundred?" the kid asked. "A thousand?"

Now Babe did try to think about it, and shrugged. "Probably more than a hundred," he said. "Certainly less than a thousand."

And the kid said, "And you trust every one of them?"

Exasperated, Babe said, "I don't even *know* every one of them. What difference is that supposed to make?"

"There's all those cars down there," the kid said. "Just sitting there. Mostly, nobody cares about them. They've got the *keys* in them, Babe. More than one hundred people know they're there."

Babe shook his head. "And why," he said, "did it just happen to happen *now*, when you people are in the building? Free run of the goddam building."

"Well," the kid said, "if I was working up in your midtown offices, and I knew all these cars were down here, and I had a key to the building, and I knew you were working down here with this gang of criminals, wouldn't I think maybe this would be the perfect time for a new set of wheels?"

Troubled, Babe looked at Doug. Troubled, Doug looked at Babe.

Dortmunder said, "The fact is, we all live right here in Manhattan. We're not going anywhere that needs cars. *Four* cars? I don't even need one car."

Doug said, "Babe? I think they're telling the truth, I really do. What's the advantage to them? And look at all the great footage we got."

Babe could be seen to waver. "I don't know," he said.

"I do," Tiny said. Turning to Dortmunder, he said, "This isn't working. We seen ourselves on the little screen, we got our twenty-four hundred except for the taxes, it's time to get out of here. We got some real capers we could work on. No more of this make-believe."

The kid said, "I think Tiny's right."

Stricken, Doug said, "No! John? Andy? *You* don't want to give up, do you?"

"As a matter of fact," Kelp said, "and now that the kid brought it up, I think I do."

Dortmunder suddenly felt lighter, in all his parts. It was as though a low-grade fever he'd had, that he hadn't even realized he was suffering from, had broken. They'd done a lot of this reality thing, they knew how it worked, who needed any more of it? "I think," he told Doug gently, "I think what you got here is an extremely short reality series."

Babe said, "Now hold on. There are contracts involved here. Obligations."

"Take us to court," Kelp advised. Turning to Dortmunder, he said, "Ready, John?"

"Never more."

Darlene had now apparently figured out which way she was going: teary. "Oh, please," she wailed. "You can't stop now. We did so much great footage. You should *see* Ray and me on the lake in Central Park, it's the sweetest thing you ever saw in your entire life."

"That really was a terrific scene, John," Ray said. "If you saw that scene, you'd definitely want to keep going with this show."

"Then it's a good thing," Dortmunder said, "I didn't see it. Good-bye, Doug."

Kelp said, "What is it people say? It's been real."

The four of them headed for the stairs. Behind them, Doug cried, "But what if we sweeten the pot? Why don't you guys get an agent? John! How do we keep in touch?"

37

MONDAY AFTERNOON, Stan decided it was time to let the rest of the guys in on what he'd learned down on Varick Street. It was going to be a blow to them, it was going to dash a lot of their hopes, but they'd be better off knowing it sooner rather than later. Stan hated to be the bearer of bad news, but he really had no choice.

The fact is, there was no caper there, not on Varick Street. Last night, having time on his hands and a little curiosity that had been building for quite a while now as to the contents of the rooms in Knickerbocker Storage, Stan had paused before removing that lovely pink Chevy Corvette from the ground floor to go upstairs, ease his way into a couple of the storage rooms, and just have a look at what they might be taking with them on the night.

Which turned out to be nothing. Crap. Wicker hampers full of old clothes, some of them clean. Tired scratched equipment for every known sport. Girly magazines from the fifties, for God's sake. Boxes of framed photos of weddings; how many times should you get married before you're ready to stop keeping a record? In a word: no dice.

It was only right to tell the guys. Their smart move, once he brought them up to speed on this, was to quit that reality series and get back to the real world. Out there somewhere, there was still dishonest work to be done.

He himself would be hitting Varick Street just one more time, to pick up that nice green Subaru Forester with the camera mountings replacing the front passenger seat, a minor flaw that he knew Maximillian's crack garage crew would have no trouble eliminating. But all that would be much later tonight; between now and then, it was time to make a meet.

When he tried, he couldn't manage to make contact with any of them directly, which meant they were all still laboring away in the vineyards of reality, but he did get to leave messages for them, after one false start.

The false start was that, the first time he phoned John, there was nobody home at all, and of course John wouldn't know an answering machine if it reared up and spat him in the eye, which it would. But then, when he called Andy's place, the phone was answered by Anne Marie, Andy's live-in friend, and after he identified himself and they used a minute in small talk he said, "Would you tell Andy I wanna get the guys together, I got some news for them they're gonna wanna know."

"Sure, Stan. Where and when?"

"I think we need to visit the OJ at ten," Stan said. "Kind of like a reentry portal to the actual world."

"I'll tell him," she promised, and he went on to call Tiny's number, where J. C.'s answering machine said, "This is the J. C. Taylor voice mail. Mr Taylor is unavailable at this moment. Your call *is* important to us, so please leave your name and number after the beep. And have a nice day. Or night."

Giving this machine the same message he'd given Anne Marie, Stan added, "I don't think the kid has a voice mail, so maybe, Tiny, you can tell him what's what. And if any of us finds himself in a living room somewhere, maybe we oughta pick up an answering machine for him. It would be a nice thing to do, and he'd actually use it."

After that, he paused for a refreshing beer, tried John's number again, and this time got May, whose, "Hello?" was delivered on such a rising curve of mistrust that he hastened to say, "It's Stan, May, how you doing, it's just me, Stan."

"Oh, hi, Stan. We haven't seen you for a while."

"I been working different parts of the street from the rest of the guys," Stan said. "But I picked up some info here and there that I think everybody oughta know, so I'm asking people to make a meet tonight at the OJ at ten."

"I'll tell John," she promised. "You're sounding good, Stan, How's your Mom?"

"Terrific," Stan said. "She's out with her cab right now, but she'll be back pretty soon."

"Tell her I said hi. And I just got back from the Safeway, so what I'm gonna do is sit down and put my feet up."

"Good idea," Stan said. "I'll probably do the same."

Five in the afternoon. All over town, people were sitting down and putting their feet up. Stan, too.

38

WHEN DORTMUNDER WALKED into the OJ at ten that night, Rollo was off to the right end of the bar, in conversation with a tourist. There were many ways to tell he was a tourist, such as the binoculars and camera both hanging from straps around his neck, the sunglasses pushed up onto his forehead, the many-pocketed camouflage jacket with the maps jutting out of most of the pockets, his pants cuffs tucked into the top of his heavy-duty hiking boots, and the fact that he was trying to pay for his beer in euros.

Rollo was having none of it. "We only do American money," he explained. "It isn't worth much, but we're used to it."

"%#&_#&%$★@ @¼&%#$," said the tourist, and went on holding out the colorful little piece of paper.

Meanwhile, to the left end of the bar, the regulars were discussing the Internet. "It's the biggest scam in the world," one of them was saying. "I mean, why go through all that?

The first thing you gotta do, even before you start, you gotta go out and put good cash money right down and buy this adding machine kind of thing."

"Computer," a second regular suggested. "They call it a computer."

"Sure," said the first. "And what does it compute? It's an adding machine."

"Well," said the second regular, "I think it's more than that. I mean, I don't know this myself, but the way I understand it, this machine connects to everything everywhere. Somehow."

"So?" said the first regular. "My phone connects to everything everywhere. My television connects with everything everywhere."

A third regular now joined the discussion, saying, "Just last week I got a wrong number from Turkey. The guy wanted me to reverse the charges. I told *him* what to reverse."

Meanwhile, the tourist, still waving his euro, was now trying blandishment. "&%$&&@★+, &&%$)★★," he wheedled, with what he apparently hoped was a winning smile.

It lost. "If it isn't green," Rollo said, "I got no use for it. Pass that thing at the UN or somewhere."

To the left, a fourth regular had joined the conversation, while Dortmunder waited patiently in the middle, resting his forearms on the bar, reading the labels on the bottles across the back, remarking to himself how few of them he thought he'd be able to pronounce. This fourth regular began by announcing, "It's all another government giveaway to the big farm interests, like those subsidies and pushed-up crop prices and all that stuff. If you do sign on to this Internet thing, you know what they make you do? You gotta sign up for shipments of salty meat!"

The second regular veered around as though he'd just seen an iceberg. "You do?"

"It's true," the fourth regular insisted. "I read about it, I read about it a couple times. People got all this meat, they don't know what to do with it."

The first regular, doubtful, said, "I think you got something wrong in there."

"No way, Jose."

The first regular lowered an eyebrow. "Do I look Hispanic to you?"

"I dunno," the fourth regular said, undaunted. "Lemme see you dance the mambo."

"Keep it down over there," Rollo said. Many years of experience had taught him the precise moment for a calm but firm intervention.

The fourth regular kept his mouth open, but perhaps spoke something different from what he originally intended. "All I know is," he said, "the government's overdoing all this crap. They're intruding on everybody's lives. They're sticking their nose in everywhere."

"The camel under the tent," said the third regular, the one with the pal in Turkey.

This comment was met with such a profound silence that Dortmunder could clearly hear that the tourist had now decided to get on his high horse and was demanding his rights, or respect, or a fair hearing, or a retrial, or something, all in a firm voice punctuated by a fingertip, from the hand not holding the euro, bonk-bonk-bonking the bar. "%#$&&," he said. "★&+@%%$# %&★++%$, $%#&@1/4★★& $%& +★%$# ★$%&$+@@."

Rollo at this point held up a hand palm outward in the universal traffic-cop sign for "stop." "Hold on," he told the tourist. "I got an actual customer here, one that doesn't deal in wampum." Turning to Dortmunder, he said, "You're the first."

"We're five tonight," Dortmunder told him.

"I know, the beer and salt told me. Let me give you the makings for you and the other bourbon."

During this exchange, the regulars had been wondering if a blog was something you could catch and the tourist was giving Dortmunder the fisheye as though suspecting somebody around here was trying to jump the line.

If so, it was successful. Rollo slid the tray with the glasses and the ice and the Amsterdam Liquor Store Bourbon— "Our Own Brand"—along the bar to stop in front of Dortmunder, but then he said, "Hold on."

"Hold on?"

Rollo was looking over Dortmunder's shoulder, so Dortmunder turned and here came Tiny and the kid. "Just in time," Dortmunder said.

"Which means somebody's late," Tiny commented.

The tourist didn't like it that an entire crowd seemed to have taken his place at center stage, but he was bewildered as to what to do about it. Holding up his euro to show it to the three of them, he said, "&%*\$*@, &*\$@+ *&%*+," his manner now showing a plea for international friendship here, some common fellowship, human understanding.

Tiny reached out and tapped the tourist on the binoculars. The tourist flinched, and looked alarmed. Tiny told him, "What you want to do is, when in Rome, don't be Greek."

The tourist blinked. All languages, even his own, seemed to have deserted him.

Rollo, having been busy, slid Tiny his bright red drink and said to the kid, "What'll it be tonight?"

"Well, I think I'd just like a beer," the kid said.

Rollo, deadpan, gave Dortmunder a lightning-fast look that said, "I believe our little boy is growing up," then turned and drew a draft as Dortmunder picked up his tray and Kelp, arriving, said, "I'm a little late, let me carry that."

"Yes," Dortmunder said, and, empty-handed, led the way toward the regulars, who were now trying to figure out if the Internet could look back at you.

"Wait a second," Kelp said.

So they all stopped, and Kelp turned to the regulars to say, "The answer is yes. Just a little while ago there's a woman right here in New York City, she works for the Apple Store, you know, the computer store, and somebody burgled her apartment and took a lot of stuff including her home computer. Now, she's very savvy about computers, and she knew a way, from another computer, how she could talk to her computer and tell it to take pictures of where it found itself. So it did, and there's the two guys who boosted it, so she took their pictures down from the other computer and gave them to the cops, and pretty soon the cops got the perps and the woman got her computer and her other stuff back, and the moral of that story is, do not commit a crime anywhere near the Internet."

Kelp nodded at them, to be sure they'd followed his story, and then said to the others, "Okay, let's go." And the four of them took off around the regulars, who were sitting in a row there now like an aquarium full of thunderstruck fish, and on down the hall, where the kid said, "Andy, that's cool. Did that really happen?"

"Yes," Kelp said. "And let it be a lesson to you."

Solemn, the kid held up his beer glass in a toast to lessons learned. "It is," he said.

39

AROUND THE BACK ROOM TABLE, they sorted themselves by order of appearance, Dortmunder facing the door, Tiny and the kid flanking him with their oblique views toward the door, Kelp first closing the door and then taking the chair beyond the kid, with its oblique view away from the door.

As they settled into their places Tiny said, "Stan is the one called this meet, and Stan is the one that isn't here. I call this rude."

Dortmunder said, "There's probly an explanation."

Tiny lowered a brow at him. "You always think the best of everybody," he accused.

"Not always," Dortmunder said, and the door opened and Stan came in.

"Uh-huh," Tiny said.

Stan, closing the door, saw he had a choice between the chair next to the irritated Tiny or the chair with its back fully to the door. As he hesitated over these selections, he said, "Sorry I'm late, but I got an explanation."

"I thought you would," Dortmunder said.

Stan put his beer and his salt on the table and his body on the chair next to Tiny. "This time a year," he said, "you got your tourists, that flood just picking up, you got your Europeans with their luxury apartments in Manhattan just opening them up for the new season, you even got your American travelers wanna see is New York as scary as their uncle said. So this time a year," he concluded, "I don't take the Belt Parkway. It's fulla sightseers that don't know how to drive in New York. Or anywhere else."

Kelp said, "This is the explanation?"

"This is the preamble," Stan told him. "I just want you to know I know what I'm doing. So on city streets, I know where the construction is, I know where the national pride day parades are, I know where the strikes and the demonstrations are, so I pick my route. Tonight, I come up Flatlands and Pennsylvania and Bushwick and the LIE to the Midtown Tunnel, because inbound isn't that bad in the evening hours, and then up the FDR to Seventy-ninth and through the park. This is the plan."

"This isn't a plan," Tiny said. "This is a travelogue."

Dortmunder said, "Tell us, Stan. What went wrong?"

"It's all working," Stan said. "I'm all the way to Manhattan, I'm on the FDR. There's pretty thick traffic, but it's moving along. I'm in the middle lane and I see, maybe three cars up in the right lane, this Honda that the left front wheel comes off."

That got everybody's attention. Kelp said, "What? It just

fell off and lay on the ground?"

"Hell, no," Stan said. "It kept going. And the Honda has this balance, so it keeps going, too. But the wheel's going faster than the cars, and when the guy driving the Honda sees this wheel pull out in front of him, he panics."

Tiny nodded. "Many would," he said.

"So he hit the brakes," Stan said. "And there goes his equilibrium. He's doing fifty, his left front hits the roadway, all at once he looked like six Hondas going in six different directions all at once, including straight up. It was like a dance, only fast. And now everybody else's hitting the brakes, and the Honda's all over the road, and when it finally stops it's blocking all three lanes, with parts falling off and scattered around the general neighborhood. All the traffic from behind is pressing way up, there's no way to go forward, and there's no exit anywhere near there. We're stopped."

The kid said, "What happened to the wheel?"

"It kept going," Stan said. "It was in front of the crash, so it just kept going. Unless it took the Triborough it's in Westchester by now."

Dortmunder said, "What about the guy in the Honda?"

"Well, I guess he's all right," Stan said, "only the Honda has kind of closed around him so he can't get out. Eventually they had to cut him out, so that was another delay."

The kid said, "Who cut him out? The cops?"

"No," Stan said. "The cops got there first and just stood around and made phone calls. Then the ambulance, that can't do anything because this guy's like a canned ham and they still gotta open the can. Then the fire department shows up and they got this special machine for opening up vehicles at times like this that things have gone a little worse than usual."

"Well," Dortmunder said, "there was no way you could plan for that."

Stan said, "Oh, you can *plan* for anything, that doesn't matter. The point is, though, they finally got us outa there and the rest of it was a snap. Even the bicycles popping wheelies on the park transverse weren't a problem. But I'm late, and I'm sorry, and that's the reason."

"And you got," Tiny said, "something to tell us."

"Yeah, that's why we're here."

Kelp said, "We also got something to tell you, but you called the meet, so you go first."

"Okay," Stan said. "While you guys've been playing with the reality people, I've been dropping into Varick Street a little later at night."

"We know that," Kelp said.

"Oh, yeah?" Stan shrugged and said, "Well, anyway, last night I decided to take a look at Knickerbocker Storage, and I know that's what we got our hopes fixed on, now that the cash for Europe thing doesn't work out, but the truth is it's no good. I hate to tell you this, guys, because I know you're counting on it, but there's just no caper there."

"That's funny," Kelp said. "That's the same news we were gonna tell you."

"Not that funny," Tiny said.

Stan said, "So you guys saw it, too, all that crap in the storage place?"

"No," Kelp said. "We didn't look in there. That was always supposed to be the fake thing anyway, so we could go after the cash going to Europe. But that didn't work either, so finally we just walked off."

"We walked off," Tiny said, "because we were accused of stealing cars."

"Oh," Stan said.

Kelp said, "If you planned to go back there tonight, bring a toothbrush."

"So that's over, is what you're saying," Stan said. "The whole reality thing. And we all knew it at the same time. So now what we got to do is figure out what we *are* gonna do."

Kelp said, "Anybody got any prospects? Anything might help?"

Stan said, "Hold that for a minute. All that storytelling, I used up my beer." Rising, he said, "Anybody else? Kid?"

"Sure," the kid said.

"Tiny?"

"I'm okay," Tiny said.

Kelp said, "John and me, we've got this bottle."

"Fine," Stan said. "I'll be right back."

Holding his empty glass, he turned and opened the door, and Doug was standing there. Doug's anxious expression switched to pleased surprise and he said, "Stan! When'd you get back?"

Stan closed the door.

40

No. They couldn't do that. They couldn't just ignore him, could they? Doug stared at the closed door, right there in front of his nose, and he couldn't believe it. He'd *seen* them, the four guys sitting around the table just exactly like the OJ back room footage they'd shot, plus Stan right there in the doorway, and the next thing, Stan slams the door. Right in front of him.

They can't do that. They can't pretend they're not in there, not after he *saw* them. Did they think he'd just go away? Well, he wouldn't go away. He couldn't go away. He needed those guys. He needed *The Heist*, now more than ever.

When he'd discovered, this afternoon, how circumstances had changed, and how much he now needed *The Heist* to get itself up and running again, he'd tried to think of some way to get back in touch with the guys. He'd known immediately there would be no gain in trying to work through Stan's Mom. She'd just brush him off and promise to pass on a message and then go out and drive her cab some more.

He couldn't have that. He needed to talk to the guys themselves, he needed to explain to them what dire straits he was in, call on their better natures, convince them to come back to *The Heist*, no matter what. But how could he reach them?

When all of a sudden he'd thought of the OJ, the real OJ up there on Amsterdam Avenue, and realized that place was almost certainly going to go on being their hangout, because people are creatures of habit and like to go back to where they've already been comfortable, he wondered, very briefly, if he dared go there and lie in wait for them. It was brief because what choice did he have?

But would that be going over a line, somehow, moving into some private space of theirs, slipping into the completely unacceptable? Would he be testing the limits of their nonviolence if he were suddenly to appear among them at their own personal OJ?

Well, it didn't matter, he just had to do it. So he made himself come to the OJ tonight a little after ten, half-hoping this would not be a night when they were present here, and when he walked into the place he saw the bartender in patient but apparently indecisive conversation with a foreign person who appeared to be unequipped in English. This distraction had made it easy for Doug to slide on by the chattering habitués at the left end of the bar and hurry down the hall to that closed back room door. When he leaned against it, ear to the old wood, he could just hear the murmur of voices, but not what they were saying.

They were here! His heart pounding, Doug tried to decide what to do. Should he just barge in on them and hope to talk fast enough so they'd understand his problem before they threw him out? Or should he simply knock on the door, like any normal visitor, which might provoke who knew what kind of response? Or should he leave them their private space and go back out to the bar and take a table there and order a drink—yes to that part—and wait for them to come out, in hopes that then and there he could talk to them, persuade them, convince them?

It was an impossible situation. He stood there, indecisive, trying to find some ray of hope in any of the options before him, stood there who knows how long, and all of a sudden the door opened, and there was Stan, of all people, with the other four seated at the table behind him. Doug had greeted Stan with honest surprise and pleasure, and Stan had responded by slamming the door in his face. (Well, closing the door, but still.)

He had to go forward. He could not retreat. And he could not simply wait for them to open this door again; that might be hours from now. He had to force the issue, dammit, force the issue. Firmly he reached out and turned the knob and opened the door.

They were all seated now, at all the chairs except the one with its back to Doug. "Guys, I'm sorry I—" Doug started, and all five of them reared back to point in various directions and tell him in various loud and pungent ways to get lost.

"I *need* you guys!" he cried. "I'm in terrible trouble. Please, just listen to me. Let me tell you what happened."

Something in his desperate manner caught their attention, if not their interest, or their sympathy. They looked at one another, and then Tiny said, "You wanna tell us a story."

"A story? I—" Then he nodded, quickly. "That's right," he said. "I want to tell you a story."

"Then you go back out there," Tiny said, "and you tell Rollo, you came here to see what the boys in the back room will have, and they will have another round. And these two will have another bottle. All on you."

"Oh, I know that," Doug said, but couldn't resist adding, "all on the production. No problem. I'll be right back."

When he hurried out to the bar, the foreign gentleman was gone and the bartender was picking up random glasses from the backbar, wiping them a little bit with a small towel, and putting them down again. Doug caught his attention, made his request, handed over his credit card, got it back, and the bartender slid over to him a tray containing a bottle that claimed to contain bourbon, two draft beers, a glass of gin and tonic and ice and lemon peel (his own addition), and a glass of red liquid that was undoubtedly not cherry soda.

"Tell them I'll grab the trays later," the bartender said.

"I will. Thank you."

The tray was too heavy and too tippy to carry one-handed, so Doug carried it in two hands, which, at the other end of the hall, meant the only way to deal with the door was not to knock on it but to kick it, which seemed aggressive but couldn't be avoided. So he kicked it, gently, and Stan, on his feet again, opened to him and said, "Good. That's good. You did good. Sit there."

So he sat with his back to the door and said, "I really appreciate this, fellas."

"Tell us the story," Tiny said.

"All right." Doug lubricated a bit with gin and tonic and said, "Just to give the highlight, *The Stand* fell apart. Today. While we were downtown."

Andy said, "Fell apart? The vegetable stand?"

"No, the whole show." Doug needed more lubrication. "All at once, Kirby, the younger son, the one that wanted to come out of the closet on a G-rated series, all at once he runs off with a human cannonball from some cheap one-ring circus going through those small towns up there. At the same time, the older son, Lowell, the shy intellectual on the show, decides to go into a Buddhist monastery up in Vermont with a vow of silence, and, needless to say, no telephone. And what apparently set them both off was because the parents, with no warning at all, announced they're getting divorced, because she's in love with the family plumber and he's tired of northern winters and he's taken a job managing a chain motel in Tahiti. They're all gone, there's nobody there to run the stand, and the truth is, it was never a viable business anyway, the only reason to have a stand like that in a location like that was because of the show. So now it's gone and we've got nothing."

Tiny said, "Do something else."

"I'd love to do something else," Doug told him, "but you'd be amazed how many topics have already been covered by reality shows. Undertakers. Plastic surgeons. Long-distance truckers. Polygamists, though tastefully. And besides, I've still got another problem."

Andy said, "I know this is mean to say, but somehow I can't get enough of your problems, Doug. Lay it on us."

"Before we knew you guys were gonna ankle," Doug said, "we put together a rough cut of the season so far and showed it to the next level of bosses, up at Monopole, and they love it. They think it's gonna be a breakout. They're already selling it overseas."

Everybody took a minute to absorb that, and then the

kid said, "That guy Ray you sent us, the ringer—"

"He really does walk on walls," Doug said.

"We know," the kid said. "And we also know he really is an actor, and the reason he was there was to spy on us and report to you."

"Well, I wouldn't phrase it like *that*," Doug said. "Besides, what does that have to do with anything?"

"Cast us all with actors," the kid said.

"Great idea," Andy said. "You're not showing our faces anyway."

"But that isn't reality," Doug objected. "That isn't the way it works."

John said, "Why not? How real is reality anyway?"

"Real enough," Doug said. "If we use actors, then it's got to be a scripted show, so then we need writers, and all at once we're into unions and all kinds of other expenses and it prices us right out of the market. The whole point of reality shows is to give the networks a way to fill airtime on the cheap."

John said, "Okay, I see your problem, so now let me tell you *our* problem. There's no robbery there."

Doug didn't grasp that at all. "But," he said, "you agreed Knickerbocker Storage would be bound to have—"

"It doesn't," Stan said, in the flat tone of one who knows.

"It was always a fake anyway," John said.

Doug said, "A fake? Why? How?"

"Well, mostly," Andy said, "it's your fault."

"Oh, not something else," Doug said.

John said, "You remember, way back when, we're trying to figure out what job you'd like to make a movie of, and I said something about cash, and you said you never saw cash anywhere—"

"And then you hiccupped," Andy said.

Doug looked at him. "I did?"

"We both noticed it," Andy said. "All of a sudden, you remembered where you'd seen cash, and you tried to cover up for it."

"So it looked to us," John said, "that Combined Tool, down on Varick Street, was the most likely place you saw cash. Because it was the most high-tech door locks in America. So that's why we said Knickerbocker Storage, so we could knock over Combined Tool while you're taking pictures of Knickerbocker Storage."

"Oh, my God," Doug said. "And that's why you had to pretend Stan wasn't involved any more, because we knew his last name and how to find him."

"But then it turned out," John said, "we were right but we were wrong. Cash going to Europe, like we thought, but not kept on Varick Street, just in the suitcase of the German guy staying overnight, every once in a while. We can't use that, cash comes in, goes right out, we never know the schedule. We need cash *there*, right there, all the time. So that's why—"

John stopped and frowned at Doug, who suddenly felt guilty or self-conscious or something. "What?" he said. "What?"

John looked at Doug but spoke to Andy. "Did you see that?"

"I sure did," Andy said.

"Even I saw that," Tiny said.

Grinning, the kid said, "Give us the good news, Doug."

"Good news? What do you mean?" But already, Doug understood. Somehow, he'd given himself away. The same as last time, they'd read him, quietly but intensely. Oh, what did they know now?

Andy said to John, "You think it's in the midtown offices? That's another set of problems."

"Well," John said, "probly what we'd do, we'd dismantle an elevator, maybe with two-three people inside it, then use the stairs and blow the office door out while security's going nuts over their elevator. Choose a doctor's office on a lower floor, spend the night there, go out in the morning with the incoming personnel."

Andy said, "Depending where this cash is."

"Well, yeah."

Andy gave Doug his brightest most cheerful look. "Where is it, Doug?"

"Please," Doug said. "Don't do this. You're asking me to commit a crime."

Andy said, "You're asking *us* to commit a crime. And you're gonna profit from it."

"But I . . ." Doug said, and ran down.

He didn't know what to do. Nobody had lured him into this. He'd lured himself into it. But how could he get out of this mess without losing *The Heist*? And how could he save *The Heist* without putting himself into terrible trouble? He reached for his glass, and to his shock it was empty. A few tiny ice cubes, a curl of lemon peel.

What to do? He didn't dare leave this room to get another drink. But how to go on without one?

John said, "That empty? Have some of ours. We got plenty." And he pointed at the "bourbon" bottle.

Doug shook his head. "No, John, I couldn't—"

"There's ice cubes in the bowl," Andy offered. "Calms the taste. Just put the lemon on that tray there."

"Go ahead," said John.

So Doug dumped out his lemon peel, dropped in a few ice cubes, and poured out a few fingers of the brown liquid.

Meanwhile, returning to the business at hand, John said, "If there's cash up in the midtown offices, and if it's there all the time, or even most of the time, then maybe we could work something out to get our hands on it, and you can still make your show."

To stall, Doug sipped from his glass, and immediately his face puckered up like a pine tree knot. He blinked away sudden moisture in his eyes and said, "You guys drink this all the time?"

"Only on occasions," John said.

"Well, my respect for you has just increased," Doug said.

"Thank you, Doug."

Andy said, "Where in the office is it, Doug?"

Doug sighed. No escape. "Not in the office," he said.

John said, "Someplace *else*? We figured, either midtown or Varick Street."

"No, you were right," Doug said. He was suddenly very tired, as though he'd been undergoing severe interrogation for a week. He swallowed a bit more of the brown liquid and sighed.

John said, "You mean, it *is* on Varick Street? But Muller just brings it overnight and takes it away."

"No," Doug said. "This is other cash. I've never met these people, I understand they're very dangerous. Even Babe keeps out of their way. They're from somewhere in Asia, Malaysia or Macao or somewhere like that."

"Tell us about it, Doug," Andy suggested.

"Asia's the new opening-up market," Doug told them.

"It's very Wild West out there, all the big companies have local teams to take care of local problems. You know, even in Russia you gotta hire a Russian that's gonna know who you bribe and who you don't have to."

"This is what we were figuring," John said.

"Well, that's what it is. We have to keep cash available because you never know when there's gonna be a change in government or your contact gets murdered, or whatever. We can't keep cash *there*, too dangerous, so we keep it here, on Varick Street, and a few of our Asian—associates, I guess—they have access to Combined Tool, and when there's an emergency they come and take. When things go wrong over there, they go wrong all of a sudden, so that's why we have to have that money handy. *Please* don't ask me where it's kept."

"No, we wouldn't, Doug," Andy said. "You'd be going too far to tell us something like that."

"Besides," the kid said, "we oughta do *some* of our own work. Right, guys?"

Solemnly, the guys all nodded their agreement.

Doug tried to keep his eye on the prize and ignore the crocodiles around his ankles. "Does this mean," he said, "you'll come back to the show?"

"But just to film Knickerbocker Storage," Andy said. "None of this other stuff."

"Oh, I know. I wouldn't want to . . ." And he let the sentence trail away, afraid to find out what he wouldn't want to cause to occur.

"We could even make it tomorrow morning at ten," Andy said.

"Oh, I think two," Doug said. "After lunch. I'll need to get everything set up."

His glass seemed to be empty again, somehow. Rising, he said, "Whatever happens, I'm glad we'll be going on with it."

They announced similar feelings, and Doug turned to the door, and the kid said, "Doug Fairkeep?"

Confused, Doug turned around. "Yes?"

"That is you, right?" the kid said. "Doug Fairkeep?"

"You know that," Doug said. "What's the point?"

The kid held up his cell phone. "If it should happen, someday," he said, "that a cop, or a boss of yours, listens to this conversation, we'd want him to be sure he knew who he was listening to."

Andy said, "You see, Doug, you coming here to the OJ like this, and seeing Stan here, we understood we had to get to a place where you weren't a threat to us any more than we were a threat to you."

"I see," Doug said. "Don't lose that phone, kid."

"I won't," the kid promised.

In the cab going downtown, Doug believed he now understood the sensations felt by a person slowly sinking into the grasp of an octopus. Play dead, he told himself.

But how?

41

WHEN KELP AND Dortmunder and Tiny and the kid walked into the fake OJ Tuesday afternoon at two, Doug and Marcy and Roy Ombelen and Rodney the bartender and the camera crews were already there, clustered around the left end of the bar, where in the real joint the regulars reigned. As they approached the bar, Rodney was saying, "No way Shakespeare wrote those plays. He didn't have the education, he hadn't been anywhere, he was just a country bumpkin. An actor. A very good actor, everybody says so, but just an actor."

Doug said, "Isn't some duke supposed to be the real guy?"

"Oh, Clarence," Rodney said, in dismissal.

"I heard that, too," Marcy said. "That's very interesting."

"No, it wasn't him," Rodney said, scoffing at the idea. "In fact, if you study those plays the way I did, you'll see they couldn't have been written by a man at all."

Marcy, astonished, said, "A woman?"

239

"No sixteenth-century guy," Rodney said, "had that kind of modern attitude toward women or instinctive understanding of the woman's mind."

One of the camerapersons said, "My husband says it was Bacon."

Another cameraperson, dripping scorn, said, "They're not talking about meat, they're talking about Shakespeare."

"Sir Francis Bacon."

"Oh."

Roy said to Rodney, "I venture to say you have someone in mind."

"Queen," Rodney pronounced, "Elizabeth the First."

Kelp and Dortmunder looked at one another. "You build it," Kelp murmured, "they will come."

Turning, Doug said, "Oh, there you are."

"Here we are," Dortmumder agreed.

"Can you start without me?" Kelp said. "I got a little gippy tummy this afternoon."

"Oh, sure," Doug said. He had a slightly manic appearance this afternoon, as though he'd forgotten and taken his medication twice. "You go ahead, we'll be setting up for a while."

So Kelp exited the set, rounded the corner, and headed for the stairs. This was the top floor, so he only had to go up the one flight to the roof door, to check into what they'd done to refix the lock and alarm now that he'd told them about its being rigged. Whatever they'd done, Kelp was ready to disarm it right now, from inside, with the various equipment in his various pockets.

And they hadn't done a thing. Was that possible? The rerouted wire was taped exactly where Kelp had left it. The lock was still nonexistent.

Hadn't they believed him? Or maybe they'd just had too many other things on their minds. In any case, it did make life simpler. Kelp opened the door, looked out at the roof, closed the door, and hurried back downstairs to the non-OJ.

Doug met him as he came into the set. "You okay, Andy?"

"Oh, fine," Kelp said. "Just one of those little things, you know, it comes along and then it goes right away."

"Stress gets to everybody, Andy," Doug said.

"Yeah, I guess so. Oh, there's my bunch."

Marcy and the rest of the cast were now clustered at one of the side booths, and Marcy waved to Kelp and called, "Come on over, Andy, we're working out the story line."

The story line. 1) You go in. 2) You take what you came for. 3) You go out. If civilians are present, insert 1A) You show, but do not employ, weapons.

Marcy's story line would be a little more baroque. Kelp went over, found a sliver of bench available next to Tiny, perched on it, and Marcy leaned in to be confidential, saying, "I hope you held out for a lot more money."

"Oh, sure," Kelp said. "You know us."

Because, of course, Marcy didn't know anything. She didn't know why they'd left, and she didn't know why they were back. So, as with the reality show, she was making up her own story line, which was perfectly okay.

"What we need, in the next couple weeks of the show," Marcy told them, "is some sense of menace. Not from you guys, some other outside force."

Dortmunder said, "Like the law, you mean?"

"No, we don't want to bring the police in until the very end of the season. The escape from the police will be the great triumph, and it'll make up for you not getting the big score you were counting on from the storage rooms."

Kelp said, "Oh, we're not getting that?"

"It's a little more complicated than that," Marcy said. "I don't want you to know the story too far ahead, because it can affect the way you play it. But I can guarantee you, the escape from the police will be *the* climax of the first season."

"I'd watch it," the kid said.

"For a menace from the outside," Marcy said, "what do you think of another gang going after the exact same target?"

Kelp said, "Wasn't that in a Woody Allen movie?"

"Oh, it's been in dozens of movies," she said. "That's all right. Nobody expects reality to be original. People will see that, and they'll laugh and they'll say, 'Just like the Woody Allen movie, and here the same thing happens in real life.'"

Dortmunder said, "That's what they say, huh?"

"Oh, people get very caught up in these stories," Marcy told him. "It's like their own reality, only better. More interesting."

Tiny said, "Where does this frightening other gang come from?"

"Well," Marcy said, "we were hoping you all might know some people."

Tiny said, "People to muscle in on our score? Point them out."

Marcy looked troubled. "You don't like that idea."

"Not much," they agreed.

"Well, Babe suggested," Marcy said, sounding unconvinced, "maybe one of you double-crosses the rest of the gang, sells you out to the owner of the storage place."

Dortmunder said, "Get Real is the owner of the storage place."

"Well, yes." Marcy nodded, but wasn't happy. "Whenever there's a problem like that," she said, "Doug says we'll work around it, but I don't see how we could work around that one."

Kelp said, "Just for curiosity's sake, which of us did you tap for the Judas?"

"We hadn't decided," Marcy said. "We thought we'd leave that up to you."

"Then I guess we'd vote for Ray," Dortmunder said.

"That's right," Kelp said. "He's already got the experience."

Marcy blushed. It was an uncomfortable sight, because she didn't do it well, but just came out all blotchy, like measles, or a face covered with cold sores. The others looked away, giving her a chance to get control of herself, and she coughed and said, "Most of us didn't really think that was a good idea, anyway."

"Most of you were right," Tiny said.

The clatter of the elevator was heard, rising through the building. "Oh, that'll be Babe," Marcy said.

Dortmunder said, "Coming to shut us down again?"

Marcy laughed, as though that had been a joke. "He's coming with Darlene and Ray," she said. "That's the other thing we're going to do, to build suspense. Today— Oh, wait," she shouted. "That's too loud."

It was. They all waited. They couldn't see the elevator from inside the set, but they could hear when at last it stopped.

Marcy, talking more rapidly now, said, "You're all going to

243

be in here, at the bar, just talking, and it would be nice if you could be reminiscing, you know, about other robberies you did. How you found out the target was there, and how you did it, and how you got away."

"And how," Tiny said, "the crime remained unsolved until now."

"Well, I expect you to change some details," Marcy said, and Darlene and Ray and Babe came into the joint.

Babe was in a good mood for once. "Hello, all," he said. "No, I'm not here to shut you down."

"That's too bad," the kid said. "There's a matinee I wanted to see."

"Ha ha," Babe said. "Marcy, did you try out those ideas on the guys?"

"They don't seem to like them," Marcy said. "And they don't have any other gangs they'd like to work with."

"And the traitor in their midst?"

Nodding at Ray but talking to Babe, Dortmunder said, "That's already been tried."

"Oh, now," Babe said.

Marcy said, "I was just starting to tell them about the action today. All of you are in the bar here, including Darlene, and you're all just talking about your old successful robberies, with changes, of course, with changes. And then a mysterious man comes in and sits in the back there, back near where the door would be if there was a door."

"That's me," Babe said.

"Everybody becomes aware of him because he's just watching people, but nobody knows who he is."

"Mine is one of the faces we can show," Babe said. He sounded modest about it.

"And then the camera," Marcy said, "the camera sees,

and so do the people at home, that *Darlene* knows who he is, and doesn't want anybody else to catch on. Is he her father? An ex-husband? A hitman, sent to kill her by somebody from her past? She seems to be afraid of him, right, Darlene?"

"I've been practicing," Darlene said.

Marcy approved. "Good." To the others she said, "So this is a mystery and some suspense, and we'll run it out as long as we can. But for today, you all just become aware of him, but don't do any big reactions, don't try to talk to him or anything like that. Okay?"

"You want us to be cool," the kid said.

"Exactly."

So everybody agreed with that idea, and then Babe said, "I've been around these shows a few years now, even dreamed up a couple of them, but I've never actually been in one before. Seemed like a good time to get my feet wet."

Roy Ombelen said, "And we're very glad indeed to have you among us, Babe. And now, lady and gents, if we could begin with Rodney in place, and Tiny and Judson sitting at—"

"Oh, that's me," the kid said. "I almost forgot."

"I believe in names," Roy told him. "In any event, you'll both be at the bar, chatting with Rodney, nothing important, and then you other four come in all together. Now, Darlene, I need you at the left end of the group along the bar, so when Babe comes in you'll have a clear view of him. The group chats—"

"About the hits of yesteryear," Kelp said.

"Even so. Now we'll be doing an existing storefront entrance for Babe's coming into the bar from the street, so at the moment that's supposed to happen, Darlene, I'll snap my fingers. You look over that way, toward the pretend door, and you see him. You're startled, and then you cover up, and the conversation goes on. Everyone all right with that?"

Everyone was all right.

"Good." Roy turned to Babe, saying, "Now, you don't look at anybody, you just come in and walk to the right end of the bar, away from the others. Rodney, you go to Babe. He orders a beer, you give him the can and the glass, he pays you and goes back to that table there, and you go back with the group. Okay?"

Everybody was still okay.

"We'll probably," Roy said, "have to take a break at that point to relight that table, but up till then, you people just do your conversation, that's the ostensible focus of our scene. Okay?"

Still okay.

"Very good. Places, please."

So everybody slid once again into reality. Kelp found it an easy place to be, no difficult demands, just talking like tough guys. Nobody even thought about cameras any more.

Kelp watched Darlene, and she really did a nice job of it. A real actress, she knew how to get the effects with really very small moves.

Meanwhile, the group cut up old jackpots, the bank in the trailer, the emerald they had to keep going back and getting again and again, the ruby that was too famous to hock so they had to put it back where they got it, the cache of cash in the reservoir. The time just seemed to go by.

★

Walking up Seventh Avenue with Dortmunder when the day's work was done, Kelp said, "I didn't think Babe was very good at that stuff."

"I know what you mean," Dortmunder said. "He was too stiff like."

"He doesn't have a natural ease in front of the camera."

"Well," Dortmunder said, "his is really a very small part, it won't matter much."

"And the rest of us," Kelp said, "can carry him."

42

STAN DROVE the GMC Mastodon hybrid from where he'd found it, alone and unattended on a dark side street in Queens, across Northern Boulevard to the Fifty-ninth Street Bridge to Manhattan, the quickest most direct route after midnight, which this was, making today Wednesday, three weeks since the Wednesday since they had first heard of the existence, from Stan's Mom, of Doug Fairkeep and reality.

Once in Manhattan, Stan paused at various street corners to pick up some friends. By the time he turned westward onto Fourteenth Street from Park Avenue, he had Dortmunder to his right and Kelp beyond that, with the kid in the usually roomy backseat making do with whatever was left over after Tiny came aboard.

"Even late at night," Stan explained, as they drove toward Varick Street, "I can't just park forever in front of that building. There's still some tunnel traffic at any hour, so the cops come by a lot to keep it clear, and if a cop decides to tell me to move along he just might also decide to have a look at my paperwork first."

"We know how it works," Dortmunder said.

"Good." Stan braked for a red light, and never even glanced at the patrol car parked in the bus stop. "What I'll do," he said, "I'll let everybody off and then just go around the block until I see you all."

"Fine," Dortmunder said.

"If it turns out," Stan said, "you have a little problem and I shouldn't wait around but just go home, try to open that garage door. Like a signal."

Kelp said, "What if we wanna give you a signal you should come in and help out with something?"

"I don't think we're gonna need that signal," Stan said.

There was no more discussion along those lines, and then they reached the building, hulking dark in the middle of the block next to the well-illuminated bank building stretching to the corner. Stan drove past the GR Development building to the darker big structure at the next corner, where he stopped. His passengers all got out to the sidewalk there and, as Stan drove off to begin his orbits, the kid did a whole lot of quick stretches and bends to counteract the effects of spending the last half hour squeezed between Tiny and the ungiving flank of the Mastodon.

Meanwhile, the others followed Kelp around the corner. They were going in the same way Dortmunder and Kelp had slipped in two weeks ago. At the small side door, Kelp bent briefly over the lock meant to protect from pilferage the deep fryers, menu holders, and microwave ovens of the restaurant supply wholesaler who called this place a living. The kid had caught up by the time Kelp was pushing open the door to lead the way inside.

The stairwell, as they now knew, was on the far side of this building, across all these unemployed furnishings. Trooping through, guided by the pink light from the wall clock at the rear of the showroom and then the dim lights at every level of the stairwell, up they went to the sixth floor and into the offices of the olive oil importer who would provide the window through which they could step onto the GR Development roof.

That door, down into Get Real, had still not been restored to service, so they simply went in and down the stairs. At the second floor, Combined Tool, Dortmunder and Tiny stopped, while Kelp and the kid continued on down to the massed vehicles on one.

With one flashlight, held by the kid, they threaded through the cars to the rear door and out, where they now had to work with only the light that New York City's sky continued to reflect down onto the crowded jumble below. Over there in the corner was the ladder, which they quickly moved into place, slanted up to beside the pantry window. Kelp climbed the ladder as the kid held it, and when he was in position he took the handled suction cup from one of the pouches in the rear of his jacket, fixed it into place against the middle of the pane of the lower half of the window, and took out the glass cutter he'd purchased new, with his own money, at a hardware store on Bleecker Street yesterday afternoon.

This was the tricky part, to cut and not break. He started at the top, which was the hardest to get at, running the cutter horizontally in as straight a line as possible along the glass, as near to the top rail as he could get, the cut angled just a bit toward the wood.

Because he didn't want to have to do finicky after-work

with the window almost completely free, he went back and cut the same line a second time, then did the same kind of cut down both stiles, first on the left, then on the right. He was aware of the kid watching him from below, but kept his concentration on the work at hand.

The slice across the bottom was the hardest. Having cut just a few inches along that line, he felt he had to hold on to the suction cup handle, just in case the pane decided to fall out before he was ready. Left hand holding the handle, left elbow braced against the jamb, he slid the cutter across once, then twice, then pocketed the cutter and leaned a little forward pressure onto the glass.

At first he thought he hadn't done enough, but then, with unexpected speed, the pane angled backward into the room. Kelp needed both hands on the handle and both elbows down against the stool in order to keep control of the glass, which was pretty heavy, particularly from this angle. Holding tight, he lifted the pane up and away from himself, then lowered it into the room. Partway, he switched his left hand to grip the glass at the top, keeping away from the fresh-cut edge.

Tink, the glass said, when it touched the floor, but landed with no harm. Kelp used both hands to reach in and down and move the pane to the left, leaning forward against the handle. Then he rattled the ladder to get the kid's attention, looked down, and waved that he was going in.

It wasn't easy to get through the glassless window. There were metal shelves to both sides of it in there, but they were a little too far away to give him much help. Mostly, he had to try to slither on his belly, using first elbows and then knees to keep himself clear of the strip of sliced glass below him. From time to time he'd stop to shift position, then inch a little farther along the way, until at last he could firmly grasp a metal shelf on the right and use it to bring his legs the rest of the way into the room.

Down below, the kid would have gone by now, leaving the ladder in place. He would go back up with Dortmunder and Tiny to wait for Kelp to disarm the door and let them in.

Kelp studied himself and found a new roughened area on the front of his jacket, but no other signs of his recent close embrace of cut glass. He stepped through from the pantry into the kitchen, which was moderately illuminated by all its appliance lights, and crossed it to the dark doorway leading into whatever room was next.

When he felt around this doorway in the dark, he found it came with a door, now open against the wall. He closed the door, so he'd be able to switch lights on in here without being seen from outside, then found the light switch, which worked a ceiling fixture.

With light and privacy, he turned to see where he was, and the man sitting up on the sofa bed pointed a Glock at him and said, "Halt."

43

K ELP HALTED. "Whoa," he said. "You scared me. I
didn't know anybody was here."

"No, you did not. You will put your hands on top of
your head." The man was Asian of some kind, not the
slender delicate Asian of the coastal countries, but a larger,
meatier, mountain country Asian, a guy who looked as
though he came from a long line of professional wrestlers.
This must be one of the Asians Doug had told them about
just today—or yesterday—and now, immediately, here he
was, as big and dangerous as promised, plus a Glock pistol,
an efficient-looking blue-gray watchdog with its one
unwavering eye fixed on Kelp.

Doug had never met these people, and was glad of it.
Even Babe, he'd told them, kept out of their way. And
here was Kelp, in the guy's bedroom in the middle of the
night.

So how many of them were here? And what could Kelp
do about it? Raising his hands to rest palms down atop his

head, "I'm sorry," he said, "I thought I could sleep here tonight."

The man in the bed wore a white T-shirt and was partly covered by sheet and blanket. His right knee was lifted, beneath the blanket, with the butt of the Glock resting on the knee, the hand holding the Glock as still as a statue.

At the moment, he was in an investigatory phase, before deciding what to do about Kelp's existence in his bedroom. He said, "Why would you sleep here tonight?"

"I missed the last train to Westin," Kelp told him. "That's happened a couple times before, and I crash here for the night."

"Here," echoed the man. "And who are you?"

"Doug Fairkeep. I work for Get Real."

The man shook his head; the Glock didn't move. "What," he said, "is Get Real?"

"We produce reality television," Kelp told him. "This is our building, GR Development. GR; Get Real."

"That is not the company."

"Oh, you mean Monopole," Kelp said.

Now the man nodded, but the Glock still didn't move. "Yes, I mean Monopole."

"They own Get Real. But that's who I work for."

"Not many persons are permitted to enter this apartment."

"At Get Real," Kelp said, "it's only Babe Tuck and me."

"I have heard the name Babe Tuck," the man said.

"I'm glad of that anyway," Kelp said. "Listen, okay if I put my hands down?"

"Andy!" came a half-whispered cry, muffled by

distance and the closed bedroom door but audible just the same.

Kelp decided to react big. Jumping a big sideways step farther from the door, though keeping his hands atop his head, he said, "What was *that*?"

"I heard that," the man said. "You have someone with you?"

"No! Do you?"

"I do not." Frowning with deep suspicion, he said, "You will open the door."

"Open the door?"

"Andy!"

"I don't know," Kelp said. "There's somebody out there."

The man climbed out of the bed, the Glock never stopping its surveillance of the space between Kelp's eyes. He wore tan boxer shorts. His legs were strong and mostly hairless. He said, "Open."

"I'll stand behind it, all right?"

Now Kelp lowered his hands, put both of them on the doorknob, and pulled the door slowly open.

This time, the "Andy, what's happening?" was a little louder, and identifiable as the kid. The goddam kid.

The man with the Glock said, "You go first."

"Oh, boy," Kelp said.

It seemed to him a reasonable amount of fear would be the most plausible reaction to show at this point, so slowly he went through the doorway, peering in obvious fright to left and right. The man followed, switching on the kitchen lights, poking the Glock into the small of Kelp's back to move him along, and Kelp said, "Listen, I need a weapon."

"A weapon?"

Kelp turned to look at the man, who was even larger and more intimidating when standing up and standing close. "I don't know what's out there," Kelp told him, "and neither do you. Maybe it's more than you can deal with all by yourself." He pointed to the row of frying pans hung from hooks above the island in the middle of the kitchen. "Okay if I carry one of those?"

The man gave a very small headshake. "What good would it do?"

"Make me feel better," Kelp said. "Safer. Let me take that one there."

Impatient, the man said, "All right, take it. But then you go first. Through that door." Meaning the pantry.

"Absolutely," Kelp said. He took down the frying pan, a nine-inch cast-iron model, satisfyingly heavy. "This seems good," he said, hefting it in both hands, then swung it sidearm with all his might into the side of that head, just above the left ear.

The man dropped like a sudden avalanche. The Glock chittered across the tile floor to smack into the dishwasher. Kelp slapped the frying pan down onto the island, grabbed the Glock, turned it around so he wasn't aiming it at himself, and paused to look at the man, who had returned to dreamland, lying on the floor on his right side, right arm extended as though showing the way.

There had been no more Andy's since the kitchen lights had been switched on. Now, carrying the Glock, Kelp raced to the pantry, and there was the kid, on the ladder, just outside the breached window. He waved the Glock. "Get outa there!"

The kid stared wide-eyed at the pistol. "What'd you— Where'd you—"

"Go, dammit! I'll tell you at the door."

And Kelp raced away, to be sure his patient was still sleeping—and still breathing—and then to hurry on to the apartment door.

44

DORTMUNDER AND TINY had grown tired of each other's company, seated here on the hard stairs outside Combined Tool. Dortmunder himself was fairly slow to impatience, but it wasn't comfortable to be around Tiny when that gentleman was beginning to feel fed up, so what Dortmunder wished, he wished they could get on with it.

They had waited what already seemed a long time before the kid came back up the stairs to report that Kelp had cut through the window with no problems and was on his way now to open this door here. And then they waited some more. And then they waited some more.

And then Tiny said, "Kid, go see what's up."

"Okay, Tiny."

And now they were waiting some more.

"If we could get that motorcycle up here," Tiny said, "maybe we could drive it through the door. Or maybe the wall beside the door. Sometimes walls are easier."

"That might work," Dortmunder said. "We'll get the kid to drive it. I think there's a helmet with it."

"No matter." Tiny looked down the stairwell. "I don't think he could drive it up the stairs," he said. "We'd have to push it."

And the apartment door opened and Kelp stood there, waving a Glock. "Come in, come in," he said, as though *they'd* been the ones dawdling. "Prop the door open for the kid."

So they entered the living room and, as Dortmunder put a table lamp on the floor to block the door from closing, Tiny said to Kelp, "You have a gun. In your hand."

"The Asians Doug told us about," Kelp said. "One of them's here."

"Where?"

"Right now, asleep on the kitchen floor."

"An odd place to sleep," Tiny suggested.

"That's where we were," Kelp said, "when I hit him with the frying pan."

The kid, out of breath, barreled into the room and shoved the lamp out of the way of the door. "You have a gun," he told Kelp.

"I know that," Kelp said. "Come on, I don't wanna leave him alone."

So they trooped through a few more rooms, all as tasteful and anonymous as the living room and all, being interior rooms, comfortably air-conditioned. Dortmunder went second into the kitchen, following Kelp, and there on the floor, as advertised, was one of the largest Asian men he'd ever seen. Not in the Tiny league, but big enough so you wouldn't want to argue with him.

Dortmunder noticed the frying pan on the wooden

island in the middle of the room and said, "You hit him with that."

"Right."

"Is he alive?"

"Yeah," Kelp said. "I checked. I figure he'll be out for a while."

"So we should find the money," Tiny said, "and go."

"It'll be in some sort of safe," Dortmunder said, "disguised as something else." Looking around, he said, "I think it'll be in the kitchen."

Nobody else liked that idea. Tiny said, "Why?"

"Because," Dortmunder told him, "everybody will think it's in the bedroom."

"*I* think it's in the bedroom," Tiny said. "So I'll look in there, and you can look around at this kitchen here all you want."

"Thank you."

"And," Tiny said, "you two guys look around the rest of the place."

"I kind of like that living room," Kelp said.

"I have no opinion," the kid said, "so I'll just look around."

So the three of them left Dortmunder with the unconscious Asian. He considered the man. Find something to tie him up? No; the guy seemed really out, and the quicker they found the cash and got out of here the better. So, merely glancing from time to time at his silent companion, to be sure nothing had changed over there, Dortmunder considered the room.

It was a well-appointed kitchen. A wide double sink, with doors beneath fronting stored cleaning products. A big refrigerator, with two doors above, freezer on the bottom. A big six-burner gas stove with two ovens beneath, both of them really ovens. Two dishwashers, one large and one small, next to one another. Cabinets mounted on the walls above the counter, and more cabinets under the counter. A broom closet, full of brooms.

Dortmunder opened all the cabinet doors, and behind every one of them was a cabinet, most of them less than half full, a couple empty.

The island was a rectangular wooden block on wheels. He moved it to the side and studied the tile floor under it, and it was nothing but a tile floor. He opened both dishwashers and they were both dishwashers.

Had he been wrong? He'd just believed that people wanting to conceal a safe in this apartment would use the kitchen. It was little more than a matter of faith, but it was a faith he didn't want to give up.

He checked everything again. All the cabinets were cabinets, none with a false back. Refrigerator refrigerator. Freezer freezer. Dishwashers dishwashers. Stove stove. Broom closet broom closet.

Wait a minute. He opened both dishwashers for a third time, and this time he pulled out the top racks of both, and the top rack of the smaller dishwasher was only half as deep as the other.

Aha. He closed both dishwashers, tugged on the front of the smaller one, and nothing happened. He studied the controls on the front of the thing. One control turned it on and off, the other two dealt with the length and purpose of the cleaning cycles. Leaving the on/off off, he turned each of the other two controls forward and back, slowly, bent over the counter, listening very hard.

There. A satisfying little *click*.

Now he tugged on the front of the machine and it rolled out into the room, trailing wires and flexible pipe. And behind it, across the rear half of the space, was the front wall of the safe. A dial in the middle of that square face asked him if he knew the combination.

Not yet, but don't go away.

Dortmunder left the kitchen, moved through the apartment, and found the kid in the very soothing pastel-colored dining room, turning the large heavy dining room chairs one at a time upside down, staring at all those identical bottoms, and putting them back.

When Dortmunder walked in, the kid looked at him, maintaining his stoop, and Dortmunder said, "Get everybody. I found it. In the kitchen."

He didn't even bother to gloat.

45

Now they all deferred to Kelp. Seated cross-legged on the floor in front of the safe, the displaced dishwasher next to his left elbow, he removed various small tools from here and there in his jacket and arrayed them on the floor in front of himself.

Dortmunder said, "You know this kinda safe?"

"I would say," Kelp said, "the conversion in here was about fifteen years ago. That's when this kind of safe was popular. Well, it's still popular with me."

"Can you get in without leaving any marks?"

"It'll take a little longer that way, but sure. How come?"

"Let's see what's in there."

So Kelp donned his stethoscope, ooched himself a little further in under the counter, and, while pressing the stethoscope to the face of the safe, began slowly to turn the combination dial.

Clong. They all turned to look, and Tiny was putting the

frying pan back on the island. "He was stirring," he said.

"He shouldn't have done that," Dortmunder said.

"Quiet," Kelp said.

So they shut up and watched, and Kelp painstakingly did his turns and his listenings, then ooched back out from under the counter and said, "I think so. Let's see."

A handle stood to the left of the dial. Kelp grasped it and turned it down to the right, and the safe said *chack*, and yawned open.

"There we go." Kelp sounded pleased, but not full of himself.

"Nice job," Dortmunder said.

They all stooped to look in at the metal box, which was three-quarters full of greenbacks. They were all neatly banded into stacks, but the pile of stacks was thrown in there every which way, making it hard to get a sense of what they had.

"They're pretty messy, these guys," the kid said.

Dortmunder said, "When Doug described them, I thought they wouldn't be people to clean up after themselves a lot. Andy, what are they? Hundreds?"

Kelp reached in to root around among the stacks. "A lot of hundreds," he said. "Some fifties. Some twenties."

Tiny said, "Dortmunder, you have something in mind."

Dortmunder said, "We take half of it."

Nobody could believe that. Tiny said, "All that cash, and we leave half of it?"

"They don't know how much they've got in there," Dortmunder said. "Andy didn't mess up their safe. We were always gonna put that window back together anyway, so we do that. We take half, we put everything back the way it was, and there's no sign anybody was ever here except a little glass cutter line on the window nobody's ever gonna notice and the bump on that guy's head."

"Two bumps," said Tiny. "Three, if he stirs again."

Kelp said, "Your idea is, they don't know we found the money, so nobody's after us for anything."

"And," Dortmunder said, "we can still collect the other money from the reality people."

"I like this," Kelp said.

"Just a second," Dortmunder said, and turned to the under-counter cabinets, where he'd seen a clump of super-market plastic bags. He took out four, doubled them for more strength, and passed them to Kelp. "Take most of the hundreds," he said, "a lot of the fifties, and some of the twenties. Leave it still looking kinda full and very messy."

"You know," Kelp said, "I'm getting a little cramped under here."

"I'll do it," the kid said.

"Good."

Tiny lifted Kelp to his feet by his armpits. As the kid got into position to transfer bundles of cash to the plastic bags, Kelp said, "If we're gonna go ahead and finish the reality thing and take stuff out of the storage rooms, I've been thinking, I might have a guy to take it all off our hands."

Dortmunder said, "What kinda guy is this?"

"He does big box stores full of crap," Kelp said. "He can always take a consignment."

"What's his name?"

"He doesn't have a name, that anybody knows. He's called My Nephew."

"I've heard of this guy," Tiny said. "He's not somebody you ask to hold your coat."

"That's true," Kelp said. "On the other hand, he doesn't pay by check."

"How's that look?" the kid said.

On the floor beside him now, the two pairs of plastic bags bulged with cash. The interior of the safe, depleted, still contained a lot of cash, messily arranged.

"Good," Dortmunder said. Slowly, he smiled. "You know," he said, "every once in a while, things work out. Not exactly the way you thought they would, but still, they work out. Not bad."

When they counted it all later that night in Dortmunder's living room, counting it quietly because May was asleep elsewhere in the apartment, the total came to 162,450 dollars. After some quick computations, the kid informed them this meant 32,490 dollars apiece.

Definitely, a profitable evening on Varick Street. "I begin to believe," Dortmunder said, "that a jinx that has dogged my days for a long long time has finally broken." And, for the second time in one day, he smiled.

46

Doug's horrible Wednesday actually started pretty well. Marcy and the gang were adding story complications down on Varick Street, the other production assistants, Josh and Edna, were working under an open assignment to come up with other reality subject matter, the debacle that had been *The Stand* was now filed and forgotten, and the only reason to come into the midtown office at all was that's where he was expected to be. Also, although he would never have admitted it to anybody, he had the irrational but obsessive conviction that during the daylight hours the apartment was haunted, by people who had lost their jobs.

He was reading Josh and Edna's latest bad ideas—but they were trying—a little after eleven that morning when Lueen stuck her sardonic head into his office doorway to say, "Your master's voice."

"I serve no master but my art," Doug told her, but went off to see what Babe wanted.

Babe wasn't alone in the room. Seated facing him across the desk, back to the door, was someone Doug initially took to be a Sikh in a white turban. Babe nodded toward Doug and said to this gentleman, "Here's Doug Fairkeep now."

The man uncurled in a savage rising spin to his feet, shoulders hunched, fists clenched, the face he now showed Doug convulsive with rage. He's not going to punch me, Doug thought in terror, he's going to turn me into an oil spill.

Then the man's implacable forward momentum abruptly disappeared, like smoke, and he rocked back on his heels, opening his hands as he said, "That is not him."

Babe said, "That is Doug Fairkeep."

"He lied."

"The man last night, you mean. That's what I assumed."

First clearing his throat to be sure he still had a voice, Doug said, "Babe? What is this?" And he now could see that the man was not a Sikh in a turban but some sort of Asiatic in a thick bandage around his head.

"Mr Mg was staying on Varick Street last night," Babe said.

"Asleep," accused Mr Mg. He was still very angry at *somebody.*

"A man who apparently didn't know Mr Mg was there," Babe went on, "came in, turned on the light, said he was Doug Fairkeep and that he sometimes slept there when he missed his last train and—"

"Never," Doug said. "Never any of it."

"I know that, Doug."

"Never slept there. Never went in there on my own. Never take trains anywhere."

"Hit me with piece of iron," Mr Mg said.

Babe said, "Mr Mg was treated in the emergency room at St. Vincent's this morning, then came up here to tell us about it."

Doug said, "How'd he get in?"

"He did not break in," Mr Mg said.

"Doug," Babe said, "that's the part I don't get. Whoever this was, he has a way to get into Combined Tool without forcing anything."

"Babe," Doug said, "*I* can't do that. You're the only one I know can do that."

"Well, Mr Mg as well," Babe said. "Some other of our overseas associates."

I just told the gang about these Asians, Doug thought. He said, "Babe, do you think it was *The Heist* gang?"

"Of course I do," Babe said. "But how could they pull that off? You tell me."

"I can't," Doug said. "What'd they get?"

"Nothing," Babe said.

"I looked carefully," Mr Mg said. "Nothing is gone. The money I put in my suitcase earlier, still there."

Doug said, "And the, uh . . ."

"The safe?" Babe shook his head. "If they did look for it, they didn't find it."

"I examined," Mr Mg said. "Not touched."

"Well, that's good, at least," Doug said, and it was, because if they'd gotten the money Babe would have hounded them all, made their lives a living hell. Then he had another thought and said, "Was it reported to the police?"

"Nothing to report," Babe said, "Nothing taken, no breaking and entering."

"I do not talk with police," Mr Mg said.

Doug asked him, "What did you say in the emergency room?"

"Fall in shower. Twice."

"Oh. Well, I'm sorry, Mr Mg, I really am, but there's nothing I can do. Babe, is there anything I can do?"

"No, that's all right," Babe said. "Mr Mg just needed to see you, that's all."

"Well, here I am," Doug said. "Nice to meet you, Mr Mg. Safe flight."

He turned away, but Mr Mg said, "Doug Fairkeep."

Doug turned back. "Yes?"

Mr Mg nodded. "He knows your name," he said.

The next problem was even worse, and came in the form of a one-two punch. First the news came, in midafternoon, that with only the one show, *The Heist*, in production, and with nothing on the air, and with nothing in development, Get Real was being eliminated. Its assets would be folded in with its superior, Monopole, and all of the staff, except for Babe and Doug, would be let go.

Babe had come to Doug's office this time, to pass along this latest bad news, and was still there when Lueen extended her snakelike head into the doorway and said to Babe, more respectfully than she ever addressed Doug, "Mr Pockell on one, sir, for you."

Pockell was an executive with Monopole. Babe stood beside Doug's desk to take the call, saying, "Yes, sir," and then, in shock, "What?" and then, in horror, "Oh, no!" and then, in almost unheard-of panic, "I'll be right there."

He slammed down the phone and would have run from the office but that Doug said, "Babe? What's up?"

Babe halted, stared at Doug, and shook his head. "I don't think there's any way to save it this time," he said. "This comes down from *way* on high. Get Real has no more assets to fold into Monopole. *The Heist* is scratched."

47

DORTMUNDER, ignoring the lights, ignoring the boom mike dangling in midair above his head, ignoring the camera brushing his cheek, said, in his tough-guy grunt, "There's too much tunnel traffic by that place. You can't keep a getaway car hanging around there."

Kelp, also hulking over the backroom table, said, "But you gotta have a getaway car, or how do you get away?"

Tiny, who didn't have to do anything more than go on being himself, said, "If you're gonna steal a getaway car, while you're at it steal a pair of walkie-talkies."

Kelp said, "But people can listen in on those things. You got no privacy."

The kid, whose television persona was baby-face killer, said, "So talk in code."

Kelp said, "What code?"

The kid shrugged, "Red sails at sunset," he said, "means come pick us up now."

Dortmunder said, "If you're not gonna give the address, why do code?"

"Then don't do code," the kid said. "I don't care."

"Cut," said Roy, and when everybody turned to look at him he beamed upon them all and said, "Fine. Delovely. Everybody take a break now while we reposition the cameras and the walls." To Marcy, observing behind camera two, he said, "Very nice, Marcy. Played even better than I expected." Because Marcy was the one who'd worked out the bit about the walkie-talkies and the code.

Marcy blushed in gratitude and pleasure, and the kid led everybody in giving her a nice if ragged round of applause. She was really very helpful, Marcy, very useful to actors who weren't really actors.

"Okay," Roy said. To the crew he said, "Position three." To his cast he said, "Five minutes."

Dortmunder and the other performers rose and stretched and moved out of the backroom set as the crew came in to move everything around. It was funny how this worked, physically. You felt fine while you were doing it, just going along easy, no problem, but as soon as Roy called *cut* everybody was stiff and sore, yawning and scratching themselves. Maybe it had something to do with concentration, like when Kelp was examining a safe.

It was late afternoon now, and Roy would have time for only one more setup today. He was trying to fit a lot in because the schedule was that this was to be their last week at the back room or the hall, though the OJ set would stay up for more use later on.

Next week they'd be doing exteriors in this neighborhood. Since they'd use cameras hidden in cars and wouldn't mind filming civilians who happened to walk by while they were shooting, the term in the television business seemed to be that they were "stealing" the shots. Not exactly.

The gang and Rodney moved toward the comfortable chairs in the OJ set, and all at once the racket of the elevator sounded, receding from their level downward. It faded and stopped, and then started again, and neared, and very soon stopped again.

Kelp looked at Dortmunder. "Stopped on two," he said. Combined Tool.

"Be ready," Dortmunder advised.

"Oh, I am."

It had been agreed it would raise too many suspicions if Kelp were to plead illness or offer some other excuse not to show up here today, but if by chance last night's Asian were to enter the place he would recognize Kelp at once, so what Kelp would do, in that circumstance, was make himself scarce. "That gippy tummy again," he said, and shook his head.

They sat comfortably in the false OJ, Rodney distributing cans of Bud, but there wasn't much conversation. Most of them were waiting for the elevator to do something.

There: racket, racket, racket, getting nearer. "Watch my seat," Kelp said, and rose, and walked out of the OJ set.

The elevator racket got as loud as it was going to get, and then it quit, and then Kelp came walking back around the edge of the set, shaking his head. As he sat across the table from Dortmunder and in front of his beer, he said, "Not him. Other friends of ours," and around the corner came Doug and Babe.

From the instant they appeared, everybody could see

from their faces that there was trouble ahead. They both looked grim; death in the family grim.

Babe saw the expressions on the group watching him, nodded, and said, "Doug, get Roy in here, will you?"

"Sure," Doug said. He was carrying an attaché case, which he put on a nearby table.

"Oh, and Marcy."

"You know, Babe," Kelp said, as Doug went off on his errand, "every time you come here it's to shut us down."

"Those other times," Babe said, "I was acting out of anger, and I was wrong. This time, I'm following orders, and if those people are wrong, and I think they are, there's nothing I can do about it."

Doug came back, followed by Roy and Marcy, Roy not concealing his irritation and impatience, but also not noticing the atmosphere in the room. "Babe," he said, "I must say I have very little time here."

"Roy," Babe said, "I have to tell you, you don't have any time left at all."

Roy frowned. "What?"

"They're shutting us down," Babe said. "In fact, they're shutting the whole company down. As of now, Get Real no longer exists. This building will go to Monopole. The lease on the midtown offices will be given up. And *The Heist* will never be aired."

Roy said, "But you told us the bosses loved it."

"At Monopole," Babe told him, "they did. They were already looking for foreign sales. They sent it up to the level above them, Intimate Communications, and *those* people loved it so much they sent it on up to TUI, even though they didn't have to, not yet, and TUI ordered everything shut down."

275

Roy said, "Remind me. What's TUI?"

"Trans-Global Universal Industries. They're into a lot more than television production, and the CEO there now is a man named Gideon, who is a morality crusader. No porn, no excessive violence, no profanity, nothing you couldn't show a ten-year-old. A dull ten-year-old. Wholesome stories with wholesome morals tucked into their wholesome endings." Voice dripping scorn, Babe said, "*The Heist*, it seems, glorifies criminals."

"So what?" said Kelp.

"It does not," cried Roy. "It shows the human side of the criminal life. It shows the hard work, the thought—"

"Glorifies criminals," Babe said. "Once you've said those words, that's like a magic incantation, it's the end of the discussion."

Rodney the bartender said, "Because *The Heist* glorifies criminals, they're shutting down the whole company?"

"Well," Babe said, "*The Stand* is gone, and there's nothing else on deck, and Get Real was too expensive an operation not to have anything come out of it. So Doug and I are going to be working for Monopole, and the rest of the staff, I'm sorry to say, is out."

Marcy, sounding tremulous, said, "You mean I'm fired?"

Doug answered. "Nobody's fired, Marcy. It's just that none of those jobs exist any more."

"And now," Babe said, "I have a little more business to conduct with just the gang, so if everybody else could grab a seat somewhere outside, this won't take long, and we can all leave together."

Rodney the bartender said, "Am I in this, or out of this?"

"Just the gang," Babe told him.

The former Rodney removed his apron and dropped it on a chair. "It's been fun, folks," Tom LaBrava said, and he and Roy and Marcy, all downcast in their own separate ways, left the ersatz OJ for the final time.

Dortmunder said to Babe, "What about the human fly and Darlene?"

"They weren't going to be taping again until the exteriors next week," Babe said, "so we phoned them. They already know." He turned to Doug. "Doug?"

"Right," Doug said, and opened the attaché case he'd left on a table. "We have contracts with you guys," he said, "that called for a twenty-thousand-dollar payout per man, plus per diem, some of which has been paid." Taking papers from the case, he said, "These are forms in which you acknowledge the series has been canceled and will never be on the air, and you're accepting ten thousand a man in cash as full and final payment for your work on *The Heist*."

That's why they stopped at Combined Tool, Dortmunder told himself. They're about to give us some of the cash we left behind. And in a few weeks we'll go back and take a lot more, and not worry much about neatness. Glorify criminals. And?

Doug was now showing the cash in the attaché case and saying, "The forms are made out in the names you gave Sam Quigg, so just sign those same names. All that matters is it's really your handwriting."

This is a little too much like wages, Dortmunder thought, as he and the others went over to sit at that table and sign the forms in three places, initial in two, and receive ten thousand dollars in banded bundles of hundreds and fifties, which they then concealed on and about their persons.

Nobody was interested in long good-byes. The crew left their cameras and other equipment behind, and then the whole crowd gathered together onto the elevator for the final sink down to the ground floor.

As the garage door was being lifted, Dortmunder glanced at all those parked vehicles over there, some of which Stan would certainly be driving in the weeks ahead. So it hadn't been a total loss.

Out on the sidewalk, a limo appeared for Babe and Doug, to whisk them away. Roy and Tom LaBrava and the crew walked off with their right arms raised, looking for cabs. Tiny led the way toward the corner around which his own limo lurked.

Nearing that corner, Dortmunder looked back and saw that Marcy was still standing there in front of the building, at a loss. "That was too bad about Marcy," he said.

"Yeah, that's tough," Kelp agreed.

"She was really a great help to us."

"Yeah, she was."

They took another couple of steps and Dortmunder said, "We might could get together and give her some of what we got."

"There's an idea," Kelp said, and kept walking.

Dortmunder almost stopped, but then he too kept walking, on around the corner. "Oh, all right," he said.

Dreaming Up America

RUSSELL
BANKS

SEVEN STORIES PRESS

New York · London · Melbourne · Toronto

FIRST TRADE PAPERBACK EDITION NOVEMBER 2009

SEVEN STORIES PRESS
140 Watts Street
New York, NY 10013
www.sevenstories.com

In Canada:
Publishers Group Canada
559 College Street, Suite 402, Toronto, ON M6G 1A9 Canada

Library of Congress Cataloging-in-Publication Data

Banks, Russell, 1940-
Dreaming up America / Russell Banks.
—Seven Stories Press 1st ed.
p. cm.
ISBN 978-1-58322-838-8 (hardcover)
ISBN 978-1-58322-891-3 (paperback)
1. National characteristics, American.
2. United States—Civilization.
3. United States—History.
I. Title.
E169.1.B2218 2008
973—dc22
2008011099

Book design by Pollen, New York
Image research by David A. Zuckerman

College professors may order examination copies
of Seven Stories Press titles for a free
six-month trial period. To order, visit
www.sevenstories.com/textbook or fax on school
letterhead to (212) 226-1411.

Printed in the United States of America

9 8 7 6 5 4 3 2 1

contents

Author's Note
vii

Reel One
THE EARLIEST SIGNS OF
AN AMERICAN SENSIBILITY
1

Reel Two
THE POWER OF WORDS
19

Reel Three
CONQUEST OF THE IMAGINATION
37

Reel Four
OF MAN AND MACHINES
53

Reel Five
A VERY PECULIAR INSTITUTION
69

Reel Six
THE DARK SIDE ONLY GETS DARKER
89

Reel Seven
THE SHIFTING CENTER
101

Reel Eight
WHAT FOR, WHERE TO
115

List of iLLustrations

Pages xii and xiii
LOUIS HENNEPIN, MAP OF NORTH AMERICA, 1697
National Archives of Canada

Pages 16 and 17
PAUL REVERE, PRINT OF BRITISH TROOPS SHOOTING
AT CROWD IN BOSTON MASSACRE, CA. 1770
Library of Congress

Pages 34 and 35
THE BIRTH OF A NATION, D. W. GRIFFITH, 1915
Photofest

Pages 50 and 51
THE GRAPES OF WRATH, JOHN FORD, 1940
Photofest

Pages 66 and 67
HANGING OF CAPTAIN WIRZ, 1865
Library of Congress

Pages 86 and 87
THE GREAT DICTATOR, CHARLES CHAPLIN, 1940
Photofest

Pages 98 and 99
TOWN MILITIA, MARTINVILLE, ALABAMA, CA. 1925
Private Collection

Pages 112 and 113
THE SIEGE, EDWARD ZWICK, 1998
Photofest

Author's Note

Perhaps this should be called a "speaker's note," since *Dreaming Up America* began as a spoken text and not a written one. It was occasioned by an invitation to me and my fellow American novelist and friend, Jim Harrison, from a French documentary filmmaker, Jean-Michel Meurice. He wanted us to play talking heads in a film he was making for the French television channel, Arte. The film, Monsieur Meurice explained, was to be about American history as told by American cinema—from *The Birth of a Nation* to *Blackhawk Down*. Harrison and I were to construct a counter-narrative and between us provide a two-hour corrective to the version of American history that French people were most familiar with, that is, the cinematic version. Its title was to be *Amérique notre histoire.*

Jean-Michel Meurice is a charming man who speaks better English than either Harrison or I speak French, and we agreed to participate in this project, not because we were particularly eager to correct the French view of "notre histoire," but because he invited us next time we were in France to visit his home on the Mediterranean near Toulouse, where he promised to cook his legendary bouillabaisse using mussels and oysters harvested that very morning. He also appealed to our literary egos by insisting that our versions of American history, as novelists, would be superior to any historians' versions. We did not disabuse him of this notion.

It would take only a single day of our time, he added, and he would bring his crew to the United States and film us in our homes, me in Saratoga Springs, New York, Harrison in Montana. We would be seated against a blue screen, while Jean-Michel himself stood off camera and asked each of us separately a series of questions that were designed to let us ruminate and, if we wished, to fulminate on specific aspects of American history. Clips from the films were to be cut into the documentary later. His questions would be edited out, à la Ken Burns, so that Harrison and I would appear to be sitting across from each other at a table waxing garrulous, while scenes from *Across the Wild Missouri,*

Captain Blood, and *Sergeant York* played behind us. "You may digress, if you wish, and bring to the subject whatever comes to your mind," he said. Not a wise invitation to a novelist, when you've only got two hours of film time available.

On a raw morning in February, Jean-Michel and his crew arrived in Saratoga Springs and for eleven hours filmed my responses to his brief, open-ended questions. Film is an ongoing dream, and history is another kind of dream, regressive, perhaps, like memory. In this case, both dreams were generated by the same reality, America, and the collision between them stimulated me more than I had anticipated. The typed transcript of my responses to Jean-Michel's questions turned out to be nearly one hundred pages long, which, using a French voice-over, he ultimately edited down to about a half-hour of film time.

My French publisher, Marie-Catherine Vacher at Actes Sud, read the entire transcript and had it translated by Pierre Furlan, who translates most of my fiction into French. In October 2006, in conjunction with Arte Editions, it was published as *Amérique notre histoire*, released at the same time as Jean-Michel's documentary. The book and the film were well received, and as there are now several other translated versions of the book in the works—Spanish, Italian, and so on, there seemed no reason not to publish it in the original English. I'm grateful to Dan Simon and his Seven

Stories Press for their willingness to take it on. For the American edition, I expanded on some of the ideas and eliminated some of the redundancies, but not all, since we wanted to preserve the flavor of a spoken text. Which brings me back to my opening remark, that this is a speaker's note as much as it is an author's note. I must beg the reader's indulgence, therefore, of certain stylistic infelicities that would pass unnoticed if uttered by a talking head in a documentary film, especially one that lasted the nearly eleven hours that it would take to speak the entire text. Perhaps Jean-Michel Meurice did me a favor by leaving all but a half-hour of the transcript on the cutting-room floor. If so, then I direct you to the DVD of *Amérique notre histoire.*

Dreaming up America

MAP OF NORTH
AMERICA, 1697

THE EARLIEST SIGNS OF
AN AMERICAN SENSIBILITY

B EFORE WE start to think or talk seriously about our American values, there are a few things I want to say about the first colonists, the first Europeans residing in North America. We have to remember that they came from different parts of Europe and that they came to North America with very different ideas about what they wanted to do here. The English colonists came to New England in search of religious freedom, with a fundamentalist Protestant vision of their own mission and with their own religious and political agenda. The Dutch came to the area where I live—New York, Manhattan, the Hudson Valley—strictly for commercial reasons, to fish and to trade for beaver and lumber, not for reasons of religion or freedom or politics. The Spanish sailed into the Caribbean, to Florida, to the coast of the Gulf of Mexico, and into Mexico for gold, and had no particular ambitions to make a community or colony.

There were all these different motives and very different values associated with each of them. At the very beginning of the colonization of America—which we'll do well to remember wasn't the same as the beginning of America, since the place these Europeans "discovered" was inhabited already—these differences between the English, the Dutch, and the Spanish established at the start a world of potential conflict between the spiritual intentions of those fleeing inhospitable European societies on the one hand, and the commercial ambitions of those seeking profitable opportunities on the other. Was America going to be a haven, a miraculous place where you could build a Protestant City on a Hill? Or was it a vast continent ripe for pillage and exploitation, a bottomless storehouse to loot for the enrichment of Europe—Spain, Holland, France, and England?

So when we speak of the values of the first colonists, we cannot lump them together. It depends on who we're talking about. *Which* colonists? And since for various reasons they grouped themselves together geographically, it also depends on *where* we're talking about. Is it the southern United States, the coastal regions along the Gulf of Mexico and the Caribbean? If so, the dominant values driving early settlement were coldly materialistic and exploitative. If we're talking about the middle colonies like Virginia, Maryland, New York, and Pennsylvania, then the dominant interests were more narrowly commercial: trading, fishing, lumber, tapping the region for its products. And in New England from the time of the earliest colonists, issues of religion and of creating a new spiritual haven were front and center, not simply the accouterments of commerce or exploitation.

Gradually, of course, those ambitions began to merge. In the South you saw materialist ambitions justified by religious and spiritual aspirations and principles. In New England you saw spiritual and religious ambitions begin to fade as the colonists seized the opportunity to exploit the region's natural resources economically. So that by the early eighteenth century enough blending had occurred for Americans, the colonists, to no longer think of themselves as Europeans. By then the braiding together of the two strands had begun to form a national culture, a shared sense of national values. But at bottom these were still conflicting values. And I think that as we move forward in this discussion we'll see the inherent conflict between those two sets of values come up again and again and again.

I spoke of the point at which the pioneers stopped feeling European. But I don't know that they ever felt

European as such. When they first arrived on our shores, their separate national identities were stronger than any single overarching European sense of identity. In the sixteenth and seventeenth centuries, the Spanish colonists felt Spanish more than they felt European. The French felt French more than European. And the English felt English, not at all European. So we have to make that distinction at the beginning. The question is, at what point did the English colonists stop feeling English? At what point did the Spanish colonists stop feeling Spanish, and the French stop feeling French? It didn't all happen at the same time. And what's interesting is that the types of governance that were established for each country's colonies helped determine how they identified themselves initially and the pace at which their new American identities evolved.

The English managed to set up administrative structures that provided a great deal of local autonomy, in New England particularly. And in Virginia and throughout all the English colonies, there were local legislative bodies, local governors and public officials who operated rather independently from the mother country, whereas the Spanish and the French still ruled much more closely from home. In Quebec and in the French colonies, for instance, and even in Maryland, which existed briefly as a French colony, and in Louisiana, when the French ruled, they ruled from home, as if their colonies were branch offices, whereas the English decentralized authority to a much greater extent, as if their colonies were franchises.

Therefore most New Englanders by the mid- to late seventeenth century, the 1680s and '90s, felt more American than English. They stopped feeling English much earlier than the French and Spanish stopped feeling French and Spanish. In Quebec, for instance, where even today they feel more French than Canadian, there's still that pull from the mother country, and I think this was also true at the time for the Spanish and the Dutch. It's an interesting question, but once again it shows us that you can't generalize about the early colonists unless you acknowledge their multiple places of origin. We don't just have one mother country. We have many dueling mothers who all play a significant role in creating us.

And of course African origins were very important in this period. There were vast numbers of Africans present from the start, in the South particularly, but throughout the colonies. After all, until the 1830s there were slaves in New England, slaves in New York and New Jersey. It wasn't just in the South that Americans owned slaves. So we have to consider the influence of African values, African culture. It's just below the surface at the start, necessarily so, but it's there. The African factor was profoundly operative, and it was influential to an extreme degree on the dominant white culture, especially in the South, so we have to acknowledge that strand, too. The very same culture that would have its flourishing in the twentieth century with the blues, with jazz, and in the visual and language arts, was already a force in the eighteenth century and especially throughout the nineteenth century when Africans made up a significant portion of the American population.

Was there an early form of the American Dream? I can't say there was *one* American Dream. There were several dreams to begin with. There was El Dorado, the City of Gold that Cortez and Pizarro dreamed of finding. And then there was Ponce de Leon's dream of the Fountain of Youth, where you could start life over again, and the New England Puritan dream of God's Protestant utopian City on a Hill, the New Jerusalem. There were at least three distinct dreams in the beginning.

The religious dream of the City on the Hill, where you could live a life that was pure and uninfected by European cosmopolitanism, was almost a pastoral dream, one in which you could become a natural human being living a holy life under the eye of God. And you could only do it here, in the New Jerusalem. You couldn't do it in corrupt old Europe. It was only possible in the New World.

The dream of the City of Gold, where you discovered untold wealth, was a dream of glory in the service of the Old World. You melted down the gold, poured it into bullion, and shipped it back to enrich the crowned heads of Europe. It was a powerful material dream, and it was this dream that became the model for the exploitation of the New World, although it was the least transformative of the three.

The dream of the Fountain of Youth may yet prove to be the strongest of the three, since it carries within it the sense of the new, the dream of starting over, of having a New Life. It's essentially the dream of being a child again, and it's the dream that persists more strongly than the other two and is today perhaps the most vivid of the three. We can think of there being three braided strands, or perhaps three mutually reinforcing dreams: one is of a place where a sinner can become virtuous, free from the decadence of the secular cosmopolitanism of old Europe; another is of a place where a poor man can become wealthy; and a third is of a place where a person can be born again.

The three together are much more powerful than any one of them alone. And they are there at the inception, at the very beginning of colonial America, side by side at first, specific to the three separate regions, but gradually merging. By the late seventeenth and early eighteenth centuries they come together, just as the colonies themselves begin to come together. As the northern colonies in New England begin to attach themselves to the middle colonies—New York, Pennsylvania, Maryland, Virginia—and then the southern colonies—

South Carolina, North Carolina, Georgia—begin to draw together, and as the English more or less achieve military and economic control and establish a kind of cultural hegemony across the eastern seaboard, you see the three dreams merge.

Forging America's idea of itself

AS AMERICANS from New England moved west into Ohio and Wisconsin and into the far northwestern territories, the first building they put up in every newly settled village was a white church with a steeple. The second building was the town hall, where everyone voted. In other words, the two pillars they carried with them were their form of representative government and along with that the notion that God was central to the community. The third building was the schoolhouse. The fourth was probably the bank. No brothels or saloons till much later, of course.

Religious fundamentalism and the idea of God are as central to our social and political organization as our vaunted democratic institutions. It has to do with the particular Protestant sects that settled in New England in the seventeenth century and made God central to the political organization there. It was not made central anywhere else—not by the French in Quebec and the north of New England, and not by the Spanish in Florida and the Caribbean. Catholic priests accompanied the Spanish and French colonists, yes, but they were not central to the political life in the same way as the Protestant ministers were in New England. So that's where I think it begins, the notion that God is an American. It begins in New England. And the degree to which the seventeenth- and eighteenth-century New England village is the primary source and model for our American social democracy and provides the template for representative government in America, the degree to which that form of democracy came to be practiced across all the thirteen colonies, is the degree to which God is central to American political thinking and American political and social discourse. It's the main mark of the ascendancy of the New England form of political comity.

Which brings us to the question of taxes. Why did the issue elicit such a strong response, such a violent reaction, in 1776? I don't think it was a simple matter of taxes per se. It was taxation without representation. That's how it was phrased. They weren't simply rebelling against taxes. They were rebelling against control from abroad by the English Parliament and Crown. By the late eighteenth century—the 1750s, '60s, '70s—New

Englanders had gotten used to representing themselves in their own towns, their own counties, their own colonies. They elected their own officials, passed their own regulations, and taxed themselves. In other words, they had already by then cut the umbilical cord between the mother country and the colonial child, and in this they were far ahead of the other colonies.

Remember, politically speaking, the American Revolution has its ideological and intellectual roots mainly in New England. But in economic terms, it finds its energy and roots in the South, in Virginia and Maryland and the Carolinas. There, to the landed gentry and the slave holders, given the size and scale and wealth of the plantation system in the South, it made economic sense to become a distinct nation independent of the mother country. As inevitably happens, when the wealth produced by a colony seems to be returning from the source to the mother country, the colonials feel cheated. To no small degree, they were right to feel cheated.

So again there was a mixed set of motives—more idealistic, ideological, and political motives in the North, and more commercial and economic in the South. But they served each other's needs. The North gave the South the ideological, intellectual, and political rationale for independence. The South gave the North the economic means and justification, and the belief that, should the colonies unite, they could survive independently without the mother country. That's why they pulled together. Simply, the South couldn't survive independence without the North; the North couldn't survive without the South. So these thirteen separate and disparate colonies managed to unite out of both practical and ideological reasons. From there they managed to pull off an extraordinary war of independence and successfully separate themselves from what was, at the time, the most powerful nation on earth.

Was our War of Independence a revolt or a revolution? I think it was a true revolution, because it articulated, for the first time and for all to use, the most radical concept of democracy then on the planet: the idea of representative government—governance obtained without a monarchy of any sort, without a nobility, without any rank of nobility; governance by and for the governed. Though it took a decade before the French managed to apply that radical concept to their own situation, it should be noted that the vocabulary and ideals for the American Revolution come straight out of the European Enlightenment. America's so-called founding fathers, Thomas Paine, Thomas Jefferson, Ben Franklin, James Madison, and so on, took their vocabulary from European Enlightenment thinking. They articulated it on the ground and institutionalized it in Philadelphia in 1776 and again in 1787 in our founding and guiding documents: the Declaration of Independence and the United States Constitution. It was a revolutionary concept at that time, a radical break with the European notion of comity and authority. Yes, it was to some degree, by today's standards, an elitist movement. Most successful political movements are. The ideas and the expression of those ideas came from the top down. And yes, only white men with property were qualified to vote. Several million slaves were excluded from this process. Women were excluded. And in the dispensation of proportional representation in Congress, each slave was to count as three-fifths of a person, which gave the South a numerical bulge sufficient to balance against the more populous North. So by definition it was elitist many times over. But at the same time it was established that there would be no nobility and no monarchy, giving life to what was essentially a populist notion. Imbedded in the words chosen carefully by those white men were concepts of freedom and inclusion that would in time carry weight and intentions far beyond anything the founding fathers may have intended. If we go back to that moment in time, to 1787 when the Constitution was ratified, we have to admit that those early Americans produced some very radical documents. We have to wait until a decade later, in France, to see anything as radical as that again. The French gave the Americans the vocabulary, the Americans created the institutions to express that vocabulary, and then the French took the institutions back a decade later. The Americans took the theory, made it pragmatic and applied it, and then the French brought the applications back home and, in a more radical form, put them to use there—a cycle that's characteristic of both cultures, one we've seen over and over in many different fields of human endeavor. And today, two and a quarter centuries later, we are still waiting for the inspiring words in those radical documents to have their full effect.

⟡

AMERICANS HAVE tended to misread and understate how difficult and long was the war against the British army, because the Civil War, when it was over, quickly became a great distorting screen or scrim for us. When you read documents, including letters and so forth, written by Americans *before* the Civil War, where they're looking back towards the Revolution barely half a century earlier, Americans viewed the Revolutionary War with greater clarity of thought and with greater understanding of its costs and sacrifices, its duration and difficulty, than they did after the Civil War. The Civil War threw such a huge shadow across America and the American imagination that it was difficult, after the war, to look back and imagine what it must have been like to conduct and finally win that Revolution, that seven-year war against the British.

Our War of Independence was fought by untrained soldiers, laymen, farmers, and mechanics, led by young men in their twenties and thirties, with very few supplies and arms, against the largest, best-trained, most professional army in the world. Through the tactical brilliance of George Washington and several others— and the support of the French, and the Marquis de Lafayette, and other Continental Europeans as well— they were able to prevail. It was extraordinary. And it was not at all inevitable or even likely. It wasn't something that you could have predicted at the time. And right up to the very end of the war it looked as though the Americans would not prevail.

Speaking of the Marquis de Lafayette, he lived a very long life, and in 1824, about ten years before he died, he returned to the United States for a triumphal tour to all the places he had been during the war, starting in New York and making his way to the South, the middle Atlantic states, north to Boston, and all the way up the Hudson River to Saratoga, where I live for much of the year. In each place he was greeted like a conquering hero. No foreigner at that time, and perhaps no foreigner since, has ever come to America and been received with such jubilation and excitement and vast crowds as when Lafayette returned. What that shows us is that a whole generation later he was still seen as a grand hero, a hero of the first order. That's how powerful the memory of the war and the image of Lafayette's role in it were in the American imagination in the years leading up to the Civil War. But if Lafayette had lived long enough to show up today in New York, or at any time after 1861, he wouldn't draw a very big crowd. Only a couple of curiosity seekers and history buffs would turn out to see him. He'd be disappointed. The role of Lafayette, and with it the memory and true meaning of the Revolutionary War, have diminished to the point where they are lost now, mostly forgotten, part of a past to which we're no longer connected.

The BLOODY MASSACRE perp

BRITISH TROOPS
SHOOTING AT
CROWD IN BOSTON
MASSACRE, CA.
1770

in King——t Street B———— on March 5 1770 by a party of the 29th. REGt.

BUTCHER'S HALL

Engrav'd Printed & Sold by PAUL REVERE Boston

THE POWER OF WORDS

R ALPH ELLISON, the great American novelist, refers to the Declaration of Independence and the Constitution as "our sacred documents," as if they were biblical, as if they were divinely ordained. And Americans generally do view the Constitution and the Declaration of Independence essentially as divinely ordained and sacred in some way. Perhaps it's because of the poetic, almost biblical language of the Declaration of Independence, and because of the institutions embodied in the Constitution. They sound more biblical than legalistic. Those two documents, more than any other writings, unite the elements at war in the American imagination and American culture, and in the divided American public—the warring elements being racial, cultural, economic, regional, and historic.

I spoke earlier about a few of these conflicts. It is only through the Declaration of Independence—the extraordinary brilliance of it, both the precision and the vagaries of it—and the beautiful, delicate balancing act that the Constitution lays out between the three branches of the government—the executive, the representative, and the judicial—that we're able to bring together these conflicting elements that lie at the heart of the American imagination and the American past. I think it's by means of an intuitive recognition of that fact that we Americans regard the documents as sacred. Even Ralph Ellison, a black novelist in the mid-twentieth century, a man who knew better than most how far we still have to go before they will be in full effect, could nonetheless refer to them as "our sacred documents," for they embodied the guiding principles of all Americans, his as much as mine.

It's fascinating to contrast the United States Constitution with the constitutions of our individual fifty states. Each state has its own constitution, usually a litany of laws. It's the same with most national constitutions—the new constitution of Iraq, or the French Constitution, for example. They're deliberately oriented to a specific people, place, and time. But the American Declaration of Independence has a poetic loftiness that universalizes its ambitions. It speaks of mankind as much as of Americans. And the institutions laid out in the American Constitution are so decorously balanced that it manages to universalize our country's political structure, too. Both of our founding documents really are extraordinary acts of creative genius.

AMERICA WASN'T always nationalistic, consistently and purely, the way we have become in the late twentieth and early twenty-first centuries. There was the tumult of conflicting impulses, especially leading up to the Civil War, when roughly as many Americans wanted to break away from a unified national identity as wanted to extend that national identity. Southerners wanted to split off early on and go their own way, hoping to pull Cuba and the Caribbean into their sphere of influence. Northern New Englanders at different times wanted to join Canada. Texas set itself up as a separate nation in the 1840s, and California was briefly a separate nation.

It was really only after the Civil War that the United States became America the nation-state. There was a shift there in terminology, too, moving from being the United States of America to "America," from being a fairly loose consortium of separate but united states, pulled apart at times, pulling together at others, into something that was a single word: America. Which is a very different kind of creature than the United States. It's more nearly mythical and points a bony finger back to the European discovery of the continent, remaking that "discovery" in its image, no longer true to the facts of the matter in all their complexity. It was the Civil War that turned our flickering national identity into a sacred flame. And that was reinforced in the twentieth century when America became a player on the world stage, starting with the Spanish American War, as we call it, which involved the taking over of Cuba and the Philippines and expelling the Spanish from their sphere of influence in the Caribbean.

In the twentieth century, when America became a central player on the world stage, our national identity got another push, right through the century and up to the Cold War. Of course at the end of the Cold War, America emerged as the single dominant power in the West, however brief our star turn may be. By then our national impulses were running at full throttle. But we do well to remember that this was never all that we were. The separate impulses that have driven us drive us still. Keep in mind that we began fleeing and resisting empire, and our national identity didn't start out strong—in fact, it started very weak—so it may not be our true nature after all, and surely it is not permanent.

WITH THE rise of nationalism, of course, has come all the other forms of idiocy that reinforce the identification with, and worship of, the state. That danger always lies at the heart of nationalism. Racial purity, the notion of religious purity, cultural hegemony—these sick social needs emerge almost inevitably and everywhere from nationalism. W. H. Auden called nationalism a disease, and it is a disease. You can see it clearly in films, because the advent of the American film industry early in the twentieth century happens to coincide with the ascendance of nationalism in America. The first great American film is *The Birth of a Nation*, which equates the birth of our nation with the achievement of racial purity in the era of Reconstruction, the 1870s to the 1890s. The bloody, brutal work of the Ku Klux Klan is a horrific, shameful episode in our history, yet right there in our first cinematic self-portrait it's presented without apology. It's even made a point of pride. It cannot be ignored that *The Birth of a Nation* is an extraordinary film—one that's loathsome ethically, and that's politically and spiritually loathsome as well, and yet artistically it's great. It's like a Leni Riefenstahl Nazi propaganda film, yet it's also the fountainhead of what is perhaps the most extraordinary art form to be developed in the twentieth century.

So our words—the words of our founding documents—have had their work cut out for them. Not only must they stand against the disease of nationalism, and the dreams of glorious wealth through exploitation, they must also withstand the visual siren song of what has become our mythmaking industry in Hollywood and elsewhere, which has occasionally been subversive, but more often serves the pleasure of the powers that be.

Again and again in America today the beliefs of Christian fundamentalists—which are not only biblical but full-on apocalyptic, including as they do the nearness of the End Time and the Second Coming of Christ—are an increasingly large component of the American character. The fundamentalist vision, representing now a very wide swath of the American people, those who have not been embraced by any other orthodoxy, who live in "fly-over" country and are not the consumers or even the citizens that media mavens and opinion-makers in New York, Los Angeles, Washington, DC, and San Francisco like to think about, hearkens back to that inherent conflict I was speaking of earlier, between the institution of slavery and the promises of the Declaration of Independence and the Constitution, between the

Plantation and New Jerusalem. It took a civil war to resolve the conflict between the materialistic, racist reality of slavery and the essentially spiritual language of the Declaration of Independence and the Constitution, an inherent conflict that could only be resolved by means of the most costly war, in terms of human life, in our history. And it continued to be fought long after the war was over, through the years of Reconstruction, which *The Birth of a Nation* portrays, well into the twentieth century, all the way up to the 1960s and the civil rights movement. We—we white people—thought the conflict was resolved, in legal terms, and also in emotional and psychological terms. The promise fulfilled. But the truth is, it still hasn't been. The question of who can claim to bear our spiritual mantle as Americans still has not been answered.

The narrative of race

THERE IS an argument, generally coming from the Right, most persistently from the South, that the Civil War was fought over states' rights. And in a sense that's true. There was a central political issue, a constitutional issue, to be settled. But the states' right they were fighting for was the right to own slaves, the right to own other human beings. If it had been the right to tax themselves or raise their own militia or set aside public lands, no one would have gone to war over it. But it was the right to own slaves. So at the heart of it, the Civil War was a conflict about race, and that conflict lies at the heart of American history. Race is our great central story. Our ur-narrative. Everything returns to it, because in it is contained the larger question of where we stand in relation to our God and whether in the end we are moral animals or not. This is why a founding document that contains language that addresses this issue can be sacred in the same way to a black American and a white American.

The narrative of race began when the first Europeans arrived off the shores of the Caribbean islands and Florida, off the shores of Jamestown, Virginia, and off the shores of New England, where they met the dark-skinned people who happened to reside here already, people whom the Europeans chose to deal with in the majority of cases as less than human, treating them instead as human chattel, as being less worthy of natural respect and kind treatment than draft animals like horses or cattle. The rationale was twofold: first, that the economic usage or exploitation of them wouldn't have made sense unless they could be seen as lesser creatures, and second, because they were not Christians.

So from the very beginning, racial differentiation was situated at the hot center of the American imagination. And it's still there. It's still central. Our most terrible wars have been fought over it. Our most important political conflicts have been waged over it. Nearly every political campaign comes down to it, even today. Our economic lives are shaped by it. Our views of the rest of the world are determined by it. How we treated Southeast Asians in the latter part of the 1960s and early '70s, how we're dealing today with the Arab world, how we treat Africans—it all comes down to race in some fundamental way. I don't mean to sound overly reductive, but when you lift the rock of American society and you look under it, you almost always see race. It's at the dark heart of our conflicted nature. We are in a sense a schizophrenic people. I don't mean that we have a split identity, but we have a deeply conflicted, self-canceling identity. We're at war with ourselves. And this explains, I think, why we so often march off to war against others—as horrific as foreign wars are, they are much easier for us at home than it would be to face the internal battles of being at war within ourselves. Anything to avoid the war within ourselves that is still actively forging our identity, a war whose outcome hasn't been decided yet; and until it is, we won't really know who we are. That is what people mean, I think, when they say that we are still a young nation.

⟨ornament⟩

THERE IS no American Revolutionary War work of fiction that everyone has read. And so our Revolutionary War isn't alive in the American imagination. Interestingly, there is an English book about the French Revolution that everyone's read or seen the movie adaptation of, and that's Charles Dickens's *A Tale of Two Cities*. Because of it, the French Revolution as a symbol of popular violence is very much alive in the American imagination. The vision of The Terror comes from England to the United States in the nineteenth century, and it sticks. It's a fearsome image to us. I don't think Americans really have any particular historically informed view of the French Revolution. We don't know very much about it, and most of us probably couldn't even date it. Nor do Americans have a visceral idea of our own revolution, of the suffering or the violence involved; instead it has been sugar-coated and cerebralized almost to the point where people think of it as nothing more than a great big roundtable discussion about freedom and representation, instead of the knock-down drag-out brawl of guerrilla warfare through shifting alliances and class conflict between rich and poor that it really was. And the closest thing we have to that sense of upheaval isn't our own revolution, but instead the French one, which thanks to Dickens has been represented to Americans imagistically by the movies and in literature. And it's an image that terrifies people who feel somewhat unstable to begin with. If you feel slightly unsure of what the proper role of citizens should be, and you see this vision of democracy unleashed—mob rule, terror, class war—then you react with fear. I really do blame it all on Dickens. If it were not for that novel and the film made of the novel, I don't think Americans would view the French Revolution any differently than the way that we do the Russian Revolution. And the Russian Revolution, even though it brought Communism into the world and was a hundred times more brutal, doesn't terrify us.

The Russian Revolution strikes us as merely fascinating, whereas the French version strikes us as threatening, and our very own revolution somehow doesn't strike us as fascinating *or* threatening. Quite the opposite. Boring and comforting. And I believe that in the vividness of the French Revolution to us, in the vividness and the emblematic power of it, you can see something that is very much alive today in America, though not much talked about, which is our fear of democracy taken to its extreme. We who are educated and opinionated and lead comfortable lives here in the US, where the quality of life for the middle class and the upper class provides, despite looming problems, opportunities for a secure, self-aggrandizing way of life, we fear the loss of social control that extreme democracy represents. We don't fear Communism, Leninism, or even Stalinism as much. The notion of an oppressive and restrictive totalitarian society doesn't have the same chilling vividness for us as the chaos of pure democracy, and that we associate with the French Revolution.

THE FIRST American immigrants, not counting the colonists, came over unwillingly: they were the enslaved Africans, who didn't come here out of any volition of their own. But they were still, after all, immigrants. And they were the first to arrive in large numbers from more or less the same region of the world, which happened to be West Africa, rather than Europe, so we have to count them and must remember that when we talk about waves of immigrants the Africans were the first. I think too often we don't want to consider them as such, and in denying them their identity as immigrants from someplace else, we assign to them the identity of slaves and the descendants of slaves. But slavery wasn't their identity, it was their circumstance. It was not who they were, but what was done to them.

After the Africans, huge numbers of immigrants from Europe started to arrive in the middle of the nineteenth century, first a great many thousands from Germany, but then mostly immigrants from northwest Europe—white Protestant Christians who were relatively easily assimilated, even if they weren't middle class. And then came the Irish, who were mostly poor and Catholic, coming to a Protestant country, as it was then, a literate country, and they were for the most part illiterate. They arrived in great numbers in the 1840s in flight from extreme poverty, just seeking the fundamentals—food, shelter, clothing—seeking little more than a chance to survive and, if they were lucky and plucky, to thrive. And that became more or less the pattern for a long period of time, seventy-five or more years. The Chinese arrived from Asia in as great a number as the Irish. Then came the Eastern Europeans, the Jews, the Poles, Italians, Greeks, and so on.

In each case they brought with them their own cultural norms from their country of origin, which they then tried to integrate with the norms of the Americans already in residence here, with greater or lesser degrees of success. It was more difficult when the immigrants' religious practices were different—Catholic instead of Protestant; Buddhist, Muslim, Confucian, or Hindu instead of Christian—or when the immigrants were seen as racially different.

There is an interesting book called *How the Irish Became White* by the historian Noel Ignatiev. It describes the parallels between the essentially racist early portrayals of the Irish in American newspapers, in American writing and in early films—as a sexually reckless, self-indulgent, musically inclined, happy-go-lucky people—and the way that African Americans were portrayed in the same period, and even until recently. The same kinds of stereotypes and prejudices were applied to both groups.

When I was growing up in the 1940s and '50s, my father and other Anglo-American men of his generation used to refer to Italians as "Guineas." I never knew what a Guinea was until I was an adult and saw that it was a nineteenth-century word for Africa, and thus for Africans. What that means to me is that as recently as the 1950s, Italians and other Mediterraneans were seen as racially different from us white folks. Even as a kid I thought this was very weird. But we Americans use racial stereotypes in order to talk about anyone who is different in any way—culturally different, religiously different, linguistically different. It doesn't matter. We'll find a way to enshrine the difference in racial terms.

This goes back to what I was saying earlier about the obsession with race in the American imagination. Each wave of immigrants has had to deal with this American obsession. Even when they were white, they had to deal somehow with the ancient and profound racial anxiety that lies at the center of the American psyche. Jews coming from Eastern Europe certainly felt it. Greeks felt it, Italians felt it, and today Hispanics feel it. Black Americans felt it for the longest time and may have the deepest understanding of it. Our racial anxiety could be amusing, it's so ridiculous, if the way it has been inflicted on people weren't so horribly cruel and brutal.

THE BIRTH OF A
NATION, 1915

CONQUEST OF
THE IMAGINATION

M OST IMMIGRANTS who arrived in the USA had no intention of going home. Only the Cubans have thought of going home in some imaginary post-Castro era, as if that one man were a historical aberration, rather than part of that country's long march towards revolution, and his death will return their country to some pre-revolutionary state. But when other immigrants came to America, not only did they invent a new life, moving in powerful, irreversible ways to start life over, they also ended their old lives. They cut themselves off from old languages, cultural associations, ethnic and religious ties, and created new ones. It's very important to understand this process if we're going to grasp how the US was able, over the last 150 years or so, to absorb wave after wave of very different kinds of people. It didn't matter whether they came from Korea, India, South America, Greece, Africa, Poland, or Ireland—that same process operated. A new identity was embraced, an old identity was discarded. The interesting exception, as I said, has been the Cubans, who put themselves in a holding pattern. In their minds, when Castro dies they'll return home. Consequently, they haven't assimilated. Mexicans in Manchester, New Hampshire; Nicaraguans in Portland, Oregon; Vietnamese in Houston, Texas, have been assimilated; but Cubans in Miami have not. They've kept their bags packed.

In Europe over the last twenty-five to forty years, the migrations have mostly been from Islamic countries, and Europeans are dealing not so much with immigrants, as with migrants who have a dream of going back and who, like the Cubans, strive to maintain the ties and cultural connections to the mother nations, their places of origin. And that has made it much more difficult to embrace the newcomers, as we have seen over recent years particularly.

I can't say exactly why it's been so difficult in Europe otherwise, except to say that this may not be exceptional. It may be the rule. And it may be that the American example, as it has stood for the last one and three-quarters centuries, may be the exception. For the fact is that when people come to the US they are coming to a place where the mythology of starting over is so powerful as to be, paradoxically, the very essence of what it means to be American. Throughout most of our history this has been the draw. You didn't just come here to make money to send home until you yourself could return. America was not simply a place to find employment; it was a place to start your life over. It goes back to that very early version of the American Dream that we were trying to describe. Central to the original American Dream is the idea of starting over. It was economic, too, yes. You could improve your financial life and your lot in life. And it was also a virtuous place. You could live free and with dignity, certainly. That too was part of the myth. But along with those material and spiritual aspects there was also the central myth of starting your life anew, of being a child again—remember the Fountain of Youth. That's a very powerful lure. And it worked. It really does work. Because if you're going to start over, you have to kill the past, and Americans are great at killing the past.

LOOKING AGAIN at books, at literature—because I feel the books that last open a window into the soul of our people—so many of our favorite novels and films are about acquiring a new identity, about changing one's life. Go west, young man or woman! Go south! Light out for the territory! Hit the road, Jack. Change your identity, reject your past, and become a new person. Not necessarily a powerful person, although that's always a possibility in America, but a new person. The novels and the films of the open road are all about that. It's a kind of film and novel that's specific to America— getting in a car and going west, or getting in a covered wagon and going west, or getting on a raft and going down the river, and changing as a result, becoming a different person.

The two most powerful American novels from the nineteenth century are Herman Melville's *Moby Dick* and Mark Twain's *Adventures of Huckleberry Finn*, and they both involve a transformation, a spiritual transformation. One is a search starting in New England that leads across the Western oceans on a quest to kill a great white whale. The other is a search by a white boy and a black man for racial clarity on a raft floating down the Mississippi River. *Moby Dick* is a story of an obsessed, monomaniacal white man in charge of a racially mixed crew, and race is a big factor in its unfolding. There's a kind of intimacy between the races that's pointed to and celebrated in the novel, and in the film, too, a story about following a possibly mad captain into the Western sea in search of a white whale—a total abstraction, an absolute truth, a religious truth, let's say. These vivid adventure tales describe rites of passage through hundreds or thousands of miles of travel and across the great psychological expanse of the racial divide that have been central aspects of the American experience from the very beginning.

It is intriguing to consider how the American conquest of the West differed from the Europeans' colonization in Africa and elsewhere during the nineteenth century. There are obvious similarities, and there are interesting differences. The West, to Americans in the East, right from the very beginning, only seemed an extension of the East. It was not a different continent that belonged to someone else and that needed to be conquered somehow. Going out and taking control of the West and settling it was our "Manifest Destiny." It was a way, perhaps the only one available at the time, to live out our destiny as Americans. And the West was ours from the start. It wasn't just a place in the imagination, an *ultima thule* at the far end of the world. You can see it in the very first colonial maps, where they extend the states of Connecticut and Virginia and various other states deep into the continent—when they didn't even know what was out there. It was made legal and binding with the Louisiana Purchase from France in 1803, when Americans acquired ownership of the enormous tract of the West, and President Jefferson sent Lewis and Clark to make their exploratory passage through it, to report back to Washington what, in fact, we had actually purchased. So it's not the same thing as the

English, and the French, and other Europeans out looking for the source of the Nile or the Congo and seizing control of the continent from the Africans in order to establish colonies. Americans felt they were exploring their own backyard. Never mind the fact that there happened to be all these native people—hundreds of thousands of them, maybe even millions, living in societies that were in some ways just as civilized and in some ways more civilized than European societies—living across that vast tract that Americans regarded as their own backyard, the backyard of New York and the backyard of Virginia. So when Americans moved west they weren't colonizing; they were simply making themselves at home. It involved a very different mentality. And they were dislodging the people that lived there as if *they* were the invaders. The native people were not regarded as the owners and caretakers of this vast piece of real estate. They were seen as trespassers on our property. In some ways, though, our colonizing history runs parallel to the European colonization of Africa with a vengeance; it starts with the Spanish American War, conquering the Philippines, colonizing Cuba and parts of Asia, and colonizing parts of Central and South America and the Caribbean. Thanks to our nineteenth-century takeover of the West, our colonial ambitions got slightly postponed, and unlike the Europeans' colonial ambitions, didn't begin to be realized until just prior to the beginning of the twentieth century.

Still, our earlier conquest of the western half of North America, factually and economically, bore an astounding resemblance to European colonization of Africa and elsewhere. But not in how we viewed it or represented it to ourselves. In a way, the Western movie genre makes that point. In the movies it's never a story of colonization. It's a story of taking what is legitimately destined to be your own and establishing governance and residence in it. The first thing you have to do is clear these blasted Indians out of it. The next thing you have to do is build a fort so that you can establish a military base for the protection of the citizenry from the Indians who are left. And then you put up a log cabin and a fence, and you put cattle and sheep inside the fence, and you plow the fields and plant corn and wheat. So there's this gradual domestication or taming of the wilderness. That's the operation that's going on in the American imagination. And of course what these films do, what all films do, is dramatize and reinforce what's already in the viewers' imagination.

In our collective imagination, the Indians are seen as part of the untamed wilderness and have to be expunged in some way. Then you're free to cut down the forest and use the logs to build the fort. That way you'll have cleared a field or two, where you can build a house and raise domestic animals. You can almost see the whole mythologized history of civilization unfolding in a typical Western movie. We went from being hunter-gatherers to farmers to villagers. And then we built cities. It's a fascinating genre if you look at it that way. That is how I think Americans view the move West. We were taming our own wilderness, domesticating it, making it fit for the American nuclear family. Which of course is always white, middle class, with 2.4 children.

To Americans, this vivid and powerful sequence of images somehow goes to the heart of the American Dream. You can go west. You can find land and build a home. You can establish a free and democratic, supportive community, and you can start your life over. One of the things that is true in all those classic Western movies is that there's very little reference to where the settlers came *from*, whether they came from Boston, Philadelphia, or Atlanta. They don't refer back; they're always going forward. The Western movie embodies the American Dream in very significant ways. And the forces which obstruct or deflect the American Dream from its realization in the Western are often presented in racial terms, as Indians or Mexicans, manifestations of the Other. They're not the forces of civilization, as we say. So usually the plot unfolds from the point where the savage or the non-Christian or the non-white Other is making it difficult for us to establish domestic bliss as ordained in the US Constitution, the Declaration of Independence, and maybe the Bible, too.

Ultimately—and it gets tricky here—the path to the American Dream has become a tortured path. It has led to our building an empire. The small engine of one person's dream of starting over has somehow morphed into the mighty engine of Manifest Destiny, of empire. From that point of view, it may be a psychotic dream, no less powerful for that—more powerful, rather, but unhealthy, an expression of dysfunction and disease. It is psychotic, in a way, to think that you can start your life over, that there's no such thing as the past. It's a kind of madness to think that you can always improve your life, financially, economically, generation after generation, with each generation succeeding further, and not recognize that this is simply an impossibility, one that ultimately, inevitably, like any Ponzi scheme, will lead to failure. And the economic demands and expectations that back this distorted dream are always going to be in conflict with the ideals of democracy. They demand and expect one person to trample on another. This conflicts with the democratic ideals in our sacred documents and in our hearts.

The great wide open spaces where we raised cows and sheep and grew vast fields of corn, rye, and wheat provided a kind of motor to drive the empire. But then the industrial might of the cities—midwestern cities like Chicago, and Detroit, and Cleveland—became the motor that set the wheels of empire turning. You had to find consumers for all this. And that required another kind of empire, a more mundane one based on the European system: simply the exploitation of other people's raw materials and labor. As a result, starting in the late nineteenth century, in Central America in particular and in South America, later in Asia and Africa and then in the Middle East, Americans got very deeply involved in gathering, controlling, and exploiting raw material and labor in other parts of the world. It was the traditional European model for empire, the new and improved version. More recently, with the increasing globalization of the economy, American corporations and successive administrations of both parties have worked very hard to ensure that we are at the center of the world economy, controlling as much of the raw processes as possible, more than any other single country in the world, with the possible exception of China, so that now the US is situated at the center of the globalization tsunami. We're doing it in a way that's familiar to us, as the continuation of the impulses we acted on in the late nineteenth century in the movement west, as if it all already belonged to us through Manifest Destiny, as if the whole world now were our backyard, and as if others who might be there already were trespassers.

There's the old American story of the three generations, one that goes back all the way to the American Revolution, to John Adams, a founding father and president. In the story the first generation is a laborer so that the second generation can go to college and become a professional person so that the third generation can live a life of leisure, or maybe become an artist.

So the first generation basically sacrifices itself for the benefit of the second, and the second generation in turn sacrifices itself for the benefit of the third. All done willingly, because the belief in progress goes very deep, the belief that the sacrifice will reap a bountiful reward, a willingness to give up one's life that I don't think is as deeply imbedded in the European imagination. And you still see it today. You see wave after wave of people from Mexico and the Caribbean, from Africa, Asia, Central and South America, who are willing to work very hard for a lifetime at menial jobs in order that their children can get an education so that they don't have to do menial work, they can become lawyers and doctors and professional people, so that the third generation can go to university and study the fine arts, the humanities, philosophy, and so forth.

I taught at Princeton University for many years, and it was always the case. I taught the ambitious children of Indians, Koreans, Jamaicans, and so on. The parents had sacrificed and sometimes humiliated themselves working at menial jobs so that these children could go to university, and they were all studying medicine, law, business, those sorts of professions. And you know that their children in turn, when they go to university, will study music and art, philosophy, the humanities. That succession, that commitment to change over the course of several generations, provides a lot of energy, a lot of momentum, a lot of labor and life-long personal sacrifice for at least two and sometimes three or more generations.

The people who changed the world in the early twentieth century were not the Rockefellers and the Carnegies and the Fords. It was the people who worked for them who changed the world. The workers provided industry with the power. The half-dozen people at the top who made the great fortunes—the Fords and the Rockefellers, the Astors and the Carnegies—they didn't provide American industry with its strength. It was the millions of Americans who worked on the assembly lines, in the mines, in the fields, in the shipping yards, on the docks and the railroads, and so on. They were the ones who changed the world. That's why I'm still talking about the American Dream. Because there is an ongoing battle for the right to restore that dream or see it replaced by the dream of empire.

Rockefeller didn't believe in the American Dream, but everyone who worked for him did. He believed in the dream of empire. Ford didn't believe in the American Dream, but all those guys assembling Model Ts and Model As down on the assembly line, they did. Those Irishmen and those Italians and those Greeks, they did. All those Hungarians and Poles in the steel yards in Pittsburgh working for Carnegie, they're the ones who changed American society. Carnegie didn't. They sacrificed and worked very, very hard for many, many years. For generations. And the dream they believed in was still believable, because it was human-scale, focused on individuals, and strengthened through family ties and in local communities and labor unions. It wasn't the distorted and corrupted dream of Empire.

So of course my American heroes are not the Carnegies and the Fords. They're the people in the mines and on the assembly lines, in the steelyards and on the docks. They're the people who laid the railroads across this country, the Chinese, and the Irish who were digging the canals. Every society has its captains of industry. Europe had its captains of industry in the first two decades of the twentieth century. What Europe didn't have was that enormous labor pool willing to sacrifice itself in the workplace, a labor pool that was for the most part literate—that's important as well—who forged our national identity as a nation of immigrants, with not one but many identities, who came together to sacrifice and to build.

THE GRAPES OF
WRATH, 1940

OF MAN AND MACHINES

AMERICANS HAVE always believed in the almost spiritual beauty of machinery. Our early heroes are people like Benjamin Franklin. If we put Ben Franklin on the same pedestal as we do George Washington, James Madison, and Thomas Jefferson, it's not because of his statesmanship, although Franklin was in fact a great statesman. No, we honor him because he was a classic American tinkerer, a true mechanic in the most basic sense. And better yet, a self-taught American mechanic.

Other American tinkerer heroes include the Wright brothers, Robert Fulton and his steamboat, Thomas

Edison, and of course Henry Ford. But the Henry Ford we admire is not the international industrialist; it's the young mechanic in the back of a Detroit garage putting together the first Model T by himself. We like to think of ourselves as a country of mechanics, self-taught, by and large. So, yes, we do idealize technology, but the object of our worship isn't the wizardry and magic of technology, but almost the very opposite. Americans have a home-spun and down-to-earth curiosity about the ways of the physical world and the mechanics of nature and a complementary belief that they can be known and controlled.

American likes and dislikes, which are after all important clues to our identity, were never incidental or coincidental. We're very pragmatic and materialistic as a culture. Consequently, we admire mechanics—not abstract scientists or intellectuals, but applied scientists and the writers of adventure stories about whaling ships and runaways on a raft. And we have been that way from the very beginning. You can go back to the sixteenth and the seventeenth centuries in American history and see how the first settlers were cut off from the European sources of early industrial production. They were in the wilderness, or on the edge of the wilderness, in Virginia, in New England, in New York. They had to make do with what they had, and they didn't have much. They had to cut down the trees; they had to build bricks from the riverbank clay; they had to work with what was literally at hand. So there developed a tremendous affection and respect for the mechanic and the handmade machine. This was how we conquered possibly our fiercest adversary, the wilderness, not the mythical one but the real wilderness of seventeenth- and eighteenth- and even nineteenth-century America, vast and unbroken, spanning nearly every possible extreme of climate, weather, and geography.

By the time our handmade machines have evolved into assembly lines, by the time we have access to highly technological industry, we've got a jump on the rest of the world because we've brought with us a profound affection for both the mechanic—we like and admire Bill Gates and Steve Jobs more than the billionaires who made theirs speculating with other peoples' money—and for the technology the mechanic creates and utilizes. We're not superstitious about it the way some cultures are. We don't look down at physical work. And we don't look down at the mechanic or the engineer. We admire them. In a way, that admiration, genuine and heartfelt, has given us an advantage in the industrial and post-industrial eras.

In the 1930s, with the development of economic liberalism and a number of specific very important social modifications, there was a cascade of significant changes in American society, along with a concomitant change in certain traditional values. They occurred because of the Depression and our collective response as a society to that crisis. They occurred because of the failure of the great industrial fortunes to provide a social network that could endure a breakdown in the capitalist economic system. As a result of extreme widespread poverty, rather than the accumulation of wealth by a small segment of society, there occurred a change in traditional social values and a rise in liberal values and the belief that government had a responsibility to care for the welfare of its citizens.

Up to this point, until Franklin Roosevelt, until 1932, the idea that there must be a social net, administered by the federal government, by which the society as a whole looked after its weakest members, or to put it more exactly, looked after weak and strong equally, wasn't operational in American society. The New Deal and the establishment of certain institutions, like Social Security and so many other protective agencies that still function today, were created and came almost at once to seem natural and permanent. But at bottom what really took place first was a shift in our view of government's responsibility to the people. It was poverty, the poverty of the Depression, and the collapse of the capitalist economy that challenged those traditional nineteenth-century American assumptions and values and changed them—permanently, we thought.

Look at a film like *The Grapes of Wrath*. It portrays that period, the terrible poverty of that period, with enormous sympathy. It focuses on the little man, saying that he is an important person—this person who's lost his land, who's lost everything and is drifting west. He's impoverished and bitter; he doesn't have a home. And he's presented with great sympathy. You wouldn't see a movie like that in the 1920s. You wouldn't see the poor portrayed that way, not even by Chaplin. You don't see it until after the Depression, when core social values have shifted. In the 1940s you can look back at the Depression and the poor of that period who suffered so terribly, in the Dust Bowl and so on, in an extremely sympathetic way.

In the 1980s, during the presidency of Ronald Reagan, democracy and capitalism got married. This is something I remember clearly. They were no longer just compatible, they were seen to be the same, a single blended unit, inseparable. It was called Free Market Democracy. Of course now it's become the official guiding ideology of America, and it is spoken of as if it were always the case, as if it's written into the Declaration of Independence and the United States Constitution. But the first time we heard it articulated and expressed as a virtue was by Ronald Reagan in the 1980s, and then it became the new American ideal. Now it's how we justify conquest, how we justify economic exploitation, how we justify invasion and occupation. In his claims, it already existed as a main element of American political and economic ideology in the 1920s and even before. You see it in the era of the first Roosevelt, Theodore, at the turn of the century, where he claims to simultaneously export capitalism and democracy to the Philippines. As if the one provided a home for the other. It goes back even further than that. In the 1820s Americans created the country of Liberia in Africa. From the creators' point of view it was going to solve the problem of race in America because they were going to be able to send the Africans back to Africa. But the founders of Liberia also thought they were making Africa safe for the three Cs: Christianity, Capitalism, and Civilization. And today the same monstrous fantasy conjoining faith, profit, and progress into a holy alliance lies behind the melding of Capitalism and democracy for export. We're making Iraq safe for the three Cs: Christianity, Capitalism, and Civilization. Woodrow Wilson thought that if you took one, you got the other, a two-for-one deal. When you got Capitalism you got democracy. The bonus was that you also got Christianity and Civilization. It's a fantasy, a self-serving fantasy, of course. And it's also pure hucksterism, pure salesmanship, like the selling of dubious remedies from the back of a wagon. America has always been the home of hucksterism and extreme salesmanship.

Speeches made by George W. Bush in his first presidential election campaign and certain speeches made by others in the Republican Party at the time were anti-Wilsonian in spirit and intent. The Republicans presented themselves as noninterventionists, if not downright isolationists. But now, in the second Bush administration, they've come to justify their policies in very much the same way Woodrow Wilson did, with a belligerent foreign policy that is highly interventionist and brash, one which even many Republicans, members of the president's own party, are highly uncomfortable with and in some cases openly against.

The two earliest justifications for the European presence in North America were materialism and idealism. And the marriage of capitalism and democracy is a way to bring those two conflicting impulses together and ignore their inherent contradictions. The first version of the United States Constitution, before it was amended to eliminate slavery, demonstrated the same failed struggle to resolve the conflict between those two ideas. Abraham Lincoln said it, that there was in our Constitution an inherent contradiction between the ideals of democracy and the institution of slavery. Slavery meant submission to an economic and materialistic view; democracy articulated an idealistic one. When you marry capitalism and democracy you are trying to avoid that contradiction.

Politicians shift their rhetoric in order to suit their needs. They have always done that. So how did America in recent years shift from a tentative kind of isolationism to full-blown interventionism? You can see the former in the Bill Clinton years, in his reluctance to get involved in the Balkans, for example, ignoring the crisis in Rwanda and elsewhere. And in George W. Bush's campaign against Al Gore in 2000, Bush advertised himself as the presidential candidate who was not involved in nation-building and regime change and all that. His rhetoric was even more isolationist than his father's or Clinton's. But Bush wasn't the only one. We have over time swung back and forth between an isolationist impulse and an interventionist impulse. It has depended on our perceived economic needs, even though both isolationism and interventionism have always been justified and rationalized in idealistic terms. We justified intervention in Cuba and the Philippines in 1901, '02, and '03 in idealistic terms, when in fact we were playing catch-up with the European empire-builders. We justified staying out of World War I in isolationist terms because we weren't threatened militarily. But when our transport of goods to Europe was being threatened by German attacks on American shipping, we came into the war. It was economic, but we typically used the rationalization that we were rushing to the fight to save Europe. Nonsense. We were rushing to save American shipping. Why did America intervene so late? It simply wasn't in our economic interest to intervene before then. Foreign policy in the US, despite the rhetoric, has historically been driven by economics. It's always been the case. Because we are such a nationalistic people we're free to look on our relations with other countries in pragmatic and self-serving terms. Because we have a hierarchy of values that is based on nationalist priorities, we see our values and our needs as more important than those of anyone else on this planet. Nationalism gives you that right. Nationalism breeds exceptionalism. So whatever happens to the Europeans or to anyone else on this planet is not as important as what happens to us. And when we say that we are exporting democracy and doing it in order to save the world, it sounds lovely. It's probably the only way you can get the American people to go to war, to sacrifice themselves. But in fact we go to war for our perceived economic needs. It's historically the case. Our isolation is physical to begin with, and it has allowed us until recently to feel as though we were not threatened militarily by another country. We're not threatened by invasion from Canada or Mexico. And the seas have also protected us, until very recently. Because of that physical isolation, our sense of ourselves in relation to the rest of the world has been one of fearlessness—that is to say, we had no fear of being invaded. If you're going to convince Americans to march off to war, you've got to make them feel they're threatened with imminent invasion. Witness the response to the attacks of 9/11. Bush and company got Americans to go to war by making us feel threatened.

In the early years of World War I, because of the attacks on our ships by German submarines, we were losing our ability to ship sold goods to Europe and to buy goods from Europe. The only thing that would sway the Congress and the Senate into declaring war was the belief that the American economy was under threat—that they couldn't ship cotton from the southern states or all those munitions that they manufactured in the factories of the North.

You can profiteer in wartime. People always make a lot of money in a war making and selling all those uniforms, tanks, weapons, bandages. There's a tremendous market for the products that get consumed in wars. So it was not to save Europe. It was surely not to save France from the Germans. Americans loved Germans in the early twentieth century.

So why does George W. Bush run America's foreign policy counter to the Republican Party's political ideology of the past fifty years? Because he has to. Bush has to resort to that kind of rhetoric in order to justify American sacrifices. Otherwise he couldn't get the American people to go on the march. He's tapping into that idealistic, religious, and nationalistic sense of self-importance, invoking it for his own reasons, of course. We've really gone back to the Eisenhower era, to the pre-containment years of the early Cold War. In talking about the call of history, Bush is trying to sound like Franklin Roosevelt in 1942. Because he's desperate. He's reaching for that particular brand of rhetoric because there is no other way to get the American people to make the sacrifices they have to make, no other way to get them to accept the brutal atrocities that we have committed, in this war in Iraq and elsewhere, and to throw overboard the essential rights that were promised to us, and by extension to everyone, in those sacred documents. We have to be made to feel that there's a cause worthy of those sacrifices, and so what Bush has been trying to do is instill in us that feeling for the cause, to make us feel that we're riding out on a white horse to save the world. We're making the world safe for those three Cs: Christianity, Capitalism, Civilization. He uses code to refer to Christianity, uses "free market" to refer to Capitalism, but feels comfortable invoking the word Civilization at will.

Meanwhile, the cause he is invoking simply isn't there. To embrace his ideology we must learn how to completely ignore the facts of our involvement in Iraq and to show an almost absolute disregard for the priorities of other peoples or other countries in the world. And yet, whenever other politicians or the Democrats or some in the media have attempted to call the President on the carpet, and to point out his utter disregard for the underlying facts, so far it hasn't seemed to stick. He isn't being impeached. His popularity is down, yes. But he seems to have brought the country down with him.

Woodrow Wilson had much the same problem that Bush has. His response was expressed a little more coherently and was perhaps a little more intellectually sophisticated than Bush & Co.'s. Wilson was, after all, a man of some education and a higher degree of literacy than Bush, perhaps. But essentially it came down to the same thing. It's been expressed differently over the years.

We mustn't forget that John F. Kennedy was responsible for the beginnings of the Vietnam War. It happened under his watch. He was a supposedly liberal Democratic president, but nonetheless he used the same rationale that Bush uses as he goes marching on today in Iraq. Wilson and Kennedy were more eloquently expressive than Bush, to be sure, but the same message was there. The underlying ideology was basically the same.

Do I think that our leaders are that cynical? Yes, I do, frankly. I think, however, that they have a system of beliefs such that they are convinced that this war is for the universal good; it is universally good to do whatever will benefit them and their friends. Reagan used that great phrase, "trickle-down economics." It was believed, and still is among Republicans, that if you gave tax cuts to rich people, eventually these benefits will trickle down to the poor, and the poor will be enriched from the rich people's having enjoyed a tax cut. A wonderful fantasy. It sounded too good to be true, and it was. We're still waiting for some of the enormous wealth that was generated by this subsidy to the richest Americans to trickle down. Of course it never did, so they gave another tax cut to the rich. The rich said, Don't worry, it's trickle-down economics; it's going to come down to you. They actually believed that. The rich believe that what's good for them is good for everybody.

I've spent hours talking to retired CIA agents who were involved in some of the worst atrocities—assassination of people like Patrice Lumumba, insurrections, coups, regime changes in places like Greece, and so on, around the world. Horrible things. And when they think you're part of the club, these old guys will sit there and talk about it fairly openly, because they think it was for the good of everybody. It was good for everybody that we went in there and knocked off Lumumba, because if we hadn't we would have had a Communist regime there. If we had a Communist regime in that central, very rich region of Africa, then the Communists would have had a foothold in Africa and da-da-da-da-da. It's a long, very old and tired story. We had to kill the Diems in Vietnam, too. It was good for everybody. The list of the leaders we have killed for the good of everybody isn't a short list, and of course the world is not a better place because of those assassinations. The world and our role in it is far worse because of them.

There was a film made a couple of years ago of the Graham Greene novel about Americans in Vietnam, *The Quiet American.* It's a beautiful portrayal of American self-serving innocence. Not quite cynicism, willful naiveté, usefully self-serving naiveté. And I think that's what this class of American politicians, captains of industry and so forth, have, a self-serving, useful naiveté. It allows them to rule conscience-free. It allows them to invite the poor, the blacks, the Hispanics, and so on, to sacrifice their children and to pay for the whole operation. The rich are not paying for this war. The poor are paying for this war, one way or another, and dying in it.

HANGING OF
CAPTAIN WIRZ,
1865

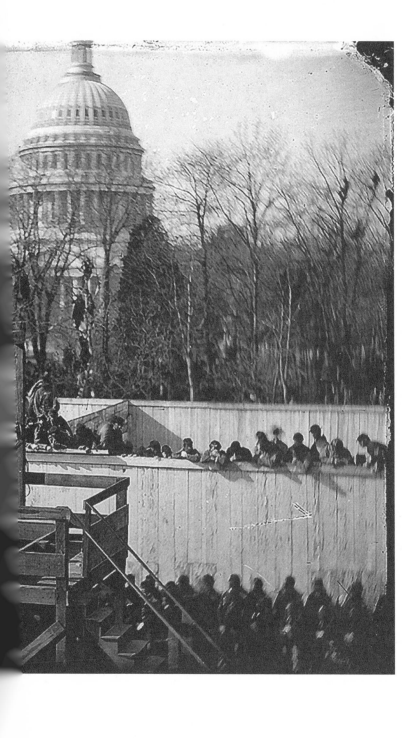

A VERY
PECULIAR INSTITUTION

THE PRESIDENCY of the United States is a very peculiar institution. It's not a person, but a persona or "role" that a person fills or plays. And our president, in some ways even more than a monarch, represents in some very personal way the imagination and the mythology of the people who have elected him. We choose presidents, but we do not choose them on the basis of their experience or even their political views. We choose them based on how well they tap into our basic beliefs, how expressive they are of our own deepest national mythologies.

Woodrow Wilson, John F. Kennedy, Richard Nixon, Jimmy Carter, Ronald Reagan, Bill Clinton, and both George Bushes on some level all share this characteristic—they tap into and express back to us our deepest American mythologies. And mythologies are not necessarily highly intellectual or highly intelligent. They are basic, primal almost. You can tap into them from any point along the spectrum of education or intelligence. The presidency is the only seat of government where power resides in one person, and it is also a symbol of American personhood and American power. Both real and abstract, both factual and symbolic. And George W. Bush wouldn't have been elected if he hadn't managed to convince enough people—not a majority, as we know, but enough people, in enough places in the United States—that he was the exponent of their deepest, communal desires.

The same thing was true for Wilson, so we should not be surprised when he and Bush sound alike, even though one says it more eloquently than the other. The same thing with Kennedy. We should not be surprised when some justification Bush offers up reminds us suddenly of something Wilson or Kennedy said. Kennedy justified, for instance, the foiled invasion of Cuba. He condemned the Bay of Pigs invasion of Cuba only on pragmatic grounds; the invading force had not been well enough prepared. And he explained away the assassination of the

Diems in Vietnam and the beginning of the build-up of American forces in Vietnam.

I mean, this was John F. Kennedy, supposedly our most enlightened president of modern times. But we shouldn't be surprised when one president ends up sounding an awful lot like another president, even one with a very different level of education and native intelligence and so forth, because they were both chosen by the American people for the reason that they seemed to be the living embodiment of our deepest ideals and desires, no matter how contradictory those ideals and desires were.

No president or prime minister or monarch has quite the same role as the American president. He's part pope, part chief executive, and part monarch, and yet he's not any one of those things alone. There is a projection of religious or spiritual beliefs onto the president, a projection of belief in the president's possessing inherited, divinely endowed powers, like those of a monarch. But there is also trust and belief in the president as a pragmatic chief executive who gets things done. All these requirements are placed in our one and only president. Other countries divide them up. They have a king, and then they have prime ministers. Or they have a president and a prime minister, as they do in France. They divide the symbolic roles from the executive. From the beginning, we Americans have blended them. I think that goes back to our Revolutionary War, when there were very few models for parliamentary democracy around, and the temptation, which was very strong, was for us to replace one King George with the other King George, George Washington. Washington had to forcefully say, "I will not be your king." So, okay, we'll make you a president who has an extreme amount of power.

We provided Washington with a long term, four years. And until after Franklin Roosevelt, when the Constitution was amended to limit the office to two terms, those four years could legally be extended to twelve, sixteen, twenty. We left open the possibility of a monarch-like president. The role of the presidency was created to be an extraordinary role. And in a time of empire the president has the capacity to become imperial, to become an emperor. You see this happening now in the conflict between Congress and President Bush over his enthusiasm for suspending the rights of privacy and so forth, his insistence on acting in a unilateral way. We have become an empire, and in an empire the president moves in the direction of becoming an emperor. It's frightening! This may be the dark view of American history, but it is the view of history that is being promoted by the very people I'm talking about, those who wield power in our world today.

Homeland

LOOK AT how the map of the world changed after World War II. The powers that be in America felt it was in their interest to establish a balance of power in order to keep any single European nation from dominating Europe after the war. One way to do that would be to make sure it was possible for Germany to check France and also England. The Americans were playing the old balance-of-power game, making a series of realistic political moves to achieve that balance.

Despite Lafayette, our historical relationship with France was never the sibling relationship that our relationship with Germany was. And is. Culturally, Germany was a Protestant country and, especially in the early part of the twentieth century, the United States thought of itself as a Protestant country. Germany was a northern European country, and the United States at that time thought of itself as a northern country. So there was what I can only call a sibling affection between Germany and the US in the early twentieth century that lasted right up to the American involvement in World War II, up to 1941 really, before which we were not willing to see Germany's threat clearly.

And then right after the war ended the old relationship was renewed. It's interesting, the difference between the way America treated Japan after the war and the way we treated Germany, with the Marshall Plan for instance, allowing Germany essentially to re-arm, whereas that was forbidden to the Japanese. There was a different kind of control exerted over Japan after the war than over Germany. I think that was because there was a persistent identification with Germany, one that was much stronger than our identification with Japan, certainly, or even with France. It is interesting that whose side we were on wasn't the determining factor. Racial differences, or what were perceived to be racial differences, were certainly factors in the case of the Japanese. And the cultural resonance we felt with Germany, as well as certain geopolitical considerations, and other more psychological ones.

In the American mythology of Europe, France is seen as feminine and Germany as masculine, and Americans see their own country as masculine. There is a kind of male bonding with Germany. The French speak of the "mother country," and Germans speak of the "fatherland." Americans use neither and refer instead to the United States as our "homeland." What's interesting is just how distinct each of those three is, how different the nuance. So after the war, both mythology and realpolitik brought us back to our old closeness with Germany, which probably wasn't what anyone would have predicted, considering how recently we had been sworn enemies.

Acting on a world stage

ACTING ON the world stage in a spirit of partnership is a perennial problem for the United States. Accepting membership, parity, or equality with other countries in any international organization, for example, is something we have always found to be enormously difficult. Partly it's because of our unbridled nationalism and the belief that there are no higher priorities than our priorities; partly. it's the historical feeling of being distinct and separate from Europe and other parts of the world and seeing their quarrels as parochial, so not wanting to become dragged into them or involved in them in any way. There is that sense of our being special and distinct on the one hand, and not wanting to become embroiled in quarrels that are seen as belonging exclusively to Europeans, Africans, or Asians on the other.

But most importantly I think it's a refusal to allow what we regard as our national destiny to be in any way affected, shaped, or controlled by other nations— by any other single nation or by any congress of nations. When you have a strong sense of your national destiny, it's practically a religious mission, a divinely-ordained sequence or narrative that won't tolerate revision. You certainly don't want to let anyone else interfere with that.

Shattered dreams

YOU HAVE to go back to the founding colonies in New England to understand the persistence of that belief in God lying, standing, or sitting just behind this, that, and every other political and social or political act. American objections to and mistrust of international organizations like the League of Nations and the United Nations are connected to the fact that in our minds we already have all the partnership we need through our special relationship with God. And indeed the objections and mistrust come more from the religious right than the secular left, and they come from rural America—the South and the Midwest—more than from the East and Northeast or the coast of California, because those are the more religious regions, and from their point of view there is an antireligious taint to these international organizations.

And I guess it would not be unfair to say that American diplomacy just after World War I was instrumental in laying the groundwork for the emerging world conflict, the rise of Nazism, and the inevitability of World War II. It's so easy to sit here and look back fifty or seventy-five years and say they should have known. It's a cheap game to play, and I'd rather not do that. But as I said, Wilson and others started out on that path for reasons of state and with a mix of motives. They were trying to be practical. But some of it was psychological, some of it was imagistic—how they perceived other peoples' roles, how they perceived their own roles. And that blend is what always drives people's political actions. It's all driven by a blend or a braid of motives, never by one single motive. Which means that things didn't have to happen they way they did. The aftermath of World War I didn't have to lay the foundation for the start of World War II. It's true for individuals, and it's true for nations as well. We never do anything for one single reason. And as individuals we're rarely conscious of most of the reasons behind our behavior.

In the presidential administrations of Harding and Coolidge and Hoover in the years leading up to the Crash of 1929, it was felt that what was good for business was good for America. Pure and simple. No apologies needed. Those administrations worked hand-in-glove with American businesses. That was a reckless, enriching period for a whole class of people. It was a bubble economy, however, and with the Crash of 1929, the bubble burst. All those fortunes that were based on speculation disappeared overnight, and all the people whose jobs and livelihoods depended on the continuing expansion of that bubble were out of work. Mortgages were called, loans were called. It was a society running on debt and inflation and speculation. It all came crashing to a halt, and there was enormous suffering as a result. The images of the suicides of the Wall Street brokers—investors and presidents of corporations leaping off skyscrapers into the streets—while quite vivid, don't really describe the pain and suffering and loss of a much larger class of Americans, mainly the working class.

As factories shut down, banks called their loans in, and family farms and homes were taken over. You began to see images of that transition in movies by the late 1930s. I mentioned earlier how in the 1930s, with Roosevelt, there was a dramatic shift in values and political ideology. Because the number of people who couldn't care for themselves was so vast, there was no other place to turn than to the government. For the first time a majority of Americans came to believe that it was the government's responsibility to care for the poor and the elderly and the sick—those who couldn't care for themselves. During that period, from 1932 to World War II, there was a dramatic and historically significant shift in values in America that was forced upon us and made us a better nation and a better people.

We've always had a boom-and-bust economy. There have been booms followed by depressions approximately every thirty years going right back to the early nineteeth century, largely because our capitalist economy is based on speculation and borrowing, on optimistic anticipation of return and growth and expansion. That's the kind of capitalist economy that evolved here. It's a free-wheeling, barely controlled, speculative economy. And in the 1920s the scale simply grew too great for the system to recover when it got roughed up, and so it quickly fell apart. There are now certain guidelines and controls, put in place in the 1930s, which are designed to keep speculative growth of the economy under some restriction. So they claim. But one wonders if, in fact, it's true—that a depression like that, a crash like that, can't occur again. I'm not so sure it's true, especially when so much of our economy today is based on money that's been loaned to the US by the Chinese and by European investors, those loans passed on to the average wage-earner. We're carrying an incredibly huge debt as a nation, and if someone starts calling in that debt, if the world starts using euros instead of dollars as the basis of the oil economy, for instance, if petro-euros are used instead of petro-dollars, the American foreign debt is going to be called, and the economy may indeed crash again.

So the possibility of a crash is still there, I believe. But it was there right from the beginning of the existence of a national economy, at least from the 1820s, let's say, the time of the creation of the National Bank under Andrew Jackson, and then remained essentially unchanged into the twentieth century. This boom-and-bust economic structure has been operating at warp speed, all through the 1980s—the boom of the '80s followed by a dip in the '90s into the Bush *pere* years, booming again in the Clinton years, and deflating again during the Bush *fils* years. That's the kind of economy we've inherited from the nineteenth century, so I don't think it's something that appeared in the 1920s, but rather was already shaped early on and wasn't able to flex or shift to meet changing demands. A certain awareness of its fragility appeared in the 1930s, a consciousness of the dangers of the boom-and-bust economy. The Roosevelt administration glimpsed the implications across the board, especially with regard to the poor and the middle class, and how vulnerable they were to it. That consciousness changed our social values and our understanding of political and government structures and responsibilities.

⟨ornament⟩

HOW DOES all this affect the American Dream? There was in fact great confusion about the American Dream in the 1930s, because it no longer seemed possible for a man or a woman to rise in wealth, to rise up out of the working class into the middle class and beyond. For the first time, that ascent started to look like a very dim possibility at best. You saw it reflected in the movies in some ways, with the gangster-as-hero, with sympathetic portraits of gangsters played by stars like Humphrey Bogart and James Cagney and Edward G. Robinson and so on. It would be hard to imagine those types of heroes in movies prior to the Depression. In the 1920s or earlier, there weren't any Robin Hood figures robbing the rich to help the poor. The early movie heroes weren't that kind of outlaw. Instead, we got glamorous and romantic pirates, as played by Errol Flynn in *Captain Blood.* We got down-and-out gangsters, killers, snarling tough guys. Antisocial figures, really bad guys, but sympathetically portrayed. And for the first time they're at the center of American movies, and at the center of American novels, too. The noir films are very closely related to the kind of noir novels that were being written at that time by Dashiell Hammett and others. It's interesting to think about them as a possible reaction to the demise of, or the fading power of, the American Dream.

In the noir film, the whole narrative sequence, the scenery, and the sets all contrived to make the literal darkness onto which the story was projected, the view of the city as a threatening, dark environment: nothing optimistic in the imagery there. Then, at the center of the story, the violent antisocial type appears as the hero, the morally corrupted detective. Think of Bogart in *The Maltese Falcon*, and dozens of other movies like that. They were men who were morally unstable, but not morally unsure; they had what today we would call low self-esteem, and yet were piercingly clear about the morality or lack thereof of their actions. They were compromised in some way and saw themselves as compromised. In this way they were expressive of a period, the 1930s, when moral certitudes—when all certitudes—were under threat. And the noir films in some ways were a response to that.

Generally, prior to that point in American history, I think Americans felt they were perennially at the beginning of a great and clearly lit future. But with the Depression, sudden disillusionment set in—not just disappointment, but a profound challenge to our most basic belief system. And in some ways Franklin

Roosevelt was the perfect president for that moment, because he could reinvigorate that old vision of the City on a Hill and of a nation that was at the beginning of a great history, rather than at the end of one. He was able, I think, to forestall a lot of that confusion and despair.

Nonetheless, we see that confusion and despair reflected in the noir genre in an extraordinary way. As in almost every case of equal-and-opposite responses to trauma, the trauma of the Depression produced one response in the noir film, but on the Left, the Depression also gave rise to the figure of the heroic worker. Of course there was the long-running tradition of Proletarian fiction, with Theodore Dreiser and John Dos Passos, back to Stephen Crane and others, but this was more of an anti-heroic tradition. In the 1930s you got the heroic worker figure for the first time in American film, in American fiction, and in American intellectual life, with a neo-Marxist or even an overtly Marxist perspective on the worker, a romanticizing of the worker. And indeed this proved to be the only time in American history from the beginning to the present when American intellectuals and artists, novelists and filmmakers, were seriously engaged with Marxist ideas and a dialectical view of history. Even in the 1960s they never again reached that point, unless perhaps in a very parochial way on college campuses. There were some individuals, like Herbert Marcuse and so forth, who were prominent on the Left in the 1960s, but intellectuals were generally were no longer universally of the Left. Opposition to the status quo was by then single-issue opposition, against the Vietnam War, for instance, or racial segregation, rather than in systemic opposition to the society as a whole, Communism versus Capitalism and so on, whereas in the 1930s, across the board, intellectuals, artists, filmmakers, and academics were by and large committed to a Marxist point of view. And that was an extraordinary blip in the history of American art and thought and politics.

You had two kinds of responses to that diminished dream. One was the sympathetic portrayal of the outlaw, real outlaws regarded in the press and across the country as heroic figures, like Willy Sutton, the bank robber, or John Dillinger, or Bonnie and Clyde Barrow. Killers and thieves regarded as heroic figures. And of course the films reflected that. And there was the other response to the diminished dream, which was the response of the Left. For the first time in the United States, intellectuals, serious artists, filmmakers, novelists, and so on, had more than a casual flirtation with Marxism and the radical Left. For the first time, capitalism was seen as a failed system, especially by intellectuals. It was no longer unfashionable for intellectuals and artists to be politically engaged. John Ford's movie *The Grapes of Wrath* (1940) came at the end of this period, based on John Steinbeck's 1939 novel by the same name, and you could say it was the culmination of this response to the economic chaos and suffering that the Depression had brought on.

I think these were two equal and opposite responses to the same historical phenomenon. The noir film, gangsters as heroes, antisocial figures, and outlaws as heroes on the one hand, and workers as heroes and the poor and suffering as heroes on the other. It's a really interesting and linked response to the same phenomenon.

THE GREAT DICTATOR,
1940

THE DARK SIDE
ONLY GETS DARKER

AMERICANS WERE not on the whole concerned about the rise of Nazism in the period leading up to the war, or even at first during the war, the period of the late 1930s through to 1941. I spoke earlier of the prevailing view of Germany in the United States going all the way back to the late nineteenth century, how Germany was viewed as a kind of natural sibling to the US, along with England, nearly as close as that; whereas France was viewed more as a cousin than a sibling. And I described how this had to do with Germany being a northern, Protestant, Anglo-Saxon country, whereas

France was somehow seen as Mediterranean, Roman Catholic, Latin, and greatly different therefore from us, and that there might be racist tints to that, a sense that we white, Anglo-Saxon, Northern European, Protestant nations had to stick together! So I don't think what was happening in Germany in the 1930s was as frightening to the US as it would have been had it happened elsewhere, because we trusted them a little more. Also, most of the victims so far seemed to be Jews, and no way was the US going to come to the defense of Jews at that time. Especially if it was going to cost us money. The other thing was our sense simply of the physical distance between the drama being played out across Europe and ourselves. Remember that the distance across the Atlantic Ocean was far, far greater then than it is now. The preferred means of transportation was still an ocean liner rather than a plane, and so it was a question of weeks of travel, not hours. It wasn't hard in those years leading into the war for Americans to say, This doesn't concern us.

What we're talking about here, of course, isn't how Europeans actually *were*, but how Americans imagined them to be, and what distinctions Americans made between the French and the Germans, English and Irish, Spanish, Italians, and so forth. We did make distinctions, and they weren't based much on reality. They were based on mythology, on how we imagined ourselves and other countries over generations, and on our limited experience of various countries. We'd had greater exposure to the English than to other Europeans, from our shared language, if nothing else. There's greater familiarity and comfort when two nations share a language or a religion, and until recent years we believed that we shared both a language and an essentially Protestant Christian religion with England–not Ireland, however–and shared that same religion with Germany.

If language and religion were factors at play in our dealings with European nations in the late 1930s, so was race. Since we imagined ourselves as a white nation–we were not a white nation and never have been, of course, yet we have always imagined ourselves as one–we engaged with the Anglo-Saxon countries more comfortably than with others, even those that were also nominally white. These were superstitions, prejudices, and stereotypes, but that's how the human imagination functions. Superstitions, prejudices, stereotypes–mythologies, in other words–are its lifeblood.

The war in Asia, with Japan, was generated by the attack on Pearl Harbor, which was perceived very similarly to how, today, we perceive September 11–as an indefensible act justifying an all-out counterattack. The war against Germany was caused by a somewhat different sequence of events, and I think the United States was slow to intervene for various reasons. As I've said, it was easier to rationalize and justify Germany's behavior in the 1930s, even the rise of Nazism. There were a great many Americans who were very sympathetic towards Nazism.

Philip Roth published a successful novel acknowledging the historical fact that there were so many Americans who were pro-Nazi in the 1930s that, if Charles Lindbergh had run, we might have elected a pro-Nazi president. These were not just German-Americans who'd recently crossed the border in order to pursue the American Dream. We're talking about Charles Lindbergh, Henry Ford, William Randolph Hearst, Joseph Kennedy—very influential Americans with large followings. And one doesn't have to look very far from home to find it. My parents were of that generation, and I would say that my parents—who were decent, hard-working people, but not very politically sophisticated or educated—saw nothing particularly wrong with the rise of Nazism, nothing threatening in any way. I'd say they were average American voters—working people, Christians, Scots-Irish, not German—typical of their generation in many ways. All this made it very difficult to get the United States to go to war against Germany before being directly attacked by Japan.

Contrary to what many people think today, Hollywood directors and actors weren't quick to support the war effort. There was instead a desire to continue with business as usual and stay out of the war. They thought, What's that got to do with us? It's way over there in Europe. The film industry in the early 1940s was slow to react. Only in the later years of the war did they come up with a commitment to help fight it—and that was induced largely by the federal government in Washington going to the studios and saying that they needed to contribute to the war effort; they needed to make films that would inspire patriotism and demonize the Germans, demonize the Japanese, and so forth. Hollywood turned American soldiers and pilots into heroic figures for us. Films in the 1940s, starting around 1943, in some cases used actual war heroes like Audie Murphy, a Medal of Honor winner. *Sergeant York* and films like that turned real heroes into movie heroes. So, yes, the movie industry put on the uniform, but belatedly. And then it forgot to take it off.

Charlie Chaplin, with *The Great Dictator* in particular, was a special case. But Chaplin wasn't American. He was English. He was also a man of the Left, and he was very unpopular for it. *The Great Dictator* became a classic film, but it never had popular success. At the time it was made, it was regarded as the nadir of his career. He was no longer the tramp, but the tramp was what we loved him for, not for being the director of *The Great Dictator*. Making *The Great Dictator* was courageous, especially because it wasn't motivated by popular opinion. Using the most popular medium without seeking the endorsement of the audience is always courageous and difficult, and it often destroys your career. It wasn't long after that that Charlie Chaplin moved abroad. He was in a sense kicked out of the house. But his film was the exception rather than the rule.

American involvement in World War II reinforced national unity in the United States. War always does that, reinforces national identity and pride. It's tribal, after all. It affirms and asserts one's tribal identity, and that certainly occurred during World War II. American identity was affirmed in a very powerful, uniting way, particularly coming out of the Depression, when that sense of unity was not so strong.

And there was a great deal of pride in the outcome of the war, after all, with America viewing itself as the savior of Europe, to some degree rightly so. Had the Americans not intervened in Europe in 1941, it would have been lost to the Nazis. The modern history of Europe would have been very different. So there were lots of reasons for that affirmation of national identity during and after the war. That was when this notion of America being the "only light that shines in the night" really came forward. Here we'd come to save poor benighted Europe from itself! Riding to the rescue! That's how Americans viewed themselves in those years and afterwards.

At that time, in the American imagination the world was divided up between those who were free, which is to say the Americans, and the slaves of dictators, who were the Europeans. We might have looked over our shoulder and seen that our immediate close neighbors and numerous others were free as well, but we tended to see only ourselves on our hill, with the light shining brightly in the night.

That sort of black-and-white division of the world into the free and the enslaved that arose out of World War II was so seductive and powerful that it carried over into the Cold War. The Cold War simply picked up where World War II left off. And again the metaphor of those who were free and those who were enslaved, those who lived in the light and those who lived in darkness, was extended very neatly beyond 1945 to the end of the Cold War. It's a rather convenient split. Even after the end of the Cold War it's been resorted to countless times as well, almost like a sales pitch that the older generation of salesmen has told you will work every time.

They're not wrong. You see it today with George Bush's rationalization of the war in Iraq and throughout his policies, particularly in the Middle East. To save the world from itself. This refrain reappears every now and then, but not with the kind of intensity and ease as it did for the colonial powers in the nineteeth and twentieth centuries. That missionary zeal of saving the poor benighted man and woman sitting in the darkness from themselves has not been a consistent American response to the rest of the world. More often than not, we've been comfortable with our isolation. It's a natural fallback position for Americans.

THE PERIOD we're going through right now in the US, in terms of Iraq and the Middle East particularly, in many ways isn't an aberrant period at all. It's typical of America's view of our proper relationship with the rest of the world. Not even the intensity of our involvement is aberrant. Look at Panama, at Vietnam, at Korea. Or, in the nineteenth century, at the Philippines, at Cuba. We are and historically have been very involved in other parts of the world, exploiting people and lands as much as any other colonial power, in Asian, African and South American countries. But in the American imagination we're only doing that to avoid leaving them to their own terrible troubles. So there's a conflict between the reality of the nineteenth century–between the nature of our involvement with Mexico, the Caribbean, Liberia, West Africa, and later our involvement in the Philippines and in Asia in the earlier twentieth century–and the rhetoric and imagery we use to describe that involvement. So much of American violence arises because of the conflict between the reality of our lives and the perception of our lives, the way we imagine ourselves. This goes back to the early colonists in New England and Virginia and the Carolinas, who were basically committing a kind of genocide against the native people, but claimed they were saving them for Civilization, Christianity, and Capitalism. In fact they were killing them and stealing their land, but they never looked at it that way. So there was a huge conflict between what they said they were doing and what they were actually doing. And that kind of conflict in any human being, in any people, makes for a predictable, explosive violence. D. H. Lawrence said, "The essential American soul is hard, isolate, stoic, and a killer." He was pointing at the consequences of the American split between perception of self and reality. The killer is someone who would rather take a life than have to resolve that conflict between self-perception and reality.

TOWN MILITIA,
MARTINTOWN,
ALABAMA, CA. 1925

THE SHIFTING CENTER

THE MARSHALL Plan and overall US policy with regard to Europe after the war was shaped to an extraordinary degree by the Cold War, that is, by our fear of the Soviets around the world. The focus was most clearly on Europe by the late 1940s and into the '50s and then expanded from there as expanding Soviet influence became America's obsession. It was the McCarthy period in the United States. Paranoia and fear of Soviet expansion drove most of our foreign policy.

The Marshall Plan wasn't idealistic, although that's how it was sold to the American people who had to pay for it. American taxpayers paid for the Marshall Plan, just as they paid for the gigantic build-up of our military after World War II, a full-scale embrace of militarism that continued into the 1950s and beyond. In order to justify the expense that was coming out of the pockets of all Americans, you had to make people afraid, and the only thing handy was the Communist menace. Having divided the world neatly into the free and the enslaved during World War II, it wasn't a big jump to continue to divide the world into the free and the enslaved in the next few decades either. The battle lines moved to Eastern Europe and the Congo and Southeast Asia and Israel, and the planet turned half dark, half shining.

At the same time, the center of the cultural world was moving from Paris to New York. American jazz was internationally recognized as arguably the first new twentieth-century art form. American movies became the dominant mode of popular filmmaking. American painting, the New York School, replaced Paris. It looked like art but was by and large a matter of economics. The money to buy those paintings was now for the first time available in New York; the money to finance those movies was available in the US. And it was not available in Western Europe. The economic engine of the United States was at full throttle, and I think that's what made it possible for the center of modern culture to shift from Paris and London to New York and Los Angeles in the 1950s. Follow the money, as they say.

Of course the cultural conversation continued to flow back and forth. There were fresh and continuing challenges to American dominance, and they usually depended upon economics. France in the 1960s was moving economically in a direction where it could finance and distribute films, and there were filmmakers in France to challenge the Hollywood films. But then very quickly the young American filmmakers—Martin Scorsese, Francis Ford Coppola, and that whole group of young turks—learned from the French New Wave film-makers and absorbed their influence and replaced it with their own. But whatever back-and-forth there has been over the years, it's almost always been shaped by financial factors. For a brief period Germany became the center of painting, because they were able to afford to buy and house those grand paintings of the 1970s and '80s. Now Americans are buying those paintings again. There are unavoidable, direct links between economics and culture, especially when we're talking about those aspects of culture that are expensive to produce—films, public music, theater—or to own, like paintings and sculpture.

It wasn't necessarily a reflection of the quality of the work so much as it was a reflection of the prestige of the culture itself. Following World War II and in the 1950s, American values and institutions enjoyed high prestige in Europe. And it really wasn't until the Vietnam War—the late 1960s, early '70s—that Europeans began to seriously question American values. We were blessed during the 1950s and '60s to be admired by Europeans. I think we began to look a bit more cursed in the late '60s, early '70s, with the Vietnam War and the Europeans' perception of the continuing racism in the United States. Then we saw a shift in Europe away from the prestige of American filmmakers and of American artists. America began to look more threatening to the Europeans. It was in this period that the French started to protect their film industry against the invasion of American films, which had begun to look like a threat to them economically and culturally. So they started to protect themselves against the expansion of American culture, and consumerism generally, and American economic control. But even so, during the period between the 1950s until the early '70s, America looked pretty good to Europeans.

The economic power that was being exerted by the Americans, together with our dominance in culture and what I think the Europeans perceived as our political stupidity and our neurotic fixation on the Communist threat, began to create a negative preponderance of facts that made us look threatening in the European imagination. Once Europeans began to see some of our faults, they found we had many others. They noticed our racism, not just in the South but across the United States. And they saw poverty, in Appalachia and also in the inner cities of New York,

Detroit, Philadelphia, and other places. The turmoil and brutality that erupted in the late 1960s and early '70s, with the assassinations of Kennedy, Martin Luther King, and Malcolm X, and the urban riots— that whole sequence of events altered the European perception of America in a significant way. Where before we had looked to them like the golden child, we now began to take on a somewhat different appearance. The United States now looked like a bully, out of control, violent, angry, short-sighted. No longer were we the brilliant innocent.

⚜

THAT YOU can make something and sell it everywhere, everywhere on the planet, turn it into something everyone desperately wants, would be one way of describing the American reality, the one that has grown out of the one strand of the American Dream that was the dream of wealth accumulation, the one we said was the least transformative of the three strands of the American Dream, the strand that leads back to old Europe, except that now the crown heads can be anywhere or nowhere. It is the modern version of the dream of Conquest. Finally America conquers the world simply by selling material goods to every single person across the globe with money to spend.

That was Henry Ford's dream, wasn't it? Going all the way back to the Model T and the Model A, the first assembly line designs, his dream was to create cars that would be sold across the planet, across all barriers, classes, languages, national borders. That's the same for McDonald's, the same for Starbucks, where the least transformative, easiest-to-access form of the American Dream is manufactured. It's about making the one American product that everyone wants. And it's not just about dollars either, although of course selling and making money is very much the point. But McDonald's and Starbucks and, of course, Coca-Cola are also about being loved and admired by the world simply for being themselves. That Coke bottle is a great metaphor for the true apotheosis of the American Dream. What a dream! There's some kind of blissful stupidity in that impulse. If people just try Coca-Cola, they'll love me! They'll love America! If they just try a Big Mac, they'll love America. If they just try Disney World, they'll love America. If the Iraqis try democracy, they'll love America.

Well, yes, we might be making a little money on the side, but that's not the point, we say. The real point of the soft drinks, fast food, and entertainment is to show you, show the world, how good these things are that we make, show you how much you can love them and, by extension, us.

WHEN I spoke earlier of the Cold War, I think I left out something important, which was the effect of the Cold War on Europe. When you divided the world in half, as we did during the Cold War, Europe itself was halved. Eastern Europe became part of the dark half and Western Europe became part of the sunlit half, and the leadership of the sunlit half economically and militarily was generated by the United States. So during the Cold War, NATO became the creature of the United States and American arms manufacturers. Even though France and England had nuclear weapons, the United States was regarded as the primary custodian and manufacturer of both nuclear and conventional weapons. I think that political and military factors had a great deal to do with the shifting of military and cultural allegiance from Europe to the United States in the postwar years, in particular the 1950s and '60s when the Cold War was at its most intense. And I don't think it had as much to do at that time with marketing. Later in the 1980s, and certainly at an accelerated rate in the 1990s, and now, with the globalization of the economy, it has come to have everything to do with marketing.

The technological developments that came about in the 1980s changed the means and ways and techniques of outsourcing, in manufacturing as well as in the service economy, and in inventory control. These developments shifted marketing techniques and controls in a radical way in the '80s, and we haven't really begun to perceive the implications of that. Maybe there are some filmmakers out there who are putting it together, in Europe and in the United States. Maybe novelists and writers are beginning to sort out the implications of these huge economic and technological changes. Most aren't really aware of the scale of these differences, despite the fact that they have far-reaching implications, and will for many, many years, for generations.

One in three American children between the ages of eight and eighteen has a TV set in his or her own bedroom. American teenagers watch TV three hours a day. These are recent statistics from *The New York Times*. If, as a child, you have a television set in your bedroom, and you watch three hours of television a day, this has to have an effect on your perception of yourself, of reality, and of the larger world. So when you speak of younger Americans you're talking about people whose sense of reality is determined largely by a version that is at best highly filtered and at worst completely distorted. An unstated fact in those statistics is that one-third of the time that they're watching television, they're really watching advertisements for consumer goods, for products. So their minds are being organized around a need for these products. Their brains are being altered.

We know that the brain adapts to sensory input and chemically alters itself to accommodate that input in some way. So we know that's happening, and it's happening worldwide, most particularly in the United States itself and increasingly in the rest of the so-called Western world. It's useful to remember that it was during the 1950s that television was introduced into the daily life of Americans. What really happened was this: we allowed the salesman into the sanctity of the home. Because programming on television exists solely in order to sell products, television is a salesman, pure and simple. Advertising doesn't exist in order to get programs on television; it's the other way around. Programs exist in order to get consumer products advertised on television. And in the 1950s we let the salesman into the home. We started with the salesman in the living room. Then a few years later the salesman became a babysitter for the children. And now that salesman is in the bedroom with those children for three hours a day. So we've basically turned our children over to the purveyors of consumerism—the manufacturers and purveyors of sneakers, of clothing, toys, video games, junk food, and eventually, of course, of beer and liquor, drugs, and automobiles.

We've done something that has never been done. As a species we have been required to protect the young, because it takes a long time for the human child to become an adult human, longer than any other species, all in order to learn how to deal with human socialization. In ancient times, as the species evolved, we protected the young first from the weather, from the saber-toothed tigers, from the amoral forces of the universe, protected them until they were able to protect themselves. In the modern era the amoral forces of the universe are primarily economic. Thus we have all those jokes about keeping the salesman out of the house, slamming the door on the salesman's foot. This is really about protecting the young and the vulnerable, those who can't distinguish between advertisement and reality. Those jokes and cartoons implied a serious challenge by the salesman to the sanctity of the home. But when we brought the television into the home, we basically brought the salesman into the home. We brought the saber-toothed tiger into the cave and said, *Make yourself comfortable by the fire.* And now we leave the salesman babysitting the children while we step out the door and go off to work at McDonald's and Wal-Mart.

It's a very dangerous situation. We've colonized our own children. Having run out of people on the planet to colonize, run out of people who can't distinguish between beads and trinkets and something of value, having found ourselves no longer able to swap some beads and axes for Manhattan Island, we've ended up colonizing our own children. We're now engaged in a process of auto-colonization. The old sow is eating its own farrow.

We've dismantled that City on the Hill that was largely spiritual and replaced it with El Dorado, the

fantasized City of Gold. We've become the conquista-
dors of our own suburbs. Actually we've done it all while
claiming not to know what it is that we've done. It is
very possibly the end of the Republic. We're seeing
something different take place now, something alto-
gether new on this planet—a fascist plutocracy presid-
ing over a world population of disenfranchised and
distracted consumers and would-be consumers.

THE SIEGE, 1998

WHAT FOR, WHERE TO

THERE IS a statement attributed to me: "We became a dreamer of homicides." What I originally said was translated into French, then translated back again, like this entire text, and I think what I said originally was, "We became a nation of homicidal dreamers, murderous dreamers." I was trying to point indirectly to that age-old conflict between our material goals and our spiritual justifications that lie at the heart of the American Dream, and also now at the heart of American history. That conflict has made us murderers over and over again. Thus the true American is a killer. The true

American is a cynical, materialistic grabber on the one hand, reaching for gold, yet he has an idealistic, even religious, sense of mission. When you tell yourself that big a lie and you call it a dream, you're going to end up committing acts of violence. It's the nature of human psychology. If it's part of our mythology as a people, then as a people we're going to act violently. And we have historically done exactly that, beginning in the sixteenth century when the Europeans first arrived off the coast of Florida, off the coast of Virginia, off the coast of New England. We were killing people and saying that we were doing it for some higher good. Not only that, we also said we were doing it for their own good!

I regard nationalism as a kind of secular religion, a substitute religion, where the state itself and one's identity as a citizen of the state takes on a religious intensity and passion. I suppose there is a lack that's highlighted by that identification. It has behind it the notion that one's identity as an American is some kind of ultimate definition of oneself and, therefore, without it one has no identity of one's own. One's citizenship isn't merely one's group identity, it's one's essential identity.

Nationalism can do that to you. It can strip you of your individuality. And in periods of strong, nationalistic fervor in the United States, it has taken on a stubbornly religious quality. I don't think this is peculiar to us, though it is something we have periodically had to deal with. One of the healthiest and most important aspects of our American system of government is the separation of religion and the state, the sharp distinction between our legal and political system on the one hand and our religious ideas and institutions on the other. One of the things this allows is great religious tolerance; but another thing it does is demystify national identity, to secularize it. To me, this is a very good idea, something much to be desired, that the framers thoughtfully included in our national idea from the beginning.

⁕

IN THE period after September 11, 2001, there was a strong surge of national ambition and fervor. There was a plethora of American flags, from bumper stickers to flags hung on the sides of houses, on storefronts, on highway overpasses. You saw American flags everywhere. Here we are now, more than six years after 9/11, and that patriotic fervor is still controlling our thinking, our basic sense of ourselves, our personal and collective identities. To me this is a frightening thing. There is nothing positive about it. I'm at one with the poet W. H. Auden, who spoke of nationalism as a sickness, a self-imposed hallucination. To make your national identity, your citizenship, your passport, a part of your essential sense of yourself is as destructive as any hallucination. When it's a mass hallucination, it's really dangerous.

The flag has become sacred. It is as sacred to Americans as the image of Mohammed is to the Muslims. We have state laws against burning the flag or defacing the flag. These laws are solutions in search of a problem, of course. But even so, every year there's an attempt to amend the Constitution to make it a criminal act to deface or burn the flag. It's treated as if the flag were one of St. Francis's fingers or a remnant of the true cross or something like that. It's ridiculous, and, what's more important, it's very dangerous. It's tribal, and it turns the flag into a fetish object. It frightens people. And it happens periodically, when nationalism raises its ugly head, and we fall to our knees and worship the state. Politicians, of course, whip that fervor up when they want to go to war and need us to make sacrifices, financial, economic, and others—let's sacrifice our children!—that otherwise we would never make. If we weren't able to have that deep blood identification with a national fantasy, we would not be willing to sacrifice our children.

Nationalism is no longer such a necessity to Europeans living adjacent to one another as part of the European Union. Centuries of dueling nationalisms and the trauma of World War I, World War II, the Spanish Civil War, and the Cold War were sufficient to disabuse most Europeans, the Balkans aside, of the virtues of nationalism, whereas here in the United States our relative isolation has allowed us to continue to nurture the

impulse. We haven't had to deal with neighbors with powerful national identities. Mexico and Canada are not
threatening to the United States and its national identity.
Canadians are almost apologetic of theirs. Mexico has
long been regarded by Americans as our poor deraci-
nated neighbor to the South. So we haven't had to com-
pete with the closest neighboring countries. Also the
United States' experience of World War I and World War
II and even the Cold War was primarily in the European
theater and in Asia. We came out of those wars, particularly World War II and the Cold War, with an inflated
sense of self-importance and with our national pride
reinforced by those experiences.

MAYBE WE'RE more dependent upon nationalism
today simply because we're a country that was invented
out of many parts. We have no ancient history as a
nation or a people, so perhaps our national identity is
more of an artifice, and you defend an artificial identity
much more aggressively than you defend an authentic
identity. The Israelis are like the Americans in this way,
exceedingly nationalistic and religious, and perhaps
it's because their and our identities are both artificial.
They have disparate parts, people arriving from all over
the world, with different languages, different races,

different histories, personal and otherwise, with each new arrival being transformed into a new person by their presence in a new land. That's very artificial. Not many Americans can trace their roots to someplace within these fifty states for longer than three generations. A small number can, of course, but most can't go back three or four generations without visualizing their ancestors in the old country, wherever that may be for them. They start looking around and saying, Well, yeah, they came here from Poland or Korea, India, Mexico, Africa, Italy, Germany, and so on. I just go back one generation myself. My father was Canadian, and three of my four grandparents were Canadian, so I'm a first generation American. You cling to your national identity more strongly when you have no good reason for it to exist.

It's interesting, and maybe more problematic, for the French and the Germans and Europeans generally, because the bond of language, of shared cultural assumptions and religions, is no longer sufficient to establish national identity. And I think that the increasing number of immigrants—different racially, culturally, religiously, linguistically, and so on—in France, Germany, and England, is raising these issues of national identity in an unexpected and threatening way, raising them in ways it's not in the United States, because our national identity has, from the very beginning, been a merging process in all those areas—race, religion, language, ethnicity, land of origin. We've been merging from the start. *E pluribus unum* is on our coins: "Out of many, one." So rather than having a sense of identity preceding the arrival of the immigrants, we always were a country with an inflow that was integral to who we were.

In some ways it's a model, but I don't know that it's a model Europeans can copy. I don't think you can pick up this template and say to Europeans, this is what you ought to do with your immigrant people who are becoming so numerous—7 percent, 8 percent, 10 percent—whom you seem unable to assimilate. I don't think anything from the United States that has to do with immigration can serve as a useful model for Europe, because our histories are so radically different. We began as an invention. We began as a merging, as a merged people. We are essentially a Creole nation, a mixture, and we have been that way since our very conception. And I don't think that's true of any European country. In fact I doubt it's true of any country on the planet except for the United States and possibly Canada, except that Canada does not have the same powerful sense of its own national identity. Canada is a federation, and in many ways it still views itself as an ex-colony. Look at their coins with the imprint of the British monarchy.

THE LAST thing I want to do is to predict what is going to happen. And I mean that in both senses. Both that as I approach the end of this conversational text this is the thing I want to do, the thing I want to do last. And also that it is something I'm reluctant to do at all, since it isn't as if there's enough information here to know yet what's going to happen, so in a way it's an empty exercise, a purely speculative exercise, however tempting.

I think most Americans believe that, whenever we want to, we can still withdraw back from the world to the City on the Hill; that interventionism and being involved in the rest of the world militarily, economically, and so forth, is a choice, rather than a necessity. If threatened, if the war goes sufficiently wrong in Iraq or Afghanistan, for instance, we can pull back our troops, pull back our military engagements, and do just fine on our own. I don't think that's true, but I think most Americans believe it is. Therefore, in the next presidential campaign, in 2008, the degree to which we should be involved in Iraq, militarily and economically, will be a significant question that people will be voting on. And I think that most Americans, most politicians, will argue that we don't need to be there. We don't need to be in Iraq; we don't need to be in Afghanistan; we don't need to be involved in the so-called free trade agreements we've been pushing in Europe, in Africa, in Latin America; we can take care of ourselves just fine. I see a new period of isolationism arising as a result of the war in Iraq. And the truth is, of course, that we should have thought of those choices beforehand, because undoing what we have wrought isn't as easy as we might like to think.

There was a great hue and cry a year or so ago against George Bush and the Bush administration's decision to lease our port security to a company based in the United Arab Emirates. Suddenly we were saying, What are we doing, letting our ports be guarded by companies from the UAE? Our ports here in America should be guarded by Americans! And both sides of the aisle, Democrats and Republicans alike, were arguing against the free market global economy when they said that. They found themselves against the principle that has guided us financially on the international stage for decades. But if we can outsource our service economy to India, then we have to accept the fact that there are other countries and companies that are coming to work here as well. But suddenly there was a hue and cry against it. What we're going to see over the next five to ten years is a return to the isolationism of the past, for both good and bad reasons. The perception that we cannot continue with the Iraq war, that we cannot control events the way we think we can, that the world is a more complicated place than we'd been told, well, that's a wake-up call and a good thing. But at the same time I think we're also going to be saying we don't need the rest of the world to survive—economically, diplomatically, militarily—that we can take care of ourselves just fine, thank you. And that's a bad thing.

Further, willed isolationism ignores the presence of China—economically, militarily, diplomatically, culturally. It also ignores the future potential of India. And it ignores the simple facts of technology and its impact on the world economy. But I think that nonetheless we're falling back into isolationism, and in many ways it will be harmful to us, culturally and economically. But at least we'll kill fewer people.

YOU HAVE to see the United States as the creation of a conflicting set of impulses—spiritual, ethical, and materialistic. Despite that, or perhaps because of it, we've managed in the process, by means of the American Constitution and the Declaration of Independence, to create one of the most extraordinary political organizations on the planet. Through those documents alone we have integrated those two warring impulses more usefully than through any other existing political or social institution or structure. They have served as a bridge, incredible and unprecedented, joining together in one place in two texts all our spiritual and earthly human impulses. The texts are sacred in the sense that they tie the two together. Through them it is possible to imagine a delicate balancing act that better serves both our strengths and our weaknesses. There is a tension, a dynamic tension, between them. Sometimes that conflict takes a self-destructive route, as it has since 9/11, and at other times it gets expressed as a creative impulse, and thus we feel it as a strength.

For me, everything in the American enterprise comes back down to that dualism. This indeed is what we are blessed and cursed with, a dual identity. America has been a dualistic, and thus a contradictory, enterprise from the very beginning. Today this is played out in every theater and operation in which the United States is involved, whether economic or military, diplomatic or cultural.

But there is never just one key to understanding the American character. Whichever aspect you may be looking at, there are nearly always at least two more keys hidden there. Materialist? Yes, indeed. Religious, spiritual, idealistic? Yes, indeed. It's not one or the other. It's not one dominating the other, except periodically. It's a dialectic, an ongoing one. Our brand of democracy has lasted for almost 200 years, over two centuries. It's the oldest continuous democracy on the planet, and the reason it's lasted this long is really due to its embodying a conflict that is so destructive—and it is truly destructive—and also so creative.

Both impulses arose in Europe. The idealistic or religious impulse arose in Europe and was behind the search for freedom of religion that led the settlers to New England. The search for gold, the materialist impulse, also arose in Europe. Both of them came from the mother countries. How they met and combined in the New World was the surprise, a fresh chemistry, something profoundly different from anything that had existed before. Without the Native Americans who were here before us, who greeted us and taught us necessary skills for living in this new world, we'd be more like the Europeans. Without the Africans, who were brought into this New World as the first immigrants, as slaves for several hundred years and then as second-class citizens for another hundred years, we'd be more like the Europeans. When I speak of America as a Creole nation, I am not speaking only of the waves of immigrants that came after, but of the very seed of us that was and has always been in the mixture. So it is both ironic and revealing that our national obsession, looking outward and away, has always been a racial obsession, since in my view the seed inside us was always closer to that complex brew than it ever was to the picture we had of ourselves as white, Anglo-Saxon, Protestant Northern Europeans.

When I look at us Americans, I feel I see people I know well. We aren't mixed together in a "melting pot." Nor do we live behind walls to protect ourselves from outsiders, since our own identity as outsiders is deeply imbedded within us. Instead I begin by recognizing that the way this country was formed, and the way it is

still coming into being, is a powerful, combustible combination of energies. We would do well to recognize
that we haven't yet finished making ourselves, and that
we can still take mindful control of that process. Our
American history is taking us somewhere. We just don't
know where yet.

We're sitting here today in Saratoga, New York.
York, of course, is an English name. But Saratoga is an
Iroquois Indian word. Originally, this place was called
Sarachtoque, which means "hillside of a great river," or
"place of the swift water." Half the place names in New
York are Indian names. Ours is a true Creole culture,
and it would be very interesting for us and for the world
around us if one day we came around to seeing ourselves in all our component parts, acknowledging
finally the only identity that's ours.